DEFENDER
RAPTOR

THE PROTECTION, INC. DEFENDERS SERIES

Defender Cave Bear
Defender Raptor

THE PROTECTION, INC. SERIES

Bodyguard Bear
Defender Dragon
Protector Panther
Warrior Wolf
Leader Lion
Soldier Snow Leopard
Top Gun Tiger

DEFENDER RAPTOR

PROTECTION, INC: DEFENDERS.

2

ZOE CHANT

TABLE OF CONTENTS

CHAPTER 1   1
CHAPTER 2   13
CHAPTER 3   24
CHAPTER 4   32
CHAPTER 5   39
CHAPTER 6   50
CHAPTER 7   62
CHAPTER 8   64
CHAPTER 9   77
CHAPTER 10   90
CHAPTER 11   106
CHAPTER 12   111
CHAPTER 13   127
CHAPTER 14   141
CHAPTER 15   171
CHAPTER 16   186
CHAPTER 17   188
CHAPTER 18   197
CHAPTER 19   205
CHAPTER 20   213
CHAPTER 21   219

CHAPTER 22   234
CHAPTER 23   244
CHAPTER 24   246
CHAPTER 25   250
CHAPTER 26   259
CHAPTER 27   275
CHAPTER 28   284
CHAPTER 29   300
A Note From Zoe Chant   305

CHAPTER 1

In retrospect, Dali should have been more suspicious of the pigeons.

The park where they lurked was unfamiliar territory to her. In the year since she'd been forced to leave the Navy, she'd spent every minute doing physical therapy, job-searching, or working. She wasn't an "I have important things to do but it's a beautiful day so I guess I'll blow off my responsibilities and stroll through the park instead" type of person.

But she also wasn't the type of person who'd refuse to do a favor for her own grandmother. When she'd visited for dinner the night before, Dali had confessed that she'd been fired again and she needed to find a new job immediately.

Grandma had fixed her with a stern look. "You never used to make your job into your whole life. Yes, you worked very hard. But when you weren't working, you had fun. You spent time with your friends. You read books. You climbed rocks—"

Dali didn't intend to call attention to her prosthetic left hand, but she couldn't help glancing down at it.

Grandma followed her gaze, then raised it back to Dali's eyes. "You *laughed*. How long has it been since you laughed?"

"I haven't had much to laugh about."

"So go see a funny movie!"

"Really, Grandma?"

"You know what I mean. Go on a date! Get a pet!"

"I'd need to meet someone I liked to go on a date," Dali said. "And I don't have time for a pet."

Her grandmother shook her head and sighed. Then she got up and left the room. When she returned, gold flashed in her hand. Dali recognized her lucky necklace, the one she'd worn when she'd met the man who would become Dali's grandfather. It was an antique, heavy and intricate, a family heirloom whose origins even Grandma didn't know.

Grandma draped around Dali's neck. "Here you go. May it bring you luck."

"I can't take—" Dali had begun.

Her grandmother cut her off with a wave of her wrinkled hand. "It's not a gift. I expect it back when you come for dinner next Sunday. In the meantime, take a break. Don't look for a job tomorrow. Instead, wear the necklace and a pretty dress—do you still have that red silk dress?"

"Yes." It had been years since Dali had worn it, but she'd lost weight while she'd been recovering, and she was sure she could fit into it.

"Good. Put it on, take a walk in the park, smell the roses, and remember that you're a beautiful, smart, strong woman with your whole life ahead of you. Promise me you will."

Grandma had so much faith in her—more than she had in herself. Dali, her eyes stinging with unshed tears, had promised.

So she'd gone to the park in a scarlet cocktail dress and a pair of cute black shoes, and she'd tried to enjoy the roses. But she was too conscious of the weight of Grandma's heirloom necklace around her throat and the weight of her prosthetic at the end of her left arm. The first was a promise she couldn't fulfill, and the second was a reminder of everything she'd lost. They weighed maybe one pound put together, and yet they were a heavier burden than any pack she'd ever carried on duty.

How could she have her entire life ahead of her when the Navy had been her entire life?

How could she be satisfied selling products that nobody needed when once she'd been a small but essential part of something as huge and important as the Navy?

Images of the day that had changed everything flashed before her mind's eye. Her phone waking her up with "Girls Like You"—if she heard that song play now, she had to leave the room. Braiding her hair without looking in a mirror—there was another thing she couldn't do anymore. Her prosthetic hand had no sense of touch, so she needed to watch it to get it to move correctly. Now she used a pair of mirrors to braid and pin up her hair.

She was so distracted by her own depressing thoughts that she didn't notice the pigeons until four of them swooped down and landed on her shoulders, flapping their wings and sending a cloud of tiny gray feathers into her face.

She had a moment of heart-jolting shock, but she didn't scream. She didn't run. Nor did she wildly flail at them. Instead, she fell back on her training and stood absolutely still, processing the situation so she could calmly decide what to do about it rather than reacting in mindless panic.

This isn't a war zone, she told herself. *You're not under attack. These are pigeons. They're harmless. People must feed them.*

Silly people. Who'd want pigeons all over them? Dali was about to take a quick step forward to dislodge them when she felt the catch of her grandmother's necklace open.

The next thing she knew, the weight had left her neck and she was watching with astonished outrage as four pigeons flew away with Grandma's priceless family heirloom.

"HEY!" Dali yelled at the pigeons. "Get back here!"

The pigeons, clutching the gold necklace in their scaly feet, flapped steadily away.

She stooped, grabbed a small rock with her right hand, and hurled it at them. Her aim was as good as ever. There was an anguished squawk and an explosion of feathers, but the necklace didn't fall.

The pigeons veered upward, out of rock-throwing distance, and vanished behind a skyscraper. Dali pelted around the back. But by the time she reached it, the birds and Grandma's necklace were long gone. She stood alone, sweating and furious, in an alley that reeked of garbage.

So much for smelling the roses.

"The pigeons stole your necklace," the police officer repeated. He clearly found the phrase extremely amusing, because that was the third time he'd said it.

She glared at him. He avoided her gaze… by staring down her cleavage. Dali wished she'd gone home and changed her clothes rather than marching straight to the nearest police station in a party dress. Then she reminded herself that it wasn't on her to hide her body, it was on him to be professional.

Dali cleared her throat loudly, making his head jerk up. "That's right. Shall we get to the paperwork?"

"You want to press charges against *birds?*"

She kept a tight grip on her temper. "I want to press charges against whoever trained the pigeons to steal for them. Just like if someone trained a dog to bite and sicced it on their enemies."

A cop at another desk glanced over his shoulder and remarked in some bizarre accent, "Oi! Pigeons stole me necklace!"

It took her a moment to realize that the accent was supposed to be Australian, and he was making a "dingoes ate my baby" joke. She was not amused. "Since you two seem incapable of taking my theft report seriously, I want to speak to your watch commander."

"I'm the watch commander," said Officer Pigeons Stole Me Necklace, dropping the accent and replacing it with a sneer. "And I assure you, we're taking your complaint exactly as seriously as it deserves."

Dali's temper flared. "I'm a veteran of the US Navy, and let me tell you, if you were working on *my* ship—"

Officer Pigeons Stole Me Necklace let out a high-pitched screech, then dove under his desk.

She folded her arms, unimpressed with his theatrics. "If you think that's going to distract me…"

"A rat!" yelped Officer Pigeons Stole Me Necklace, crawling rapidly out from under his desk in a most undignified fashion. "A rat bit my ankle!"

The other cops rushed to his side, examining his ankle and peering under the desk. Dali stayed where she was, wondering whether this was yet another stupid joke or if he was on drugs and had hallucinated the rat. Then she saw a furry gray animal dart away from the desk. Before she could get a good look at it, the little creature scurried out the door.

Raising her voice, Dali said, "I'm reporting this office to the police commissioner for failure to take a crime report, *and* to the health department for the rodent infestation!"

Without waiting to see whether that pack of uniformed idiots had heard her, she spun around and marched out the door.

Her anger carried her for a few blocks. But by the time she'd finished mentally writing the complaints, its heat had died away, leaving her with nothing but ashes. She'd lost Grandma's precious necklace, which had been handed down for generations. And the only reason Dali had been wearing it to begin with was that Grandma had wanted to make her feel better. It was her fault twice over.

What do I tell her? Dali wondered. She knew her grandmother wouldn't blame her, but somehow that made her feel worse rather than better.

She started to walk past a gloomy alley, the sort people got mugged in, then turned around and marched on in. It was a shortcut, and she wasn't about to let herself be ruled by fear any more than she already was.

Dali half-hoped someone *would* try to mug her. She might not have fought in combat, but she'd gotten the same training as everyone else. And while she wouldn't want to test her prosthetic hand against a human jaw, that still left her with one hand and both feet. Any mugger that messed with her deserved the ass-kicking she felt perfectly capable of handing out.

Something small and gray flew into the alley.

A pigeon? Dali thought. *A trained, thieving pigeon?!*

She lunged for it. It darted away, then stopped and hovered. And that was when she saw that it wasn't a pigeon.

"No way," Dali muttered aloud. "That's *impossible.*"

The impossible creature meowed.

Dali stared incredulously at the little animal. She took in every detail, searching for the one false note that would prove that it was an elaborate puppet or a special effect or a drone in a fur coat or anything other than what it appeared to be, which was a gray kitten with a pair of translucent, rapidly beating dragonfly wings, hovering a good five feet above the ground. The wings made a soft buzzing sound.

Cautiously, Dali passed her right hand over the air above the kitten, feeling for hidden strings. There were none. The kitten's bright blue eyes followed the movement of her hand. When she let her hand drop, it flew forward, landing on her chest with all paws outstretched.

"Ow!"

The kitten clung to her dress with its sharp little claws. The buzzing sound stopped as it closed its wings neatly over its back. Once they were folded up, they became almost invisible except for a rainbow shimmer and a faint tracery of veins. And without the distraction of the wings, Dali recognized that soft shade of gray. The kitten was none other than the police station's "rat."

"Did you bite that nasty rude policeman?" Dali asked.

The kitten purred and butted its head into her cleavage.

Dali took that as a yes. "Good for you!"

Her disbelief vanished at the very solid feeling of the kitten's head smacking into her cleavage. She cupped the kitten in her right hand. Its fur was very soft. It released her dress, settled itself in her palm, and purred even more enthusiastically.

"Hey there, cutie pie," Dali murmured. "Are you a boy or a girl?"

There was no response from the kitten, but it wasn't like she'd expected one. She lifted it high and nudged aside its tail with her left hand. It was a girl.

Now that Dali had more of a chance to look at the kitten without being distracted by the wings, she could appreciate all the adorable details. The kitten had a triangular head and slim build, much like a Siamese. In fact, Dali realized, she also had colored points like a Siamese: rather than being the same shade of light gray all over, her face and ears and paws and tail-tip were a darker gray with a bluish tinge.

"I think you *are* a Siamese," Dali said. "Or bred from one, anyway. Weren't they owned by royalty? Maybe I should call you Princess. Princess Absolutely Adorable?"

The kitten spat indignantly.

"Or maybe not," Dali said, trying not to laugh too hard at the kitten's injured dignity. She was so pretty, though, with those sky-blue eyes and fur like a cloudy morning, that Dali wanted to give her an equally pretty name. "Cloud?"

Cloud purred and began to lick her hand with a little rough tongue.

"Where'd you come from, Cloud?"

Unsurprisingly, Cloud did not reply. But when Dali thought about her question, she came to some very unsettling conclusions.

The dragonfly kitten must be some kind of genetic engineering experiment, created in a private or government laboratory.

There was no way scientists would have randomly released a *dragonfly kitten* into the city, so she had to have escaped. Which meant they'd come looking for her soon… if they weren't already searching for her.

Labs dissected and experimented on animals. God knew what they'd do to her if they got her back. The absolute best outcome was that she'd be locked in a cage for the rest of her life.

Cloud nibbled her fingertips and purred some more. Dali had always loved cats and regretted that her career had prevented her from having one. She'd rather lose her other hand than let this precious little darling come to harm.

She moved with the decisiveness that had been her hallmark back in the Navy. In a second, Dali had popped Cloud into her purse and was striding through the alley, holding her right hand over the opening as if it was casually resting there. Her heart was pounding, her senses on high alert.

A tiny sound, the faintest scrape of a metal against concrete, instantly flooded her with adrenaline. Dali hit the ground and rolled, clutching the purse and Cloud to her chest and protecting them with her body.

Something small and dark pinged against the ground, missing her face by inches.

A bullet, she thought, already rolling again. But she'd heard only a faint hissing sound, not even the muffled pop of a silencer.

Another hiss, and something bounced off her prosthetic hand. She caught a glimpse of it before it rolled away. It was a black dart, not a bullet. A tranquilizer dart?

Dali half-rolled, half-lunged behind a metal dumpster. She rose into a crouch, catching her breath, and saw that it concealed a narrow crawlspace between buildings. She crammed the purse and Cloud into her blouse and crawled through.

If Cloud starts meowing, we're dead, she thought. *But if she keeps quiet, we might be able to get away.*

She could feel the kitten's trembling and rapid heartbeat, but Cloud was silent. Dali emerged from the crawlspace into another alley. She staggered to her feet and ran, darting from alley to alley until she finally came to one that ended in a busy, crowded street.

She leaned against the wall, catching her breath. No one seemed to be chasing her. Either she'd lost them, or they'd given up. For now.

Dali slung her purse back over her shoulder and left the alley, trying to blend into the crowd. It was a typical Refuge City street, full of old people, young people, parents with small children, hotdog carts, skateboarders, bicyclists, cars, trucks, dogs on leashes, one loudly protesting cat on a leash, a woman doing cartoon sketches for tourists, and a frantic-looking young father jiggling a howling baby. What she did not see were any people who looked like they might shoot darts at people or experiment on kittens.

Which didn't mean they weren't there, of course. It wasn't like they'd be wearing white coats stamped with WINGED KITTEN EXPERIMENTS, INC.

Once upon a time, Dali would have felt entirely equal to the task of protecting a helpless creature under her care, no matter what stood in her way. But now she felt small and alone and inadequate. It was bitterly ironic that the last time she'd have felt confident enough to protect Cloud herself, she'd also had as many people as she possibly could have wanted to pitch in, all of them smart, professional, and highly trained.

But she couldn't call on her old Navy buddies now. Some were dead. Some were deployed. And if she contacted any of the rest, they'd want to know why she'd left the Navy. *They'd* know she could still do her job with a prosthetic hand and a few scars. And then she'd have to tell them…

The thought of revealing the awful truth made an all-too-familiar tightness close around her chest, squeezing her heart and lungs. She forced herself to breathe deeply and rhythmically until the threat of a panic attack subsided.

Like everything else in her life now, this situation was something she'd have to deal with all by herself.

If she brought Cloud to her apartment building, she'd potentially be putting her neighbors at risk. And they weren't all tough like Dali. Most of them were more like Esther, who must be at least eighty and brought Dali homemade bread once a week. Or like Tirzah, who never did anything more strenuous than tooling around the neighborhood in her wheelchair. Tirzah's fiancé Pete was a veteran… but his thirteen-year-old daughter lived with them. And there were other kids in the building. Dali couldn't do anything that might endanger them.

And then there was Grandma's necklace. Dali had exactly one week to get it back before their next dinner, when she'd have to confess what had happened to it. But who could help her retrieve it when the police weren't willing to help her and she wasn't willing to call her Navy buddies?

That was when she realized that she could leverage one problem to solve another.

Tirzah and Pete both worked at Protection, Inc: Defenders, a private security agency. Pete was a bodyguard and Tirzah did cyber security. Tirzah was smart as a whip, and Pete was a veteran Marine. Dali didn't know much about the agency and had never been to the office, but if they both worked there, it had to be good.

Instead of going home to the apartment building, Dali could go straight to the Defenders office and ask for help retrieving her necklace *and* protecting her kitten. She'd take Cloud with her, so both her neighbors and Cloud would be safe, and Dali could prove to the Defenders that the kitten was real.

There was no feeling quite so satisfying as that of taking a complicated mess and creating order out of it. She hadn't felt this good since… well, since she'd been in the Navy, where she did that every day.

Smiling to herself, she took out her phone and looked up the address of Protection, Inc: Defenders. Then she took the subway, keeping her right hand firmly on Cloud inside her purse. The dragonfly kitten was curled up and seemed to have dozed off, to Dali's relief.

She emerged from the subway station and blinked in the bright morning sunlight. The subway had dropped her off right in front of the Defenders office, but the first thing that caught her eye wasn't the building, but the gigantic billboard beside it. Swooping crimson letters accented with gold announced:

THE FABULOUS FLYING CHAMELEONS!
World-famous circus on a special US tour!

The rest of the billboard was crammed with iconic circus images: seals balancing balls on their noses, lions leaping through hoops, trapeze artists flying through the air in spangled leotards, a ringmaster with an immense curled moustache, a clown juggling teacups with a cat perched on his head, and more. Much more. So much more that it made her feel slightly dizzy.

The poster was old-fashioned, but it brimmed with playfulness and joy. Everyone looked so happy, even the animals. Maybe especially the animals. Dali had never been to the circus, but looking at the poster made her want to go. Maybe once she got the necklace back, she'd buy two tickets and take her grandmother. It *would* be nice to have some fun for a change.

She took the elevator up to the Defenders lobby and rang the doorbell. There was no answer. She turned the doorknob, expecting it to be locked, but it opened. She stepped inside. And tripped over something directly in front of the door.

Normally, she'd have thrown out both arms to keep her balance. But her right hand was inside her purse with Cloud. Dali staggered, her left arm flailing.

A hand shot out and caught her by the shoulder. "Easy."

She looked up into the angular, unsmiling face of a tall man with auburn hair. The instant she'd caught her balance, he released her and stepped backward. Fascinated, she watched him step neatly over the thing she'd tripped over—some weird contraption involving a box, a lever, a mass of tangled string, and a carrot—without first looking to see where she'd kicked it.

"Merlin's not here yet," the man said. "Give him a couple more minutes."

Who was Merlin? Puzzled, Dali said, "I think you've mistaken me for someone else."

"No," he said. "I haven't." And with that mysterious statement, he walked out the door, leaving her alone.

Who *was* that guy? He'd looked more like a college professor than a bodyguard. And what in the world had he been talking about?

Dali looked around the lobby in baffled annoyance. This was the office of a respected private security agency? Where was the receptionist? Where was the office manager?

Where was the *cleaner?* The coffee table was stacked with files and papers, plus a half-drunk cup of coffee and a paper plate with half a bagel—not a bagel sliced in half, either, but one with teeth marks. There was a circuit board on the sofa, not to mention the box-and-string thing in the middle of the floor.

Most bizarre of all, a wire live trap was stuck halfway out a window, baited with a strip of bacon, a whole egg, an oozing chunk of honeycomb, and a plastic cup half-full of what could only be Kool-Aid.

Dali stared at the trap for a long moment, unable to believe her eyes. What in the world were they trying to catch? It was too small for raccoons or possums, but too big for mice and rats. And what kind of animal drinks Kool-Aid?

This complete shambles of a workplace couldn't help her. If anything, it needed to be rescued from itself.

Dali turned to leave, with no idea of where she was going to other than *away.*

That was when Cloud leaped out of her purse, her dragonfly wings buzzing madly, and made a beeline for the bacon.

"No!" Dali yelled.

But she was too late. The door of the trap slammed shut.

CHAPTER 2

"I just want to get some coffee before I go to work," Merlin said. "That's a totally normal thing! It shouldn't be this difficult!"

The normal flow of sidewalk traffic abruptly broke up as everyone within hearing distance of Merlin edged away. Oops. He hadn't meant to speak aloud.

"I love my new… tiny… earpiece phone!" Merlin said for their benefit. "You can't even see it's there!"

Traffic resumed. Merlin, reminding himself not to move his lips this time, sternly addressed his inner raptor. *We're getting some coffee, then we're going to work. No arguments!*

His inner raptor bounced up and down like a toddler having a sugar rush on a trampoline. *Offices are boring. Let's run into the middle of the street and play in traffic!*

Merlin actually took a step toward the street before he regained control of his body. Determinedly, he veered into the Starbucks and took his place in line.

A few people glanced at him, making him tense until they looked away. For the millionth time since he'd been experimented on and given the power to make people see him as whoever they expected to see, he wished he had control over it. Or at least that he could tell when it was operating. As it was, he had no idea if his power was off and they'd perceived him as a customer in line at Starbucks because that was what he was, or if his power was on and they'd perceived him as a Starbucks customer because that was what they expected to see inside a Starbucks.

At least it only worked on people who didn't already know him. If he risked being perceived as a client or an enemy or God knows what every time he went into the office, he'd lose his mind.

"Ark ark ark!"

For the briefest of instants, his heart leaped at the thought that when he looked down, he'd find a tiny seal at his feet. He could see it already: an adorable mini-seal that would swim in his sink and bathtub and—

Merlin looked down, and saw a small boy making seal noises and playing with a plastic figurine of a seal balancing a ball on its nose.

Maybe it's a magical plastic seal that'll come to life, suggested his raptor.

I don't think so, Merlin replied silently. *And even if it was, it'd be the kid's pet, not mine.*

The boy's mother shot Merlin an embarrassed glance. "I hope he's not bothering you."

"Not at all," said Merlin.

The boy took out another figurine, this one of a lion. In a growly lion voice, he said, "Grrr! Grrr! I'm going to eat you up!" Then, in a barking seal voice, he replied, "Ark! Ark! Not in front of the audience! They'll be traumatized!"

Merlin and the boy's mother exchanged amused glances.

"He's got a great vocabulary for his age," said Merlin.

"Oh, yes, he's very bright," replied his mother.

The boy glanced up. To Merlin, he said, "I'm going to join the circus some day. I'll be a seal trainer and a lion trainer and an elephant trainer!"

"You could join Cirque du Soliel as an acrobat," his mother said encouragingly. "But circuses nowadays don't have animals."

"A few of them still do," said Merlin. "I was raised in a circus—"

"*You* were in the circus?" said the boy, awestruck. "Were you a seal trainer?"

"No, the seals trained themselves," said Merlin. As the boy's mother placed their order, he went on, "I did odd jobs, whatever needed to be done. Sometimes I drove the clown car, sometimes I cleaned the lion cage, sometimes—"

"Were you a lion trainer?" the boy interrupted.

"No, the lions trained themselves."

"Were you an elephant trainer?"

"We only had one elephant, and she trained herself," said Merlin apologetically. "But I did hold tiny little hoops for the flying squirrels to fly through when they did their aerial act."

"Oh." The boy thought that over, then gave a satisfied nod. "I could do that."

His mother, now with their drinks in hand, smiled at Merlin. "Thank you so much for entertaining him. Are you a writer? You're so imaginative!"

"No, I'm a bodyguard. But I really was raised in a circus."

The boy's mother gave him a wink, clearly not believing a word he said. "Of course you were. Noah, say goodbye to the nice storytelling man."

"Bye, flying squirrel hoop bodyguard," called the boy.

Merlin watched them leave, a little wistfully. It was nice to have someone believe him, for once, even if that someone was four years old. None of his teammates ever believed his circus stories.

He approached the counter, trying to decide whether he wanted a cappuccino or a latte.

Coffee is boring, said his raptor. *Buy a bottle of hazelnut syrup and drink it all, all, ALL!*

"Haz—uh—" Merlin was too distracted by stopping himself from ordering a bottle of syrup to register the way the barista was staring at him. By the time he caught her expression of righteous fury, it was too late.

She hurled the contents of the venti coffee cup in her hand, drenching him in some sticky pink concoction, then slapped him across the face. "YOU! I *knew* you'd come here some day, you… you *toad!*"

It was apparently going to be one of those days. At least now he knew that his power was on. The boy and the woman in line had expected to see a Starbucks customer, and that was what they'd seen. Unfortunately for Merlin, it seemed like the barista had expected to see someone she didn't like. From her reaction, she'd been *dreading* seeing someone for quite some time.

"Right," Merlin said, backing out of slapping range. "But I'll never come back again." He was about to leave when curiosity got the better of him. Who did she think he was? Experimentally, he said, "I'm a terrible person."

"You are!" yelled the barista. "And a cheater!"

Ah-ha, Merlin thought. *She expected to see her evil ex.*

"Are you ever going to give me back my sofa, you horrible cheating THIEF?" screamed the barista.

Yes, yes he will, said his raptor. *Because we'll make him!*

Much as Merlin appreciated his raptor's sense of justice, enacting it for the barista seemed unlikely. *I don't even know who her ex is.*

No problem! His inner raptor's tail whipped rapidly back and forth with excitement. *We can find out! It'll be fun!*

The manager rushed out from the back. "What's going on here?"

Merlin began, "I'm her—"

Evil ex, evil sofa stealing ex, his raptor put in.

"Ex," said Merlin firmly. "I came in to harass her and taunt her and tell her I'd never give back her sofa that I stole. But now I'm leaving, bye!"

Before anyone could respond, he fled the Starbucks, leaving behind a trail of pink drips. With any luck his confession would excuse the barista's reaction and protect her job, but it wasn't as if he could stick around to make sure.

His raptor was bouncing around the inside of his head again. *Let's follow her home and search her house and find her evil ex's address and steal her sofa and put it back in her house in the middle of the night so she'll find it as a surprise when she wakes up!*

Merlin had to admit that the "steal and replace sofa" part of the scheme had a definite appeal. But he had other things to do that day. Such as his job. Plus, the office had a bathroom and spare clothes. He could always order coffee delivered and hide in the bathroom once he heard the knock so someone else would open the door, thus reducing the risk that the coffee delivery person would see him as their evil ex or worst enemy or a mugger or someone else who needed the coffee thrown in their face rather than handed over.

Tell your friends about your power, and then you don't need to hide in the bathroom, said his raptor.

For the millionth time, Merlin patiently explained the situation to his raptor. *That power of mine has to stay a secret.*

But your friends know you can turn into a raptor. Gleefully, his raptor added, *And that I can change my size!*

My other power is different, Merlin said. Summoning all his patience and trying to use simple terms that his raptor would understand and not be bored with, he said, *My teammates already think I'm a liar. My other power is a sort of... lying power. It makes people see things that aren't true. And I can't control it. Sure, it doesn't affect my teammates because they already know me. But if they knew about it, they'd think—*

—you have a cool power! interjected his raptor.

—I'm a liar at heart, Merlin said. *They already don't respect me. If they knew about this, they wouldn't trust me either. And that would be the end of me being on the team.*

It was a bitter fact to face, but it was the truth. And, ironically enough, truth was something he respected.

As an afterthought, Merlin added, *And they're not my friends. They're just my teammates. Friends are people who like each other.*

You like your teammates, his raptor said.

Yes, but—

And they like you!

In a way, I guess, but... Merlin wasn't sure how to explain. Protection,

17

Inc: Defenders was a team of damaged misfits forced together by shared trauma. He trusted them to have his back, but it wasn't like they went out for beer and pizza.

Tell your friends about your power, and then tell them about the sofa, and then we can steal it and give it back together, suggested his raptor. *And then you can all get beer and pizza. And ice cream! With hot fudge. And whipped cream. ALL the whipped cream!*

Merlin gave up. *We'll talk about the sofa retrieval later.*

Ignoring the reply of *No no no, now now now,* Merlin headed off to work.

The familiar sound of a bang and a yell met his ears as he approached the lobby. Past experience told him that it was his teammates tripping over things or arguing. But hope, which sprang eternal in his breast, whispered that maybe he'd finally caught a magical pet of his very own.

Yes, yes, said his raptor. *A shape-changing pterodactyl that can pick us up and fly us around, no matter how big or small we are!*

Merlin had been thinking more of an adorable winged kitten that would perch on his shoulder, but his raptor's idea did sound fun. Especially if the shape-changing pterodactyl was big enough for Merlin to ride rather than having to be dangled from its claws.

Eagerly, he threw open the door. The sight that met his eyes made him grateful that he'd gotten the idea of making traps. The live trap he'd set up in the window the night before had caught a magical pet! And what a wonderful one, too. A beautiful gray kitten with translucent dragonfly wings sat inside the trap. One paw was planted in the Kool-Aid cup and one on the honeycomb as it gobbled down the slice of bacon.

Merlin felt a delighted grin nearly split his cheeks. He'd had a good feeling about the bacon. He headed for the trap, hand outstretched, crooning, "Hello, kitty. I can't wait to take you home."

A woman stepped in front of him, blocking his path. He skidded to a stop.

Merlin had seen lots and lots of pretty women in his time, many of them in skin-tight spangled leotards, but none had ever captivated him with a single glance.

Until *her.*

Her brown eyes shone bright with intelligence, and her elegant up-swept eyebrows gave her a slightly sardonic expression that suggested an excellent sense of humor. Merlin had always been good at reading people, a skill he'd honed in his years with the circus, and he thought she looked sensible and reliable, both traits which he admired and which people had often criticized him for lacking.

Also, she had hair like midnight silk, deliciously plump cheeks, and the most kissable lips he'd ever seen. Her body was an intoxicating combination of sensuality and strength, from the firm muscles of her shoulders to the luscious curves of her breasts and thighs, and she moved with the confidence and grace of a trapeze artist.

Her left hand was a prosthetic, and her clinging crimson dress did nothing to hide the scars on her left arm and leg. Merlin recognized the mix of shiny burns and ragged tears and neat surgical incisions: she'd been caught in an explosion. She must have been in combat; her hair was tightly braided and pinned up, which was typical for long-haired women in the military. He felt no pity for her—no veteran would want that, and he was sure from her bearing that she was one—but rather a sense of camaraderie and shared hardship. Like him, she was a survivor.

And this incredible vision was looking at him with an expression very much like the one the barista had worn right before she'd thrown a drink on him and slapped him in the face.

"That's *my* kitten," she said.

"Are you sure?" Merlin asked. "It's in *my* magical pet trap."

"Yes, I'm sure!" She shot him a glare fit to wither him in his tracks. "I brought her here."

She strode to the window and opened the trap. The kitten leaped out, half the bacon still in its mouth, and flew to her shoulder. Its Kool-Aid and honey-soaked paws and the dangling bacon strip left sticky stains and oily smears on her fancy dress as it settled in and continued its meal.

The gorgeous veteran gave a regretful glance at her dress, but didn't dislodge the kitten. Instead, she petted it and said fondly, "Poor baby. You must've been hungry. I should've fed you first thing."

"Um." Merlin was rarely at a loss for words, but he wasn't sure whether he should introduce himself or apologize or ask how she'd gotten the kitten or why she was in the office—

Everything, tell her everything, suggested his raptor. *Quick, before she gets away!*

What actually came out of his mouth was, "I love your kitten. What's her name?"

"Cloud." The beautiful woman eyed him suspiciously. "You don't seem surprised that I have a kitten with wings."

Now he felt on firmer footing. "I'm not. I've seen them before."

"At a lab?"

He nodded. "But not an ordinary lab."

"I wouldn't think so," she said dryly. "Considering that it genetically engineers flying kittens."

"They're not genetically engineered," Merlin said. "They're born that way—I mean, born naturally. They're magical animals. Like pegasi."

"Like what?"

"It's the plural of pegasus. Technically pegasuses is also correct, like octopuses, but it's hard to say and it sounds wrong, so people say octopi. And pegasi. Anyway, your kitten is like a pegasus. Only a cat instead of a horse."

"Uh-huh." Her lovely eyes narrowed with doubt. "If they're magical, why were they in a lab?"

"I'm not exactly sure," Merlin admitted. "I mean, they must've been captured and taken to it, but as for why the wizard-scientists wanted them—"

"The *who?*"

"The wizard-scientists. They're a secret organization of wizards who are also scientists. They claim to date back to the days of King Arthur—"

Merlin broke off when he saw her eyebrows rise high enough to nearly hit the ceiling. "Look, you're the one with a winged kitten on your shoulder."

"Fair enough," she said, a little grudgingly.

Since that was the friendliest she'd been so far, he seized the opportunity to introduce himself. "Also, hi. I'm Merlin Merrick."

He offered his hand. She didn't take it, instead staring down at it with her eyebrows still raised. She had the most marvelously expressive eyebrows. Right now, they were very clearly conveying *I cannot believe you actually thought I'd be willing to shake your hand.*

For an instant, Merlin was hurt. Then he followed her gaze and saw that his hand, no doubt like the rest of him, was covered in sticky pink ooze that smelled strongly of artificial watermelon.

He yanked back his hand. "Okay, we'll skip the handshake. Hi. I'm Merlin Merrick."

As if against her will, a chuckle escaped her lips. Her dubious expression briefly changed to an even more enchanting one of amusement. "I'm Dalisay Batiste. You can call me Dali."

She pronounced it "dally," not "dolly." As in "to dally among the primroses," or "to dally at the fair." She had been so serious before, it made him want to coax her to dally more. Or, to use the other meaning of the word, to dally with *him.*

"I love your name," he said. "It has such a great meaning."

And there went her eyebrows again. She was going to grow eyebrow muscles if she kept this up, she was giving them such a workout. "Uh-huh. Right. What's Dalisay mean, then?"

"Pure."

Surprised, she said, "How do you know that? Were you stationed in the Philippines?"

"No, I just had some Filipino friends growing up. I meant your nickname, though. In English."

"To dilly-dally? What's so great about wasting time?"

"To dally, no dillying involved," he said. "To linger. To *take* your time, not waste it. To relax and enjoy yourself. To play."

"To…" she began, then stopped. But he knew what she'd been about to say: there was only one meaning left.

To have a love affair.

Their eyes met. Her gaze was intent, not awkward or embarrassed. Her eyebrows were challenging: *show me what you've got.* The air between them felt hot and charged, like a tropical night before a lightning storm.

Oh, he thought. *It's not just me.*

She looked him up and down, cool as a glass of lemonade on a summer day. He stood up straight and let her look. So he was dripping with watermelon slime; so what? The chemistry he'd felt with her apparently went both ways.

No. It *definitely* went both ways. Merlin could feel it, crackling between them like purple lightning in a fortuneteller's plasma ball.

Kiss her, urged his raptor. *Now, now, now!*

For a dizzying moment, Merlin thought it might happen. They had drawn close together, and her head was tilted up with those sensual lips of hers slightly parted. All he had to do was ask. All she had to do was say yes.

And then he remembered his power. Not his ability to turn into a raptor, which was *awesome,* or his raptor's ability to change size, which was great once he managed to get the size he wanted. His *other* power. The one he might be using now without even realizing it.

What had Dali expected when she walked into the office? If she was a prospective client, she'd come looking for help; had she expected a bodyguard straight out of central casting, a perfectly strong, perfectly brave, perfectly handsome hero? If she had, and if his power was affecting her, then she wasn't seeing him at all.

He couldn't let anything happen between them until he could be sure that she saw him as he was and wanted him anyway.

Merlin stepped back. It felt like a physically painful wrench, as if he'd been glued to the spot and torn himself loose. And what stung more than that was the brief flicker of hurt in Dali's eyes before she put on a don't-care expression.

No no no no no, yelped his raptor. *What are you doing?! You're rejecting her! You're hurting her feelings! Apologize and give her a sofa!*

A... what? Sometimes Merlin had no idea what his raptor was going on about.

A sofa. Exasperation at Merlin's slowness tinged his raptor's voice as he explained, *Remember how mad the barista was that her ex stole hers? Women love sofas!*

Merlin had no time to explain that logical error to his raptor. Instead, though it made him feel like a sofa had fallen fifty feet and landed right on his heart, he put on his best professional, utterly non-flirtatious smile. "I'm sorry, I've forgotten my manners. Welcome to Defenders, the east coast branch of Protection, Inc. How can I help you?"

CHAPTER 3

Dali was not often baffled, but Merlin baffled her. She could have sworn he was attracted to her. For a wild moment she'd thought he was gearing up to ask her out. And for an even wilder moment, she'd thrown caution to the winds and decided to say yes.

And then he'd backed off, dropped the flirting, and acted like it had never happened. What was *with* him?

I must have imagined it, she decided. *I'm lonely and he's hot, and that's all there is to it.*

It took an impressive amount of hotness to overcome the fact that he'd apparently tripped and spilled an entire strawberry milkshake all over himself. And was wearing a T-shirt showing a caveman riding a dinosaur with the caption MY OTHER CAR IS A VELOCIRAPTOR. Not to mention the red mark on his cheek, which looked exactly like someone had slapped him. Maybe he'd tripped, spilled the milkshake, then fallen into a wall. Cheek first.

Which was also odd, because he moved with an astonishing grace. If he wasn't trained in some traditional martial art like kung fu or aikido, she'd eat her hat. He looked very strong, but he was also light on his feet. In fact, *light* was the word for him all round: the shining gold of his tousled hair, the bright clear blue of his eyes, and his dazzling, warming smile.

Dali forced herself to stop thinking thirsty thoughts. He'd drawn a very clear line in the sand, and it said, *Don't even think about it.* He probably had a girlfriend already. An employed girlfriend with two hands and no scars, physical or mental.

"Right. I did come here for help." But she couldn't help asking one more question. "What's with the traps?"

"Remember that lab I mentioned, where I saw the flying kittens? We found a bunch of magical animals held captive there, and we opened their cages. And then we got attacked and they disappeared. But after we got back home, some of them appeared and kind of adopted some of my friends. But none of them picked me. I wanted a magical pet, so I figured if I set some traps, maybe I'd catch one."

A moment passed after Merlin had finished talking, leaving Dali feeling slightly dazed. It made sense, sort of, on its own bizarre terms. And yet…

On the positive side, she felt a lot more confident now that he would not find her story too weird to believe. All the same, she had no intention of telling him exactly why she'd gone strolling in the park with the necklace. Grandma knew why she'd left the Navy, but as far as Dali was concerned, everyone else could assume it was due to her disability. Which was, she reminded herself, more-or-less the truth.

Instead, she explained that she lived in Tirzah and Pete's apartment building and that was how she'd heard of Defenders, then plunged straight into the necklace-snatching, the police who didn't believe her, the unexpected appearance of Cloud, and the dart attack.

She watched Merlin carefully for signs of disbelief, but he showed none. He looked intrigued by the pigeons, angry over the police, delighted by Cloud, and both concerned and admiring at her escape from the alley.

"That sounds like the wizard-scientists, all right," Merlin said. "That's how I ended up in the lab. I was on patrol with Pete and Ransom and some sniper we never even saw knocked us all out with tranquilizer darts. Good for you for getting away! You must have incredible reflexes."

She couldn't help being pleased at his praise, but said, "It was only because I was expecting an attack. Whoever shot at me—or Cloud—probably thought they'd be taking us completely by surprise. I don't think I could dodge a dart again."

"You won't have to," Merlin said immediately. "I'll protect you. Cloud too, of course. Don't worry. I won't let anything happen to either of you."

His blue eyes were deep as the sky, and as steady. For all his sometimes-flighty manner, she believed that he not only *could* protect her and Cloud, but that she could absolutely trust him to do so. The relief of that realization was so intense, it nearly brought her to tears.

She blinked hard, forcing them back. "And the necklace?"

"Were the birds definitely pigeons?" Merlin asked. "Or could they have been some other birds that had their feathers dyed?"

What a weird question, Dali thought, but answered it. "They were pigeons. It wasn't just the color of their feathers. They were shaped like pigeons and bobbed their heads like pigeons."

"Excellent. Don't worry about your grandma. I'll have her necklace back before the end of the week." But though his voice sounded confident, he didn't meet her eyes.

"You know who stole it?"

"No, but I've come across this method of theft before. I know what doors to bang on. So to speak."

He was hiding something. Dali didn't know what, but she could feel it.

"What aren't you telling me?" she asked.

He blinked innocently at her. "What makes you think there's something I'm not telling you?"

The anger that had been simmering inside her for the last year, through five lost jobs, one harassing boss, and a bunch of jeering cops, abruptly overflowed. "Don't give me that bullshit. If you don't want to tell me, just say so. Don't turn it back on me."

A dead silence fell while they stared at each other, neither giving an inch. Dali waited for him to deny it and tell her she was crazy. She was suddenly glad he hadn't been flirting with her after all. The last thing she needed was to get romantically entangled with a man who'd never admit he was in the wrong, and then blame any consequences on her.

"You're right," Merlin admitted. He didn't sound angry or resentful, just honest. "Sorry. What I wasn't telling you was that I don't think your necklace was stolen by a person with trained pigeons. I think it was stolen by the pigeons themselves. That is, by pigeon shifters—people who can turn into pigeons."

"People who can turn into pigeons," Dali repeated disbelievingly.

Merlin pointed at Cloud. "Flying cat."

"You can't use that as the answer for everything," she protested.

"You have to admit though, it's a very good answer. 'There is more on Heaven and Earth, Horatio, than is dreamt of in your philosophy.' And there's the proof." He again indicated at Cloud, who had finished her bacon and was now chewing Dali's hair.

She hated to admit it, but it was indeed a convincing argument. "And you know these pigeon shifter thieves?"

"No, but I know some bird shifters who use the same trick. If they didn't steal it themselves, they can probably tell me who did. By the way, why were you all dressed up to go to the park? Were you on your way to somewhere else?"

Dali had been hoping to avoid that *why*. But as she looked into the clear blue of his eyes, she realized that she didn't mind if he knew. "I just got fired. My grandma said that instead of immediately looking for a new job, I should relax, dress up, and smell the roses. Literally."

"Why'd you get fired?"

"Same reason I always get fired," she admitted. "I tried to make some improvements at my workplace, and it turned out that everyone else liked things exactly the way they were. I was a yeoman in the Navy—that's an administrator—"

"I know what yeomen do," Merlin assured her. "I was a Marine. They take a million moving parts and busy people and different jobs, plus a *billion* pieces of paper, and they turn it into a machine that runs so smoothly that no one even notices until you get an incompetent yeoman, and then everything comes to a screeching halt."

"Yes. That's exactly what it was like." The warmth of remembered pride filled her. Even in the Navy, lots of people didn't appreciate yeomen. Like he said, the better they were at their jobs, the less you noticed them. But Merlin had noticed.

"You wanted your civilian jobs to be like that, right?" he asked. "I take it you got a bunch of incompetent idiots who didn't like hearing that things could be done better?"

"Yes. Well, that and I caught one boss harassing a temp worker. She was young and too scared to stand up for herself, so I had to do something."

"Oh?" Merlin's eyes gleamed with delight. "Tell me he'll never do that again."

"Hopefully not. I reported him everywhere I could think of."

He studied her with those bright, knowing eyes of his. "I bet that's not all you did."

"I dropped his new laptop on his foot," she admitted. "Broke them both. I was lucky he didn't press charges."

"I expect he didn't want to end up in court and have you explain why you did it. Good for you. Just imagine what it would have been like for that poor temp worker if you hadn't been there!"

Dali had only told that story once before, to Grandma. She'd said Dali had her heart in the right place but needed to keep a better grip on her temper, then lectured her all the way through dessert on how terrible it would be if she'd ended up in jail. Dali had recognized several of the scenarios from *Orange is the New Black* and pointed out that the show was fiction, only to have Grandma counter that the reality was probably even worse.

But Merlin hadn't lectured her or scolded her, or even said that she should leave justice to the professionals. Instead, he'd sympathized with the young temp, and had understood why Dali had to step in. More than understood: he'd approved.

It had been so long since she'd worked with men who respected her, or with anyone who saw the world the way she did. It made her wish she could work *with* him instead of just handing him a task and then returning to her own job search.

She couldn't say that, but she did want to let him know some of what she'd been thinking. Dali believed in encouraging people who did the right thing. But though she'd intended to say something complimentary but impersonal, what actually came out of her mouth was, "I knew guys like you in the Navy."

She shut her mouth fast, before she could say anything even more revealing. But his gaze wasn't pitying, but sympathetic. "It was a home to you, wasn't it?"

Dali nodded, not trusting herself to speak.

"I had something like that too," Merlin said.

She swallowed, forcing back any telltale tremble in her voice. "The Marines?"

"The circus."

The military was full of acronyms and nicknames. The 101st Airborne was the Screaming Eagles, sailors were called squids, and the *USS Kalamazoo* was nicknamed the *Zoo.* But Dali couldn't bring to mind any ship or unit or place that was nicknamed "the circus." Then she remembered a unit whose name sounded sort of like "circus."

"Is that what they call the Marine headquarters and service company?" she asked. When he looked blank, she said, "Headquarters and circus?"

Merlin let out a laugh so sudden that Cloud hissed in protest. "No, no. I meant an actual, literal circus. I was raised in one, you see."

"Really?" Dali asked, fascinated. "What was that like?"

He tilted his head, examining her like she was some strange but appealing creature, like a kitten with dragonfly wings. "Did you know you're the first person who's ever asked me that question?"

29

"I'd think people would ask you all the time," Dali replied, a little defensively. It was so unusual, of course she'd been curious.

"Mostly they think I'm making it all up."

"Why would they think that?"

"Well…" Merlin's voice trailed off.

Dali didn't interrupt. Even apart from his stunning good looks, his engaging manner, his unique background, and his previous experience with magical creatures—all perfectly obvious reasons for her to want to get to know him—she sensed a mystery that intrigued her. There was something about him that felt hidden, despite his open manner.

Then she realized that while she'd been waiting for him to go on, a silence had fallen. A silence in which that chemistry she'd felt earlier had come to crackling, electric life. She could almost feel the warmth of his body on her skin, even though they were standing apart.

The little details of him stood out to her as if they were rimmed in light. The unusual thickness of muscle at his wrists, which wasn't something you got from working out at a gym. The sunlight coming in through the windows that turned his hair to molten gold. His stillness now, when previously he'd been constantly in motion, even if it was nothing more than twirling the windowshade cord between his fingers.

When she finally lifted her gaze to his eyes, she caught him looking at her as intently as she'd been looking at him. No, not looking: he was staring at her. Taking her in. *Drinking* her in. She abruptly recalled that she was still in the red silk dress, which showed off her cleavage and her hips and her ass and her legs and—well, pretty much everything. And while his gaze wasn't obnoxiously glued to any particular part, there was no doubt in her mind that he appreciated the view.

Next time I see Grandma, I'll thank her for telling me to wear this, she thought.

Grandma had been right. It *was* nice to stop and enjoy the roses. And there was a rose of a man right in front of her.

Sure, he wasn't available. He'd already made that quite clear. But once upon a time, she'd enjoyed just having chemistry and looking and maybe a little light flirting, with no need for anything more to come of it.

"Can I ask you something?" Merlin asked abruptly.

"Sure."

He shuffled his feet, gave a little cough, and asked, "What color is my hair?"

Dali stared at him. "Is that a joke?"

"No." She could see from his expression that he was absolutely serious. "Just tell me, please. What color does it look like to you?"

"Like early afternoon sunlight. Like a field of ripe wheat. Like…" She broke off, hoping she wasn't blushing. It was hard to describe his hair without thinking of running her fingers through it. "Is that specific enough? I'm not a hair stylist, I don't know the technical terms."

Merlin was grinning as if she'd just handed him a million dollar check. "Great. Great. That's all I needed to know. Now there's something *I* should tell *you*…"

CHAPTER 4

Merlin wondered where he should even start.

"I have this secret power I've never told anyone about, and I asked you about my hair color to make sure it wasn't affecting you now."

"I'm a shifter, like the pigeons who stole your grandma's necklace."

"Even my own teammates never believe a word I say."

"About my circus…"

Everything, tell her everything, his raptor chimed in. *All at once!*

Maybe it would be best if he told her everything in the form of a story. Everyone loved stories. Well, everyone except his teammates, who had been known to flee the room when he began one. But maybe Dali would be different.

"I mentioned that I was raised in a circus," he began. "It all began…"

"Not that again," said an all-too-familiar voice. His teammate Pete had flung open the door and was holding it open for his mate Tirzah as she came in. In his other hand, he held a large Starbucks cup. Tirzah had another one in the cup holder of her wheelchair.

Merlin sighed. The moment was ruined, and he *still* didn't have any coffee.

"Oh, hey, Dali, what're you doing—" Tirzah broke off, stared, then burst out laughing. "You have a flying kitten! How long have you had it?"

"About an hour. I found her in an alley. Or maybe she found me."
Dali shot Tirzah and Pete a sharp glance. "You don't seem that surprised that flying kittens exist, either."

"No," Tirzah admitted. "I have one too. So does Pete. I love yours,
she's so pretty!"

Tirzah approached Dali and the kitten, then came to a jolting stop as
one of her wheels ran over what was left of his floor trap and the twine
tangled in the spokes.

"Goddammit, Merlin!" Pete roared. "You're a menace!"

Pete stooped to untangle Tirzah, then straightened up and pointed
an accusing finger at Merlin. "YOU put an obstacle in her path, YOU
get rid of it!"

Merlin, feeling guilty, took a step toward Tirzah. She held up her
hands to ward him off. "Don't come near me! You're covered in...
What *are* you covered in?"

"Watermelon frappuccino," he said absently, but his attention was
elsewhere.

"Hey, Merlin?" Dali said.

It was the first time she'd ever said his name. There was something
so intimate about hearing it from her lips, in her beautiful voice. He'd
treasure the memory always, whether they ever got a chance to act on
their attraction or not.

And then he came back to earth as he took in the rest of what she
was saying: "Why *are* you covered in watermelon frappuccino? And...
is that a handprint on your face?"

Pete, glancing over his shoulder as he cut the twine with a pocket
knife, said, "Don't bother asking Merlin questions like that. Or any
questions about himself. He'll just come out with some ridiculous
bullshit story."

"Oh?" Dali's eyebrows arched, but her skeptical look was directed at Pete, not Merlin. She turned to face Merlin to ask, "So, what
happened?"

Resigned to her disbelief, Merlin said, "I went into a Starbucks, and before I could even place my order the barista threw a drink at me and slapped me across the face."

"See what I mean?" Pete said to Dali.

Merlin liked Pete. Really. But there were times when he wanted to throw a watermelon frappuccino over *him*, and this was one of them.

Ignoring Pete, Dali asked Merlin, "Why would she do that?"

"She mistook me for her ex who cheated on her and stole her sofa."

His raptor, who had been uncharacteristically quiet up to this point, broke in. *Let's go steal the sofa back! And pour a watermelon frappuccino over the ex while he's sleeping!*

"Who you coincidentally happened to resemble enough for her to think you were him from a foot away," Pete said.

Merlin resisted the urge to flick some watermelon frappuccino droplets in his face. Instead, he gave Pete his biggest, brightest smile, and said, "When I was in the circus, we had these two trapeze artists who went by Mia and Pia Bonaventura, and performed as twins. They really did look a lot alike—especially when they had makeup and identical leotards on—even though not only were they not sisters, let alone twins, they weren't related at all. They also weren't Italian, but that's another story. Anyway, once Pia was dangling upside down from the trapeze when a traveling salesman—"

"Merlin," Pete interrupted. "There's showers in the office. Why don't you go take one?"

"Dali hired me for a job," said Merlin, who did want a shower but didn't want to leave Dali alone with Pete, who would undoubtedly tell her unfairly misleading stories about him. "To protect her and Cloud—her kitten's name is Cloud—and to retrieve a stolen necklace. I need a few more details—"

"Oh?" Pete folded his arms. Between his size and his stubborn expression and his brown hair, he reminded Merlin very much of the cave bear he could turn into. "I'm her neighbor. I should be the one protecting her."

"Guys," Tirzah said, spinning her chair so the wheels made a barrier between them. "Number one, it's Dali's choice. Number two, Roland is the boss and you really ought to run the whole thing by him first. Number three, you're not the only agents who work here."

"There was another man here when I came in," Dali put in. "Tall, brownish-red hair, looked kind of like a professor...?"

"Did he say anything weird, by any chance?" Tirzah asked, grinning.

"Yeah, he did, actually."

"Ransom," chorused Merlin and Pete.

"He didn't seem very friendly. If your boss Roland is okay with it, I'll go with one of you." Dali looked from Pete to Merlin.

Merlin had to restrain himself from saying, *Me, me, pick me*—though that didn't stop his raptor from saying it. But like Tirzah had said, it was Dali's choice.

"I'll take Merlin," she said, smiling at him. "When can you start?"

"Immediately." Half of him wanted to burst into song and skip around the room. The other half, looking ahead to what he'd have to do to retrieve her necklace, wanted to run screaming. "I mean, after my shower."

He stared deeply into Pete's eyes, trying to telepathically communicate *She doesn't know I'm a shifter and I want to tell her myself so please don't mention it while I'm out of the room, naked, dripping wet, and unable to speak for myself.*

Pete made an impatient gesture. "What?"

Merlin came to his senses. Pete might be willing to discuss flying kittens with someone who already had one, but there was no way he'd bring up the fact that Merlin was a shifter. It would be too close to admitting that Pete was one himself. And while Pete had gotten much more comfortable with his cave bear since he'd fallen in love with Tirzah, it still wasn't a topic he'd bring up of his own accord.

"Call Carter and tell him to come fix the coffee machine," Merlin said, and fled.

He took the fastest shower of all time, if you didn't count the "lightning shower" act he'd once understudied at the circus, and was done, dried, and dressed in spare clothes in less than ten minutes. When he returned to the lobby, his hair was still dripping down the back of his TEA REX T-shirt, which featured a tea-sipping T-rex dressed like an Edwardian gentleman.

Dali was sitting on the sofa next to Tirzah, both of them tickling Cloud, who was rolling around on the floor. Tirzah leaned over to stroke her fat tummy, then winced slightly and put a hand to her shoulder.

Pete, who had been rummaging through a stack of files, put them down, stepped behind Tirzah, and started massaging her shoulders.

She moved her mass of curly brown hair out of the way of his hands. "Thanks, sweetie."

"You've got a hell of a knot in there," Pete said, pressing hard. "Okay, I think I got it."

Tirzah leaned her head against his arm. "You have the best hands."

An unexpected pang of jealousy went through Merlin. That was what it was like to have a mate. It didn't mean your relationship would be free of difficulties or conflict, but it did mean that you would love each other and be there for each other. Forever.

Born shifters, like the ones he'd known at the circus, recognized their mates at first sight. But Merlin and his teammates had been made into shifters, and their wizard-scientist creators had destroyed their ability to recognize or bond with their mates. Pete and Tirzah had eventually managed to overcome that, but Merlin had no idea if that meant that all of them could, or if they'd been a special case.

He really hoped that all of them could. He couldn't think of anything more wonderful than having a mate. Though now that he'd met Dali, it was hard to imagine a woman he'd want more than her.

He shot a glance at her. She didn't look like someone who'd just been informed that the bodyguard she wanted to hire could turn into a raptor. Good. He wanted to tell her himself, preferably alone and in a more controlled environment than the office.

Why all the fuss? asked his raptor. *I'm so cool! She'll love seeing me! Who wouldn't?*

Merlin gave an inward sigh. *Because the last time I showed you to some- one who'd never seen anyone shift before, she screamed and nearly tipped her chair over.*

Tirzah was just startled, his raptor said. *She said so herself.*

Not. Yet, Merlin said firmly. A veteran like Dali would be unlikely to scream, of course. And he already knew she had nerves of steel. But all the same, he wanted to do a better job of preparation this time.

Cloud scuttled behind the sofa, and Dali followed her. Crouching down behind it, she was momentarily invisible.

The front door opened and Roland came in. The Defenders boss ran his hand through his silvering hair, looking harried.

"Merlin!" Roland flipped open his briefcase and extracted a gnawed-on report. Waving it at Merlin, he said, "How many times do I have to tell you, 'my raptor ate my report' is not a valid excuse?"

"Roland!" Horrified, Merlin flapped his hand madly at the sofa. Roland glanced at it, saw only Pete and Tirzah, and mistook Merlin's intent.

"Don't point to Pete," Roland said crossly. "Yeah, he had trouble controlling his cave bear, but he never let it affect his office work. If you turn into a raptor and it goes out of control, don't give me some long, ridiculous explanation about how once in the circus ten clowns, three seals, and the daring young man on the flying trapeze all took turns eating the white tiger's homework. If your raptor chews up your report, *you write another report!*"

Dali stood up, Cloud in her arms. Her eyebrows looked like a pair of loaded guns directed at Merlin as she repeated Roland's words: "If you turn into a raptor?!"

"Er," Merlin said. "That was what I was trying to tell you when Pete came in."

She folded her arms. "Let's get all our cards on the table. If you really turn into a raptor, I want to see it. Now."

"Wait!" Tirzah, Pete, and Roland flung out their hands and shouted simultaneously.

But Merlin didn't see any point in waiting and explaining. She already knew, so that part was out of the bag. She'd said she wanted to see it, so any delays would only annoy her. Besides, he was proud of his raptor and he wanted to show it off.

Small, he thought as he triggered the shift. *Tiny. Hamster-sized. Remember, we don't want to alarm her.*

But his raptor had other ideas. And once he began to shift, it was his raptor who had the upper hand.

BIG! he gleefully exclaimed. *We want to impress her! The ceiling's the limit!*

CHAPTER 5

Dali was not normally a screamer. But when a twelve-foot velociraptor suddenly loomed over her, with eyes like yellow lanterns and fangs like daggers and claws like scimitars, a startled shriek burst from her lips.

And then her reflexes took over. She might have been a desk jockey who'd never seen combat except for that one devastating day, but she'd been trained like everyone else. Instinctively seeking to protect those who needed it the most, she thrust Cloud into Tirzah's arms and jumped in front of them both.

"Goddammit, Merlin!" Pete bellowed.

"Shift back, now!" shouted Roland, the burly black man who had scolded Merlin over the report. To Dali, he said, "Please don't be alarmed…"

"It's Merlin, Dali," Tirzah said. "It's fine. He's just impetuous."

"That's a nice word for it," Pete muttered.

Dali's heartbeat slowed. Of course. A *veloci*raptor. She'd assumed he meant a raptor as in a bird of prey. She wasn't sure whether to be annoyed at Merlin for not warning her or annoyed at herself for screaming.

Cloud zipped out of Tirzah's arms and flew at the gigantic velociraptor, wings buzzing like an angry hornet. Hovering in midair, she arched her back and spat in its face.

The velociraptor abruptly shrank to the size of a kitten. Cloud, undeterred, dove down and pounced on it. The kitten and the kitten-sized velociraptor began rolling over the floor together.

Roland and Dali moved simultaneously. Dali snatched up Cloud, anxiously examining her for injuries to her delicate wings, while the kitten struggled and hissed, trying to return to the fight. Meanwhile, Roland gingerly plucked up the tiny velociraptor and held it up before his eyes, sighing, "Merlin…"

Reassured that Cloud was unharmed, Dali returned her attention to the velociraptor. It had sleek rather than scaly hide and was black rather than green, but otherwise, it was the spitting image of the deadly dinosaurs in *Jurassic Park*. Apart from being the size of a kitten.

The velociraptor gave a rather frantic-sounding hiss. Roland placed it on the floor and stepped back. It suddenly grew back to its full height, its head almost brushing the ceiling, then shrank, just as suddenly, to the size of a hamster. Cloud let out long "mrrrrorrrrw," which Dali recognized as a hunting howl. She clutched the kitten tight. The last thing anyone needed was a repeat of the kitten vs. velociraptor battle.

The velociraptor grew once more, this time to the height of a man. It let out a furious hiss, and then was Merlin again, clean and fully dressed in a new outfit, his wet hair darkened to bronze. "Whew. Sorry about that."

Dali stared at him. It was one thing to be told that people could turn into animals, or even to hold a winged kitten in your arms. It was a whole 'nother thing to actually see that charming, fast-talking, annoyingly sexy man turn into a giant dinosaur. And also a tiny dinosaur. And a medium size dinosaur. It was so mind-boggling, she couldn't even process it.

"I really am sorry," Merlin repeated. "Remember that lab I mentioned, with the wizard-scientists who'd locked up Cloud and the other magical creatures? And how me and Ransom and Pete—and Roland too—got kidnapped and taken there? They experimented on us to make us into shapeshifters and give us special powers. So this is all pretty new to us. Which is why I'm still a little shaky on getting my size right when I shift. *I didn't even know I could get that big!*"

Dali bit her lip, trying not to snicker. She had to be the only person there who'd thought of the double meaning, and she didn't want to come across like she had a dirty mind.

Tirzah burst into giggles. "Merlin, do you say that to all the ladies?"

"I've seen bigger," said Pete.

Roland, his lips twitching, seemed to be fighting an internal battle to not comment. He lost. "Is whatever you used prescription-only, or did you order it by mail?"

"You guys,"Merlin said despairingly. To Roland, he said, "You're the one who's always telling us we need to be more professional!"

"You do need to be more professional," replied Roland with a perfect deadpan. "Stop turning into a dinosaur in the workplace."

"I was very impressed with your size," Dali assured Merlin, grinning. "And Cloud *loved* mini-dinosaur-you."

Merlin gave in and laughed. Then he spun around with that incredible grace of his, saying, "I'm sorry, I didn't get a chance to introduce you. Dali, this is Roland Walker, our boss. Roland, this is Dali Batiste."

"Oh," Roland said, looking her over with new interest. "You're Tirzah and Pete's neighbor. You were a sailor, right? I was in the Army."

As Dali nodded, Merlin said to Pete, "How come you told Roland about her but you never mentioned her to me?"

"You were there," Pete said. "You were too busy babbling about tightrope walkers falling out of clown cars to listen."

"Tightrope walkers falling *on* to clown cars," said Merlin.

"Guys," Tirzah said peaceably. "I think she came up *once*. Roland has a good memory."

"And what can we do for you, Dali?" Roland asked.

"She's my new client," Merlin said. He stepped closer to her as he spoke, as if he might need to shield her with his body. Dali could smell the shampoo he'd used on his drying hair, an herbal-spicy aroma. She inhaled appreciatively.

41

"You mean, she'd like to hire us and you're requesting her," Roland said.

Dali recognized this kind of turf war. Given the state of the office, she was unsurprised at the lack of a clear chain of command. She moved to break the tie. "*I'm* requesting *him.* If you don't mind."

"Not at all," Roland said. "You can think of this little interlude as a Merlin's demonstration of his skills."

That reminded her of the other thing she'd heard Roland say. "Pete, you can turn into a *cave bear?*"

Pete gave a reluctant nod.

Dali turned to Roland. "What sort of dinosaur—I mean prehistoric animal—

do *you* turn into?"

"None," Roland said. "The experiments they were doing weren't just with prehistoric animals, but mythic ones too. That is, magical animals. I'm a phoenix."

Looking into his steady gaze, Dali found it impossible to doubt what he said. "And you can all change your size?"

"No, that's just me," Merlin said. "The rest of us have other powers. Also thanks to the wizard-scientists."

"I don't thank them for mine," said a new voice.

Dali almost jumped out of her skin. The tall man with the dark red hair, the one she'd met when she'd first come in, had returned without her noticing.

"And I don't need any powers to know who's responsible for… this." He waved a long-fingered hand. Dali, following his gesture, saw that the giant velociraptor had made the general mess even worse by breaking coffee cups, knocking over stacks of files, and scattering papers all over the floor. "Merlin."

"Ransom Pierce," Merlin began. "Meet—"

"Dali Batiste," said Ransom. He shook her hand. "Pleased to meet you."

"How did you know my name?" Dali inquired. "Were you standing with your ear to the door this whole time?"

Ransom looked mildly amused. "In a manner of speaking. That's my power: I know things."

"That's very… broad," Dali said.

"Yes," said Ransom, and said nothing more.

"So, do you *know* who stole my necklace? And who's after Cloud or me?"

Ransom shook his head. "Knowledge comes to me. I don't choose what I know. It's much harder to find specific information." The hard lines of his face softened a little as he said, "Merlin's the terror of the office, but he's an excellent bodyguard. You'll be safe with him protecting you."

Dali smiled, warming to him. Anyone who praised Merlin was all right in her book. "I know. Hey, everyone's been telling me what they turn into. Or showing me, in Merlin's case. So, do you turn into something prehistoric, or something magical?"

She regretted asking when his face froze over again. "Magical." Then, after a long pause, he added, "A hellhound."

What the hell—so to speak—is a hellhound? Dali wondered. But his expression forbade further questioning.

Tirzah broke the uncomfortable silence by saying cheerfully, "I'm the boring one. I don't turn into anything."

Pete leaned down and kissed her cheek. "That's because you're perfect exactly the way you are."

The door flew open as if it had been kicked, and a man in an expensive-looking suit came in. Dali couldn't see his face, as he was carrying a machine big enough to block it.

"All right, guys," he proclaimed. "I made this so *I* could have a reliable source of coffee if I happen to be here. I'll let you use it on the condition that you read the instructions I wrote for it and follow them to the letter. I'm putting it…"

The man lowered the machine, revealing his face. He was handsome, with black hair and hazel eyes that widened as he took in the state of

43

the office. He looked absolutely aghast, then pulled the thing that Dali figured must be the world's most elaborate coffee machine defensively close to his chest. "On second thought, maybe I'm not putting it anywhere. It won't last ten minutes in this madhouse!"

"No, please, Carter," Tirzah begged. "I need coffee! Put it in the tech room, it'll be safe there."

"It better be," Carter said, directing an ominous stare at Merlin. Then he noticed Dali. "Hello. I'm Carter Howe. And I don't work here!"

"Hi, I'm Dali Batiste," Dali said, baffled by his vehemence. "I'm a client too."

Merlin burst out laughing. He was quickly joined by Tirzah, then Pete.

Carter looked exasperated. "I'm not a client. I do tech work—as a favor—for the team. Occasionally. Rarely."

"Okay," Dali said, still puzzled by why he was telling her all this.

"Carter's a shifter too," Merlin said.

"Merlin!" Carter shouted.

"It's fine, Carter," said Roland. "She already saw Merlin turn into a velociraptor."

"That wasn't what I meant," Carter said.

Merlin went on, "Carter's been invited to join the team. Repeatedly. He keeps saying he's not interested, but he keeps hanging around, so it does give the impression that he works here. It reminds me of when I was in the circus and there was this girl who was also raised in it, but she kept saying she didn't want any part of the life and she refused to be part of her family's act. But she never did leave. One night, her brother sprained his ankle right before he was supposed to go onstage, and—"

"I don't 'hang around,'" Carter interrupted, glaring at Merlin. "And enough with the circus stories! Nobody believes in your imaginary circus!"

Dali felt oddly protective of Merlin. Everyone kept accusing him of making things up, but even the most outrageous things he'd told her had turned out to be absolutely true. Borrowing his own argument that one impossible thing proves another, she said, "You guys, Merlin turns into a velociraptor! Why *wouldn't* you believe that he was raised in a circus?"

"Because his stories are ridiculous," Carter said.

"More ridiculous than a flying kitten?" Dali inquired.

"If you'd been in the Marines with him and heard all his stories…" Pete began, then trailed off, looking uncertain. "I mean, I believe that the circus exists. I've seen posters for it! I just don't believe that Merlin, a white rat, and three performing seals discovered the lost crown jewels of the queen of Latveria—"

"Latveria doesn't exist," Tirzah said helpfully. "It's Doctor Doom's kingdom. I think it was Latvia. Or maybe Lithuania."

"That's what I mean," said Pete. "His stories are so unlikely, they might as well involve Doctor Doom!"

Merlin glanced from his teammates to Dali, then seemed to make up his mind. Standing up straight and looking them in the eyes, he said, "My stories are true. All of them. The one about Queen Juliana's crown jewels included. I haven't told you everything, but I've never told a lie. The circus is real. It's the Fabulous Flying Chameleons, and you can see them for yourself."

The Fabulous Flying Chameleons! Dali, delighted, imagined Merlin on that crowded, joyous billboard. In a skin-tight leotard, swinging from a trapeze…

But his teammates didn't look as happy. Instead, they looked uncomfortable, confused, and maybe even a little guilty. A silence fell.

Finally, Pete said, "Why didn't you ever say it like that before?"

"Would you have believed me?" Merlin asked.

"Yes," said Roland simply. Except for Ransom, the rest of them nodded their agreement.

Merlin's sharp gaze turned to Ransom. "You wouldn't have?"

"I didn't need to hear it from you to believe it," Ransom said. "I always knew it was all true. I know things, remember?"

Merlin's voice rose in frustration and annoyance. "Then why didn't you say so?"

Ransom shrugged. "You never asked."

An argument promptly broke out again. Dali listened incredulously. How did this team of squabbling misfits ever get *anything* done? Then Roland raised a hand and cleared his throat, and she realized that was how as they subsided into silence.

"Dali?" Roland said. "We're a small team, and we often pitch in on each other's cases. I know you've already spoken with Merlin, but would you mind telling the story to the rest of the team?"

"I'm not on the team," Carter said. But she noticed that he didn't leave. Instead, he sat down, holding his coffee machine protectively in his lap.

"To the rest of the team and Carter," said Roland patiently.

Dali repeated her story, with everyone listening intently. Merlin chimed in occasionally. When she got to the part about the black darts, she noticed the blood drain from Ransom's face, leaving it white as paper. Pete reached out as if he was going to put a hand on Ransom's shoulder, but Ransom gave him a chilly stare. Pete dropped his hand to his side.

"Them again," Carter sighed.

"At least the pteranodon guy's dead," Tirzah said.

"Pteranodon?" Dali said incredulously.

"It's a long story," Merlin said. "It all began when Tirzah here—"

A chorus of "Not now!" arose.

"The wizard-scientists went after me and Tirzah," Pete explained. "They were trying to get their magical creatures back. That's probably why you and Cloud got shot at—they were after Cloud."

Dali held the kitten close. "Well, they're not going to get her. And what about those pigeon shifters who stole Grandma's necklace? Are they the wizard-scientists too?"

"No, I'm sure they're not," said Merlin.

Roland turned to Merlin. "You seem to know a lot about methods shifters can use to commit crimes. Where exactly did you learn all that?"

Merlin shot a glance at Dali, chewed on his lip, then mumbled, more to her than to Roland, "My circus."

"The Fabulous Flying Chameleons is a *crime circus?*" Dali blurted out.

"Of course it is," Carter remarked. "What other sort of circus would have raised Merlin?"

Merlin ignored Carter and replied to Dali. Earnestly, he said, "It's not a *crime circus.* It's a completely legitimate circus which has real acts and earns real money from real ticket sales…"

"And does some real crimes on the side?" Tirzah inquired.

"And does some crimes on the side," Merlin admitted.

Dali felt like her head was about to explode. "Your crime circus stole my grandmother's necklace?!"

"No!" Merlin exclaimed, madly waving his hands as if that possibility was flying at his face like a rabid pigeon. Startled, Cloud leaped off Dali's shoulder, digging in her claws painfully, and flew as far away from him as she could get. "No, no, absolutely not!"

Everyone looked at him. Dali folded her arms and glared.

In a small voice, he said, "It can't have been anyone from my circus because none of them are pigeon shifters. But someone from the Fabulous Flying Chameleons might have told the pigeon shifter thieves how to do it."

"A crime circus," Pete said, shaking his head. "Only you, Merlin."

Merlin, looking deeply and rather desperately into Dali's eyes, said, "Financial and property crimes only! Absolutely nothing violent! And only to people who can afford it."

"Well, of course you only steal from the rich," said Carter. "Poor people don't have enough money to make it worthwhile."

"Stealing is stealing," Dali said to Merlin, ignoring Carter's sarcasm. "Just because you're not ruining anyone's life doesn't make it okay."

Once again, she expected Merlin to blow her off. Once again, he didn't. "I know. I mean, I did leave it." He hesitated, his frank gaze sliding off to the side. "Well—there were other reasons."

For a moment, Dali was frustrated. Why couldn't he just tell her… whatever it was. Then she remembered that the last thing he hadn't told her immediately was that he could turn into a raptor. Maybe he had his reasons for not dropping everything on her all at once.

"Is everyone in it a shifter?" Carter asked.

Merlin nodded. "Pretty much. We don't—they don't—have any actual animals. The animal acts are all us. I mean them."

"No wonder you were so unfazed by learning that shifters existed," Pete said. "You knew all along."

Merlin grinned. "Yep. I couldn't tell, of course."

Despite her moral indignation over the crime part, Dali couldn't help being charmed by the idea of shifters performing in animal acts. "The tigers are actually tiger shifters?"

Merlin grinned at her. "And the ringmaster cracking the whip at them is a white rat. And the elephant is his wife. Everyone shifts backstage, then comes back out and does another act in another form. It's very convenient—we only need half the people that we normally would, because every performer is also an animal. And of course no one needs to train or take care of the animals. Though we do keep cages and food for show."

It seemed to give Carter physical pain to admit this, but he said, "That's very clever. A lot of shifters hide in plain sight—I can't tell you how many people I know who are their own cats—but that's not possible for wild animal shifters in cities. But if anyone sees a tiger at a circus, well, of course there's tigers at a circus."

Merlin beamed. "Yes, exactly. It all began hundreds of years ago, in medieval times, when we were traveling jesters with dancing bears. I mean traveling jesters who *were* dancing bears. It's probably the oldest living circus in the world. And we still have a dancing bear! Not the same dancing bear, of course, or even a descendant. But the tradition—"

"Right, got it," Carter said.

Tirzah grabbed Pete's arm. "Pete, we have to go. And take Caro. And your mom. They'll love it. Especially once we tell them it's all shifters!"

"No!" Merlin exclaimed. "I, um, I might need you to do something there later."

"Merlin's right," Roland said. "No visiting the circus until the investigation's over."

"Except for you." Merlin smiled at Dali. "I have to protect you, so I can't leave your side… and you can't leave mine. How do you feel about a matinee?"

CHAPTER 6

Dali's smile was as radiant as the mid-day sun. "Absolutely!"

Yes yes yes, chimed in Merlin's raptor. *We'll go to the circus and roll around in the sawdust and swing from the trapeze and eat ALL the cara- mel corn!*

"Great! Let's go!"

"I have to drop off Cloud—" Dali began, then broke off. "Is it safe to leave her at my apartment?"

"Completely," Pete assured her. "Remember, I did the security sys- tem. We leave our own flying kittens there."

"I can monitor the building from my phone," Tirzah said. "Cloud will be fine."

Doubtfully, Dali said, "Is that enough? If you see anyone trying to get in, you're half an hour away."

"I'm not," said Roland. When she gave him a puzzled glance, he lifted his hands and made little wing-flapping movements. He was so imposing, between his size and his silvering hair and his solemn expres- sion, that the contrast between that and his flappy-hand gesture made Merlin burst out laughing.

"Phoenix," Merlin reminded her.

"Right." Dali popped Cloud in her purse and waved good-bye with her prosthetic hand, keeping her other hand in her purse.

Excitement tingled up and down his spine as he escorted her to the parking lot. Finally, he was alone with her. She'd described his hair color perfectly, so she was seeing him as he was. He didn't need to worry that he was accidentally deceiving her.

On the negative side, she had been notably un-thrilled to learn that he came from a criminal background. Not to mention that someone from his circus was probably indirectly responsible for the theft he'd been hired to solve. That could make things awkward.

He realized with a start that he was already thinking of the future. *Their* future.

Could she be his mate?

He swallowed, struck to the heart with the thought of it, just as he'd been struck to the heart by the first sight of her. It hadn't occurred to him before because normally shifters instantly recognized their mates. But Pete hadn't known Tirzah was his mate till later.

Is Dali my mate? Merlin asked his raptor.

What's a mate? his raptor replied.

Which pretty much answered that. But Merlin replied anyway. *Your true love. The person you'll love forever, as long as you both shall live.*

I like Dali, replied his raptor. *I bet she'd help us steal a sofa. You should make her some hot chocolate. Look, a blinking light!*

Merlin gave an inner sigh. Probably the whole idea of him meeting his mate, whether he recognized her or not, was wishful thinking. In theory, everyone had a mate, whether they were shifters or not. In practice, not everyone actually found theirs—shifters included.

He should just enjoy being with Dali for as long as it lasted, whether that was a day or so (a thought which filled him with gloom) or forever.

But he couldn't help hoping for forever.

When they reached the underground parking lot, he watched Dali look around with interest at the admittedly unusual selection of cars.

"I know that one," she said, indicating Tirzah's car, a Tesla that had been modified for hand controls. "And I don't see Pete's, so I assume he came with her."

In the brief time he'd known Dali, he'd seen her suspicious, disapproving, startled, heroic, protective, sad, amused, and flirtatious. There was so much *to* her— no man at her side would ever be bored. She'd been playful, too, which was a mood he had the feeling she hadn't experienced recently. Merlin wanted to let her experience it more.

Rather than heading for his car, he stopped. "Guess which is whose."

Her eyebrows arched in surprise, then pulled together in suspicion. "Is this some kind of test?"

"No," said Merlin. "It's a game. If you don't think it'll be fun, you don't have to play."

Dali smiled. "Okay. I'll give it a shot."

He watched her, not the cars, as her gaze traveled over them, sharp but also amused. Enjoying herself. He liked seeing that.

"Dark blue Volkswagen," she said. "Sturdy, reliable, not flashy. Must be Roland."

"Correct," said Merlin.

"Lipstick-red Ferrari," she went on. "That car screams 'I have a lot of money and possibly a midlife crisis.' Carter?"

"Very good!"

Dali grinned, clearly enjoying herself and enjoying his attention. Merlin couldn't believe how much she'd brightened up from the serious, buttoned-down woman he'd first laid eyes on.

Like a rose in winter, he thought. *All you see at first is the thorns. But add a little sunlight and water, and it blossoms.*

"Okay," she said. "To be honest, I got to the next one by the process of elimination, not insight. I'm guessing that generic-looking white car is Ransom's, because I *know* the tiny red one is yours."

"Excellent! A+" Merlin applauded. To his delight, Dali took a bow. As they headed for his car, he explained, "Ransom rents a new car every month. I assume so he's not easy to find or follow. How'd you guess mine?"

With a perfect deadpan, she said, "Because it's a clown car."

"I'll have you know, this is a 1969 MGB-GT. A classic British sports car, perfectly restored."

"A teeny-weeny clown car," Dali teased. "Goes with your teeny-weeny dinosaur."

"A sleek, fast mini-car to go with my sleek, fast mini-raptor," Merlin corrected her, and opened the door for her.

In fact, the MGB-GT had more room on the inside than was apparent from outside. Though it only had three doors (driver's, passenger's, and rear), two small people could squeeze into the back, or you could flip down the rear seats to get a reasonably roomy luggage compartment. It was true that it was half the size of most modern cars, but as far as Merlin was concerned, that only made it extra-cool.

"A clown car would be even smaller," he remarked as he pulled out of the parking lot. "Makes it more impressive when all the clowns come out."

"How does it work?" Dali asked. "Is there a trapdoor in the floor?"

Merlin shook his head. "No, nothing like that. You use a real car—a VW Beetle is best because they have a funny shape—and take out the entire interior. Seats, the panel separating the trunk from the rest of the car, everything. You paint over the windows so the audience can't see what's inside…"

"And then you cram in the clowns?"

"And then you cram in the clowns," Merlin agreed. "Once we tried getting in more by having a bunch of small shifters, like flying squirrels and cats and so forth, go inside while they were shifted. And then they'd shift back to human one or two at a time. Only they had to get into their clown outfits and red noses and stuff before they got out, and it slowed down the whole thing too much."

"Why didn't they put on their costumes before they got in the car?"

"Because only magical and extinct shifters take their clothes with them," Merlin said. "If a regular shifter transforms with a clown suit on, it'll either fall off or explode off. Wigs and buttons and red noses flying in all directions!"

Dali chuckled, then shook her head in wonder. "I *saw* you turn into a velociraptor, and I still can hardly believe this is all real."

"It's real," he said.

His words came out freighted with more meaning than he'd intended. She looked right into his eyes, and her steady brown gaze flooded him with sexual heat. She was so close, sitting right there next to him in his very small car. With his keen shifter senses, he could smell not only the scent of her green apple shampoo but the natural perfume of her body.

He had to tear his focus away from her. It was making it hard to concentrate on the road, and driving in Refuge City required one's full attention. Spotting a Starbucks, he said, "Want to stop for coffee?"

"I already had some. But you haven't, have you?"

He shook his head. "Not even the stuff that got tossed in my face had caffeine in it."

"Sorry, but we better not," Dali said. "I'm not sure how long Cloud will stay in my purse. But I have a coffee maker at my apartment."

A meow from Cloud prompted them to stop anyway, at a supermarket to buy kitten food, litter, and a litter tray, but they went in and out as fast as they could. Merlin resisted his raptor's suggestions to buy twelve bags of marshmallows and one each of every brand of cereal, and make *everything treats.* He scanned for danger, but saw nothing out of the ordinary. Nor did anyone mistake him for an evil ex or their long-lost true love, so he counted that as a win.

Tell her about that power of yours, advised his raptor. *Right now!*

Later, Merlin said firmly.

Everything was going so well, he didn't want to mess with it. Besides, he'd startled the hell out of her when he'd impulsively turned into a giant raptor. Surely she'd had enough surprises for one day. The "let me tell you about my weird, out of control secret power" talk could keep. She'd said herself that she could barely wrap her mind around the power she already knew about.

They parked at Dali, Pete, and Tirzah's apartment building. Merlin looked around with interest as they approached the steps. He'd heard a fair amount about it, mostly from Tirzah. Apparently it had a lot of nosy, friendly neighbors…

Dali stopped dead, looking with alarm at the people standing on the sidewalk and chatting. She whispered, "Those are my neighbors. They're going to wonder who you are."

"Leave it to me," Merlin whispered back.

As they approached the door, everyone on the sidewalk called out friendly greetings and looked curiously at Merlin. A woman flipped her cornrow braids away from her face and said, "Hi, Dali. Hi…?"

Merlin Merrick and his amazing inner raptor, suggested his raptor.

Merlin gave them all his best and brightest smile. "Hi. I'm Merlin Merrick. I'm a friend of Pete and Tirzah's from Protection, Inc: Defenders, and I'm helping Dali retrieve a stolen necklace."

When they began to exclaim in dismay, he assured them, "It was a nonviolent theft, like a pickpocketing. But police don't take those sorts of things seriously, so… enter me!"

"Come on, Merlin, I need to drop off my shopping." Dali hustled him into the elevator. When the doors closed safely behind them, she arched her eyebrows at him. "Very smooth. Not a single actual lie, and yet it left so much out."

"You get good at that when you're a shifter," Merlin said. He didn't add that you also got good at it when you're raised in… well, okay, a crime circus.

Dali let him into her apartment. For the first time since she'd left the Defenders office, she lifted her hand from her purse. Cloud leaped out. Her iridescent wings buzzed as she flew around, inspecting everything.

As Merlin watched the kitten fly, he also checked out Dali's living space. It was a one-room apartment plus a bathroom and a strip of linoleum that, with a few shelves and a space for a sink, a hot plate, a coffee maker, and a mini-fridge, functioned as a kitchen. There was nothing else in the room but a plain and narrow bed, an equally plain table with one chair, and a closet.

Cloud landed atop the mini-fridge and let out a loud meow that

Merlin guessed meant, "Feed me, human!" Dali filled a pair of bowls with kitten chow and water. They were plain white plastic, like the rest of her dishes.

There was absolutely nothing in the apartment indicative of Dali's personality. He'd have thought she'd just moved in, but then there should have been boxes.

It's like Ransom's rental cars, Merlin thought. Only Ransom, as far as Merlin could tell, was trying to avoid people who might be looking for him. Who—or what—was Dali hiding from?

Cloud gave an excited squeak, buzzed down, and began neatly eating from the food bowl. Her wings folded into a shimmer over her back and her tail curled around her side as she ate.

"How long have you lived here?" Merlin asked.

"A year." Catching his startled look, Dali admitted, "It is kind of plain."

"Like Army barracks," Merlin said. Then, realizing, he said, "Or a Navy ship."

"Yeah. I—I really loved the Navy." Dali's eyes suddenly glistened with unshed tears. She whipped around, turning her back on him, and busied herself with the coffee machine.

Merlin wanted to kick himself in the shins. She'd already told him she missed the Navy. She obviously hadn't left by her own choice, but had been forced out on a medical discharge. And he had to go and toss a handful of salt in her wounds—and then put her in the awkward position of having to try to hide being upset because he was around. Him and his big mouth.

"I'll set up the litter box," he volunteered.

He took his time doing it, to give her a chance to recover. Cloud flew into the bathroom and perched on the towel rack. He scritched the dragonfly kitten behind the ears. Cloud had either forgotten or forgiven him for the raptor incident, because she nuzzled him and purred.

"Someday, Cloud," he promised her. "Someday I'll have a sweet little kitten of my own for you to play with."

His imagination wandered as he petted her. He'd always loved cats—well, dogs too, not to mention rabbits and tigers and all furry creatures—but of all the magical animals he'd seen so far, it was the flying kittens that had captivated him. Kittens with butterfly wings and kittens with moth wings, kittens with furry wings and kittens with dragon wings. Black kittens, gray kittens, Pete's green cactus kitten. He tried to decide what kitten he'd like best, but it was impossible to choose. They were all so adorable.

At least Dali, in her apartment that she kept bare and impersonal because she'd been happiest in a bare, impersonal ship's berth, now had a kitten to comfort her. He hoped Cloud would bring her back some of the joy she seemed to have lost.

"Coffee's ready," Dali called.

He washed his hands and came out. She had recovered her composure, to his relief. The hurt was still there, undoubtedly, but she'd managed to stuff it down below the surface.

"Milk? Sugar?" she asked.

"Both, please."

Unexpectedly, she said, "Homemade cookies?"

Merlin eyed her kitchen set-up. "How in the world do you make cookies on a hot plate? You must be some kind of scientific chef genius."

She chuckled. "Hardly. My neighbor Khaliya baked them. She was the one who *really* wanted to know who you were. So, do you want them? They're snickerdoodles."

Eat ALL the snickerdoodles, demanded his raptor. Then, apparently enjoying the word, he began a background chant of *Snickerdoodle, snickerdoodle, snickerdoodle...*

"I love snickerdoodles," Merlin said. "Thanks."

Dali sat down on the bed and waved at Merlin to take the chair. It was with immense pleasure that he took his first, life-giving gulp of coffee.

Sugar, demanded his raptor.

Merlin satisfied it with a bite of snickerdoodle. Not that it was some kind of sacrifice. The cookie was fresh-baked and delicious.

Dali had also taken a cup of coffee, but obviously didn't need it as much as he did. "How come your office doesn't have a coffee machine?"

"It's had lots of coffee machines. 'Had' being the operative word."

"What happened to them? Raptor attacks?"

"Some of them got broken by Tirzah and Pete's flying kittens."

"And some of them got broken by a certain size-changing raptor?"

"Maybe one. Or two. The last one had nothing to do with me. It just spontaneously exploded."

"Someone must have forgotten to turn it off," Dali said.

"Could be," Merlin said easily, though he personally was voting for 'spontaneously exploded.'

Cloud came bouncing back in, taking long leaps and beating her wings while she was in the air, like a kung fu movie character doing weightless leaping. She landed by her food bowl and returned to crunching her kibble.

"I should get Cloud her own bowls," Dali said. "With mice on them. Or dragonflies. It's a bit of a waste of money, though. I have enough for her and me, and they're perfectly functional."

Functional, Merlin thought. *That's the most joyless word in the world.*

"You could paint the ones you have. That wouldn't cost you anything."

"It'd cost me the paint." But she gazed speculatively at her white dishes. "Though… Pete does carpentry. He might have paint he could loan me."

"What would you paint the rest of them?" Merlin asked.

"Maybe I'll get Cloud to step in the paint and make paw-prints," Dali proposed. Then, with a grin, she said, "Or I could get you to shrink down and make velociraptor prints."

It was such an unexpectedly hilarious idea that Merlin burst out laughing. "You're on. Get the paints and I'll do it. That is, if you don't mind eating off dishes I've stepped on."

"You're only allowed to step on the outside."

"I promise to keep my raptor in hand," he assured her. Inwardly, he crossed his fingers. Probably they should do the project in a very large area with nothing breakable. Just in case.

Confirming his worst fears, his raptor said, *This apartment is boring. Dali should have a fun apartment! I'll dip my feet in paint and decorate the floor for her, and then I'll dip my tail in paint and decorate the walls, and—*

Let's start with the dishes, Merlin replied.

"So, about the circus," Dali said. "You said we're going to a matinee. Should we have lunch first?"

Eat there, suggested his raptor. *Popcorn and cotton candy and hot dogs and enough soda to fill a swimming pool!*

Not a bad idea, Merlin admitted, ignoring the mental image of his raptor happily thrashing around in a root beer-filled swimming pool.

"The circus had a fair attached," he said. "It's small, but it has games and fortune telling and food stalls. Or we could go to a restaurant if you'd rather."

"I would *love* to eat at the circus. Let me change. This dress has bacon grease on it. And honey. And Kool-Aid. Um…" She glanced around, clearly realizing the problem. They were in her bedroom, so to speak. The only place Merlin could go in the one-room apartment would be the bathroom.

"I'll step outside," he said.

He waited in the corridor, imagining what Dali was doing inside. *Now,* she was going to the closet and selecting something else to wear. *Now,* she was stripping off her dress. *Now,* she stood naked in that bare room like a jewel in an empty box, her brown eyes and midnight hair and soft curves vibrant and enticing in that cold white space. *Now,* she was walking nude across the floor, her breasts moving—

The door opened. Merlin jumped. Apparently she changed a whole lot faster than he'd been imagining. And also, there had probably not been any random wandering around in the nude. In fact, probably there had been zero nudity, as she had no reason to change her bra and panties.

59

He dragged his mind away from the incredibly arousing image of Dali in bra and panties, and said, "You look great. Perfect circus outfit."

She'd changed into light blue jeans that hugged her curves, a black blouse with rhinestone-studded short sleeves, and candy apple red shoes with short wedge heels. Dali looked sexy and gorgeous, of course, but the sparkle of the sleeves and the pop of color in the shoes gave her an air of playfulness as well.

"Thanks. I pulled the blouse out of the back of my closet. Haven't worn it in years." She bent down, shooed Cloud away from the door, whispered, "I'll be back," and quickly closed it.

As they walked to the car, Merlin realized that he'd boxed himself into a corner. They were going to eat at the circus, which meant they were going straight there. He had to warn her now, or he'd leave her unprepared. She might even blurt something out, which would be bad for him and totally unfair to her.

Once the MGB-GT was moving through Refuge City's busy traffic, he said, "It's been a while since I've been to the circus. They're international, you know. And I've had a lot going on, what with being a Marine and then getting kidnapped and turned into a shifter and leaving the Marines and becoming a bodyguard and… Well, anyway, they don't know I'm a shifter."

"But they're all shifters."

"Right. But when I was with them, I wasn't one. And I haven't told them. So please don't mention it. As far as they're concerned, I'm just your bodyguard."

"Okay. But if they're shifters anyway, why don't you want them to know you're one too?" Dali asked.

"Circus politics. It's complicated." That was the truth, at least. "To be honest, I'm hoping to say hi to everyone, find out who told some pigeons how to steal jewelry and who the pigeons are, and leave."

"Sounds like an awkward family Thanksgiving," Dali said.

"That's exactly what it's like. The circus is like a giant, crazy, semi-dys-functional family. That dresses up in sequins and clown paint, turns into animals, and steals."

Dali chuckled. "Got it. Want to set up some kind of signal so if it's getting too awkward, I'll know to drag you off?"

"Yes. Yes, I *would* like that. If I cough and touch my ear, find something you really want to do somewhere else."

"Gotcha."

She was so thoughtful and understanding, it put Merlin at ease. Maybe he'd been blowing his circus issues out of proportion. Anyway, now he had an escape hatch. Everything would be fine.

But I want *to shift,* protested his raptor. *I want to show off how big I can get! And how small! And swing from the trapeze and play with the lions and try on the ringmaster's hat and roll around in the sawdust and drive the clown car and eat cotton candy. ALL the cotton candy!*

A little too loudly, Merlin said aloud, "Everything will be fine!"

CHAPTER 7

The wizard-scientist Morgana needed better minions.

She leveled a cold stare at the one who stood before her, a reputable and highly paid tracker. He maintained his usual stone-face, but she caught the tiniest nervous twitch of his hands.

"So," she said. "Let us review. I hired you to retrieve an escaped magical beast and any person with whom it came into contact. You found the beast with a person—so far, so good—and then you allowed them both to escape."

He made no excuses for his failure, which she appreciated, but did say, "They haven't escaped for long. I tracked the woman who found the kitten to a local security agency, Defenders..."

Of course, Morgana thought as he continued his report. *Such is the working of fate.*

The grand plan of the wizard-scientists required both the magical beasts and the kidnapped humans whom the wizard-scientists had intended to forge into their Dark Knights. But both beasts and humans had escaped them. And the humans had drawn together into the Defenders, while one by one, the beasts were drawn to bond with the Defenders and the people close to them.

On the one hand, that did make them easier to find. On the other hand, it made them harder to defeat. Humans were so much weaker when they were alone and isolated.

If only I had been in charge from the beginning, Morgana thought. She felt sure that if she had, both humans and beasts would still be secured within the lab, in their solitary cells.

"…so I thought you'd want me to consult you before proceeding," concluded the tracker.

"Yes," Morgana said absently. "I'll let you know if I want you. Dismissed."

As he left her presence, she gave careful thought to the problem of re-capturing the beast and recruiting her chosen Dark Knight. Unlike the last wizard-scientist who had attempted that task, she would proceed with planning and cleverness, not brute force.

Poor stupid Gorlois had charged in with all guns blazing, bringing out his chosen Knight's protective instincts. He'd only succeeded in deepening the bonds between his Knight and others. Gorlois's attempt had gone so badly that the ability to form a mate bond, which was supposed to have been destroyed in all the potential Knights, had acti-vated. No wonder he had been killed!

But Morgana would not make the same mistake. She had studied her chosen Dark Knight well, and she knew his weaknesses. Rather than repeat Gorlois's mistakes, she would use a more subtle approach. Morgana intended to systematically strip Merlin of everything he loved. And then, when he was without friends, without family, without animal companion, and certainly without mate…

Then she would make her move.

And Merlin, in his loneliness and despair, would have no choice but to accept her offer.

"Checkmate," murmured Morgana to the empty room.

CHAPTER 8

Merlin's absurdly tiny sports car was absurdly fun to ride in. He drove with the pizzazz that seemed to be his trademark, zipping in and out of traffic while talking a mile a minute. Once Dali got over thinking they were going to be squashed by an SUV at any second, she relaxed and enjoyed the ride.

She also enjoyed Merlin. With at least some of his attention on the road, she could look her fill without feeling like he'd catch her staring. His hair had dried to a striking gold that caught the sun, a perfect match for his sky-blue eyes. His tan showed off his lithe musculature, and his gestures were as graceful as a hawk's flight.

Summer man, she thought. *He's all sun and sky and freedom. Light as a bird. Nothing weighing* him *down.*

If she pursued the metaphor, that would make her the winter woman. Black hair like the bare earth under snow, brown eyes like a leafless tree, heart like a hearth where the fire's gone out. And all the weight of loss she was carrying, like snow piled so heavily that it cracks the roof.

But Merlin's lightness must have lifted her. It was as if the sheer amount of things that were impossible yet somehow real—pigeon thieves, flying kittens, velociraptors, shifters, Dali all dressed up for a trip to the crime circus—had knocked her loose from everything that pinned her down, leaving her in free fall. It was a scary feeling, but freeing, too. Anything might be possible.

Maybe Grandma was right. Maybe Dali did have her whole life ahead of her.

"...and that's how the white rat married the elephant," Merlin concluded.

Dali, who had been so deep in her own thoughts that she'd lost track of his story, only belatedly remembered that he was talking about shifters rather than actual animals. "The white rat is the ringmaster, right?"

Merlin nodded. "Maximilian Doubek. He's from Prague. His wife, Renu, is from India. We performed once in her home city, Hyderabad, but unfortunately there was a little incident involving the mayor's wife's diamond earrings, a runaway camel, and some local cobra shifters that got us banned. It all began when one of our performers, Zillah Zimmerman, who turns into a calico cat—all the Zimmermans are cat shifters—climbed a palm tree and got stuck halfway…"

His voice trailed off as he pulled into a crowded parking lot. The big top loomed ahead, a gigantic red and gold tent surrounded by fairground stalls. Dali reached for her door, but Merlin didn't move. He was staring at the big top, his hands frozen on the steering wheel, with an expression she couldn't interpret: nostalgia or longing or dread, or maybe all of them at once.

"You okay?" Dali asked.

Her words broke the spell. Merlin gave a start, and the ambivalence vanished from his face, to be replaced with a bright smile. "Absolutely!"

Dali doubted that, but she wasn't sure she had the right to pry into his emotions, especially since he obviously didn't want to share them. It wasn't as if they had a relationship. She was his client, and nothing more.

It was ridiculous of her to wish for more.

"I'll keep watch, of course," he assured her. "But you should be safe here. The wizard-scientists aren't likely to try anything with this many people around."

That hadn't been exactly what she'd meant, but she nodded. Then a thought struck her. "Hey, Merlin? If no one's supposed to know you're a shifter now, then I probably shouldn't know shifters exist, right? Or is that something you might have told me because of how my necklace got stolen?"

"Oh. Oh, man." Merlin ran a hand through his hair, rumpling it. "I'm so glad you thought of that. No, normally I wouldn't have told you. So pretend you have no idea the circus animals are anything but animals, and say I'm investigating whether someone here trained pigeons to steal. They'll know what I really think."

With that, he sprang out of the car, ran around to the side, and opened the door for her. Dali was about to tell him her prosthetic could open doors, then realized that he was being a gentleman. It made her smile. She got out, and together they walked to the circus.

As they approached the ticket booth, he said, "We'll watch the show first—that'll give me a chance to see who's still here and who's new. Then we'll talk to Natalie. She was—is—my best friend from when I was here. You'll like her."

"What kind of shifter is she?"

"Natalie's not a shifter," Merlin said. "She's an acrobat and a target girl."

"A what?"

"A target girl. It's a term in the impalement arts—"

"The WHAT?"

"The impalement arts. Stuff like throwing knives at people, shooting apples off people's heads, stuff like that. I know, the name is weird considering that the object is *not* to get impaled."

Dali snorted. "It's like if you called parachuting and hang gliding 'the plummeting to your death sports.'"

Merlin laughed. "Anyway, not everyone who works at the circus is a shifter. The ticket takers and food stall cooks and so forth are locals we hire while we're in town. Most of the permanent company are shifters, but not all. Sometimes non-shifters get born into shifter families. Max and Renu's daughter Kalpana is like that—her dad is a white rat and her mom is an elephant, but she can't shift."

"Was that hard?"

"No, it was actually lucky for her. Kalpana loves the circus but she has terrible stage fright. If she'd been an elephant she'd have been pressured to perform, but what she's really good at is behind the scenes stuff. So she only does that, and everyone's happy! Actually, I bet you'd get along with her too. She's our stage manager, which is sort of a yeoman-equivalent. I'll make sure to introduce—"

Dali held up her hand, cutting off his flow of chatter. "I meant, was it hard for *you* to grow up in a shifter circus without being a shifter yourself?"

"Oh, here we are! I'll buy your ticket." Merlin rushed to the ticket booth, wallet in hand, leaving Dali to wonder if he was deliberately evading her question or if he was just distractible.

He rejoined her with the tickets. She thanked him, and they went through the gate. The air carried the sound of laughter and calliope music, and the smell of cotton candy and buttered popcorn. Little kids were running amok, waving corndogs on sticks and blowing noisemakers and throwing Ping-Pong balls to try to win a goldfish.

"Skip the games," Merlin advised Dali quietly. "They're rigged."

"You guys cheat little kids?" Dali exclaimed, then lowered her voice.

"Nope," Merlin said with a grin. "Kids don't have money, remember? We cheat rich adults. Want to see how?"

Much as she disapproved, her curiosity got the better of her. "Okay. But I think I need to be fortified with food first. Nothing dishonest at the food stalls, right? No selling tofu as pork or pork as tofu or saying things are gluten-free when they aren't?"

"Good Lord, no," Merlin replied. "The food is exactly what we say it is. It's good, too. Not good *for* you, of course. But tasty."

As they headed to the food stalls, she noted him scanning the grounds. He'd ramped up his usual awareness, and she couldn't help wondering if it was because it would be more difficult to spot a stalker in this crowded chaos, or because he was counting down to the moment when someone recognized him.

She decided not to distract him, and instead checked out the food stalls. It was hard for a working woman to have time to eat well, but she did her best. She avoided junk food, didn't drink soda, and generally tried to treat her body well. Besides, Grandma's Sunday dinners, while absolutely delicious, were heavy on pork and deep-fried things, so Dali tried to make up for them during the rest of the week.

She stopped dead at the food stalls and parked food trucks, overwhelmed by the sheer amount of deep-fried and sugar-coated everything. Grandma would love it.

Merlin, mistaking her hesitation, suggested, "Want me to order for us both, and we can share? There'll be enough choices that you'll definitely like *something*."

Throwing health and responsibility to the winds, Dali said, "Go right ahead."

He darted from food truck to food truck and food stall to food stall, pulling her in his wake. He bought cotton candy in pink and rainbow flavors, boxes of peanuts (salted and candy-coated), lemonade and horchata and Coke, funnel cakes doused in powdered sugar, and huge soft pretzels with mustard. Just as she was about to protest that they would keel over from an overdose of salt and sugar and no real food, he went to a stall selling skewered everything and bought a giant selection of grilled meat and vegetables on sticks.

She offered to help carry the food, but he waved her away, explaining, "I'll need your hands free to unload it." She watched in amazement as he deftly balanced cotton candy stick holders on peanut boxes atop soda cups on takeout boxes until he was holding a Jenga tower of food in each hand, steady as a rock.

He laughed at her expression. "I used to help the seals with their balancing acts."

"Of course you did." Dali followed him to an unoccupied bench and table beside a roulette game.

Merlin didn't spill a drop of soda or a crumb of funnel cake, or even a grain of powdered sugar. She couldn't help wondering what else he could do with those clever hands of his and the incredible physical control he had over his entire body. He had to be *amazing* in bed. Not that she'd ever find out.

She set out the food, and they helped themselves to a little of everything. Dali started with the most meal-like of the options, the grilled meat and vegetable skewers, which were a little charred, very juicy, and nicely seasoned. But then Merlin waved a funnel cake under her nose, and the aroma was irresistible. She took it from his hand and took a bite. It was crisp-fried dough buried under a blanket of powdered sugar, hot and sweet and greasy and good. Then next thing she knew, she'd inhaled the entire thing.

"Got a bit of sugar there," Merlin said. He reached out toward her face.

Dali could have told him she'd get it herself, but she said nothing. His deft fingers brushed the tip of her nose, her cheek, and finally her lips. They felt burning hot, and even after he pulled his hand away, she could still feel his touch on her skin.

"Are we going to watch some crimes?" she asked softly, to distract herself from wanting to touch him in return.

"Absolutely," Merlin said, also speaking quietly. He indicated the roulette wheel, which was operated by a glamorous woman in her forties with sleek black hair in a 1920s-style bob. "That's Renu Doubek."

"From Hyderabad, India," said Dali, remembering Merlin's story. "The elephant who married a rat."

She realized then that he had carefully selected their table so they could see the roulette wheel, but a tree blocked them from being seen by anyone standing at the wheel. He obviously didn't intend to reveal himself to his old partners in crime until he was ready.

"Good memory. Now, see him?" Merlin gestured at a man walking toward the roulette wheel. "He's the mark."

"The what?"

"The mark—the person who has enough money to be worth cheating

69

him out of some."

"How can you tell?" Dali asked. The mark wore a T-shirt and jeans, and didn't look particularly rich to her.

"His clothes are cheap, yeah. But look at his shoes."

"They're sneakers," Dali said, puzzled.

"They're three thousand dollar sneakers," Merlin said.

"What?!"

"Really. And a five thousand dollar watch. Also…" Merlin grinned. "He looks like a jerk."

It was true. The mark had a distinctly punchable face, set in lines of bad temper and contempt. But as he came closer, it became clear that he wasn't headed for the roulette wheel after all, but was only going to pass near it.

"Too bad for the crime circus coffers," Dali said, enjoying Merlin's snicker at the phrase. "Doesn't look like he's playing."

"Oh, we—they—can fix that," Merlin assured her. "Watch."

As the mark came closer, Renu called out, "It's rat roulette time, ladies and gentlemen! Rat roulette! We can match bids of up to five thousand dollars! It's rat roulette!"

At the words "five thousand dollars," the mark turned his head. Renu stooped behind the table and lifted up a white rat. It sat tamely in the palm of her hand, its beady black eyes blinking and its pink nose twitching.

"And that's her husband, Max," said Merlin.

Dali had to bite her lip to not burst out laughing.

"What the hell is rat roulette?" shouted a thuggish-looking man in the crowd of onlookers. "And who the hell bets five thousand dollars at a goddamn circus?"

The mark stopped walking to watch.

"The mark is a man who doesn't like women," Merlin murmured in Dali's ear. "So a man yelling at a woman will get his attention. Just like a greedy person's attention will be caught by mentioning a lot of money. So Larry got him twice over."

"Larry's the man who looks like he walked off the set of *The Sopranos?*" Dali whispered.

"Uh-huh. He's Larry Duffy, one of the Duffy brothers. They don't appear in the show, so no one will recognize him later. He's what we call a plant: someone we plant in the audience."

Renu raised her voice so the entire crowd—and the mark—could hear. "Rat roulette is when the rat picks the number instead of the ball. And as for who'd bet that amount of money... Are you feeling lucky today, sir?"

Larry Duffy sneered and made a dismissive gesture.

"Let's start with a small bet," suggested Renu. "Five dollars? Any takers?"

A little girl begged to her parents, "I want to see the rat pick the number!"

"Just so long as you don't expect to win anything," said her mother with a smile, handing Renu a five. "This is only for fun."

"Are *they* plants?" Dali whispered, fascinated.

Merlin shook his head. "Nope. Someone will always think it's worth five dollars to see a rat play roulette."

Renu offered the white rat to the little girl. "Would you like to pet him for luck?"

Giggling, the little girl petted the white rat.

"Now pick a number, odds or evens, and either red or black. If you get them all wrong, I keep the five. If you get just odd/even or red/black right, I give you seven-fifty. If you get both of those right but not the number, I give you ten. And if you get the number right... That's when you *really* start winning." Renu indicated a sign that explained the details. "Ready to choose?"

"Seven, odds, and red!" said the little girl.

Renu ceremoniously placed the white rat in the center of the wheel and gave it a spin. The rat began to run around the wheel as the crowd laughed and cheered and urged him on. Finally, when the wheel came to a stop, the rat flopped down in a slot.

"And it's black and… eight!" Renu shook her head. "You were so close. Want to try again?"

"Yes!" exclaimed the little girl.

"Nope," said her mother. "Come on, Chely, let's get some cotton candy."

As they walked away, Renu called out, "Who else wants to try their luck with the rat?"

Dali whispered to Merlin, "Do you really need a shifter to do this? Couldn't you train a regular rat to stop when you give it a signal?"

Merlin smiled. "Yes."

Right on cue, Larry Duffy said loudly, "This is a scam! She's signaling the rat when to stop."

Renu folded her arms. "I assure you, I am not. The rat stops where the rat wants to stop."

"Sure he does," sneered Larry.

"Place a bet and watch me closely," Renu offered. "If you spot me signaling, you'll automatically win."

"Okay!" said Larry. He began digging into his pants pocket.

The mark frowned. "Wait. The signal is probably very subtle. You won't see it."

Larry turned his sneer on him. "I'm not blind!"

"She has to know what the bet is to signal the rat," said a teenage boy, then chuckled. "What if you wrote it down and just showed it to the rat?"

Renu looked visibly alarmed at this suggestion. "There's no need for that. I'll hold up my hands so you can watch them."

"She probably taps her foot," said the mark. He nodded at the boy. "Yeah. I like that idea."

"Sir, this is ridiculous," said Renu.

The mark stepped forward, looming over her. Aggressively, he said, "You promised to accept any bet up to a five thousand dollars!"

"Yes, but—"

The mark took off his watch. "This is a five thousand dollar watch."

"I can only accept cash," said Renu, and smirked at him like she'd won.

The crowd murmured, clearly turning on her. A few people yelled, "Take his watch!" and "Write down your bet!" The teenage boy's voice rose up clearly, "Show your bet to the rat!"

Pressing his advantage, the mark said, "If you don't let me bet my watch and write down my bet for the rat, I'll call the cops right now and bust you for running a crooked gambling operation. And then you'll lose a lot more than five thousand dollars."

Renu looked furious and trapped. Finally, she shouted, "Fine!"

The teenage boy offered the mark a small notebook and a pen.

"Turn your back," said the mark.

Renu turned her back.

Grinning, the mark wrote down BLACK EVENS 30 on a page. He showed it to the crowd, then, smirking, said, "Oh, and we need to let the rat see too."

The teenage boy scooped up the rat and held it in front of the page, then popped it back down on the wheel.

The mark folded the paper and replaced it in his pocket. "You can turn around now."

Renu turned around. She spun the wheel, saying, "Around and around and around it goes, where it stops, nobody knows!"

The white rat ran around the wheel. Dali knew what had to happen, but she still watched with all the excitement of a fan watching her favorite team playing a tournament. So did the crowd.

The wheel slowly came to a stop, and the rat flopped down on a red slot labeled 5.

The crowd gasped.

"What?!" exclaimed the mark.

"What was your bet?" Renu inquired.

"This is bullshit!" yelled the mark. "You cheated!"

"What was the bet?" Renu asked the crowd.

"Black evens thirty!" the crowd yelled.

Renu spread her hands. "What a shame. Still, no one can say where the rat will stop. May I have your watch, sir?"

"No!" shouted the mark.

The crowd's fickle attention turned on him. Now they were murmuring and scowling at him.

"Sir, do you believe the rat can read?" Renu asked.

The mark scowled at her. "What?"

As if she was explaining things to a small, slow child, Renu said, "If I'm signaling the rat, I need to know what the bet was. I didn't see the bet, though the rat did. Do you think the rat read your bet and cheated you all by itself?

Confused and angry, the mark said, "You cheated some other way!"

Renu held out her hand. "Your watch, sir. Or do I have to call the police?"

The mark looked around. The crowd was glaring at him. Several of them meaningfully took out their phones.

"Fine!" The mark took off his watch and flung it at Renu's face.

She neatly caught it, then tucked it into her pocket. As the mark stormed away to the sound of the crowd's laughter, cheers, and jeers, she said, "Who'd like to be the next to play rat roulette? I suggest that you don't bet more than you can afford to lose."

As people eagerly waved bills at her, Dali sat back. Softly, to Merlin, she said, "I feel like I watched an entire performance. The teenage boy was another plant, right?"

"Bobby Duffy," Merlin said. "Larry's nephew."

She wanted to disapprove. Swindling was swindling, even if the victim could afford it and was terrible. But she caught herself admitting, "I kind of enjoyed watching that."

Merlin grinned. "I thought you might. It *is* fun. Even if it's not something you'd ever do yourself."

There was a burst of applause, and Renu handed a member of the crowd a bill, shaking her head ruefully.

"So they get to win sometimes?" Dali asked.

"Of course. That watch could pay for everyone else to win today. The only reason they made sure the little girl didn't win was to set up Larry calling it a scam. If the girl or her mom had looked like losing would have upset them, then Renu would have made sure it was the next person who lost."

"Very clever. Did you ever run rat roulette?"

Merlin grinned. "All the time, once I was old enough."

"I feel like I'm learning so much about you right now," Dali said. The moment the words were out, she felt awkward. It sounded like the kind of line you'd say on a date. She supposed it was because they'd eaten lunch together and were about to see a show, so it felt a bit... date-like.

He gave her a sharp glance, then a slightly forced chuckle. "You already knew I was from a crime circus."

"Sure, but watching that scam showed me what you need to run something like that—you have to be spontaneous, quick-witted, able to improvise, a fast talker, and a good judge of people."

"And have a rat that can read."

"That too. So, were you born into—"

"Oh, hey," Merlin said, checking his watch. "Show's going to start soon."

Dali looked around. Nobody seemed in any great hurry, and Renu was still taking bets. "I think—"

Merlin began to talk quickly as he grabbed the empty containers and started tossing them into a trashcan with NBA-worthy accuracy. "I can't wait for you to see the show. I'm sure you'll enjoy it. Especially since you love cats. The Fabulous Flying Chameleons are the only circus in the world that has a cat act. Not big cats, regular cats. They're actually the Zimmerman family, who are also notable for having spent the last twenty years feuding with the Richelieu family, who are French poodle shifters. Nobody knows exactly how it started, but *I* think..."

As he began to spin out an elaborate theory, Dali's mind was occupied with what he *wasn't* saying.

He's hiding in plain sight, she thought. *He talks so much about the circus that you don't notice what he's not saying about the circus. Even his own teammates didn't know they were shifters.*

In fact, she remembered, his own teammates hadn't even realized the circus was real!

Dali tried to recall what he'd ever said about how he'd ended up there. *"I was raised in a circus,"* he'd said. Not *"I was born in a circus."*

He doesn't lie, she thought. *He just steers you to assume what he wants you to assume. Like Renu saying, "Do you think the rat can read?" to make everyone think that since rats can't read, the game couldn't have been rigged.*

"Anyway, you'll see both families perform," Merlin concluded. She guiltily jerked her attention back to him. "You'll have to tell me which you like better, the dogs or the cats."

"I can tell you that right now," she said.

He laughed and led her into the big top. "The best seats aren't in the front row. You want to sit close enough to see the details, but far enough to see the big picture. Here you go."

They sat down together. Dali did have an excellent view. Surrounded by excited people in couples and families and groups and alone, murmuring and crunching on snacks, her excitement rose. It wasn't just that she was about to see a circus performance for the very first time, or that it was a unique shifter circus, or even that it would be the first step in getting her necklace back. It was that like the rat roulette, this would be her chance to learn more about Merlin.

"All I need is a box of crackerjacks," she remarked.

He instantly produced one. She laughed, opened it, and offered it to him. They were still munching when the lights went down.

CHAPTER 9

The lights came up on Maximilian Doubek, the ringmaster, magnificent in his red waistcoat and immense curled moustache. "Welcome to the Fabulous Flying Chameleons, where humans and animals come together to bring you the most astounding—the most amazing—the most fabulous spectacle you've ever seen!"

Max went on, but Merlin barely heard him. He felt like he was drowning in nostalgia, both good and bad. It was as if he could see his entire past life, right there in the center of the ring.

Why past? inquired his raptor. *You could have it now!*

His raptor's words hit Merlin like a punch to the gut. His inner dinosaur was right. Merlin *could* go back to the circus. He'd known that already, but it was a completely different thing to know it as an abstract possibility, and to know it with all the glory and fun of the circus right there in front of him.

Dali nudged him in the side with her elbow. That was a touch from a very non-erotic part of the body, through two layers of cloth, and yet it felt as sensual as if she'd slipped her bare hand under his shirt. Then she leaned in, so close that her cheek brushed against his hair, and whispered right in his ear, "Is that guy the white rat?"

Her breath was warm on his skin, like a caress.

Turn around and kiss her, suggested his raptor.

Merlin wanted to. He really, really wanted to. For a dizzying moment, he couldn't think of a single reason not to. Then he came to his senses. Sure, they'd flirted a bit. But there had been a lot of water under the bridge after that. Water that contained a velociraptor. He needed to check in with Dali or at least do some more flirting first to see if she was still interested, not just randomly kiss her in the middle of a circus performance which was also a part of his job protecting her and finding her necklace.

Kiss her, urged his raptor. *Kiss her, kiss her, KISSSSSSSS HER!*

Not now, he managed.

Belatedly recalling Dali's question, he whispered back, "Yeah, Max—the ringmaster—is the roulette rat."

"And now for the Wheel! Of! DEATH!!!" Max declared.

Stagehands brought out a target wheel, which they ceremoniously placed in the center of the stage. With a dramatic gesture, the ringmaster announced, "Please give a hand to our lovely and courageous target girl, Tawny Lyon!"

"That's your friend Natalie, right? Love her stage name," Dali whispered with a snicker.

"Natalie doesn't have a stage name," Merlin said. "Tawny Lyon is a lion shifter. All the big cats have names like Leopold and Leona and—anyway, Tawny's not a target girl. Max screwed up and announced the wrong…"

Tawny Lyon walked onstage, smiling and waving. Merlin watched, bewildered, as the stagehands bound her to the wheel.

Maybe Natalie got bored and decided to do something different, suggested his raptor.

Not a chance, replied Merlin.

Natalie never missed a show, and she loved this act. She lived in the moment, and as she was always both enjoying and trying to perfect her performances, she never found them boring.

Maybe she has the flu, Merlin thought.

Then he realized something that made her absence even more

unsettling. Tawny was built on Amazonian proportions, while Natalie was short and slim. If Tawny had crammed herself into Natalie's costume for the knife-throwing act, it would be bursting at the seams. But it wasn't. It fit Tawny perfectly.

They'd made a new target girl costume just for Tawny. Natalie wasn't just taking one night off. She'd been replaced—in this act, at least.

What was going *on?*

Max set the Wheel of Death spinning. Tawny spun around and around, now upside down, now right side up, but always keeping a smile on her face.

"Oof," murmured Dali. "I'm good with boats, but that's a bit much."

"I tried it once. I threw up," Merlin admitted.

"And now for our knife-throwers!" Max declaimed.

The spotlight swung up and up, until it caught a flock of flying squirrels in full flight. They glided over the heads of the audience, furry flaps of skin stretched out and black eyes gleaming in the light. The spotlight followed them as they glided downward, over the ring, and past Tawny, still spinning on the wheel. As the first squirrel passed in front of her, it threw a tiny knife.

The audience, enraptured, was utterly silent; the *thock* of the blade striking the wood was clearly audible as the knife hit home directly over her head. Each squirrel threw a tiny knife as it passed her, until her body was outlined in miniature blades.

The audience went wild. They yelled, clapped, squealed, and stamped their feet, and Dali was right there with them. It was a beautiful sight to see.

Max stopped the wheel, leaving Tawny right side up. The stagehands unbound her. She stepped away, leaving her silhouette in knives on the board, and held out her arms. The flying squirrels swung around in a tight circle. One by one, they landed on her outstretched arms, until all but one of the flock had settled down. The last squirrel landed on her head. She sank down in a curtsey, careful not to disturb the squirrels.

The audience burst into delirious cheers and applause. But Merlin couldn't drink it in the way he wanted to. He frowned as Tawny walked carefully offstage, still covered in squirrels.

"Knife-throwing flying squirrels," Dali whispered, her soft voice full of glee.

"They're the Flying Fratellis," Merlin said absently. "That squirrel with the white-tipped tail—that's Fausto Fratelli. He and I used to have one hell of a feud going on."

"How come?" Dali whispered.

And that was yet another aspect of his past that Merlin didn't want to get into. Yet. "Watch this, you'll love it."

The Zesty Zimmermans marched out in single file, in order of size. Zachariah Zimmerman, an immensely fluffy and rather lion-like orange cat, led them. He was followed by Zillah Zimmerman, an only slightly less immensely fluffy calico. A sequence of fluffy cousins, aunts, uncles, and children followed: tabbies and tortoiseshells, whites and blacks, splotched and spotted, waving their tails as they marched in perfect precision. The last one had to be Zoe, who hadn't been old enough to perform the last time Merlin had seen the show, but who proudly brought up the rear as a teeny calico furball.

Dali gasped aloud, along with the rest of the audience. As the cats marched in formation, creating kaleidoscope-like patterns within the ring, his gaze was on her rather than the Zimmermans. Her mouth was open and her eyes sparkled with delight. Merlin drank in the sight of her uncomplicated joy. *That* was what he loved about the circus: it made people happy.

Well, the people it didn't steal from or cheat, anyway.

The Zimmermans were followed by a crowd-pleasing riding act, in which French poodles rode horses and did tricks on them, then the cats rode on poodles and did the same tricks, and finally the flying squirrels rode on cats and did the tricks again. For the grand finale, the squirrels rode the cats who were riding the poodles who were riding the horses.

"The horses are the Outstanding Ortegas," Merlin whispered. "The poodles are the Remarkable Richelieus, the cats are the Zesty

Zimmermans, and the squirrels are the Flying Fratellis."

He enjoyed Dali's delighted laughter as he explained to her, in the human acts which followed, which of the horses and poodles and cats and squirrels were also clowns and jugglers and acrobats. But she had to nudge him to get him to explain which animals the trapeze artists were; he was distracted by the realization that not only was Natalie not in the trapeze act, but the entire act had been retooled to remove her role.

Where was she? He found it hard to imagine that she'd leave the circus, she loved it so much. And if she had, why hadn't she told him?

Between watching Dali transformed by joy, resisting his raptor's demands to kiss her, wondering about Natalie, watching for any trouble he might need to protect Dali from, and plotting his approach to dealing with the circus folk after the performance, Merlin had trouble focusing on the rest of the show.

He kept having to bring his attention back to it as jugglers juggled, clowns tumbled out of a clown car, lions and tigers held a saw in their jaws and sawed a woman in half, a bear danced and rode a unicycle, a parrot answered questions from the audience, and a family of seals ("sea lions, actually," Merlin whispered) played basketball and volleyball with their noses. And more. Much more. The Fabulous Flying Chameleons believed in giving their audience value for their money.

For the grand finale, Renu came out as an elephant, along with the bear, the big cats, and the seals, and made human performers jump through hoops and do other tricks, rewarding them with treats after every one.

At last, the lights went to full black, not the dim blue used for scene changes, and then came up bright and white for everyone to take their bows. The curtain call alternated between humans and animals, to give them a chance to shift backstage.

Snickering, Dali whispered, "Is everyone getting applauded twice?"

"The ones who performed twice are," Merlin said. "If you think of it that way, it's only fair."

They waited till the rest of the audience had filed out, and then he led her down to the ring.

What are you doing? demanded his raptor. *Run away! Run away with Dali! Drive to Las Vegas with her and get married by Elvis!* As an afterthought, he added, *Take the cotton candy.*

Merlin's palms were sweating, and his raptor's stream of suggestions didn't help. He thought again of Dali's comment that it was like an awkward family Thanksgiving, and couldn't help murmuring, "You remember the escape signal, right?"

"Of course," she said. "If you touch your ear and cough, I remember a pressing engagement."

"You're the best."

He was unsurprised to see that the entire company was coming out to meet him. He'd never really believed that he'd avoided their notice. They were merely very aware, as con artists themselves, that if he wasn't greeting them there was probably a reason, and had allowed him to maintain his cover until they were in private.

At the head of the group was the leader, owner, and alpha of the circus—and most importantly, his mother.

She'd appeared in the show as Goldie the Amazing Talking Parrot and as the psychic Madame Fortuna, and was currently in her human form as a tiny woman with curly white hair and glasses with Coke-bottle lenses that gave her a slightly bug-eyed appearance. She never would state her age, but would reply to the question with a discussion-ending *"Old."*

He had a lot of complicated feelings about her, but when he saw her now, all he felt was love. The next thing he knew, they were hugging like they always had. Merlin lifted her off her feet, as he had ever since he'd been big enough to do it, and she said, "Put me down," like she always did.

Finally, Mom pushed him away, held him at arms' length, and said, "You're so thin! You haven't been eating properly. You need someone to feed you."

Merlin tried very hard not to either turn red or catch Dali's eyes. "Mom, I can cook."

"Hmph," replied Mom. "You run away, you don't write, you don't call—"

"I write," Merlin protested. "I call!"

"Not nearly enough," Mom said. She raised her voice so the entire company could hear. "If I'd known you were coming, I'd have prepared a *proper* welcome for my returning heir."

"Heir?" Dali said.

Mom gave her a distinctly suspicious glance. "Hello, young lady. May I inquire as to your relationship with my heir?"

Run, suggested his velociraptor.

Merlin wished he could. Everything was spinning out of control. He felt like he was strapped to the Wheel of Death, though hopefully with less puking.

He tried to speak as fast as possible, so no one would have a chance to interrupt him before he could get everything out. And also in the hope that he could drop enough information on both Dali and Mom that they'd be distracted from the "heir" and "relationship" questions.

"Mom, this is Dali Batiste," Merlin rattled off. "She's my client. Dali, this is Janet Gold, the owner of the circus. And my mother. Mom, Dali hired me to investigate the theft of an heirloom necklace by trained pigeons and since you have trained birds here at the circus, I thought someone here might have taught someone to train pigeons to do tricks, only whoever they taught how to teach the pigeons used them to steal instead."

Merlin gulped for breath. In that pause, he scanned the crowd. They were silent, waiting for their alpha to finish with Merlin before they greeted him or yelled at him, depending.

Fausto Fratelli looked like he wanted to shift into a flying squirrel, fly at Merlin's face, and scratch his eyes out. Renard Richelieu was giving Merlin a more subtle glare. The Duffy brothers, who were sparrow shifters and thieves, had looked distinctly irritated ever since Merlin

83

had mentioned trained birds. Kalpana, the stage manager, was smiling shyly at him from the back of the crowd. Renu and Max were clearly just waiting to hug him.

There was no one new in the company. And the only person missing was Natalie.

"Hmph," said Mom.

"Heir?" repeated Dali.

Merlin waved his hands frantically. As much to Mom and the rest of the company as to Dali, he said, "I'm not the heir. This is just a visit. A business visit. And a friendly catch-up, of course. Where's Natalie?"

To Merlin's surprise, Kalpana spoke first. Though maybe that shouldn't have been surprising; as two of the few non-shifters, she and Natalie had been close, though not as close as Natalie and Merlin.

"She left," Kalpana said.

"Left?" Merlin repeated blankly. "Left the circus? Why?"

At that, everyone broke in, talking on top of each other. In the next thirty seconds, Merlin heard that Natalie had gotten bored, had fallen in love, had decided to find herself, and had wanted to pursue acting, cooking, rock climbing, and history. From which Merlin concluded that no one had any idea.

In the midst of the hubbub, Merlin caught Dali mouthing *"Heir?"* at him.

Spotting the Duffy brothers starting to head for the exits in a "casual" manner designed to get out as fast as possible while not looking like that was what you were doing, he murmured in her ear, "Let me corner them alone."

She grabbed him by the shoulder. Her eyebrows were pulled together in a way that clearly meant business. Not even bothering to lower her voice, she said, "Nope. You and me are having a talk. Now."

"Wait," Merlin protested as she began to march him up the aisle and into the empty audience section. "I'll explain everything in the car—everyone is watching—"

Unfortunately, everyone was not only watching, they were cracking up and yelling encouragement. She didn't look back, but she could undoubtedly hear the chorus of "Yep, that's the way to handle him!" and "You go, girl!" and "Don't fall for the old 'there's a tiger behind you' trick!"

When they were halfway up the aisle—far enough from the ring to be able to speak without being overheard—she put a hand on each shoulder and sat him down in a seat. Hard.

"Ow," he protested reflexively, though it hadn't hurt. It was drowned out in a chorus of cheers, catcalls, and applause from the circus folk below.

Dali sat in the seat in front of him, leaning over the back to talk face-to-face. This put him in the embarrassing position of having to see both her and the laughing circus folk in the ring below as they talked.

"Can you please wait outside?" Merlin yelled down. "Change out of your costumes! I won't go anywhere!"

They yelled back stuff like "You better not!" and "We'll put guards at the exits!" and "I'll loan you a spoon to tunnel your way out!" But they did leave, to his immense relief. Dali twisted around to watch them go, then turned back to him.

"I've put up with your evasions long enough," Dali said. Her dark eyes seemed to gaze directly into his soul. "I want to know what's going on."

She's especially sexy when she's pissed off, his raptor remarked unhelpfully. *You should kiss her right now.*

"Shut UP," Merlin said, and realized a second later that he'd spoken aloud. "Sorry! Sorry!" Lowering his voice, he hastily said, "That wasn't to you! That was to my raptor! He talks inside my head—"

"You hear voices," Dali said flatly. He could see that she couldn't decide whether to be annoyed that he'd told her to shut up, annoyed that he was lying about it, or annoyed that his lie was so ridiculous.

"Yes, all shifters do. Well, one voice. We hear the animal we shift into. It's not really a separate being from us. It's like the voice of our subconscious. Or, well, not really 'sub' in my case. That's why sometimes

I seem kind of distractible—well, it's one of the reasons—anyway—"

"Fine," Dali said, jerking her hand to cut off that subject. "We'll talk about that later. Right now, I want you to explain this heir thing. In brief. No long stories where 'it all began' thirty years ago, no 'look, a triceratops!' Just the facts."

She *was* especially sexy when she was pissed off. Her eyes were like black diamonds, her cheeks were flushed, and even her lips had gone a darker shade of brown-pink, like a dusty peach. A peach that he'd really like to taste. It would be so sweet...

"NOW," Dali said ominously.

Merlin gathered his wits together, and told her the truth. "Mom and I aren't biologically related. She adopted me when I was a boy. She's the head of the circus, and when I came of age, she announced that she was naming me as her heir. Only I wasn't a shifter, and the head of the circus has always been a shifter. Her decision split the circus in half. It set families against each other. It caused so much trouble that I asked her to take it back. She refused. She's stubborn as hell. People were threatening to leave over it. The only way I could save the circus was to leave myself."

He stopped suddenly, his eyes prickling and his face hot. He'd managed to say that much by trying to blurt it out without thinking about it, but he could only manage a few sentences before his mind caught up to his mouth. And then all that grief and loss and frustration hit him like a tidal wave, like it had happened the day before instead of years ago.

"It was my home," Merlin said. And then his throat closed up, and he could say no more.

"I think I understand," Dali said. "The Navy was mine."

And then she did the last thing he'd have expected. She leaned over the back of her seat and put her arms around him. Instinctively, he wrapped his around her. And they sat together, holding each other, two lost people seeking and finding comfort in each other's touch. Merlin breathed in Dali's sweet-spicy scent and felt the softness and warmth of her skin. They were so close that he could feel her breathing.

He didn't know which of them moved first, or if they both moved at the same time. All he knew was that their lips were touching, then opening to each other. His hands tightened over the slippery silk of her blouse and the warm body beneath it as they kissed. Her mouth was hot and intoxicating. She wound her arms around his neck, and he felt her breathing catch. His heart was racing. He'd never wanted a woman so much in his life.

And then they both tried to get closer, and banged into something hard.

"Ow," muttered Dali.

Merlin opened his eyes, which had closed without him noticing it. He felt as if he'd woken up from a dream in a strange place. He'd completely forgotten where he was. Now he could see that they were both leaning way over, and had collided with the hard seat back that was between them.

Dali's eyes were wide, her lips parted, her hair slightly mussed. He couldn't help wondering if that was what she looked like when she was making love. Forget when she was angry, *now* when she was most beautiful.

She blinked as if she too felt like she'd just woken up. "I hope you don't regret that, because I don't."

"Never," Merlin swore.

Their eyes met, then glanced away. He laughed as he realized that they were both doing the same thing: looking around to see if there was anywhere more comfortable where they could continue making out.

"I'm afraid this is it," he said. "Also there's a bunch of circus people waiting for us outside."

"And you have interviews to do," she said, sounding as regretful as he felt. "But afterward…"

"Afterward, we have a date," he promised.

She ran her fingers through his hair, then brushed them over his lips. He kissed them. Merlin felt light as a feather, as if he might float away from sheer joy. As if his entire life had changed in the last few minutes.

"So…" Dali said slowly. "You couldn't inherit the circus because you weren't a shifter. But you're one now. Would they care that you weren't born one?"

"No, no." Merlin waved his hand dismissively. "If I shifted in front of them, they'd *have* to accept me."

The light in Dali's eyes faded. She looked uncertain now, as if bracing herself for a blow that she knew was coming, but not when it would fall. "Will you?"

Merlin heaved a sigh, and once again told her the hard, blunt truth. "I haven't decided. I love the circus, but there's been a lot of water under the bridge since I left. It's been hanging over my head ever since I got turned into a shifter. Anyway, I wanted to decide on my own. If they know I can shift now, it'll blow up everything all over again and I'll have Mom pressuring me even more."

"Wow. That's a lot." Dali put her hand on his shoulder.

Her touch was incredibly comforting. Not to mention distracting him with the delicious prospect of their upcoming date. "Let's go out and meet the family. I'll track down the Duffy brothers and see if they know your pigeon thieves. If it wasn't them, I'll at least get a start on interviewing everyone else until I find out who it was. And then…"

"Then our date." Dali grinned at him. She looked so different when she smiled, as if another, happier woman lived below her somber surface, just waiting to come up for air.

Merlin led her down the aisle and into the ring. It was the quickest way out, and he was sure she'd enjoy seeing the backstage area. As they walked across the ring, he heard the tiniest creaking sound. He looked up.

The entire trapeze apparatus, with its heavy metal bars, had somehow come loose from the ceiling and was plummeting down, directly above Dali.

Protect Dali!

Merlin didn't know if the shout inside his head came from him or his raptor. All he knew was that the apparatus was far too big for him to simply push her out of the way.

For the first time since he'd gained his powers, he was completely confident that when he shifted, he'd be the exact size that he needed to be.

Merlin became a raptor and lunged forward, shielding Dali with his body.

He was struck so hard that he felt nothing but the impact—not even the pain.

CHAPTER 10

Dali slammed into the floor. Metal crashed and clanged all around her, and a leather strap struck her shoulder like a whip. But nothing hard or heavy fell on her. Merlin had protected her from that.

"Merlin!" Dali shouted. "Are you all right?"

The huge raptor that he had become lay heavy and still atop her, pinning her legs. She twisted around frantically, trying to tell if he was breathing. Blood trickled down his head, and his eyes were closed.

"Merlin!" She sat up, her legs still pinned under the great raptor's body. Dali strained forward to reach his throat, where she fumbled for a pulse. Before she could find one, his great yellow eyes blinked open. She sagged with relief. "Oh, Merlin."

She stroked his throat and shoulder. His hide was smooth to the touch rather than scaly, velvety like old worn leather. Then it changed under her fingers, and Merlin lay sprawled across her legs, with his head in her lap and blood matting his bright hair.

He clutched at her frantically. "Dali! Are you hurt?"

"I'm fine," she reassured him. "Maybe a little bruised. Don't move, Merlin, you might have back or neck injuries."

"I'm fine," he protested, then winced. "Mostly."

He looked past her, and his expression changed from relief to dismay. Following his line of sight, she turned her head. And saw a crowd of circus folk standing behind her.

They had obviously come rushing back at the sound of the crash. Some were only half-dressed, or had been caught halfway through changing out of a costume and into regular clothes. Rather horrifyingly, one woman wore full clown makeup and a sexy black dress. Others, mostly the large predators, had shifted, so the crowd included lions, tigers, and a bear, plus a flying squirrel excitedly chittering atop the shoulder of a man wearing a shirt and no pants.

The pantless man knelt beside Merlin and began examining him, ignoring his protests that he was fine, just a little banged up.

"Are you a doctor?" Dali asked.

The pantsless man shook his head. "I'm a healer."

"What are your actual medical qualifications?" Dali inquired, barely stopping herself from adding, *"If any."*

"Zane's a paramedic, Dali, it's fine," Merlin said. "And he's had doctor-level training from other shifter medical people."

She was about to point out that unofficial training was no substitute for X-Rays when the crowd parted to make way for Janet, who couldn't move as fast as the younger people.

"You nearly gave me a heart attack," she scolded Merlin. "I thought you might be dead!"

"No, no, Mom, I'm fine," he assured her. "Everyone's making a big fuss over nothing."

"They certainly are not. Don't you dare move until Zane is finished examining you." Janet knelt beside Merlin and took his hand with a gentleness and concern that touched Dali's heart. As soon as Zane finished his examination and sat back, she turned to him. "Well?"

"No broken bones," Zane said. Dali would have been more relieved, except she didn't particularly trust the "healer's" expertise. She was also annoyed that he addressed Janet rather than Merlin. "Just cuts and bruises and the shock of the impact. He'll be fine with a little rest. His shift form was so big and strong, it protected him from the worst of it."

"Shift form?" Janet said, her eyebrows raised almost to her hairline.

A chorus of voices arose. "He turned into a dinosaur!" "A huge black lizard with fangs!" "A giant velociraptor!"

Janet held up a wrinkled hand. Silence instantly fell. "Merlin, is this true?"

"Yes. I got turned. It's a long story." For once, he didn't seem inclined to tell it immediately. Dali could see that there was a whole lot of family history behind the glance he and his mother exchanged.

Janet rose to her feet. Turning to address the crowd, she said, "My heir has returned. As you saw for yourselves, he's a shifter. I trust that there will be no more objections."

The silence was broken by a cough from Merlin as he gingerly touched the side of his head. He'd had a hell of a bad accident, whether as a raptor or not, and he was obviously in pain.

"Shall I call an ambulance, or would you rather have me drive you to the hospital?" Dali asked.

Imperiously, Janet said to the crowd, "Fetch a stretcher and take him to the infirmary."

"I don't need a stretcher." Merlin coughed again, more loudly, and again rubbed at his temple.

The cough worried Dali. Once might be dust in the air, but twice seemed significant. It could even be a sign of internal injuries.

"A stretcher!" Janet ordered, snapping her fingers. "Step lively!"

Several of the circus people hurried out.

Dali took out her cell phone. "I'm calling 911."

"No!" The exclamations came as one, from Merlin and everyone else there with a human throat.

"Hospitals aren't safe for shifters," Merlin said. "If a doctor notices anything weird and passes on the info, I could get kidnapped and experimented on."

He didn't say *again,* but he didn't have to. Reluctantly, Dali put her cell phone back in her purse. "Fine, but…"

Merlin staggered to his feet, then swayed.

She jumped up and steadied him. "You shouldn't have."

"It's done." He managed a smile, first for her, then for his mother, and finally for everyone else. "She'll take me to get help. Safe help. I know where."

Janet gave him and Dali a baleful glare. "You can get safe help here, Merlin. This is your home—your family!"

Merlin coughed so loudly that it sounded almost like a seal's bark, and pressed his entire hand to the side of his head.

That did it. No more dilly-dallying, Dali was taking him to the ER. Once he was there, she'd call his team to protect him from any kidnapping attempts.

"Come on, Merlin." They began to walk away, with her supporting him.

Over his shoulder, he said, "I'll call you tonight, Mom! I'm fine, really!"

Dali didn't want to rush him, but he picked up the pace himself, walking briskly despite periodic stumbles. When they got to his car, he fished in his pocket and pressed the keys into her hand. She opened the door and helped him into the passenger seat, then took the driver's seat.

Once she was settled in, she looked anxiously at Merlin. He was sagging in his seat, his head tilted back, his eyes half-closed. Bruises were coming up on his face in red and purple blotches, and both his head and his lip were bleeding.

Dali took out her phone to look up the address of the nearest hospital.

"I'll give you the address," Merlin said, and told it to her.

She fed it into GPS and began driving. The tiny sports car was incredibly responsive, and she didn't resist the urge to zip in and out of traffic. After all, she needed to get him to the ER as fast as possible.

"Fun, isn't it?" he said.

"Well, not now!" Then Dali looked into her heart, and admitted, "All right, it is. Or it would be under better circumstances."

"You can have better circumstances," Merlin said. "Drive it on our date, if you like."

The date! In the terror of the accident and her worry over him, she'd almost forgotten about it. At his words, the delicious anticipation, sexual thrill, and unexpected intimacy that she'd experienced with his kiss returned to her.

She didn't dare take her right hand off the wheel, and it would be too awkward to try to pat him with her left, even if it wasn't a prosthetic. She waited till the next red light, then leaned over and pressed a kiss into the side of his throat. He turned his head and kissed her back, and then she lost track of everything until a blast of angry honking informed her that the light had changed.

Dali jerked away and hit the gas, vowing not to kiss him again until she'd delivered him safely to an ER. It was obviously a driving hazard. But she was less worried that his injuries were serious now—not if he could kiss like that.

"Hey," Merlin said. "Good job catching my signal."

"What signal?"

"The signal to pull me out." When she didn't reply, he said, "I cough and touch my ear, and you come up with a reason I have to go. Though I didn't expect you to have a reason as plausible as 'I have to rush him to a doctor to treat him for trapeze injuries.'"

Dali groaned aloud. "Was *that* what you were doing? Merlin, I'd totally forgotten about the signal. I thought you were coughing and rubbing your head because you had a concussion and bruised lungs or something."

Merlin burst out laughing, then winced. "Ow. I don't think I have bruised lungs, but I'm sure I have bruised ribs. No, I was trying to signal you. I kept making it louder and bigger because I wasn't sure you'd noticed it. By the end I felt like I was barking like a seal."

"You kind of sounded like you were," Dali said. "Sorry I didn't pick up on it sooner. I was distracted by the accident."

"Accident?" The sharp note in Merlin's voice alarmed her. "That was no accident. Someone tried to kill you."

"What?" A cold stab of fear jabbed itself into Dali's belly. "How can you be sure?"

"Because I've set up that trapeze apparatus myself. An earthquake wouldn't bring it down. There's no way the entire thing could come loose unless someone *made* it come loose."

"You think someone from the circus tried to kill me?" Dali exclaimed, horrified. Then, realizing the unlikeliness of that, she said, "Merlin, are you sure they weren't trying to kill *you*? We were walking right next to each other. And you're the heir, not me. Maybe someone wants you out of the way so they can have a chance."

Then it was Merlin's turn to be appalled. "Oh, I'm sure they wouldn't—"

"You thought someone there set up a death trap for *me*," she pointed out.

"Well..." Merlin rubbed his forehead. "Either way, I don't think it's the best place for us to be right now."

"You can say that again." Following the GPS directions, Dali pulled up in front of...

...a little house in a residential neighborhood. That couldn't be right. Merlin reached for the car door handle.

"Wait," Dali said. "I must've given GPS the wrong address."

"No, you didn't."

"We're going to an ER," Dali said patiently, once again convinced that he was concussed. "This is someone's house."

"Right." Merlin gave a faint smile. "Mine."

Before she could stop him, he got out, then braced himself with a hand on the roof. Since Dali couldn't haul him back inside from the driver's seat, she was forced to get out too.

"You need to go to a hospital," she said.

"Nope." Lowering his voice, he said, "Shifters heal faster and better than non-shifters. And Zane Zimmerman really does know his stuff. If he says I just need a little rest, then I just need a little rest."

"You can't even walk by yourself!"

"Sure I can." He began to make his rather wobbly way up to his front door. Aggravated, Dali chased after him, managing to grab him by the arm just as he started to trip over the front step. Regaining his balance, he gave her a sweet smile. "Thanks, Dali."

She glared in return and said, quietly but with force, "Someone tried to kill me! Or you! How are we supposed to be safe in a regular house when you can't even stand up on your own?"

"We'll be safer than if I got kidnapped for another stay in a secret lab," Merlin pointed out. "Also, Carter did my security system, and he's a technical genius. If anyone tries to get in, not only will alarms go off that will wake the dead, but it'll send alerts to my entire team."

He was leaning against the door as if he hadn't a care in the world. Dali suspected that it was actually to make sure he didn't fall over

"And what about before your team makes it here?"

"I was a Marine before I was a velociraptor," he pointed out. "I have a gun, and I can shoot sitting down."

Dali found that more reassuring than the security system. Merlin *was* a veteran Recon Marine. He undoubtedly could defend himself and her if he was flat on his back.

He punched in a security code, fumbled out his keys and opened the front door, then stepped inside. Dali had to either let go of his arm or go with him, so she went with him. As soon as they crossed the threshold, something metal fell down and bounced noisily across the floor.

"Oops," said Merlin. "I forgot about that. Don't move until I turn on the lights."

He flipped on the light switch and shut the door. While he re-set the alarm, she got her first look at his house. She felt her own eyes bulge as she surveyed the array of cunningly constructed traps all over his house. They were similar to the one that had briefly imprisoned Cloud, and they lurked everywhere. There were even several hanging from the ceiling.

"You live here?" Dali exclaimed. "It's a death trap!"

Merlin gave her a pained glance. "They're all live traps. They're completely harmless."

"Not if they whomp you over the head!" She pointed an accusing finger at a contraption balanced on the half-open bathroom door.

"That one's mostly netting. There's nothing *to* whomp. Anyway, I have lots of stuff other than traps."

It was true. Merlin had lots of stuff, period: too much to take in all at once. Dali found her gaze fixing on small parts of it, one at a time.

A collection of little Day of the Dead figurines: clothed skeletons getting married, drinking in bars, and playing in a band.

What looked like hundreds of circus posters on the walls, not just of The Fabulous Flying Chameleons, but also Ringling Brothers, Barnum & Bailey, and, rather out of place, Cirque du Soleil.

Shelves and stacks of battered paperbacks in every genre imaginable, romance included; Dali spotted *The Gladiator Platypus's Curvy Librarian* and *Bought by the Billionaire Blink Dog* on the seat of a chair, sharing space with *The Care and Feeding of Your Kitten* and what appeared to be a teenage angst novel called *Loneliness and Other Large Molecules*.

"Do you have a kitten?" Dali asked.

"No, but I'm hoping to catch one. Or a dragonette. Something little and cute to perch on my shoulder."

Which reminded her that she had left her own kitten in her apartment. It had only been a few hours, but it felt like weeks. But she didn't want to leave Merlin alone, no matter how fine he claimed he was. Making a mental note to call Tirzah to check in on Cloud, she said, "Are you really dead-set on not seeing a doctor?"

"I'm dead-set on not staying at the circus or going to a hospital. I wasn't kidding about hospitals being dangerous for shifters." When Dali felt her eyebrows start to pull together with her intent to make sure he got medical care *somewhere*, Merlin said quickly, "Tell you what. If I'm not fine tomorrow, we can go to the office and Roland can call in some friends of his. They're shifter paramedics, from the west coast branch of Protection, Inc."

"Why not call them now?"

Merlin already looked fragile, with the bruises on his face and blood in his hair. But when he raised his eyes to hers, the vulnerability she saw in his clear blue gaze made her heart hurt. "Because my teammates already think I'm a joke. And I don't want to give them more reasons to feel that way."

"If they really do, they're dicks and they don't deserve you," Dali said. "But I bet you're wrong about that. Anyway, you got hurt saving my life! You didn't do anything wrong."

"Maybe I could've moved faster. I don't know. I…" He let out a long, fluttering breath. "I just want to stay here and not have to see anyone but you."

At that, Dali felt bad for arguing with him. He obviously wasn't in any immediate danger, and all she was doing was hassling him when he was already feeling bad.

"Hey. Let's get you cleaned up, okay?" She unhooked the net trap over the door and draped it over a stack of books for lack of a better option, then returned to Merlin and took his arm.

He leaned against her as she helped him to the bathroom. She could feel the hard muscle of his body, and she'd seen his astonishing grace and the steadiness of his hands as he'd balanced that absurd amount of circus food he'd bought for their lunch. That made it all the more alarming to see his trembling hands and feel how he leaned against her, both needing and trusting her support.

His silence worried her most of all. She'd gotten so used to his chatter. *Not just used to it,* she mentally amended. If she was honest with herself, she liked it. Merlin was charming and entertaining and fun, not to mention surprisingly thoughtful and insightful. The quiet felt so wrong.

The bathroom mat had an alarming realistic design of piranhas lunging upward from a pond, fanged mouths opened wide as if they were going to bite off your feet. But it was thick and fluffy, so she helped him sit down on it and lean back against the wall. He closed his eyes.

Dali thought he was worn out, not actually asleep or unconscious, but she still hated to disturb him. He looked so exhausted, and he'd gotten hurt protecting her. Instead of asking him if he had a first aid kit and where it was, she checked in the closest place where someone might keep one, which was the cupboard under the sink.

Something sprang out at her from within the dark cupboard. She recoiled with a yell. Merlin lunged forward, eyes still half-shut, instinctively seeking to shield her with his own body. The next thing she knew, she was lying on the bathroom floor with Merlin sprawled on top of her and a net entangling them both.

"Ptah!" Merlin tried to spit out a strand of webbing that had gotten in his mouth. "Sorry, sorry…"

He struggled to untangle them, but only succeeded in drawing it tighter. It took both their efforts to extract themselves, and by the time they were done, a trickle of blood was running down his face from the wound on his head and the bath mat piranhas appeared to have made a fresh kill.

Dali wasn't sure whether to laugh hysterically, scold him, or kiss him and make it better. "Please tell me you have a first aid kit I can get to without setting off a magical pet trap."

Merlin leaned over and slid open a drawer under the sink. Nothing jumped out or slammed shut or fell over, though she couldn't help noting that in addition to the kit, the drawer contained a screwdriver, three Snickers bars, and a plastic Tyrannosaurus rex eating a plastic pterodactyl.

The kit was not a commercial or even military one, but had obviously been hand-assembled from parts of both, plus some stuff Dali didn't recognize. She picked up a stoppered glass vial containing golden liquid, with a hand-printed label reading *"Heart's ease. For dragonsbane poisoning."*

"Dragonsbane?" Dali said.

"It's an herb that's poisonous to dragon shifters," Merlin said.

Part of her quietly boggled at the fact that she wasn't being sarcastic at all when she said, "Are there dragon shifters at the circus? Or on your team?"

"Neither. There's one on the west coast team, Lucas. And another guy on the west coast team has a mate who's a dragon shifter. Both of them have been poisoned by dragonsbane, so I figured I'd better keep the antidote around."

"Do they visit your team often?" Dali asked.

"Raluca came once. Lucas hasn't yet."

"So just in case one of them is here or you come across some other dragon, and in case they get poisoned, you wanted to make sure you could help them?"

He nodded as if it was the most logical thing in the world. She thought it was the most *Merlin* thing in the world: that he'd think of a wildly unlikely but not actually impossible chain of events, and just on the off chance that it might happen, go to what was probably a significant degree of trouble, not to mention risking people thinking he was a lunatic, so he could help someone—possibly someone he hadn't even met yet.

Dali spotted other odd things in the kit, but chose not to ask about or examine them. It was clearly an endless series of rabbit holes (which was also very Merlin), and she didn't want to get distracted from her task.

"I hope you're not too attached to that shirt," she said. "Because I think it'll hurt a whole lot less if I cut if off."

Merlin experimentally tried to lift one arm over his head, and put it down with a wince. He glanced down at his blood-spattered Tea Rex shirt, gave a regretful sigh, and said, "It's a goner away. Put it out of its misery."

She used the shears from the kit to slice off his T-shirt and tossed the scraps in the trash. His chest and shoulders were more muscular than she'd realized—he was so well-proportioned, it was only obvious with his shirt off. His golden tan and light dusting of blond hair made the blackening bruises stand out even more; just looking at them made Dali wince.

"Let me see your back," she said.

Merlin turned around. She could actually see the outline of a trapeze bar across his back, like he'd been struck with a crowbar.

That was the blow he'd taken for her.

"Are you all right?" Merlin asked unexpectedly. He turned back around, his sky-blue eyes wide and anxious as they peered into hers. "I can take care of myself, you know. You don't have to do it, and you don't have to watch. Why don't you go into the living room and read a book or—"

Dali interrupted him. She had to, or she wouldn't have been able to get a word in edgewise. "Merlin, I *want* to help. I wouldn't be here if I didn't. What got into you all of a sudden?"

He gave her a final searching stare, then dropped his gaze, his face flushing. "You went silent for a while, and it occurred to me... well... stop me if I'm being a jerk..."

"Spit it out," Dali said.

"Well, there's blood and I'm hurt and we're on the floor and I thought..." He tilted his face up again, his gaze compassionate and honest. "You obviously went through something that involved blood and injuries, and you were forced to leave the Navy even you didn't want to, and a yeoman can do the job just fine with a prosthetic hand. I figured you had to have PTSD. And it had to be pretty bad to keep you from going back. I thought maybe the blood and all was getting to you."

Dali was struck dumb. The truth so terrible that she couldn't even bear to think of it herself, the secret shame that had defined her life far more than the loss of her hand, the thing she'd thought she'd never be able to tell him or anyone, had turned out to not be a secret at all. Merlin had figured it out by himself. More importantly, he spoke of it as if it was a simple fact, not something to be ashamed of.

She felt like a shell around her heart had been cracked open with a single, precise hammer-blow. All the feelings she'd locked inside were going to come flooding out. She had a moment of terror when she realized that she couldn't stop it, and then the part of her that cared about that was washed away as well.

Her emotions were so intense and overwhelming that they clogged her throat. She sat staring at him, unable to speak, until she realized from the increasing worry on his face that he probably thought she was having a flashback. He started to reach out, then looked down at his blood-spattered hand and froze, obviously uncertain if touching her would make things better or worse.

"You can touch me," she said. "I'm not afraid of a little blood."

He put his arms around her and held her tight. Merlin was hurt himself, but he was taking care of *her*. It should have made her feel guilty, but instead she felt comforted. She relaxed into his strong grip, snuggling up against his warmth and breathing in the scent of him, the salt of clean sweat and a sweetness like he still had some powdered sugar on his fingers.

For the first time since she'd woken up in the hospital, she felt safe: safe to feel again. Dali buried her face in his shoulder and let her tears flow: tears of loss, tears of grief, tears of relief at finally being able to cry.

Merlin didn't tell her to stop or quiz her about what had happened or try to distract her with some story of his own. He simply held her and didn't let her go. His silence didn't feel ominous this time, but like a gift he was giving her: his quiet strength and caring, and all the time and space that she needed.

When she finally lifted her head, she felt cleansed. He'd spoken so matter-of-factly that she couldn't imagine him shaming or criticizing her, no matter what she told him. Merlin accepted people, quirks and flaws and all.

"I was on the USS *Greyhound*," she said. When he nodded, she saw in his lack of surprise that he'd already guessed that she'd been on it when it had been bombed. "So I don't need to tell you what happened to it."

"No," he said gently. "I know about that."

"You don't know what happened to *me*, though." Dali blew out a breath, exasperated with herself. "Never mind that. You're sitting here bleeding—my story can wait."

"I'm pretty sure it's stopped," Merlin said.

He was right, but she still didn't feel right postponing his care any more than she already had. Besides, she could probably use some distraction herself. She tore open a medical wipe. "Lean forward."

As she began cleaning the cut on his head, she said, "It was a day like any other day. One of my duties was maintaining shipboard legal records, and I was working on those files. I woke up in a hospital."

Even with his head bowed, she could see the startled flicker of his eyelids.

"Yeah," she said. "Just like that. If my hand wasn't busy, I'd snap my fingers."

"That must have been so confusing."

She nodded. "I was on a lot of drugs, and I had to have a bunch of surgeries. By the time I could understand what had happened, it was a month later. Everyone who'd died had already had their funerals, and the ship was back in service."

"You never remembered anything about the bombing?"

"I never *experienced* the bombing." She tossed away the wipe and picked up a roll of gauze. "The doctors said I was instantly knocked unconscious. The blood and fear and injured people—I missed all that. From my perspective, it was like I blinked, and I woke up in a different body in a different world."

He looked up at her, his eyes full of startled understanding. "So—"

"Hold still." Dali pushed his head back down and began winding gauze around it. She had to watch her prosthetic hand to use it, but she spared a glance for the other as well, expecting to see it trembling. But it was steady as a rock.

When she finished, Merlin appeared to be wearing a white headband. He already looked a bit like a surfer, and that made him *really* look like a surfer.

That amused her enough to give her the strength to get to the hard part. Especially since she'd need to be looking straight at his face when she did it. "You can lift your head now."

Very gently, glad her hands were steady, she took some more disinfectant wipes and started cleaning the cuts on Merlin's face. "I thought I'd grieve for my friends who died, get fitted for a prosthetic and learn how to use it, and then I'd go back to work. I didn't even think about PTSD. After all, I couldn't remember what had happened, so it wasn't like I could have nightmares or flashbacks or horrible memories... right?"

It was a rhetorical question. Merlin didn't reply, but just gave her a sad, ironic half-smile. He might not know the details yet, but he obviously knew the answer to that.

"I went back." Lifting her prosthetic, she said, "I can even type with this. Nowhere near as fast as I used to, but I learned a two-finger method that was good enough. But..."

She looked him over to give herself some breathing space. She'd disinfected everything but the cut on his lips. How had she managed to time things so she'd gotten to the hardest part of her story at the same time that she'd gotten to the hardest part of tending to Merlin's injuries? The mouth was such a sensitive part of the body, it was bound to sting like hell.

"Sorry," she muttered, not knowing if she was apologizing for hurting him or for what she was about to reveal. As she dabbed antiseptic on his lips, she said, "I kept thinking that any second, I'd wake up in a hospital. Or not wake up at all. I knew that everything could vanish at any moment and I kept waiting for it to happen. I couldn't focus on my work. I went on medical leave and did therapy, and I thought it was helping. But when I went back on duty, it was exactly the same as before. I was okay when I was off-duty, but it turned out that my trigger was being on-duty in the Navy, and nothing I did could change that."

Dali's words ran down like a car running out of gas. She realized that she was clutching the antiseptic wipe, and she dropped it in the trash without breaking eye contact with Merlin. He'd never looked away, the entire time she'd been speaking.

She'd thought having to tell that story while she was looking into his eyes would make it harder. But instead, it made it easier. She could watch him the entire time for any vestige of disapproval, contempt, or worst of all, pity at her weakness. But he never showed any of that. Instead, she saw sympathy and understanding.

"How long did you stay on, after you went back?" Merlin asked.

She hadn't expected that question, and it took her a moment to figure that out. "About four months. Not counting the medical leave."

"Four months of expecting to die at any second."

Dali nodded, her lips pressed tight together. If she thought about it too much, she could feel a ghost of that terrifying certainty.

"That's the bravest thing I've ever heard of anyone doing," Merlin said. "You're the bravest person I know."

She stared at him. "What? I was just trying to do my job, and I couldn't even do that!"

"I was a Marine, you know. So I know what it feels like to think you're about to die. But I only ever experienced that for a few seconds at a time. Added up, it was maybe five minutes over my whole career. But you faced death every second of every day, for four months. You knew it would be like that every morning when you woke up, and you got out of bed and did it anyway. I don't think I could've done that."

Merlin was unmistakably sincere, which made her give serious consideration to his words. She'd always thought of that time as a failure caused by her own weakness. But he'd reframed it as an act of courage, and that made her recall how difficult it had been to get up, day after day, and walk into what felt like certain death.

Maybe she hadn't been weak. Maybe she'd been stronger than she'd ever known she could be.

Dali felt like her whole world had once again been picked up, given a good shake, and set back down again with all the pieces in different places. But this time, for the better.

It was an incredible gift. And Merlin was the one who'd given it to her.

CHAPTER 11

Merlin's thoughts were going as fast as they always did, and his raptor was babbling on in his head like he always did, but Merlin managed to keep his mouth shut. Dali was obviously lost in thought, and whatever was going on in her mind didn't seem to be making her unhappy, so he didn't want to interrupt it. Instead, he simply sat and watched, barely daring to breathe, as the light of hope slowly brightened her face like the rising sun.

"Thank you," she said at last. "For everything. But especially what you said about going back taking courage. I never thought of it that way before. It means a lot to me."

"Thank *you*," he said.

"Oh, it was nothing," Dali said. "Just a little basic first aid."

"I didn't mean that. Though thank you for that too. I meant, thank you for believing me. And taking me seriously. And not telling me to get rid of the goddamn traps, like everyone does at work. Though I guess I can't really blame them. People do trip over them a lot. Pete's gotten his foot stuck in them twice, and Carter threatened to bill me for dry cleaning after he set off a trip-wire and it spilled carrot juice down the front of his shirt."

"Why do you want a magical pet so much?" Dali asked.

No one had ever asked him that before. They just assumed he was weird Merlin being weird, or thought they already knew because they'd heard him say things like "I want something adorable to sit on my shoulder" or "Who wouldn't want a flying kitten?" or "I always dreamed of having a miniature dragon." And that was all perfectly true. It just wasn't all of the truth.

But Dali had asked. Maybe that was why he blurted out, "Because I'm lonely."

"Oh, Merlin," she said softly.

He knew he didn't have to explain, but since it was already out there, he wanted her to understand him. "I love my mom, but we get in the same fight every time I see her. I had friends at the circus, but it's been pretty awkward since I left. Natalie was my best friend there, but she didn't even tell me *she* left. I had friends in the Marines, but they're all deployed and I'm here. The west coast Protection, Inc. team is on the west coast. And as for my team—"

Merlin had felt cold and shaky ever since he'd had two hundred pounds of metal dropped on his back, but the last of his chill burned off in a hot rush of blood as he went on, "Carter won't even tell us what sort of animal he turns into and he high-tails it in his private jet if anyone suggests he's part of the team. Ransom spends half his time locked in his office getting psychic messages from Mars or something. Pete is constantly on the verge of tossing me out the window. Roland is running the team as a distraction from grieving for a woman he met once for five minutes, whose name he never knew. Tirzah... Tirzah's cool, actually. But she's engaged to Pete so it's not like I'm ever getting invited over to dinner at their place."

He sighed. "Ugh, this all sounds so self-pitying. Forget you heard any of it. Chalk it up to loss of blood."

But Dali didn't look at him like she pitied him. "I'm lonely, too."

She put her arm around his shoulder. In that simple gesture, he could sense that she was reaching out to find and touch someone like herself. Like two soldiers under fire. Or two lonely people coming together in shared desire.

Now that he'd been sitting down for a while and she had bandaged everything that needed bandaging, he felt a lot better. But her touch still knocked him off-balance.

She knocked him off-balance. Even sitting on his floor with her braids coming unpinned and her clothes sprinkled with sawdust and his blood on her hands, she was still the most beautiful, sexy woman he'd ever seen. Actually, the messy hair made her *more* sexy, like she'd just finished having sex so urgent and frantic that her hair had gotten yanked down and she'd never even noticed. The sawdust made him remember how he'd been willing to give his life to protect her, and the blood touched him with the memory of her kindness.

You should have sex with her right now, his raptor suggested.

He kissed her instead. She responded with the same passion he felt, opening her mouth to him, seeking to claim him as much as he sought to claim her. He forgot his injuries, forgot everything but this marvelous, infinitely desirable woman who was, impossibly, right here in his arms. His breath came faster. His heartbeat pounded in his ears like a drum. He felt dizzy with desire.

And also, just plain dizzy. Black spots were dancing before his eyes.

"Merlin!" Dali's voice was sharp with alarm. He felt her hand on the back of his head, pushing it down between his knees. "Take a deep, slow breath. Another."

He breathed slowly until he felt less like he was going to pass out at any second. When he was sure it was safe to lift his head, he said, "I thought it would be extremely romantic if I was so overcome by your beauty that I actually fainted."

Dali inspected him worriedly, then gave him a rueful smile. "You got hurt saving my life. I think that's romantic enough. How about you lie down now, and we take a rain check on the making out?"

"Sounds good."

She helped him to his feet, and they made their way to his bedroom. He pointed out the traps as they went, and they got in without setting any off. He kicked off his shoes and lay down, grateful that between the circus and the Marines, he'd gotten into the habit of making the bed every morning. He'd have hated her to be grossed out by his single guy habits.

Once he was lying down, he felt a lot better. "Sorry for being such a terrible host. Help yourself to anything in the kitchen or, well, anything. I've got lots of books if you're bored."

"Do *you* want anything?"

Marshmallows with hot chocolate, said his raptor.

Between the blood loss and the leftover high from kissing Dali, Merlin's defenses were down. He started to automatically echo what his raptor had said, only managing to cut himself off a couple words in.

"Marshmallows with hot?" Dali repeated. She touched his forehead as if she thought he might be feverish.

"I'm not delirious. Remember how I said my raptor talks to me?"

Her eyebrows formed a pair of exquisite arches as she said, "Your *velociraptor* wants hot marshmallows?"

"Marshmallows with hot chocolate," Merlin said. "He's kind of a sugar freak."

She sat down on the bed beside him. "At the circus, you said he's your subconscious. So your subconscious wants sugar?"

"I guess so."

"Do *you* want sugar?"

He shrugged. "I like sweet things, sure. Not as much as he does. I put sugar in my coffee. He tells me to throw away the coffee and pour the sugar into my mouth."

Dali chuckled, then her amusement faded and was replaced by curiosity. "Why the difference?"

"You know, I never really thought about that. At the circus they say the inner animal is the most primal part of yourself. The heart, not the mind."

And the part that recognizes your mate, he thought, but he stuffed that thought down so fast and deep that even his raptor wasn't quick enough to catch it. Either his raptor was too damaged to recognize his mate or his mate wasn't Dali, and either way, he didn't want to think about it.

"Did you ever eat plain sugar?" Dali asked.

"When I was a kid, sure," he began. And then his mind raced ahead of his words. In a small voice, he said, "Oh."

"What?"

Tell her, demanded his raptor. *She needs to understand.*

If his raptor really was the deepest part of his heart, then maybe Merlin should listen to his relationship advice. And he *did* want her to understand him.

He patted the bed. "Lie down next to me?"

She immediately lay down. Their bodies fit together like puzzle pieces, molding to each other as if they'd spent a lifetime getting it just right.

CHAPTER 12

Merlin's Story

I did eat plain sugar when I was a kid. It was the only sweet thing in the house. It wasn't because my parents were health nuts. They didn't like sweet stuff themselves, so they didn't buy it. They'd never wanted me and they didn't love me, so if the only reason to do something was to make *me* happy, it didn't get done.

That's not how that story's supposed to go. Maybe the baby was a surprise, but Mom and Dad fall in love with it the moment they hold it in their arms, right? Or if they don't, it's because Dad's a wife-beater and Mom's an alcoholic and eventually the kid gets taken away.

It wasn't like that. Nobody beat me. Nobody starved me. And nobody loved me. They never said so, but they didn't have to. I could feel it.

We were in the kind of social circles where kids don't run around the neighborhood. They have playdates and classes and Cub Scouts instead. My parents didn't go out of their way to arrange stuff like that for me. If it wasn't convenient for them, they didn't happen. So I'd make friends at school, but it was hard to see them outside of school.

I never had a pet. My parents thought animals were messy and noisy and a nuisance. But I loved them. There were some big trees in our backyard, and I used to climb them and try to get the squirrels to eat peanuts out of my hands.

I read books about boys and their dogs, and girls and their horses, and kids who ran away and lived with the wolves, and kids who ran away to the circus, and kids who stepped through a door into another world where they had magical pets and people who loved them and important things to do. I wanted that so much, it felt like the force of my longing would tear a hole in reality and open up a door for me to step through.

Maybe it did.

When I was eleven, the Fabulous Flying Chameleons came to town. I saw that poster, and I wanted to step into it. I asked my parents for money to go, but they refused. I wasn't surprised, but it bothered me more than that sort of thing usually did, so I kept asking. And they kept saying no.

Finally, it was the day of the Fabulous Flying Chameleons' last performance. I'd never done this before, but I stole some money from Dad's wallet. I told them I was spending the night at a friend's house. They never even asked which one.

I don't have to describe the circus to you. You've seen it. Some of the performers and acts are different, but it's always had the same concept. And the same spirit. I remember it exactly. Not only the acts, but the smells, the seats, the bits of sawdust on the floor. I bought a hotdog and a box of Crackerjack, and I remember every bite I took.

And I remember the moment that changed my life. It was seeing the trapeze artists. They started their act with the most basic catch there is, the one where they hang from the bar by their knees and catch hands. But to me, it looked absolutely magical. They were flying through the air, trusting each other with their lives.

I thought, *They must feel so happy and free. Why can't my life be like that?*

And I thought, *Maybe it could.*

When the show was over, I snuck closer and closer to the backstage area until I could see that no one was looking. Then I climbed a ladder that went straight up the wall and got into the rigging—that's the metal structure beneath the tent ceiling that holds the lights and the trapezes and so forth. I was pretty small as a kid, so the beams were wide enough that I wasn't too scared by the height, even though it was really high. And when I lay down on a beam, I was basically invisible from below. I lay there and watched the animals come off the stage and go into other rooms I couldn't see, and the clowns taking off their shoes and stage hands packing things up.

I'd gotten the idea to go up because I'd read in a book that the best place to hide was over people's heads, because people don't tend to look there. That's true for most people, though not so much for shifters. But of course I didn't know about shifters then.

I didn't have a very detailed plan. I knew they'd have to take down the entire tent, so I figured I'd hide until everyone was packing stuff somewhere else, then come down and hide in a trunk or a suitcase or something, and hope they didn't find me until they were far away and it was too late to take me back. Honestly I don't think it was a terrible plan considering that I was eleven.

Everything about the circus felt magical. So I wasn't one hundred percent shocked when I saw a tiny orange-and-white kitten run backstage, then turn into a toddler. He was stark naked, running around laughing and yelling "You can't catch me!"

A woman came chasing after him and grabbed him by the scruff of the neck. He turned back into the kitten and yowled. She held him tight and called to the nearest stagehand, "Jeannie, can you bring my clothes to the dressing room?"

Jeannie said sure. And the woman disappeared. Her clothes fell to the floor like she'd vaporized. Then a calico cat scrambled out of the heap of clothes with the kitten in her mouth and trotted off with him. Jeannie picked up the clothes and followed her out. There were lots of other people backstage. And none of them blinked an eye.

Circus people and theatre people are pretty casual about nudity, since they have to do quick-changes backstage and dressing rooms are shared.

And shifters are casual too, because regular shifters—ones that aren't mythic or extinct—can't take anything with them when they shift. So not everyone bothered to go to the dressing rooms before they shifted.

I saw a bear turn into a woman, and a flying squirrel turn into a man. I saw two tigers and a tabby cat practice a new act all by themselves. I saw a beautiful woman tell a white rat that it was his turn to help their daughter practice her math that night. I was absolutely enchanted. I forgot about myself and my plans and just watched.

An old woman sat down on a trunk with little kids and kittens and poodle puppies and a foal and two baby seals in a semi-circle on the floor around her, and told them a story. I couldn't hear her very well, because she was on the other side from me and her voice was soft. But she'd started with "In the days of Merlin, the first shifter," and I was really interested. So I started slithering along the beam to get closer.

I didn't realize it, but once I moved out from where I was, I went in front of a light and cast a shadow. And someone saw it. The next thing I knew, a flying squirrel landed on the beam in front of me, turned into a boy my age, and yelled, "INTRUDER!"

I fell off the beam.

I was fifty feet up, and I was falling. I grabbed out in a panic, and I caught something.

It was the tightrope, and I was dangling from the middle of it. My hands hurt—I had rope burns on my palms from grabbing it without gloves—and I was still thirty feet up. And everyone was below me, looking up and shouting instructions at me and at each other.

That was when the fear of heights hit me. I knew that if I fell, I'd die. I was so scared, I couldn't even scream.

Then a parrot flew up. I didn't see where it had come from, but it circled around a few times to make sure I saw it. Them it flew up and perched on the tightrope next to me. It opened its beak and squawked, "Hold on!"

I gulped. "You can talk?"

"Yes," said the parrot. "Haven't you ever heard of talking parrots?"

I nodded.

"I'm going to help you get down," the parrot said. "But you'll have to be brave."

"I can be brave," I said, though I sure didn't feel brave.

"Good boy!" squawked the parrot. "Did you see the show?"

"Yes. It was wonderful."

"Now, don't look down. Just answer. Do you remember the net beneath the tightrope?"

Even though she'd warned me, I nearly did look down. But I caught myself just in time. Then I felt stupid. Why was I so scared when there was a net below me?

It didn't help, though. I was still terrified. There were tears pouring down my face. But I said, "Yeah, I remember the net."

"It's there in case anyone falls," the parrot said. "But if you're stiff when you fall, you can get hurt. You need to relax your whole body and fall light as a feather. Then you'll just bounce. It's actually fun, if you fall right."

I wasn't sure I believed her, but I nodded. By then I'd been hanging for a while. My hands burned like fire, and my arms felt like they were being pulled out of their sockets. I was scared to let go, but I didn't know how much longer I could hold on. I said, "Should I let go now?"

"Not yet," the parrot said. "First I need to teach you how to fall."

I don't know how I managed it, but I hung on while she told me to relax my toes, then relax my feet, then my lower legs, and so forth.

Finally, she said, "Now when I say relax, I want you to relax your hands and fingers, and let go. Relax!"

I let go. I fell, but it wasn't terrifying any more. I saw her skimming down after me, and when I hit the net, I was relaxed, and I bounced. I sat up and said, "That *was* fun!"

"I told you it would be," the parrot said from her perch on the rim of the net.

The circus people were all clustered around, cheering and clapping. Some of them were crying, though I didn't understand why till later.

It was the last performance, so they'd been taking everything down and packing it up. When I fell, they'd already dismantled and packed up the net. As soon as they saw me, they ran to unpack it and get it in place. But it took a while. The parrot sat there calmly talking to me and distracting me the whole time they were putting up the net, and made sure I didn't let go until it was safe. She saved my life.

I didn't know that then. But I did know that she'd kept me company and comforted me when I was scared to death. If she hadn't been a parrot, I'd have hugged her.

"Excuse me for a moment," said the parrot. "I need to get dressed."

She flew off, and someone carried her clothes after her. Some other circus people helped me out of the net. They made a fuss over me and Zane Zimmerman checked me over to make sure I wasn't hurt.

Once I relaxed enough to notice more of what was going on, I saw the flying squirrel boy who'd made me fall standing off to the side, glaring at me while his parents scolded him. They looked really mad at him, and I was glad. I realize now that he was eleven too and he hadn't known I'd fall off if he startled me, but at the time, all I knew was that he'd nearly gotten me killed.

Then the old woman who'd been telling the story about Merlin came up and sat down next to me. She introduced herself as Janet Gold, then she smiled and asked me if I recognized her.

"You were the parrot," I said. To this day, I don't know how I knew. I hadn't seen her shift, and her normal voice doesn't sound anything like the parrot's. It was just something about her.

"Yes, that's me," she said. "Did you come on a school trip?"

I realized afterward that she'd assumed it had to be that, since if I'd come with family they'd have noticed I was missing way before now, and she was trying to figure out how long it would take before a panicked teacher ran backstage looking for me.

But I was busy trying to figure out what I could possibly say to her to make her take me with her. I thought fast, and I said, "I came by myself. I don't go to school because I'm an orphan. A homeless orphan."

"Really," she said. "In this day and age."

Of course, I was as clean as any eleven-year-old boy ever is, and my clothes were what you buy for a kid when you care more about looking respectable to other parents than the kid's own taste. Which is to say, I was *better*-dressed than the average kid.

But I thought she was thinking that a homeless orphan should be in foster care, so I said, "I was in foster care, but they starved me and beat me and made me live in a closet. So I ran away to live on the streets. Uh, but this gang has been trying to recruit me, only I didn't want to sell drugs, so I saw this circus and I thought it would be a good place to hide from them, and that's why I was in your rafters. The gang's probably still waiting outside, so I better not leave just yet."

"Better not," she agreed. Now she was smiling. "It's a cold night, and you've had a fright. How would you like some hot chocolate?"

"Yes, please," I said.

Janet tapped the person closest to her, who I recognized as the ringmaster. He had a huge twirled moustache and he looked very impressive. "Max? Will you get the boy a nice big mug of hot chocolate, please? With marshmallows."

He went off without a word. He didn't even look annoyed on being sent on an errand.

"Are you the boss of the circus?" I asked.

"You're a very observant boy," she said. "Yes, I am."

"And you can all turn into animals?"

"Well, most of us can." I caught just a flicker of a glance she gave to a girl with long black braids who'd been listening to her tell the Merlin story.

"Can you teach me?" I asked. I was so eager that I grabbed at her sleeve. "I want to be a tiger! Or, no, I'd rather fly. Can I be a parrot, like you?"

She shook her head. "I'm afraid you have to be born that way."

Max came back with a mug of hot chocolate. It not only had marshmallows, it had whipped cream and even rainbow sprinkles. Max can be a bit full of himself, but he's a good guy and he's great with kids.

It *was* a cold night, and I'd had a shock, so the heat and sugar made me feel a lot better. It was also really great hot chocolate. Max had hit the gourmet stash for it, and used real milk instead of water.

I'd mostly been paying attention to Janet, but a whole lot of circus people were standing around watching us. While I drank the hot chocolate, she turned to them and said, "The boy is bright. He's agile. He got backstage and into the rigging without any of us seeing him, he didn't fall until he was startled, and he wasn't frightened until he actually fell. He enjoyed hitting the net. He's articulate, quick-witted, and has an excellent line of patter considering his age. He's excited by shifters, not frightened."

Nobody had ever said such nice things about me before, or paid so much attention to me. Sometimes teachers said I was smart and a good student, but they always added stuff like "when he calms down and focuses" or "when he actually does the assignment instead of something he thinks is more fun."

"I want to speak to him alone," Janet said. "I'll call you back in when we're ready—and I want all adults to be present. In the meantime, please discuss it amongst yourselves."

They went out, leaving us alone. Part of me was so hopeful, I was about ready to explode. The other part was sure it was too good to be true. I was so keyed-up, my throat closed up. I had to put down the hot chocolate even though I hadn't finished it.

"You want to stay here, don't you?" she asked.

"Yes," I said. "Please."

"I know you told me some lies," she said. When I started to protest, she held up her hand. "I'm not angry. Lies aren't always bad. But I have some decisions to make now, and I need to know the truth to make them. I can promise you that I'm not going to toss you out just because you have parents who don't beat you or starve you. Okay?"

"Okay." It came out in a whisper.

"*Do* you have parents?" she asked.

I nodded.

"When do they expect you to come back?"

"Some time tomorrow," I said.

"Do they abuse you?"

I shook my head.

"What's wrong with them, then?" she asked.

"They don't love me," I said. And I started to cry. She put her arms around me, and let me cry all over her beautiful embroidered jacket.

I'd always wondered, before that moment, if maybe the problem was me, not my parents. Maybe they did love me after all, but something was wrong with me that made me unable to feel it. And if that was true, I'd always wondered if I'd ever feel that someone did love me. If it was even possible for me to experience love.

We'd only just met, but I could feel that Janet loved me already. And I loved her too. We looked at each other, and I knew I didn't have to be afraid. She wasn't going to kick me out.

She knew it, too. Janet patted me on the back, and said, "I don't know if you've noticed, but I never asked your name."

"It's—" I started to say, but she put her finger to her lips.

"A lot of people change their name when they join the circus. They're starting a new life, so they give themselves a new name. You don't have to, but if you want to, you can."

Once she explained it, I did want to. And I knew exactly what name I wanted.

"I'm Merlin," I said.

She looked taken aback, then she laughed. "Did you hear my story?"

"Just the first sentence," I said. "But I know who Merlin was. He was King Arthur's magician."

"He was much more than that," Janet said. "But it's an excellent name. Do you have a last name to go with it?"

I shook my head.

"Shall I pick one for you?"

"Yes, please."

"A lot of circus people have first and last names that start with the same letter. It's called alliteration, and it makes them nice and memorable. The same first two letters are even better. Or maybe the first three…" She thought for a moment, then said, "Merlin Merrick. How's that sound?"

"It sounds *fabulous*," I said.

She laughed. And then she changed my life.

She called everyone back in, and she said, "Now that I've spoken to the boy, I've decided not to hold a vote. I'm taking him in and raising him myself."

When directors want to have "crowd murmuring" sounds, they tell the actors to say "rhubarb, rhubarb," because it'll sound like murmuring but you won't be able to pick up the actual word. Well, there was a lot of murmuring when she made that announcement, and I couldn't pick up the words. But I could tell the emotion. They were completely shocked.

"No questions, no arguments," she said. "It's done."

She swept her gaze over them, and they went silent. To me, she said, "Tell them your name."

I said, "My name is Merlin Merrick."

She said, "Please welcome our newest Fabulous Flying Chameleon, Merlin Merrick!"

And they all applauded. Well, almost all of them. The flying squirrel boy didn't. And I could see that some of the adults weren't very enthusiastic. That only barely registered with me at the time, I was so overwhelmed at the thought of living in a magical circus and having Janet instead of my parents. But afterward, I remembered it.

Afterward, I learned a whole lot of things I didn't know that night.

Janet—you know, I'll just call her Mom now that you know who I'm talking about—is the circus boss, but she's something else too. She's the alpha. It's unusual for shifters of different species to have a single alpha, but it can happen when they're all working together. That means that she can overrule them all in a way that goes way beyond being able to fire them. She can dominate them, like an alpha wolf in a regular wolf pack.

Normally, new members who aren't born into the circus are only accepted by a vote of the entire company. Two-thirds of them have to vote yes, and Mom's vote doesn't hold any more weight than anyone else's—though her recommendation does, of course. But there had been times when she'd held a vote and had been overruled.

The decision on me had to be made fast, because it'd be less than 24 hours before my parents would notice I was missing. Mom didn't want to chance me being voted down as not a shifter and too much of a risk of attracting police attention, and she thought it would make everyone angry if they voted against me and *then* she overruled them. So she didn't hold a vote. She just announced her decision, and she used her alpha dominance to stop them from arguing. That had a lot of repercussions later on.

But that night, I stuck by her side while they packed up everything, dismantled the rigging and the tent, and loaded it all into a couple of train cars. I tried to help, but mostly I just got underfoot.

The circus travels on its own train. The "pie car" is the kitchen and cafeteria. They have cars with animal cages and food. Mostly they're empty, but every now and then someone will request to inspect them to make sure the animals are treated right, and then everyone shifts and gets in them until the inspector leaves.

I was not only going to live in a circus, I was going to live in a *circus train*.

The living quarters were small but cozy, with beds that folded out from the walls at night and folded up during the day. Janet unfolded one, made it up, and put me to bed. In the morning, I woke up in a different state, with a different name, a different life, a different family, and a different home.

I'd never been happier.

I caused a lot of trouble behind the scenes, because they not only had to scramble to come up with fake papers for me, they had to head off a high-profile missing child investigation. First they had me call my parents to say I was spending another night at the friend's house, to buy some time. Then they tracked down my dad's sister, who was an off-the-grid survivalist who was estranged from the rest of the family, and had me call again to say I'd run away and was spending some time with her.

They finally made up one of the lion shifters to look like her—it's amazing how much you can do if you're really good at stage makeup—and did a video call with both of us in blurry video with me doing most of the talking, where I said I was staying with her and she said she'd teach me the important things in life. To be honest, it was a plan that could only work if I was right that my parents really didn't care about me and would be just as happy to have me gone.

It worked perfectly.

I wasn't so much sad as relieved. I'd always thought they didn't want me, and it turned out that I'd been right all along. It sounds awful, but it was a kind of awfulness I'd been living with my whole life, and now I knew that I wasn't crazy and the problem was them, not me.

And now I had a mom who loved me so much that she'd taken one look at me, and turned her entire life upside down for me. Mom had never married or had kids. But she moved me into her train car quarters, gave me half her space, and never ever made me feel like she didn't want me there.

Nobody had to sit me down and explain to me that it was a crime circus. If I hadn't figured it out from how they already knew how to create fake identities, I would have the first time I saw the rat roulette trick. I just thought it made them even cooler. Especially when I was learning how to do stuff like pick locks and be a lookout for jewelry-stealing sparrows.

And that wasn't all I learned. I couldn't shift, but I got to try everything a human could do. I was best at acrobatics and trapeze—I might not have wings, but I could still fly through the air—and I couldn't wait to be old enough to be the human partner for rat roulette.

I don't want to sound like everything was perfect. The flying squirrel boy, Fausto Fratelli, couldn't stand me and the feeling was mutual. We got in fist-fights, I'd play pranks on him, and he'd break stuff and try to pin it on me.

It was too bad because there weren't a lot of kids my age—most of the rest were a couple years older or younger. The only other one was Kalpana Doubek, Max and Renu's daughter. That was the girl with black braids who Mom had looked at when I asked if I could learn to shift. Everyone thought she and I would be best friends because we were the same age and we both couldn't shift. That didn't happen. She was super nice but a lot more mature than me. She was kind to me in an older-sister way, not a buddy way.

A couple months after we joined, near the end of our US tour, I saw a girl my age sneak in without paying. She was really clever about it, too. She tagged along with a big family, and joined them and got away from them with perfect timing so neither they nor the ticket taker noticed. But I noticed.

After the show, I went up to her and struck up a conversation. We hit it off right away, like kids do sometimes. Her name was Natalie, and she had sort of a similar background to the one I'd made up. No getting locked in closets, but she really was an orphan, and she really had run away from a group home—though just for the day. She was planning to go back after the performance. I asked her if she liked it there, and she said no, but she had nowhere else to go.

I told her all about the circus—everything but that they were shifters—and she asked if I could talk my mom into letting her join too. So I took her to Mom and asked.

Mom was less thrilled than I was with the idea, but she asked Natalie what she thought she could do that would be valuable to a circus. Natalie did some backflips and cartwheels, which were pretty good considering she'd never had any actual lessons. And of course Mom saw how well we got along. So she said she'd present Natalie to the company for a vote.

I begged Mom to just tell everyone Natalie was in, like she had with me. But Natalie said no. She was only a kid, but she understood social stuff a lot better than I did. She'd had to, from growing up in a group home. She told Mom it would be better if she went ahead and did the vote.

That was when Natalie won Mom over. The two of them put their heads together, and they decided to say that Mom had discovered her, not me. I was a little put out—like I said, I didn't understand people like they did—but I agreed.

Mom called the company together and presented Natalie to them. She told them how she'd spotted her sneaking in like a pro, and had her demonstrate her acrobatics. She said that if Natalie disappeared, everyone would assume she was just another runaway. And she said Natalie and I were already friends and we could keep each other company… maybe for life, wink wink nudge nudge.

That convinced some of the company who hadn't liked how Mom had strong-armed me in. If they were stuck with a non-shifter from a non-shifter family, they'd rather have him grow up to marry another non-shifter than into one of their families.

That wasn't going to happen. Natalie and I were close, but like siblings, not childhood sweethearts. I'm pretty sure Mom knew that from day one. But she was good at saying the right thing to make the company vote like she wanted. They did a private ballot with bits of paper, and she got in.

And then they told her about shifters. Well, Mom showed her. That was fun.

I could talk all night about what it was like growing up in the circus, but I'll save it for later. Short version is Natalie became an acrobat and a target girl, and I was an acrobat and a jack of all trades.

Everything was great until I turned twenty-one. And then everything fell apart.

Mom was in good health but she was old when she adopted me. She wanted to eventually retire from running the circus, and just keep doing her fortune teller and psychic parrot acts. But she needed some-one to take over, and she'd never named an heir.

She named me.

The circus blew up. Half the company either agreed with her decision or didn't but was willing to respect it, and the other half was absolutely dead-set against it. As alpha, she would normally have the absolute right to name her heir. But the circus had never had a non-shifter as its leader.

The other problem went all the way back to when I'd first joined. I was the only person who'd ever joined without the company getting a chance to choose me, and some of them still resented it. Fausto Fratelli got his entire family and some friends to petition for him to be the heir, which is also something that's not done and only pissed Mom off even more.

I went to Mom and told her I was happy being a trapeze artist and assistant clown and so forth, and to pick someone else. Preferably not Fausto. She refused. Said it was her decision and she was sticking with it and I shouldn't let myself be intimidated by a bunch of squirrels.

The entire Fratelli family threatened to quit. The Richelieus—they're the French poodles—said they'd go with them and start their own circus. Zack and Zara Zimmerman, who were twelve at the time, snuck into the Richelieus' train car in cat form and peed on their pillows.

It was a disaster, and it just kept snowballing. Our performances were suffering. The Duffy brothers got careless stealing jewelry and we had to break them out of a birdcage in a high rise.

I realized that I was endangering the entire circus. I got in a huge fight with Mom. I told her if she didn't name someone else as heir or at least take back that it was me, I'd leave. She said she wasn't going to allow me to be peer-pressured out of my rightful position and I'd be glad later that she hadn't let me.

I thought I could force her hand if I left. I thought once I was gone for a while, she'd *have* to name someone else, and then I could come back and just be an acrobat and a squirrel ring holder and so forth. But she stuck to her guns.

I even joined the Marines, so she'd know I'd be gone for at least four years. But she wouldn't relent. Said I could come back and take over the circus once my term of service was over. Every time I see her, we get in a huge fight over that goddamn heir thing. I can't go back until she drops it, and she refuses to drop it.

And now...

I guess I have a circus to inherit. If I decide to take it.

CHAPTER 13

Dali and Merlin had been lying with their arms around each other the entire time he'd been talking, but when he finally stopped, she squeezed him tighter. It was not only to give him comfort, but to satisfy her own impulse to hang on to him. He'd told her part of his story before, but it was only now that she fully understood how much the circus had meant to him. Why *wouldn't* he take it, now that he finally could?

I only just met him, she thought. *How can it hurt this much to know that I'm going to lose him?*

Part of her didn't want to discuss it. But the other part, the part of her that would always be a veteran even if she wasn't in the military now, refused to let herself shy away from a necessary task just because it was difficult and painful.

"You're a shifter now," she said, keeping her voice steady. "Would it still split the company if you went back?"

"I doubt it," Merlin replied. But he didn't sound as overjoyed at the prospect as she'd expected. "Some of them will still be pissed off because they don't like me or they're still seething over how I got in, but those weren't the objections they actually stated. 'He bugs me' isn't a good enough argument."

Dali made herself ask the question. "Do you want to go back?"

"Yes, but…" He ran his fingers through his hair until they hit the bandage. "Ouch." He looked into her eyes and seemed to search for something, then dropped his gaze with a sigh. "I don't know. It's complicated. I was telling the truth when I said I hadn't decided."

Dali hated it when she'd geared herself up to do something hard, and then it turned out to not actually resolve anything. She liked it when she knew where things stood. Now she felt even more unsettled than before.

He gave her a bright smile. "Hey, I feel a lot better now that I've rested a bit. If I make some hot chocolate with marshmallows, would you share it with me?"

"I don't think I've had hot chocolate since I was..." Dali searched her memory. "Eighteen. My grandma would fix it for me when I came home from school in the winter."

"Did you like it then?"

"Yeah, I used to love it."

Merlin sat up, then stood. Dali watched him closely, ready to catch him, but he seemed much more steady on his feet. "Want to find out if you still do?"

"Sure."

She followed him into the kitchen. It was distinctly homey, and reminded her a bit of her grandmother's until she looked more closely.

In addition to canisters of regular coffee, he also had chicory coffee from New Orleans and canisters whose handwritten labels read "elderflower-rose hip infusion," "fireweed tea," and "purple corn drink."

A magical pet trap was hidden behind the tackiest wine holder Dali had ever seen—not that she'd seen a lot of wine holders, to be fair—which was a rooster lying on its back and clutching the bottle in its claws.

A basket of apples and oranges also contained a bizarre fruit like a cross between a lemon and a tentacle monster.

"What in God's name is that... that citrus squid?"

Merlin chuckled. "It's a Buddha's hand. You use it like lemon rind, for zesting or marmalade. Or you can candy it."

He indicated a little bottle labeled "candied grapefruit peel" on a wooden spice rack. The rack contained all the usual spices and herbs, plus some she'd never even heard of. What were chervil, idli podi, and za'atar? Then she spotted one she hadn't seen in years.

"My mom had this," Dali said, indicating a bottle of pandan leaves. "She used them to flavor cakes and puddings and things like that."

"Oh, nice. I love Filipino desserts." He opened the bottle and offered it to her. "Smell."

Dali inhaled the scent of pandan, that unique aroma like vanilla infused with herbs. She could almost see her mother beating cake batter in the kitchen. Dali rarely talked about her childhood, but Merlin had shared so much, she wanted to share something in return.

"Dad was in the Navy," she said. "He met Mom when he was stationed in the Philippines, and took her back to America. He was gone most of the time, so she raised me by herself. In the Philippines, she'd had this big family she was really close to, but in America, she was alone on a Navy base with a bunch of Navy wives she had nothing in common with. When I was eleven, she got divorced and moved back home."

"Eleven," Merlin said. "The start of a new life for both of us."

She gave him a wry smile. "You liked yours better than I liked mine. The way Mom felt about America was the way I felt about the Philippines. Where she lived was really rural. It was too different. I couldn't adjust. I look like my mom, so people were always surprised and disappointed on some level when I acted like a foreigner. But I *was* a foreigner. And I was always going to be. I felt completely alone."

"That sounds so hard."

"I stuck it out for a year, and then I begged to go back to Dad. I absolutely idolized him—wanted to be just like him. Only he was on a ship most of the time. He and Mom worked it out so I could go back to America and live with his mother. I'm still really close to Grandma. She's gotten a bit frail, so she's in retirement housing, but she can still cook and we always have dinner together on Sundays." Dali hesitated, not wanting to remind Merlin of his awful biological parents, then said, "They all loved me a lot, to get that to work out. I never doubted that."

Merlin, intuitive as always, heard what she wasn't saying. "But…?"

"But I ended up not seeing much of Mom and Dad. I love them, but they're more like distant relatives than parents. Literally distant. When I think of my family, really it's Grandma. She was more of a mother to me than my own mother. Like you and Janet, I guess."

"And she made you hot chocolate."

Dali smiled. "Just like Janet. Are you making me the same hot chocolate you got?"

"Nah. My tastes changed a bit when I got older. It's just my raptor that's still hung up on pure sugar."

"Is he really your subconscious? Or is he more like your inner child?"

"A little of both, I guess. Though… I think maybe he's starting to grow up."

He took a slab of chocolate and a metal container from a shelf with a wild variety of unusual snacks. Dali spotted chocolate-dipped potato chips, guava cookies, elk jerky, and multiple flavors of Pocky before he closed the cupboard.

Catching her expression, he said, "Want any of that? My snacks are your snacks."

"No, thanks." Then, unable to resist at least mentioning it, she said, "Chocolate-dipped potato chips, seriously?"

"They're delicious. Salty and sweet. Like salted caramel ice cream." As Merlin tried to convince her to try the potato chips, he proceeded to make the fanciest hot chocolate she'd ever seen. He melted the chocolate over a double boiler, then whisked it into heated whole milk, sprinkled in spices, and finally asked her, "What flavors do you like with chocolate, if any? Peppermint, orange, raspberry, more chocolate, vanilla, hazelnut, chili pepper…?"

Dali was tempted to say "more chocolate," but there was nothing she loved more than mint chocolate chip ice cream. "Peppermint."

Merlin opened the container. She peeked inside and saw a rainbow of marshmallows, large and clearly homemade. He selected a bright pink one and topped her hot chocolate with it. "There you go."

"You didn't make those yourself!" she exclaimed.

"Sure I did. It's not that hard so long as you make sure not to try it when it's raining. The air gets too damp and they don't solidify. I learned that the hard way. It was pretty gross, like rainbow-colored Elmer's glue." Merlin selected a red marshmallow and topped his own drink with it.

"Is that raspberry or chili pepper?"

"I don't know. They both came out the same shade of red. Guess I'll find out." He lifted his mug in a toast. It had a velociraptor painted on the side, and the curled tail formed the handle. Hers had a design of scampering cats, also with a tail forming the handle. "Cheers."

"Cheers."

They clinked their mugs together and drank.

"Ah-ha," said Merlin. "Raspberry."

The hot chocolate was rich and sweet, but not too sweet. It brought up childhood memories, but it wasn't a child's drink. The flavors were too complex for that, with heat from the spices and sharpness from the peppermint. It was sensual and surprising and playful, all at once.

"It's wonderful," Dali said. "It's very… you. Grandma always says that cooking is an expression of who you are."

"She's very wise," Merlin said. "And now I want you to cook for me."

"Right now?" Dali asked, startled.

He laughed. "No, I meant in general, so I can taste who *you* are. Though if you wanted to make something now, I have enough ingredients that you probably could."

Once he mentioned it, she realized that she was hungry. Which wasn't surprising; when she glanced out the window, she saw that the sun was setting. And she did want to show him who she was.

"You're on," she said. "But we're, uh, staying here tonight, right?"

They had to stay together so he could protect her. But after the kissing in bathroom—and at the circus—and the kissing she was tempted to do right now, the question had an obvious double meaning. Dali braced herself for either an awkward discussion or him assuming that *of course* they'd have sex.

"It'd be more comfortable than your apartment," he said. "And safer than a hotel. The sofa folds out."

"Sure. Sounds good."

And just like that, it was decided. No awkwardness, no assumptions, no pressure to decide right now who'd sleep where and whether they'd do more than sleep. For all his complicated life and booby-trapped house, Merlin was surprisingly relaxing to be with.

"Let me make a phone call," Dali said. "I need to get Tirzah to take care of Cloud."

"Can she get in your apartment?"

Dali began to smile, realizing that she knew something he didn't about their mutual friend. "I can always call the apartment manager and ask him to give her the keys. But I don't think it'll be necessary. Did you know she's my landlord?"

"What? I thought she was a tenant."

"She *might* be a tenant," Dali said. "But I don't think so. When I first came to the building to look at apartments, Tirzah just happened to be there when the manager showed it to me. She introduced herself as a tenant. The manager told me the rent, and I said I was sorry, but I couldn't afford it. Tirzah coughed really loudly—"

"Like my seal bark?" Merlin asked.

"Very similar," Dali replied. "I didn't think of it at the time, but it was pretty fake-sounding. As soon as she did, the manager said he'd misspoken and was talking about the rent for a larger unit, and *this* one cost much less. I signed on the spot—the new rent was a fantastic deal, and it's a great building. Really nice neighbors."

"If Tirzah's secretly picking them, they would be. How did you figure it out?"

"The rent checks go to an off-site landlord no one's ever met, and

Tirzah's always around when prospective tenants were looking at apartments. If you tell her about a problem with the building, it gets fixed right away. I eventually asked another tenant, and he said they were all convinced that Tirzah owns the building. 'She's the best landlord we've ever had,' he said. 'So if she likes to think we don't know, well, we just let her think that.'"

Merlin cracked up. "That is so Tirzah. I'm sure you're right. Well, I'll join the conspiracy to not tell her everybody knows. Let her enjoy her 'secret.' But let's find out for sure. Don't mention calling the manager to ask him to give her your key, and see if she gets in anyway."

"I feel like a rat playing roulette."

"Fun, isn't it? I'll call my mom while you're doing that. She'll want to know I'm fine." He heaved a sigh. "And she'll want to know all about how I became a shifter and why I waited this long to tell her."

Dali leaned over and kissed him. "Good luck."

"Thanks, I'll need it." He kissed her back and vanished into his bedroom, then poked his head out. "Oh—please don't tell Tirzah the details of, well, anything yet. I need to report it to Roland, and if you tell her she'll tell Pete and Pete will tell Roland and—"

"My lips are sealed." Dali called Tirzah on her cell phone. "Hey, Tirzah. Would you mind taking care of Cloud for a bit? Merlin and I are staying at his place—"

"Oooooh," Tirzah said. "That moved fast!"

Dali had been so focused on not letting Tirzah find out about the trapeze attack or Merlin's circus issues or that Dali knew she was her landlord that she'd entirely forgotten to not let her find out that she and Merlin were… whatever they were doing. She was so blindsided that she couldn't think of a single thing to say.

"Not that I'm judging," Tirzah said quickly, apparently mistaking Dali's silence for offense. "I'm happy for you! For both of you. Seriously, I think it's awesome. Merlin is so much fun, and he's really a sweetheart. Pete's mom and daughter both love him. Any man who's adored by thirteen-year-olds and grandmas has to be a great guy."

133

"I didn't think you were judging me," Dali assured her. "Look, you're not wrong that we've got something going on. But I don't know where it's going yet. And okay, yes, I'm spending the night, but it might be on the sofa bed."

"I don't thiiiiiink so," Tirzah sang out.

"No, really," Dali protested.

"I was kidding you, Dali. Sort of. No matter what, you won't be on the sofa bed because Merlin would never ever let you take it. You're sleeping in his bed tonight whether he's in it or not." Tirzah snickered. "Though I will say that if lithe, blond, and chatty was my type, I definitely wouldn't kick Merlin out of bed!"

"Yeah, he's incredibly hot, and I'm sure he's great in bed…"

"He used to be an acrobat," Tirzah put in. "Just imagine what he could do!"

"Oh, believe me, I've imagined," said Dali. "But it's so complicated. There's all this stuff going on that I can't tell you about because he wants to keep it private for now, but it makes me wonder if we could have a future together. And I get the feeling that there's even more that I don't know about because I haven't asked the right question yet."

"Pete wasn't very forthcoming either when we first got involved," Tirzah said. "Every time I thought I knew all his secrets, something new would come out. He didn't even tell me he was a dad!"

"Do you feel like you know everything now?"

"Oh, definitely. And to be fair, I didn't tell him everything about me right away either. It took patience and trust, and those don't come overnight."

It was such a relief to be able to talk to Tirzah, even if Dali couldn't tell her all the details yet. When Dali had moved into her building, Tirzah herself had been adjusting to being newly disabled. They'd had plenty of satisfying mutual gripe sessions about inaccessible buildings, condescending doctors, and movies where the disabled characters always died at the end. And now they had yet another thing in common: a shifter man in their lives. Not to mention a flying kitten.

Dali was about to ask about Cloud when Tirzah said, "Has he said anything about mates yet?"

"Mates?" Dali echoed. "You mean his teammates?"

There was a brief pause. "Yeah. His teammates. I know he and Pete have clashed a bit—a lot—but Pete really does care about him. Is the stuff Merlin doesn't want you to talk about because he thinks his teammates would give him a hard time?"

"Some of it, yeah. I think you're right, he's making it into more of a big deal than it really is. Anyway, I was calling to ask if you can take care of Cloud for me. She's in my apartment, and I have everything she needs there."

"Of course," Tirzah replied. "I can't wait to introduce her to our kittens, but I'll hold off till you're there. I'll just go down myself with my laptop so I can keep her company for a bit."

Dali suppressed a chuckle. Tirzah had a master key, all right. "Thanks. I appreciate it. Hey, say hi to Pete and Caro for me."

They chatted a bit more about lighter, more ordinary subjects: Caro's science fair project, an upcoming family vacation with Pete's mom, and Dali's plans to try rock climbing again with adaptive gear.

They'd just said their good-byes when Merlin came out of the bedroom, looking tired. "Looks like your conversation went better than mine did. Mom went ballistic on me over not telling her I was a shifter for six months—"

"You've been a shifter for *six months* and you never told her?" Dali exclaimed.

"Yeah," Merlin said glumly. "I can't decide if that was a bad idea or the bad idea was telling the truth now."

"I don't think telling the truth is ever a bad idea," Dali said.

Merlin looked at her for a long moment, then said, "Did you get a chance to check out my fridge? It's pretty well stocked up. I found this great butcher who learned his craft in Tuscany almost thirty years ago. He told me this funny story about how when he was still an apprentice, a guy in town decided he wanted to have a turkey stuffed with a chicken stuffed with a quail stuffed with an egg stuffed with an olive stuffed with a…"

Patience and trust, Dali thought, and let him tell his story, which *was* funny. He showed her his fridge, freezer, and cupboards, all of them stocked with a wild array of ingredients from every culture Dali had ever heard of, and several she hadn't.

But in the end, she went with the tried and true: simple things she could do well. She found two steaks, rubbed them with salt and pepper and olive oil, and seared them in a pan. For a side, she made greens sautéed with a bit of bacon for flavor. And since she had the pandan leaves right there, she searched both her memory and Google for the recipe, and produced a reasonable approximation of her mother's pandan chiffon cake.

Dali had never done much cooking, so it was a little nerve-wracking fixing dinner for a man who made his own marshmallows. She'd also never enjoyed it enough to cook just for herself, though she'd liked helping her mother or grandmother, so she'd spent the last year subsisting on ramen and takeout when she didn't have anything Grandma had made. But having Merlin help her made it fun. He did all the tasks that were difficult with a prosthetic or that just needed two people, and he kept her company.

There was something distinctly sexy about Merlin in the kitchen. The heat gave his skin a glowing quality, and the moisture made his hair curl. She kept getting distracted by watching his hands as he beat cake batter or chopped with slightly scary speed. He was so competent and confident, so dexterous and quick, and his hands reflected that. She could easily imagine him hanging from a trapeze and catching his partner's hands as she flew through the air.

Dali wished she'd tried learning trapeze before the bombing. There was no way her prosthetic, which attached by suction, could stand up to the force exerted by a trapeze hand catch. But even if she had learned before that, she hadn't known Merlin then. Having him catch her in mid-air could never be more than a fantasy.

There were other things she could do with him that didn't have to stay fantasies, though.

He had fallen silent. She could feel the sexual tension between them sizzling in the air like the steaks sizzling in the pan. Every time they brushed up against each other, which was often as it was a small kitchen, it felt like an electric shock.

When they sat down to eat, the meal that Dali had worried was too simple turned out to be exactly right. Everything had come out beautifully—the steak juicy and flavorful, the greens cutting the richness, and the pandan cake light and fluffy—but it was all familiar and uncomplicated, a meal that could be enjoyed solely as a sensual pleasure without having to adjust to something new.

"What did you think?" she asked when they were done.

"Other than 'absolutely delicious?'" Merlin asked. "It made me think of craftspeople who spend a lifetime learning to do one thing perfectly, like sushi masters in Japan or woodworkers in Germany. I know you said you don't know how to make very many things, but you don't need to. You made that dinner with focus, attention to detail, and respect for the ingredients, and it came out perfectly. It was straightforward and honest and close to your roots, and... is it weird to call food sexy if you're not eating it off someone's naked body?"

The thought of Merlin eating something off her naked body dazed her enough that she only barely managed to get out a "No."

"And sexy," he concluded. "Very you."

"So, you tasted who I am?"

He caught her double meaning. All teasing gone, he replied in a low voice that sent shivers of desire up and down her spine. "Yes. I did."

He put his hands on her shoulders, his fingertips stroking her throat. No one had ever done that to her before, and it made her catch her breath. "Shall I do it for real now?"

Desire threatened to sweep her away, to make her agree to all sorts of unwise things just because she wanted them so much. For the first time in her life, she truly understood the meaning of temptation. The part of her that was sensible required her to say no. Every other part of her—her heart, her soul, and especially certain parts of her body—was already saying yes.

As soon as his job with me is over, he's going to run away to the circus, the sensible part of her thought. *And I'll never see him again.*

I should tell him that kissing him was a mistake, she thought. *I should tell him I want to keep things strictly business between us from now on. It'll be less painful in the long run.*

Then she remembered Grandma telling her to enjoy the roses. A rose only lived for a few days; did that mean you should walk away from its perfume, just because it wouldn't last?

Dali recalled her old fear that at any instant, she could wake up in a hospital with everything changed. But this time, rather than sending her spiraling into panic, it made her think, *If I knew that when I went to sleep tonight, I'd never wake up again, what would I do now?*

"Yes," she said. "Yes, Merlin, I want you."

He went down on his knees before her, then looked up. The intensity in his eyes spoke of the ferocity of his desire, but there was a depth there too. An unspoken commitment, like her own: *if this was my last day on Earth, this is how I'd want to spend it.*

"I've never wanted anyone more," he said. His voice had dropped lower. She thought she could feel its vibration in the air, making her tremble like a plucked guitar string. "Only you."

She put her hands on his shoulders, feeling his acrobat's muscles flex as he bent to take off her shoes. She started to stand, so she could get out of her pants, but he glanced up at her and shook his head. Merlin, still kneeling, placed his palms on her hips, took a deep breath, and lifted her. Dali gasped; in that position, it was an extraordinary feat of strength, and that alone was one hell of a turn on.

Then she realized something, and giggled.

"What?" said Merlin.

"I still can't get my pants off."

He glanced from his hands to her waist. "Oh."

She was still laughing as he lowered her back down, but it was as much with giddiness as anything else. She felt as effervescent as champagne. When he put her down, she stood up, caught his hand, and pulled him to his feet. "That chair's not comfortable enough anyway. Let's go to bed."

They made their way back to the bedroom, where Dali quickly stripped off her pants and underwear, then sat down on the edge of the bed. "As you were."

Merlin knelt again. *Like a knight at the feet of his queen*, she thought.

If he was a knight, he was one without armor. He'd stripped himself bare to her, as she had to him. And as he kissed his way up her inner thighs, they parted without her conscious intent, opening her body to him as she'd already opened her heart. Every touch of his hands and his hot mouth sparked an inner fire in her, a hunger and a need that only he could satisfy. And satisfy it he did, sending her to the brink and beyond.

She fell back on the bed, gasping and flushed, satisfied and yet ready for more. He followed her, his eyes like the blue heart of a flame, his sweat-damp hair curling like strands of gold. She stripped off his clothes, wincing once more at the bruises.

"I'll be gentle," she said.

Merlin laughed. "Don't bother."

She could see for herself that what he was feeling was nothing even remotely like pain. He took off her blouse, then her bra, and kissed her breasts until she was on fire with need, to touch and be touched, everywhere. Their bodies slid against each other, his hard, hers softer, both hot as flame. Her hair came down and hung around her face, and he ran his fingers through it.

They took their time exploring each other's bodies: every soft curve, every hard angle, every freckle, every scar. His touch set her aflame with desire, and she burned even hotter to hear him gasp at hers. His hands were every bit as strong as she'd experienced, and deft as she'd imagined. But more than that, he paid attention to her reactions just as she did to his. She could feel that he loved seeing her pleasure as much he loved feeling it himself. And she felt the same way.

She wanted to go on forever like that, but she wanted more as well. The first time she tried to say so, he slipped a finger inside her, and then she lost track of what she'd meant to say for a long stretch of helpless, trembling bliss.

"Good hands," she murmured, overcome.

He kissed her, and his hardness pressed against her in a way that drove her wild all over again. She lifted herself to him, and he thrust into her with a strength and control that made her gasp. They moved together like one body, seeking not only pleasure but a communion of hearts. And then harder, wilder, fiercer, until they came together in a burst of ecstasy like love made into white-hot light.

"I always thought 'I felt fireworks' was just a saying," Dali murmured at the end.

Merlin kissed her, his mouth hot and sweet and loving. "I felt them too."

CHAPTER 14

A crash from the living room sent Merlin rocketing out of bed, adrenaline surging through his veins. Dali was also scrambling to her feet. She glanced in dismay at her prosthetic hand, which she'd taken off before they'd gone to sleep and placed on a table, then grabbed an elephant-shaped bronze bookend with her right hand.

Merlin put his finger to his lips and gestured to her to stay where she was. He took a split second to decide whether he wanted to confront the intruder with a dinosaur or with a gun.

Me me me, said his raptor, pushing to take control. *I'm much more intimidating!*

But it was another consideration that made the decision. Merlin had a lot of faith in Carter's alarm system. The fact that it hadn't gone off suggested that whoever had gotten in was also a technical genius... or had used magic. If they were a tech genius, they probably had a better gun, but he bet they didn't have a velociraptor. If they'd used magic—say, if they were a wizard-scientist—they could probably make his gun melt or turn to stone or something, but a raptor would be harder to deal with.

Just slightly bigger than man-size, Merlin told his raptor. *So we can fit through the door.*

As usual, his raptor had different ideas. Just as Merlin triggered the shift, it gleefully exclaimed, *Tiny! We'll sneak up on our enemy and chomp his ankle before he even sees us!*

Merlin was abruptly much closer to the floor. In fact, his head was now level with Dali's ankle.

Merlin and his raptor fought an inner battle, with Merlin shoving his size upward and the raptor stubbornly pushing it down. He shot up to horse height, then down to French poodle, then down to mouse, and finally achieved his original goal of slightly bigger than man-height.

He glanced back at Dali. She was pressing her hand to her mouth to suppress any audible laughter, but he could see it dancing in her eyes.

There was another crash from the living room, this time closer to the bedroom, followed by a strange buzzing sound. That sobered them both up in a hurry.

Merlin threw open the door and darted into the living room, betting on his speed and the intruder's shock at being attacked by a dinosaur to win the fight.

The intruder wasn't human.

Merlin skidded to a stop. An animal the size of a Saint Bernard was bumbling around his living room, bumping into furniture. It had very fluffy fur—bright blue fluffy fur—and a pair of dragonfly wings which were far too small for it to fly with, though they were beating rapidly enough to produce a buzzing sound.

A bugbear, Merlin thought. He'd never seen one, but he'd heard about them. What in the world was it doing in his living room?

The bugbear had its head stuck in one of the flying kitten traps. As he watched, incredulous, it walked straight into a small table and bowled it over. It sat down in a plaintive attitude and pawed at the trap. Its oversized paw failed to get the trap off, but succeeded in knocking a pillow off the sofa.

I need to be human to get the trap off, Merlin told his raptor. *That creature is—*

A friend! His raptor was bouncing up and down. *Yes, yes, set it free and then we'll play!*

Merlin returned to his human form with no trouble at all.

"It's safe, Dali," he called. "It's just a bugbear!"

He approached the bugbear slowly and cautiously, talking soothingly. "It's all right. I'm not going to hurt you. I'll just get that trap off your head, and then you can be on your way."

The bugbear swung its head toward him, knocking over a chair. But it didn't make any angry or fearful moves. Merlin unsnapped the catch, then lifted the kitten trap off the bugbear's head. Like its body, its head was something like a bear's and something like a dog's. It had huge, mournful-looking brown eyes, like a basset hound's.

The bugbear gazed up at Merlin with what he could swear was gratitude, then reared up on its hind legs. As Merlin started to jump back, the bugbear's immense paws landed on his shoulders. They both went over backward, knocking over another table. The next thing Merlin knew, he was lying on his back on the carpet with the bugbear licking his face.

The sound of Dali's laughter rose up. He looked up at her wryly. "Are you going to stand there and laugh at me, or are you—yecch!" The bugbear chose that moment to lick Merlin on the lips. Shielding his mouth with his hand, he said, "Or are you going to help me up?"

Still laughing, Dali extended a hand. Merlin took it and hauled himself into a sitting position. The bugbear gazed up at him mournfully, climbed into his lap, then attempted to climb further up.

That was when the penny dropped.

"Did you come here for *me?*" Merlin asked.

The bugbear made another determined attempt to climb on to Merlin's shoulder. When that failed, it snuffled at his hair, shoved its cold nose into his neck, stuck its tongue in his ear, and finally gave a huge sigh and rested its head on Merlin's shoulder.

Merlin was enchanted. He stroked the bugbear's fluffy blue fur and scratched behind its bear-like ears. The bugbear flopped over on its back on the floor, with all four legs splayed out like a dead bug. Merlin rubbed its—his—furry belly. The bugbear's stumpy tail wagged vigorously as he gave little snuffling grunts, like a bear eating a jar of honey.

"He's yours, all right," Dali said. "No regrets over not having something tiny and adorable to sit on your shoulder?"

"Why would I? He's plenty adorable, and he *tries* to sit on my shoulder. Not his fault he's too big!"

The bugbear looked up at Merlin with his perpetually sad eyes and licked his hand.

"What a good bugbear," Merlin said, giving his ears a tug. "Best bugbear! Let me give you a name… A name to strike fear into the hearts of your enemies!"

The bugbear rolled over, got up, and began shambling around the room. His tiny dragonfly wings fluttered delicately as he nosed at everything. A stack of books on a chair fell down with a crash.

"Yes," Dali said dryly. "You give him a name fit for that very dignified and terrifying creature."

Merlin laughed. His heart was so filled with joy, he felt like it might burst. Every book he'd ever read as a kid about a boy and his dog or a boy and his bear or even a boy and his horse came rushing back to him. *Gentle Ben, Big Red, The Black Stallion.*

Now he was a man and his bugbear. It wasn't exactly what he'd imagined.

It was even better.

"Blue?"

The bugbear's wings buzzed rapidly as he lifted his head. He trotted to Merlin and sat down at his feet, looking up expectantly with his big mournful eyes.

Merlin stroked his furry head. "Your name is Blue."

Blue seemed satisfied with this. He turned away from Merlin and shoved his nose between Dali's knees.

She gave him a pat on the head. He licked her hand. To Blue, she said, "Hello, cutie." To Merlin, she said, "Congratulations, you caught a magical pet. I thought you said they were all little, though."

Merlin couldn't stop grinning as he gazed down at Blue. "The ones I saw were. But I didn't see all of them. You couldn't see into the cages, so we were just unlocking them as fast as we could. Then we got ambushed and they all disappeared, including the ones that were still in their cages at the time."

To Blue, he said, "Like you!" To Dali, he said, "Actually, Ransom did say I should build bigger traps. But I thought he was just messing with me. I should apologize." To Blue, he said, "When I bring you in to the office so you can meet the team!" To Dali, he said, "We have to go in this morning anyway so I can report to Roland."

Dali gave Blue a doubtful glance. "Merlin, he's huge. How are you going to get him to the office without everyone seeing him? Would he even fit into your car?"

"He'll fit," Merlin assured her. "He's not as big as he looks, he's just furry. If he was wetted down, he'd only be about the size of a German shepherd."

His raptor broke in impatiently. *I want to play with him! Now, now, now!*

"But first, I should make sure Blue's used to my raptor."

Dali punched his shoulder. "You mean you want to roll around on the floor with him as a velociraptor. Admit it."

"I admit it," Merlin said, grinning.

Before he could shift, a buzzing filled the room. It was similar to the buzz of Blue's wings, but came from above. Cloud swooped down and landed on Dali's shoulder. Blue looked up at her hopefully, wagging his stub of a tail and buzzing his wings, which were only slightly larger than hers. The gray kitten folded her wings, arched her back, and hissed at the bugbear.

"Stop that, Cloud," said Dali. "Hey, how did she get in here? Did you leave a window open, Merlin?"

Merlin shook his head. "I think magical creatures can get in anywhere they want. Last year we kept getting one in our office, no matter what sort of security system Carter set up. When we found them in the

145

lab, their cages weren't just locked, they were locked with shiftsilver. It's a kind of metal that stops magical shifters from changing form or doing magic. And I guess it stops magical animals from escaping. Or getting in, probably. Though I don't know why anyone would want to keep them out."

"Maybe they're not all as harmless as yours."

Merlin shrugged. "Mom always said that if you leave them alone, they'll leave you alone. Normally they're very shy, so you rarely encounter them. I never saw one in my life till we rescued the ones at the lab."

Cloud launched off Dali's shoulder, swooped low, and swatted Blue across the nose.

"Hey!" Dali exclaimed. "That's not nice!"

Cloud flew away with Blue galumphing after her. From his expression, he'd taken that as an invitation to play.

Now! Merlin's raptor demanded.

Merlin didn't try to control his size, but simply shifted. He was unsurprised to find himself the exact size of a bugbear.

Everyone thinks my size control is terrible, Merlin thought. *But my raptor has perfect control of his size. It's my control of him that's terrible.*

But that gloomy thought quickly vanished as Blue leaped at him. Merlin and Blue went rolling over and over on the floor together as Cloud darted in and out, swatting them, and Dali cracked up watching them.

Too bad she can't shift, his raptor remarked.

Merlin felt his face crack into a fanged grin. *So what?*

He pounced on Dali, careful not to use his claws. She wrestled back, then was buried under fur as Blue leaped on top of them both. They rolled around on the carpet, grappling and laughing, while Cloud kept up her guerilla-style aerial attacks.

They broke apart when Dali's phone rang. She extricated herself from the pile on the floor to answer it. "Hello?"

Tirzah's panicky voice came over loud and clear, even though she wasn't on speakerphone. "I can't find Cloud! I went in this morning and—"

"It's fine, Tirzah. Cloud's with me. She showed up this morning..." Dali pointed to Blue and made a questioning expression. Merlin shook his head. He wanted to surprise everyone with his wonderful pet. "Anyway, I'll see you soon. We're about to come to the office."

Merlin shifted back to human form, after a brief bobble in which he became a velociraptor the size of a turkey.

Dali hung up. She glanced at Blue, who had flopped down on the sofa. It wasn't quite wide enough for him, and he was sliding off it in slow motion. "Are you sure you want to bring him to the office? Even if he fits in the car, you still need to get him out of the house. Wouldn't it be safer to leave him here?"

Merlin was dying to show off Blue to his team. But when he tried to think of a better reason, one immediately came to mind. "We're going to the circus after the office, and we can't have Blue and Cloud trailing after us there. They'll be a huge distraction. And now that we know they can follow us, we probably shouldn't leave them alone because they might get bored or lonely. But at the office, they'll have people to keep them company."

"Good idea. I don't want Cloud flying around looking for me." Dali whistled, and Cloud flew down and landed on her shoulder. "Do Pete and Tirzah's flying kittens stay put because they're keeping each other company?"

"Probably, but they also bring them to the office a lot. They keep them out of the tech room because Carter has a lot of fragile, expensive stuff in there. But they've been trained to become invisible to everyone who doesn't already know about them—"

"What?"

Merlin nodded. "The west coast office of Protection, Inc. figured it out. Apparently all magical animals can do it. But it takes a month or so to teach them, like any other kind of training."

Dali scritched Cloud behind the ears. "Just wait till I train you and take you out in public. Any necklace-stealing pigeons will get the surprise of a lifetime!"

Merlin chuckled. "Shower together first?"

"Absolutely."

They shut the bathroom door firmly against any rampaging winged pets, and Merlin removed the bandage on his head.

Dali let out a startled breath. "You told me, but it's another thing to actually see it."

He glanced in the mirror. The cuts on his face and head were no more than pink lines, as if they had been made a week ago rather than the day before. His bruises were visible but had faded from black to a faint purple.

"If I'd been a shifter during the bombing…" Dali began, then swallowed. "Do I want to know?"

"Yes, I think so." When she gestured for him to go on, he said, "You'd have recovered faster. But that's all. Serious injuries still leave scars. And even shifters can't re-grow lost limbs. No, I'm wrong. There's one way they can. A lizard shifter who loses their tail can re-grow that. In their lizard form, I mean."

Dali's wistful expression vanished as she burst out laughing. "I would hope in their lizard form!"

"Oh, I don't know. Imagine what kind of trapeze acts you could do with a prehensile tail."

She gave his butt a playful smack. "I'm glad you don't have a tail."

They got in the shower together. Merlin could hardly believe his luck as he helped Dali shampoo her hair and soap her back. This strong, honest, courageous, absolutely gorgeous, incredibly sexy woman was dallying with *him.*

The streaming water turned her hair to liquid silk. It reminded him of the night before, when it had come undone and flowed over her back. Stroking it, he asked, "Do you ever wear it down?"

"Sometimes. Maybe I will today. You can roll the roof down and I'll let the wind blow it around and we can both pretend we're in a Bruce Springsteen song."

He could have replied, but he was too busy kissing her. He could never get enough of her—the soft heat of her lips, the bounty of her breasts, the elegance of her neck, the curve of her belly, the smoothness of her unmarked skin, the strength and courage marked out in her scars. It was all *her*, just as the food she'd cooked for him had been *her*.

He lifted her up, because she'd enjoyed that the night before. She let out a delighted gasp, then said, "You're not going to slip and break both our necks, are you?"

"Never," Merlin promised. "I'm an acrobat, remember? I can walk a tightrope. And I can stand on a shower floor."

He'd have put her down if she still seemed nervous, but all tension left her body at his words. Her trust in him lit a fire in his body and heart. She bent forward to kiss him, and her hair made a silken curtain around them. He shifted his weight, still holding her up, and slid inside her. The fire within him blazed up, higher and hotter, so intense that it would have been unbearable if it hadn't been so perfect and ecstatic and right. Afterward, they clung to each other, and let the water wash them clean and new.

While Dali put on her hand, Merlin selected his T-shirt for the day. In honor of Blue, he chose a blue one with an image of a T-rex reading a book and the caption THESAURUS REX.

"Do you own any clothing without dinosaur jokes?" Dali inquired.

Merlin grinned. "Everything that's more than six months old."

"Mind if I borrow some? The clothes I wore yesterday are all covered in sweat and blood and sawdust."

"My clothes are your clothes," Merlin said immediately, opening his closet and drawers. "I don't know what you can do for pants, though."

Dali pulled out a pair of his blue jeans and held them up. "They'll work. You're taller, but I'm broader in the hips and that'll take up the slack."

She wriggled into his jeans, belted them, and rolled up the bottoms. Then, after poking through his non-dinosaur shirts, she selected a plain black one that hung down to her hips like a tunic. "Well? Do I look all right, or is it Walk of Shame time?"

Seeing Dali wearing his clothes was incredibly sexy and almost painfully intimate; he'd been lonely for so long that her presence made him feel raw and vulnerable, like he'd immersed frostbitten hands in warm water. But when he thought of saying so, he was seized by the conviction that he'd be tempting fate, and she'd somehow be taken from him.

He put on a bright smile and said, "More like Walk of Sexiness. Help yourself to my wardrobe any time."

In the living room, Cloud was perched on the back of the sofa and hissing at Blue, who had slid almost entirely off the sofa except for his left rear leg. He looked vaguely perplexed by this situation.

"How are you getting him into the car?" Dali asked. "He's awfully conspicuous."

I could get big and block everyone's view of him, his raptor suggested.

"I know!" Merlin raced back to the bedroom, where he dug around in his closet until he found the hairy yellow coat, which he triumphantly brought into the living room.

"What IS that monstrosity?" Dali asked. "It looks like someone skinned a Pokémon."

"I'm not sure exactly. I found it in the closet when I moved in."

"And you didn't throw it out?"

"I thought it might come in handy some day. And I was right!" He whistled to Blue, who scrambled up and shook himself. Merlin tenderly draped the coat over the bugbear, placing the hood over his head, and buttoned the middle row of buttons under his belly. Blue shook himself, sending up a cloud of fake fur, but failed to dislodge the coat.

"There we go," Merlin said triumphantly.

Dali's eyebrows did not convey the confidence Merlin felt. "You know, Merlin, my mom told me that when I was a toddler, she shooed me out of the kitchen because she was boiling water. Five minutes later, a blanket with a toddler shaped lump started slooooooowly crawling into the kitchen. I guess I figured if I was beneath the blanket, she couldn't see me."

Merlin laughed. "It'll be fine. It's only a couple yards to the car. Anyway, it's early. Probably no one will even be up yet."

Shaking her head, Dali popped Cloud into her purse. Merlin called to Blue, and they went out.

Halfway down the walk, one of his neighbors came out, watering can in hand. She stared at Blue. "Is that a dog? In a fur coat?"

"Yes," Merlin said. "He's a Hairless Boxerdoodle. Very susceptible to colds."

He had always thought his little MGB-GT was the perfect size, but when he'd bought it, he hadn't anticipated having a bugbear the size of a Saint Bernard. Let alone a bugbear the size of a Saint Bernard wearing a thick fake fur coat.

Blue put up with Merlin's attempts to cram him into the back seat with gloomy dignity, but he kept pouring bonelessly out of it. Merlin wrestled with him and also with the coat, which didn't want to stay on. At one point the coat somehow transferred itself from Blue to Merlin, and then Merlin had to frantically try to put it back on Blue, now in a very cramped space, before anyone saw. When he was finally done, a visible cloud of yellow fake fur hung in the air.

When Merlin got into the driver's seat, he found Dali laughing silently with actual tears running down her face. She wiped her eyes and said, "Wow. I don't think I've laughed that hard in years."

If he had made it his life's goal to get her to laugh until she cried, he couldn't have done any better. And that certainly seemed like an excellent life goal. Her cheeks were flushed and her eyes were bright, and her damp black hair, which she'd left down, was tumbled around her shoulders and back.

"You're beautiful when you're laughing," Merlin said, and kissed her, tasting the salt of her tears. "And also when you're not, of course."

She kissed him back, and said, "And you're hilarious when you're trying to cram a bugbear in a fake fur coat into the back seat of a tiny British sports car."

"Only hilarious? Not sexy?"

She gave him a wicked smile that instantly reminded him of last night after dinner. And also this morning in the shower. "Men who make me laugh are the sexiest of all."

"Speaking of that," Merlin said. "I assume you don't want me to tell the guys... or do you?"

"Tirzah may have already figured it out," Dali admitted. "But to avoid any awkward conversations, let's not mention it right now. Not that it's a huge secret. It's just... early."

For once, they were on the same page about secrets. Much as he would have loved to share his happiness with everyone he met, it *was* early. And his team was guaranteed to make anything awkward. "Absolutely. My lips are sealed until you tell me otherwise."

When he pulled into the Defenders parking lot, he saw that everyone's cars were there, even Carter's. Merlin was delighted. Now he could show off Blue to everyone!

I'm hungry, said his raptor. *Forget the office. Let's go to a candy shop.*

It was only then that Merlin realized that in the excitement of Blue's arrival and getting him disguised to go out, Merlin had forgotten breakfast. He'd even forgotten coffee.

"Are you starving?" he asked Dali. "Or jonesing for caffeine?"

She shrugged. "I'm all right. We can grab something on the way to the circus."

"I can find something to tide us over at the office," Merlin said. "We have food stashed all over."

"Don't you have a kitchen?"

"Yeah, but I was keeping stuff for the magical pet traps, and Roland brings food and then gives it Ransom and then Ransom doesn't actually eat it, and Tirzah likes to stash cookies all over so she doesn't have to go fetch them, and Pete stores MREs in weird places in case of emergency, and Carter hides fancy food because he thinks we'll steal it."

Dali gave the *I can't believe this* slow head-shake that seemed to be her general response to his team. "You guys need help."

"I try," Merlin protested. "But they mostly don't seem to want it.

Anyway, I'll scrounge up something for us."

He ran around to open the door for her, then helped Blue out of the back seat. The bugbear came loose like a cork from a bottle, nearly sending Merlin over backward and leaving the fur coat behind on the seat. Blue shook himself, sending yellow and blue hairs flying, then ambled after them.

"Pete will be especially happy to see Blue," Merlin said. "I can take down all the traps he keeps tripping over."

Dali opened her purse, and Cloud flew out and perched on her shoulder. The only person in the lobby was Carter, who was bent over a computer. He glanced up, greeted Dali, and gave a pre-emptive glare to Merlin.

"Tirzah and I are installing a security patch on the office computers," Carter said. "So don't turn them off or unplug them. They need—what the hell is that?!"

Blue, a little way behind them, had poked his head into the room. He gazed sadly at Carter, as if he'd had his feelings hurt. Merlin stroked his head, then his neck and back as more of him emerged. Once he was all the way inside, he began wandering around the lobby, sniffing things.

"This is Blue," Merlin said. "He's a bugbear and he's my new pet."

"Good Lord," exclaimed Carter. "Did you catch him in one of your traps?"

"Sort of," Merlin said. "Isn't he adorable? Hey, where is everyone?"

"Pete's in the tech room keeping Tirzah company," Carter said, not sharing his thoughts on Blue's adorability. "Roland's in his office, on the phone with a prospective client. I assume Ransom's in his office too, but I haven't seen him."

Blue found some interesting scent beneath the coffee table and tried to crawl under it to get a better sniff. The table, which was not remotely low enough for him to fit, began to tip over. A bunch of magazines slid off, and Carter had to grab his computer to rescue it from the same fate.

Cater glared at Blue. "Shoo!"

Blue backed out hurriedly. His big blunt claws caught the power cord and yanked it out of the wall. The computer screen went black.

Carter's howl of outrage could probably be heard in outer space. "MERLIN! Your beast just ruined hours of work!"

Blue clearly sensed that he'd done something wrong. With a distinctly guilty expression in his sad basset hound eyes, he rubbed up against Carter's legs, snuffling and nuzzling him in apology. The expensive black fabric of Carter's pant legs instantly acquired a layer of real blue hairs and yellow fake hairs, and Blue's rapidly flapping dragonfly wings sent more upward to decorate his shirt and jacket.

"MERLIN!" Carter yelled again. "Get this creature away from me!"

Merlin glanced at Dali. She was leaning against the wall, and tears of laughter were again streaming down her face. Much as he appreciated the sight, there would clearly be no help forthcoming from that department.

"Stop yelling," Merlin said. "You're making him think he needs to show you how sorry he is."

Carter subsided into seething silence as Merlin pried Blue off his legs. Just as he did so, Tirzah came in with her black flying kitten, Batcat, perched on her left shoulder, and Spike, Pete's flying cactus kitten, on her right. "What happened to—"

Cloud arched her back and hissed. Batcat did the same, and spat for good measure. Spike let out a warning yowl. Dali and Tirzah snatched at their kittens, but they had already launched themselves and were zipping around the office, yowling and hissing and clawing at each other. Tirzah was too low, in her wheelchair, to catch a kitten in mid-air, so Dali went for Cloud and Merlin went for Batcat and Spike.

"Unbelievable," Carter remarked to the room at large, making no effort to help. "Every time I think this place couldn't possibly be more of a madhouse, someone proves me wrong."

After several minutes of hot pursuit and a few broken coffee mugs, Dali held a flapping, spitting kitten by the scruff of the neck, and

Merlin had one in each hand.

"I love your kittens," Dali said to Tirzah. "What are their names?"

Tirzah beamed. "The black one is Batcat—she's mine—and the green one is Spike—he's Pete's. Spike's a cactus kitten, and he can—"

Spike lunged for Cloud, driving a cactus spine into Merlin's wrist.

"Ow!" Merlin yelped.

Ransom flung open the door to his office. His auburn hair was disheveled, and he was shading his eyes with his hands as if the light hurt them. "Will you all be quiet?! I have a migraine."

"Sorry," Merlin said.

While some knowledge came to Ransom without pain or effort, he tended to get migraines—or worse—if he tried to learn a specific thing. Which made Merlin wonder what information Ransom had thought would be worth the price.

"What were you trying to figure out?" Merlin asked.

Ransom hesitated, then said, "Whether it's possible for a shifter to give up their animal, and if so, how."

"Oh, I know that," Merlin said. "There is a method. It's dangerous and difficult and painful, but it does get used sometimes on the absolute worst shifter criminals. Of course no one would ever do it voluntarily—who'd want to lose their animal? Anyway, you start by—"

"*Now* I know how it's done," Ransom said ominously. "My question is, how do *you* know about it?"

"I heard about it at the circus."

The look in Ransom's dark eyes could strip paint. "So I gave myself a migraine finding out something I could have just asked you about?"

"Er... yes," Merlin admitted. He couldn't see how this was his fault, but Ransom was sure looking at him like it was. "Anyway, why did you want to know?"

Ransom stalked back into his office without a word. He didn't slam the door, but shut it in a manner which conveyed that under better circumstances, he would have.

"Merlin, what happened to your face?" Tirzah asked.

"A trapeze fell on me."

Tirzah's face scrunched up as she tried to parse this. "You mean you fell off a trapeze?"

"No, I mean the whole trapeze apparatus fell from the ceiling. On me."

"Of course it did." Carter stood up and tripped over Blue, who had again glued himself to Carter's legs in an attempt to show how very very very sorry he was. "Will you get that creature *off* me?!"

Tirzah, who had evidently been too distracted by kittens to notice Blue before, nearly fell out of her wheelchair. "What *is* that?"

"It's Blue," Merlin.

"I can see that," said Tirzah. "But what is it?"

"Blue is his name," Merlin explained. "He's a bugbear, and he's my magical pet! Isn't he a sweetheart?"

Blue sneezed on Carter's thousand-dollar shoes.

"MERLIN!" Carter yelled.

Merlin saw Blue decide he must have done something wrong again. In a show of regret, he lay down on Carter's shoes and rolled over, exposing his belly.

Dali cleared her throat. "Merlin, how about we go find something to eat?"

"Good idea," said Tirzah. "That'll give Carter and me a chance to start over without, um, interference. While you're at it, can you lock the kittens in separate rooms?"

"Consider it done." Merlin wanted to get out as fast as possible, but Blue didn't do fast. He and Dali were forced to exit the room at Blue's top speed, which was a put-upon slow trot. Once they were out the door, Dali kicked it shut behind her, and Merlin groaned. "What a disaster."

"Carter seems a little high-strung," Dali said. "So does Ransom. Good thing you've got steady, sensible people like Tirzah and Pete to balance them out."

"Yeah," Merlin said glumly, thinking of the many times Pete had gone ballistic on him. "Good thing."

He deposited Batcat and Spike in Tirzah's office and Cloud in his own, then showed Dali the break room.

"Merlin, this room has a complete kitchen," Dali said. "Why is it buried under all this... stuff? Why are there files in the cupboards? And what on earth happened to the microwave?"

"Oh, Carter was tinkering with it and it exploded," Merlin said.

That was fun, said his raptor.

"He has bad luck with stuff he didn't make or program himself," Merlin added.

He spotted Blue heading straight for a magical pet trap baited with salmon jerky, and hurriedly removed the jerky, gave it to the bugbear, and shoved the trap into the oven. Noticing Dali's incredulous expression, he said, "It's fine, no one ever uses it."

"Do you have a bathroom?" she asked. "Or should I wait till we get to the circus?"

He showed her to it—she seemed relieved that it was the one thing in the office that was in perfect working order and not buried under a layer of junk—and returned to the break room, determined to find her some breakfast. He'd stashed some emergency granola bars somewhere in there, but he couldn't recall exactly where. As he searched for them, he discovered a powdery gray-green ball that had perhaps once been an orange under the sofa, three MREs stacked atop the water cooler, and a box of fancy chocolate cleverly hidden inside the dead microwave.

Eat the chocolate, demanded his raptor. *Eat ALL the chocolate!*

Merlin's stomach growled. He was frustrated with himself for failing to provide Dali with basic necessities like breakfast and coffee, for being unable to find the granola bars he'd hidden himself, and over his encounters with Carter and Ransom. Carter *had* warned him not to turn off the computers, and Merlin's pet had made more work for him. He'd meant to tell Ransom he'd been right about the size of his magical pet, but he'd not only failed to do that, he'd ticked Ransom off in the bargain.

What was he even doing on this team where nobody liked him and he couldn't seem to do anything right? Not everybody had been his friend at the circus, but a lot of people had, and he'd fit in so much better. And now that he was a shifter, he *could* go back.

But if he did, would he lose Dali? She wasn't a shifter, which would definitely make it harder to fit in. She was so grounded and practical and down to earth, which were all wonderful qualities that were in distinctly short supply at the circus. Though maybe the Fabulous Flying Chameleons could use more people like that. And though he doubted she'd want to perform, there was plenty to do in terms of management.

On the other hand, she was honest and upright, and it was a *crime circus.* Or at least a circus that committed some crimes on the side. And even if it had been a completely law-abiding circus, it was still a circus. Dali didn't seem the type to toss aside her entire life to join the circus.

Carter came into the break room, looking exasperated and holding a lint roller, with most but not all of the fur removed from his suit. "I need chocolate if I'm going to have to re-do everything from the beginning," he announced, seemingly to the room at large but, Merlin suspected, mostly to him.

Pete came in. He stopped dead at the sight of Blue, who was lying on his back in the middle of the floor, clutching the salmon jerky in two paws like an otter and gnawing on it blissfully.

"My God," Pete said. "Tirzah described that thing, but somehow that didn't actually prepare me."

"He's so much cuter than you imagined, right?" Merlin asked.

Pete did not deign to answer that.

"Hey!" Carter exclaimed. "Who ate my truffles?" He whirled accusingly on Merlin, brandishing an empty box of fancy chocolate. "It was that beast of yours, wasn't it?"

"No—" Merlin began.

"He's halfway between a dog and a bear, isn't he?" Pete said, peering at Blue. "A bear can unwrap a chocolate bar and eat it without even tearing the wrapper."

"Yes, but—" Merlin said.

"You need to keep that beast on a leash!" Carter exclaimed.

"He—"

"Chocolate is poisonous to dogs," Pete said. "Is he enough like a dog that we need to call a vet?"

Dali and Tirzah came in, both with scratches on their hands and their hair disarrayed.

"Sorry," Dali said to Merlin. "You must've thought I'd fallen in!"

"The kittens got out, and Cloud started fighting with Batcat and Spike," Tirzah explained breathlessly. "We had to lock them in Merlin's magical pet traps."

"So they're finally good for something," Pete said.

Roland came in, holding a file. "Everyone, a client—" He stopped and stared at Blue. "What's that?"

"It's Blue," said Merlin.

"I can see that it's blue," said Roland. "But what is it?"

"Not the 'Who's on first' routine again," groaned Carter. "Roland, his name is Blue and he's Merlin's chocolate-stealing menace of a pet!"

Before anyone else could speak, Merlin put in, "Carter, I ate your chocolate." Everyone turned to stare at him, reminding him of an illustration in a children's book of George Washington's family standing around a chopped-down cherry tree. "I'm really sorry. I barely even noticed I was doing it. I was hungry and stressed and my raptor told me to—"

Merlin had meant to continue with, "but that's no excuse." Before he could, Roland said, "That's no excuse!"

"I know," Merlin said. "Seriously, Carter, I apologize. I can make you homemade truffles if you like."

"Why don't you make some homemade circus peanuts while you're at it?" said Carter. Behind his back, Roland was giving Merlin an exasperated look and Pete was rolling his eyes. Even Tirzah looked disbelieving.

"You guys," Dali broke in, stepping forward to stand at his side and glare at the lot of them. "Of course Merlin can make truffles! He has a tin of homemade marshmallows in his house in twelve different flavors. They're delicious, too."

Merlin's heart warmed at her defense of him and his candy-making skills. And while he was apparently the opposite of convincing when he was telling the truth, everyone believed Dali instantly and looked abashed.

"Okay," said Carter. "You're on. I want one box of your best truffles, as soon as you get the chance. No banana, no white chocolate, no licorice."

"Deal," said Merlin.

"If you're some kind of secret gourmet chef, why don't you ever bring in homemade goodies for the rest of us?" Pete asked, aggrieved. "You sat there watching me eat an MRE for lunch last week because Batcat stole my sandwich."

"I tried to bring cookies a couple times, but..." Merlin cut himself off before he could explain that he'd suffered a raptor-fueled failure of will en route to the office and eaten them himself. "Anyway, I will now."

"I can't wait," said Roland, and this time he sounded sincerely pleased. "Merlin, do you have anything to report on your case?"

Run away, quick, suggested his raptor. *If I get really big, I could carry Dali and Blue.*

If only, Merlin replied silently. "Let's go back to the lobby and collect Ransom. I think everyone should hear this."

Ransom emerged from his office the instant they stepped into the lobby. He looked strained and pale, and took a seat in the corner without speaking. Merlin wondered what it was like to have his power. Had his power let him listen to their conversation in the break room, or showed them returning? Or did he simply *know* what was happening?

Ransom glanced at Merlin and said, "I heard everyone's footsteps, and I knew Roland would want a report from you. That's all."

Which explained Merlin's question, but raised the one of how

Ransom had known what he was thinking.

With a faint smile, Ransom said, "I'm not using any powers. Your face is just easy to read."

Which didn't make Merlin feel any less unsettled. The memory came into his mind of the only time he'd ever seen Ransom's hellhound. That huge black dog had literally stared down a dragon with his fiery eyes. What was it like to have that eerie presence inside your head?

Not fun, Merlin suspected. "Hey, Ransom, you were completely right that I needed bigger traps. I assumed you were pulling my leg, but obviously…" He waved his hand at Blue, who was making a determined attempt to climb into Merlin's lap. "I found him when he got his head caught in a kitten-sized trap. Anyway, I'm sorry I doubted you."

Ransom blinked. He seemed so startled by the apology that he was at a loss for words. Finally, he said, "He's a bugbear, right?"

"Yes. He's very friendly. Hold our your hand to him."

Ransom offered Blue his hand. Blue sniffed it, then began to lick it enthusiastically.

"See?" Merlin said. "He likes you."

"He's testing to see if you're edible," Carter suggested.

Ignoring that, Merlin forged on. "I bet you'll be next to get a magical pet, Ransom! You were there at the lab—one of them must have bonded to you."

"Just because you're living a boy and his dog story doesn't mean we all are." Ransom withdrew his hand and folded his arms. "I'm not the boy who gets the dog. I'm the boy who wasn't even in the book."

Roland cleared his throat. "Merlin? Your report, please."

With no other alternative, Merlin plunged into his story. He didn't tell them his entire background at the circus, but he did explain how he'd been adopted and how being named as his mother's heir had forced him to leave. He had to, or else Dali's theory that the falling trapeze was actually an attack on him would make no sense.

At the end of the story, Roland turned to Merlin. His steady gaze made Merlin feel like a kid in the principal's office—a regrettably familiar experience. "So, you're the heir to a shifter circus, and that's a position that's important enough that someone might try to kill you over it."

"I can't believe anyone in the circus would go that far," Merlin protested.

Ignoring that, Roland went on, "None of which you ever mentioned before." He held up a hand, silencing Merlin before he could point out that none of them had ever asked, and also that they never believed anything about the circus anyway. "I'm not criticizing you for that. But given how serious this has gotten, is there anything else about you or your past that we might need to know?"

Everyone's gaze felt like a weight on Merlin's shoulders. He wished he'd already told Dali about his other power. He *would*, as soon as they got out of the office. He felt confident that it wouldn't change how she felt about him. And he felt the opposite of confident about his teammates.

Tell them why the barista tossed a watermelon frappuccino in your face, his raptor said. *And then we can all go steal back her sofa!*

For a beast with a short attention span, his raptor could have an annoyingly long memory.

Say, 'I have this other power I've never told you about,' his raptor suggested.

"I have…" Merlin began. Then he imagined what would happen if he finished that sentence. He could see his teammates' expressions as they stared at him in horror or disgust. And those would be the looks he'd always remember when he thought about them, because it would be the last time he'd ever see them.

"…a lot of things I haven't told you," he continued smoothly. "Did I ever mention that when I was a kid at the circus, I once had to stand in for one of the performing seals? I even balanced a ball on my nose! I got a standing ovation. But it ended up causing trouble between the seal family and the cat family, because…"

"Never mind," said Roland hastily. He steepled his hands together.

"So, we have three incidents. The theft of Dali's necklace by pigeon shifters, Dali or Cloud or both of them getting tranquilizer darts shot at by an unknown party that's most likely the wizard-scientists, and a sabotaged trapeze falling on you both. I could believe that any one of those is unrelated to the other two, but it's stretching it to believe that all three are."

"I think they're all directed at Dali," Pete said. "Just because someone might have a motive to get rid of Merlin doesn't mean they actually tried to do it."

Merlin couldn't help reading some subtext into his last sentence.

Carter put in, "Or the pigeons and the trapeze were both the crime circus going on a crime wave, and Dali just happened to be in the wrong place at the wrong time when the wizard-scientists tried to retrieve Cloud."

"Do you know why the wizard-scientists even had the magical animals?" Dali asked.

"No, not yet," Roland said. "It's one of the things we're looking into, but not at a high priority. They're unusual, but, well, they're pets. Compared to the other mysteries surrounding the wizard-scientists, the magical creatures aren't that important."

Merlin petted Blue under the table, murmuring, "You're important to *me*."

Roland glanced at his watch. "Let's move this along. I'm expecting a prospective client any minute now. Merlin, I assume you're going back to the circus. Do you need any backup?"

"No, not like that." The last thing Merlin wanted was his teammates wandering around the circus, grumbling about everything. "I'd like some help information-gathering, though. Tirzah, anything you can dig up about any of this would be great—news stories about birds stealing necklaces, conspiracy theories about the wizard-scientists, anything."

"Ransom?" Dali said. "Your power is getting information, right? Could you find out who sabotaged the trapeze?"

"I could try," Ransom said cautiously. "But that sort of question—detailed information about a specific thing—is one of the hardest for me. I might not get anything useful, and even trying would put me out of commission for a while after that. Days, maybe."

"Don't," said Roland. "I'd rather reserve that for emergencies. Merlin, see what you can find with ordinary detective work first. Tirzah, get on the research."

The buzzer sounded. Roland picked it up, waving everyone into silence. "Protection, Inc: Defenders. How can I help you?"

A nervous-sounding man said, "This is Andrew Oliver. We spoke on the phone about you protecting me from a disgruntled ex-employee who's been stalking me...?"

"Of course," Roland said. "Come on up."

He hung up and snapped his fingers. "Merlin, get rid of those traps and stash Blue somewhere! Everyone else, tidy up!"

Everyone jumped to work, shoving papers and other clutter into their offices and closing the door on them. Merlin gathered an armful of traps and called, "Blue!"

Blue looked up at him and panted, making no move to follow.

"I'll get him," Dali said, and coaxed Blue out the door.

"I'll make sure the kittens aren't escaping," said Tirzah.

Merlin dumped the traps in Pete's office. When he came back in, the prospective client, Oliver, had arrived and was showing Roland photos on his phone, while Pete and Ransom and Carter looked over his shoulder.

"And that's my front door with a stake hammered into it," Oliver was saying.

"That's a statement, all right," remarked Carter.

Roland glanced up at Merlin. "Oh, meet—"

Oliver looked up at Merlin and screamed, "That's him!"

He hurled his cell phone at Merlin's head. Instinctively, Merlin caught it.

Oliver's eyes bulged as if he was about to have a heart attack. With a shriek, he bolted out the door, letting it slam behind him.

"What the hell…?" began Pete.

"Oh," Ransom said, sounding enlightened. To Merlin, he said, "So *that's* what you've been doing."

"Merlin's been moonlighting as a stalker accountant?" Carter asked. "Why?"

Merlin felt like the floor had dropped out from under his feet. And also like the ceiling had fallen on his head. Or maybe a trapeze. He felt his mouth open and close like a goldfish that had jumped out of the bowl.

He had to tell them everything. He also had to catch that poor guy before he called the police. And he had to send someone else, because he sure couldn't go himself. Carter would argue with Merlin rather than just go, Pete was too intimidating, and Merlin felt bad about making Ransom run after someone when he probably felt like his head was about to explode.

"Roland, can you please run after that guy and explain that it was a chance resemblance and I'm not his stalker?" Merlin spoke so fast that his words blurred together. He shoved the phone at Roland. "Here!"

Ominously, Roland said, "He emailed me a photo of his stalker. There's no resemblance. Do you still want me to say that?"

"Yes," Merlin said. "And hurry? He's probably about to call the cops."

"Good thing he threw his cell phone," Carter remarked.

Roland stabbed a finger at Merlin. "Don't go anywhere." With a startling grace for his stocky build, he spun around and ran after the man.

As if things couldn't get any worse, Dali burst into the lobby, followed closely by Tirzah. Merlin saw Dali's gaze go straight to him, and the relief in her expression when she saw that he was unhurt. Normally, that would have lifted his heart, but under the circumstances, it made him feel like he'd swallowed a rock.

"We heard screaming," Tirzah said breathlessly.

"What happened?" Dali demanded.

Everyone looked at each other.

"I'm really not sure," Carter said.

Pete said, "Ask Merlin."

"I can explain," Merlin said, hearing how exactly he sounded like a murderer caught standing over a corpse and clutching a bloody knife. After a silence that felt like it lasted for an hour, he said, "Um… How about when Roland gets back? So I don't have to do it twice."

The silence in which they waited for Roland to get back felt like it lasted for a year. It was only broken when Merlin, fidgeting nervously, knocked over and broke the last remaining intact coffee mug.

His raptor had no shortage of suggestions, each more appealing than the last, from *Point over everyone's heads and say "Look! A pteranodon!" and run away while they're looking* to *Shrink to the size of a mouse and hide in Roland's desk* to *Bite Pete on the ankle and run away* to *Propose to Dali and run away to Las Vegas with her and get married by Elvis and start a new life where nobody knows you.*

That last one sounded incredibly good. Merlin was only stopped from getting down on his knees by a glance at Dali's eyebrows. Those were not the brows of a woman who would say yes to a proposal. Those were the brows of a woman seriously considering a break-up, depending on what Merlin said once he said something.

Run to the bathroom and throw up, his raptor suggested. After a pause, he said, *Then climb out the window.*

"No!" Merlin said. "Stop telling me to run away! I'm staying here and facing the music!"

He only realized that he had spoken aloud when he saw everyone's expressions change from *This better be good, Merlin* to *Maybe we should call the men in white coats with the butterfly nets.*

"Everyone" included Roland. Merlin had been so preoccupied with what his raptor was saying that he'd missed his boss coming back in.

"I was talking to my raptor," Merlin said. Nobody's expression changed.

Roland folded his arms. "I convinced Mr. Oliver that we're not actually harboring his stalker inside our office. And I referred him to

166

another security agency, because he wanted nothing more to do with us. So. Merlin. What would you like to tell us?"

Merlin braced himself and told the truth. "I have another power. It doesn't work on people who know me well, just on strangers and acquaintances. It's to make people see me as whoever they expect to see. Mr. Oliver was scared and expecting to see his stalker around every corner, so that's exactly who he saw."

Roland slammed his fist down on a table, making Merlin jump. "Why on earth did you use it on him, then?"

"I didn't mean to. I can't control it—I can't even tell when it's on." Merlin took a deep breath and went on, "It took me a while to figure out that I even had it. I had to deduce it from people's reactions to me."

"Is that why you asked me the color of your hair when we first met?" Dali broke in.

"Yes. I wanted to make sure you were seeing me, not..." *A better version of me,* he thought, then said, "...someone else."

Dali looked relieved. Ransom had that satisfied expression he got when he figured something out. Everyone else looked massively pissed off.

"And why didn't you tell us about it?" Roland asked.

"I..."

Run, suggested his raptor.

But with Dali's gaze on him, he couldn't do anything but tell the truth. "It's a power that tricks people—that lies to them. I didn't want you to think I was a liar at heart."

"Oh, Merlin, no one would think that," Dali said. "You didn't choose it. You can't even control it."

"Yes, but our powers express who we are," Merlin said. "Ransom, for instance. Look at who he is, and look at the power he got."

It was the worst possible thing to say. He realized it as soon as he'd spoken. Ransom's expression froze over, and Merlin suddenly remembered that in the Marines, Ransom had been a sniper.

"You think my power expresses who I am?" Ransom spoke in a deadly cold voice.

"And mine?" Roland looked as stricken as he had when he'd been told that the woman who'd saved his life had died.

"How dare you!" Carter yelled suddenly, making Merlin jump. His fists were clenched at his sides.

Dali grabbed Merlin's hand. "I don't know what's going on, but Merlin has a job to do. For me. Tirzah, we can leave our pets here, right?"

Tirzah, looking bewildered, said, "Sure." Then, glancing around the room, she added, "You don't have to come back to the office today to collect them. If you don't, we'll take them home and you can pick them up whenever. Right, Pete?"

"Sure," Pete said. His agreeable tone had to be for Tirzah and Dali, not Merlin.

"Merlin, let's go," said Dali.

They left in record time. When they got to his car, he opened the door for her, and they both collapsed into their seats.

"Whew," Merlin said. "Thanks for rescuing me. I've never been more glad to leave a place in my life. Except maybe the wizard-scientists' lab. And my parents' home when I was a kid."

Dali put her arm around his shoulder. "I don't blame you."

As he pulled out of the parking lot, he asked, "You really don't think my power says anything about me?"

"I don't think it says anything bad. I see now what you mean about it matching something about you. But I don't think it means you're a liar. Maybe it's because you grew up in a place that tricks people, so you got the power to trick people. Or you've had a lot of different roles in your life, and now you get seen as a lot of different people."

That had never occurred to Merlin before. "You're so smart. And you're not mad at me for not telling you about my power?"

"Well—" She rubbed her forehead, clearly sorting through her feelings, then said, "Not really. If you'd let me make any decisions when you weren't sure I was seeing you clearly, you'd be out of my life like that." She snapped the fingers of her right hand. "But you didn't. You were very careful about that. It seems to me that you dealt with your power as ethically as you could."

That made him feel much better—not only that she wasn't angry with him, but that she understood that he'd never tried to manipulate her. "I *was* going to tell you. I'd meant to tell my teammates too, but, well, you saw how they reacted."

"Yeah, what was that about? They flipped out when you said that the powers match the person. So you're a bit like a hyperactive velociraptor and Pete's a bit like a bear. What's wrong with that?"

"I meant their other powers," Merlin said. "Though you're right, Pete is kind of bear-like. Hmm. Roland's a phoenix. No idea what could be wrong with that. Ransom's a hellhound—okay, I can see how that could have bad connotations. And I've only ever seen him shift once."

"What *is* a hellhound?"

"A huge black dog with fiery eyes." Merlin gave a frustrated sigh. "I wasn't even thinking about that, though. I meant his other power, the power he has as a man. We were all supposed to have two: one in our animal form, and one as a human."

"What are Ransom's?"

"As a man, information. As a hellhound, got me. I was going to say that he's a smart, curious guy who likes to know things, and he got the power to know things that nobody else does. It's very suited to him. Except it's obviously not much fun to use. Actually, it pretty much sucks." He sighed again. "Okay, I can see where I put my foot in it."

"For Ransom. What about for the rest of them?" Dali was leaning forward, intent as a bloodhound on the trail. "What sort of animal does Carter turn into?"

"No idea. I've never seen it, and he won't say. And if he has any powers, I sure don't know what they are."

"What about Roland? What are his powers?"

"His phoenix can set things on fire. He says he doesn't have any powers as a man." Merlin shrugged. "Though up till today everyone thought I didn't, either."

"*How* long has your team been working together?"

"Six months." Merlin looked gloomily out the window at a group of laughing teenagers doing skateboard tricks on the sidewalk. "And if you're thinking we ought to know each other better and get along better, you're right. We're like the Bad News Bears of shifter security teams."

"You were all kidnapped and traumatized and had your lives uprooted," Dali pointed out. "It takes more than six months to get through that kind of thing."

She, more than anyone, would know how long it takes to get through being traumatized and having your life uprooted, Merlin thought.

"You're right," he said. "I hadn't thought of it that way. Still, I'm not looking forward to setting foot in that office again. Hey, want to go straight to the circus? Mom makes much better coffee than Starbucks."

"Sure."

As they headed for the circus, he put his hand on her thigh, relishing both the sensual warmth of her body and the knowledge that she would welcome his touch. Dali leaned against him, her head tilted back so her silky hair drifted over his skin.

It was a beautiful sunny day, and the woman of his dreams was at his side. This time, surely *this* time, everything would be all right.

CHAPTER 15

After a year spent in a haze of depression alternating with a strict focus on work, Dali wasn't used to being so tossed about by conflicting emotions. As she sat beside Merlin in his ridiculously small but also genuinely cool car, she was turned on by his presence and thrilled that they were together and frustrated by the situation with his team and excited by visiting the circus and nervous about meeting his mother and pre-emptively broken-hearted that he might run off with the circus and she'd never see him again.

Focus, Dali, she told herself. *Just take it one day at a time.*

Or, considering that it was Merlin, maybe she should be taking it one minute at a time.

He pulled into the circus parking lot. It was Monday, so there would only be an evening performance that day, and they were the only car in the lot. But not the only people; a middle-aged woman was leaning against a lamp post, waiting for someone.

"Uh-oh," Merlin muttered. "That's Rosine. Rosine Richelieu, of the Remarkable Richelieus."

"She's a poodle, right? And that's the family that didn't want you as heir?"

"One of them, yeah. And she was one of the loudest of the 'shifter leaders only' faction, so..." He squared his shoulders. "Oh, well. May as well face the music."

Rosine made a beeline for them as soon as they got out of the car. Before they could even say hello, she said, "Merlin, I want you to know that things have changed. You're a shifter now. From now on, you have my full support as heir."

It was the first time Dali had ever seen Merlin at a loss for words. He opened his mouth, but nothing came out.

Rosine went on, "I'm going to talk to my family, and also to everyone who had a problem with you before. I think I can persuade them to support you now. But it'll go better if I do it privately and discreetly. That's why I came out here alone. So don't go around yet saying I support you, okay? And don't try rounding up support yourself. I'll do that for you. It'll look better coming from me."

"Uh… okay," Merlin said, staring at her like she'd grown two heads.

She nodded briskly. "I'll let you know when I've persuaded everyone who's persuadable. Until then, we didn't have this talk."

With that, she turned around and walked out of the parking lot, toward the circus entrance and fairground. They watched her go in silence.

Dali wanted to be happy for Merlin, but in her heart of hearts, she wished she was a size-changing velociraptor so she could have bitten that woman's ankle and scared her away before she said a word. If Rosine Richelieu was right about how influential she was, once she was through Merlin would no longer have any reason not to return to the circus.

"That was weird," Merlin said.

Dali forced herself to focus on what was going on right now, not on her impending heartbreak. "Well, you *are* a shifter now. Or did you think she had something against you personally?"

"Yeah, actually, I did. But also, she's not normally this sneaky. She doesn't make secret plans and talk to people privately, she says exactly what she thinks as publicly as she can." He shrugged. "Well—I guess people can change. Anyway, I'll let her do her thing. Don't mention it."

172

"My lips are sealed," Dali promised. But she couldn't help hoping that the poodle woman's out-of-character plan would fail.

They headed into the fairgrounds. The stalls were closed, and it had a slightly desolate air. Merlin led her to the train behind the big top. A pair of kittens were pouncing and squeaking, Max the ringmaster sat in a lawn chair getting his magnificent moustache trimmed by his wife Renu, his daughter Kalpana was scribbling on a clipboard, and a group of sea lions were playing basketball with their noses.

They all greeted Merlin and Dali. (At least, she thought the seal lions' barks were greetings rather than jeers.) She tried not to blush when she saw them look from Merlin to her clothes that were in fact his clothes, then shoot her meaningful looks. They knew how the two of them had spent the night, all right.

"Janet's in her room," Kalpana said. "Go get your scolding and get it over with!"

"I already got it," Merlin replied. "Over the phone. Hey, Kalpana? Last night you said something about Natalie maybe leaving because of an accident. What was that about?"

"Oh… It probably wasn't that," Kalpana said. "She left so suddenly and she didn't really explain why, so I was grasping at straws."

"What accident, though? Was it serious?"

Kalpana shook her head. "She was up in the rigging helping to set up the lights, and she got an electric shock from a frayed wire. She fell. We had the net up, of course, so she wasn't hurt. But I was there supervising, and I almost had a heart attack. It reminded me of how you fell when you first came here. Natalie left a few months later. Afterward I thought maybe it had made her decide she wanted a less dangerous job."

"Did she seem scared?"

"No," Kalpana admitted. "But you know Natalie. She never seems scared."

Merlin sighed. "No, she doesn't. I don't suppose she left any contact info?"

"No. She said she would, but she didn't. Actually, that's part of why I thought she might've gotten scared. It might've embarrassed her, so she didn't want to talk to us."

"Could be." But Merlin sounded unconvinced. "Thanks, Kalpana. Let me know if you hear from her. You have *my* phone number."

"Will do."

As they headed for the train, Dali said, "What do you make of that?"

Merlin spread his hands in frustration. "Got me. Kalpana has a lot of insight into people, and if it was anyone but Natalie, I'd say she was probably right."

Quietly, Dali said, "You never know how almost dying can affect you till it happens."

He put his hand on her back. "I know. But Natalie didn't almost die. And she wouldn't have felt like she had. What Kalpana doesn't know is that me and Natalie used to sneak out in the middle of the night and practice trapeze at the full height, way before we were allowed to do that. We fell all the time, but into the net. Natalie would've been startled, sure, but not terrified."

"What do *you* think happened, then?"

Merlin sighed. "I wish I knew."

They went into the parked train. Dali had ridden in one only a few times in her life, and was fascinated by the interior. Merlin walked her through the "animal cars," which contained the neatest, cleanest cages she'd seen in her life—unsurprisingly, as no animals actually lived in them.

"We get inspected by animal welfare people occasionally," Merlin said. "They give us advance warning, so we can show them animals in their cages. That also gives us time to mess them up a bit, have some of the kids pee in them, and so forth. You know, for realism."

Dali snickered. "I bet the little boys love that. So the animal welfare people don't do surprise inspections?"

"No, that would be dangerous if we had real animals. You don't want to have some random stranger suddenly showing up when there might

be lions and tigers training in the ring. They give us a day or so's warning, and schedule it when we're not doing a show, so they're all in their
cages."

They passed the sea lion tank, which was much more convincingly
lived-in. "Because the sea lions really do swim in it," Merlin explained.

Dali grinned to herself as they walked past. She could definitely see
why Merlin loved the circus so much.

For the first time, she wondered if she might consider following him
to it. Sure, she wasn't a shifter, but neither was Kalpana. It didn't seem
to be an issue unless you were the heir. And it obviously required an
immense amount of organization, which was Dali's specialty.

On the other hand, between Merlin's mom and Kalpana, it was beautifully run already. Dali would be redundant. And it wasn't like she
could double as an acrobat or a performing poodle.

Enjoy the roses while you have them, she told herself. *And try not to
think too much about how in the blink of an eye, it could all disappear.*

They found Janet waiting for them in her room, with coffee and three
mugs ready. She and Merlin hugged, and then he stood there fidgeting
and trying to change the topic while she fussed over him and prodded
at his head. Dali drank her coffee and tried not to look too amused. It
reminded her so much of her with her own grandmother. Maybe, once
everything was over, she could bring Grandma to see the show, then
take her backstage and introduce her to Janet.

When Merlin finally convinced his mother that he was fine, she fixed
him with a sharp, rather parrot-like eye. "I'm absolutely furious about
that 'accident.' Give me a little more time, and I'll find out who was
behind it. And they'll be out of the circus like that!" She snapped her
fingers.

"I'm not sure it was anyone at the circus," said Merlin. "An audience
member could have snuck into the rigging, dropped it on Dali, and
taken off while everyone was distracted."

"Pffft!" snorted Janet. "You think it was directed at your girlfriend?
That was aimed at you! Someone's trying to get you out of the way so

they can take over your rightful position!" She rounded on Dali, who was still mentally stuck on "girlfriend," and said, "Don't you agree?"

"Er…yes," Dali admitted. Janet's fierce protectiveness toward Merlin made Dali feel like the two of them were on the same side.

"Come on, mom," Merlin protested. "You seriously think Fausto Fratelli would do something that might kill me?"

"I wouldn't put it past him," said Janet. "Or maybe Rosine Richelieu."

"It's definitely not Rosine."

"Well, it's somebody," said Janet. "And I won't rest till I find out who. Maybe Renard Richelieu."

"Mom! It's not any of the poodles!"

Dali sensed a fight about to break out, and moved to head it off at the pass. "Merlin and I are going to talk to people here. Not interrogate them, just catch up with them and keep our ears open for any clues. He's got lots to tell them."

"He does indeed," said Janet, rather ominously. "Such as the fact that he can now shift into a giant velociraptor, which one might think would be something he could have shared with his own mother just a *little* bit earlier."

Dali, slightly frantic, said, "He can also shift into a tiny velociraptor! You should see that, it's really cool. He gets down to the size of a hamster!"

"Really?" Janet asked, intrigued. "That small?"

Merlin put down his coffee mug and said to himself, in a low but forceful voice, "Absolutely no breaking anything. Tiny!"

And then a hamster-sized raptor was perched on the bunk where he had been sitting. Both Dali and Janet gasped in delight. The tiny raptor leaped on to the table and made a beeline for the sugar bowl.

Janet picked out a sugar lump and fed it to him, remarking, "*Very* impressive. And so versatile. You could get into buildings through the ventilation ducts, then open the doors from the inside. You could hide inside a bank and memorize the combination to a vault."

Dali repressed a sigh. She'd forgotten for a while that it was a crime circus.

Merlin crammed the last of sugar into his jaws with his tiny talons, then leaped back on to the bed and became a man again.

Shooting a guilty look at Dali, he said, "Never mind the burglary applications. It was great seeing you, Mom, but Dali and I need to get going with the 'let's catch up' thing."

"How are you going to explain her presence?" Janet inquired. "If all you're doing is casual catching up with friends, you shouldn't bother with that while you're bodyguarding her."

Dali felt like an idiot. Everything had been moving so fast, that hadn't occurred to her. From the look on Merlin's face, it hadn't occurred to him either.

"Say you're dating and it's getting serious," Janet suggested. "Say you want to see more of the circus in case you end up joining it."

Behind her thick glasses, the old woman's eyes glittered with intelligence. Dali was positive that Janet had suggested that because she knew they were together and thought that was exactly what Dali ought to be doing.

Dali restrained the impulse to run out of the train car screaming.

"Yeah, that'd be easier to pull off," Merlin said. Then, glancing at Dali, he added, "Right?"

"Yeah. Sure. Let's get on that right now!" She drained her coffee mug. "Nice to see you, Janet!"

Dali fled the room, so quickly that Merlin didn't catch up with her till she'd reached the empty animal car.

"Are you really all right with that?" he asked. "You left awfully quick."

"It's fine. Just a little weird and nerve-wracking." She didn't add, *And heartbreakingly ironic.*

Merlin liked her, obviously, but she was the one who'd fallen too hard, too soon. She didn't want to dump a ton of... not love, it was way too soon for love... intense feelings on him that would do nothing but make him feel guilty about living the life that was right for him.

"You'll be great," he assured her, and kissed her. Which did nothing

177

to take away from all those *feelings*.

"Let's talk to the Duffy brothers first," Merlin said, when they'd reluctantly broken apart.

"The sparrow guys? Do you think they know something about the trapeze, or about my necklace?"

"Your necklace. It'd be nice to get it back, right? I know you wanted to before your dinner with your grandma on Sunday."

Her last Sunday dinner felt like a lifetime ago. Impulsively, she said, "Will you come to dinner with me? I've met your family, so…"

"I would love to meet your grandma," Merlin said. "I'll bring a bottle of wine. Or maybe homemade marshmallows. And dress up. No dinosaur shirts!"

Dali was about to say there was no need, then decided not to. She *did* want to see what Merlin looked like dressed up. It would either be incredibly hot or, depending on his idea of "dressed up," incredibly funny. "It's a date."

He led her to another train car. On their way, they passed a number of people who greeted Merlin with varying degrees of warmth, from chilly politeness to exuberant hugs. Rosine Richelieu pretended not to see him, which was a clear snub as they ran into her in a train corridor and had to step aside to let her get past.

Once she was gone, Dali pointed out quietly, "See? She really is putting on the act she talked about."

Merlin scratched his head. "Yeah. I'm impressed."

The Duffy brothers weren't in their room, but Tawny Lyon said she'd seen them at the fairgrounds. Merlin asked her if she'd heard from Natalie or knew anything about why she'd left, but Tawny only shrugged and said she had no idea, but she'd happily give up her job as target girl if Natalie came back.

"I have to take two Dramamine before every performance," she confided.

As they headed for the fairgrounds, Dali said, "You seem really worried about Natalie."

"She's not replying to calls or email, nobody knows where she is… It's not like her. I'm tempted to ask Ransom, but that's the exact sort of question that can really mess him up. And I don't *know* that anything's wrong with her. If I'm going to ask a teammate to put himself through hell for my sake, I'd rather ask him who tried to kill you." Merlin ran his hand through his hair, rumpling it. "Is that selfish of me?"

Dali took his hand. "Merlin, you're the least selfish person I've ever met. You're pulling yourself in all directions trying to do the right thing for everybody: me, Natalie, Ransom. Your mother. The circus. You should do more for *you*."

"That's funny." He squeezed her hand. "I could say the same thing about you. Maybe we should promise each other to do more for ourselves."

"In bed?" she asked drily.

He grinned, unabashed. "Also in the shower."

"It's a date."

They found the Duffy brothers, as sparrows, practicing squeezing through increasingly small rings held by Bobby Duffy, the teenager who had been an audience plant in rat roulette.

"Cool act," said Dali.

"Not an act," said Merlin. "The Duffys don't perform. They're practicing breaking into buildings. Or cars with the windows partly rolled down."

Dali stifled a sigh. Fun as the circus was, there was no way that she could ever join a criminal enterprise. The law might be stupid and unfair at times—the sound of the cop jeering "Pigeons stole me necklace!" echoed in her ears—but she still believed in it. She'd bent all she could in accepting that the circus's crimes weren't *that* bad, as crimes went, but they were still crimes.

"Hey, Billy! Larry!" Merlin called. "I need to talk to you."

The sparrows shifted into their human forms as a pair of jowly middle-aged guys with receding hairlines. Dali averted her eyes, but unfortunately not fast enough to miss the sight of the Duffy brothers stark naked.

"Yeah?" said a Duffy brother. She had no idea which, as she wasn't looking.

"You ever teach the necklace trick to pigeon shifters?"

"Nope," said the other Duffy brother.

"Do you *know* any pigeon shifters?"

"Nope," said a Duffy brother.

"Have you ever told anyone outside of the circus about the necklace trick?" Merlin asked patiently.

"Nope," said the other Duffy brother.

Dali was so aggravated by their utter lack of caring that she looked up. Larry Duffy had put on his shirt, but no pants. The other one, presumably Billy Duffy, was still completely naked, sitting on a bench with his legs spread wide as he leisurely unknotted his shoe laces. Dali once again averted her eyes… and saw the Duffy nephew, also determinedly looking away. And also looking very slightly guilty.

She beckoned to him. "How about we get away from the naked dudes with the dad bods?"

Bobby eagerly followed her behind the nearest food stall. "Thanks. They're so embarrassing!"

"It must be even worse for you, since they're family."

"It is," he said, with all the heartfelt sincerity of a teenager. "Thanks again for rescuing me. If I walk out on my own, they tease the hell out of me."

"Family," said Dali. "You love them, but they drive you crazy."

"You can say that again." He gave her a curious glance. "How come Merlin's asking about the necklace trick?"

"It's because of *my* family, actually. I was raised by my grandmother, and she has a necklace that's a family heirloom. She believes it's a lucky charm. Last week I got fired, so she loaned it to me to give me better luck…"

As Dali continued her story, she watched the play of emotions over the teenager's face: sympathy, realization, and guilt. It amazed her how well her ploy had worked. She'd never thought of herself as a sneaky person, but she'd set up the entire conversation to get this exact response, and it seemed to be working.

She concluded with, "My grandma is in assisted living, but she still can cook, and she makes dinner for me every Sunday. I'm really hoping to get the necklace back to her then—I'll feel terrible if I have to tell her it's gone forever."

Dali watched the kid's face. Guilt. Anxiety. More guilt.

"Umm," he said. "Sunday, huh?"

"Yes," she said firmly. "Sunday, before 6:00 PM."

He made his decision. "Can I get your email?"

She was tempted to let him do his thing, but he looked about fifteen. She couldn't let him potentially walk into danger just to retrieve an inanimate object, no matter how precious it was.

"Bobby, I want that necklace back, but I don't want you going alone into some situation that might turn violent—"

She broke off, surprised, when he laughed. "It won't."

"Are you sure?"

"Yeah. I guess I have to tell you the whole story, huh? So you won't worry I'm going to get shot by gangsters or something."

"Yes," Dali said firmly. "But I promise to keep it a secret."

He shrugged. "You can tell Merlin. Just tell him not to tell anyone else, okay?"

"Sure."

"There's a secret website for teenage shifters," he said. "I'm not going to tell you what it's called. Trust me, no one knows about it who shouldn't."

"Okay."

"So, I have some buddies on it who live here in Refuge City. They're pigeon shifters. I told them some of the stuff we do, and they tried it. I warned them not to! My family has been practicing it for years and years, and also, we're sparrows. My uncles can slip a necklace off someone's neck without them ever noticing, so they think it came undone

181

and fell off. Those idiot friends of mine flew at people and perched on their shoulders. Everybody noticed! And not only did they notice, they freaked out and flailed at them and then ran screaming!"

"Except for me," Dali said.

Bobby nodded. "Yeah. You were the only person they actually got anything from."

Normally she was proud of her ability to master her panic, but apparently that had been the one time when screaming and flailing would have worked out better. "Do they still have it?"

"Yeah. They were just doing it for fun and to see if they could, and they didn't realize your necklace was valuable till they got away with it. But they couldn't return it because they didn't know who you were. I'll email them that I found the owner, they'll give it to me, and I'll give it back to you."

"As simple as that," Dali marveled.

Bobby grinned. "As simple as that."

"You're a good guy," she said. "Thanks. I really appreciate it."

"Any time. And just so you know, I've always liked Merlin. I know heir isn't something we vote on and I'm too young to vote anyway, but I'm staying with the circus no matter what. And whatever my uncles say, I know they will too. You can tell—"

A sparrow landed on his head and pecked his ear.

"Ow!" Bobby yelped, batting at it. "Cut it out, Uncle Larry. Well, guess I'm back to work. Nice to meet you."

"Nice to meet *you*. See you later."

Dali watched him walk away. She was about to follow him when she felt a tug at her jeans ankle. A tiny raptor poked his head out of the cuff of her jeans where he'd been hiding. She burst out laughing as Merlin leaped out, scurried a few feet away, and then became a man again.

"Great work," he said. "You couldn't have been smoother if you'd been raised here yourself."

"Thanks. And hey, good work to you, too. You went straight from teeny raptor to man without any size switches in between."

"That's right. It *has* been easier lately." He seemed to listen to some inward voice.

"Is your raptor talking to you? What's he saying?"

"He says, 'You've gotten much more sensible lately. Of course I'll do what you want if it's what I want too, because I know best. Now let's go get a banana split.'" Merlin leaned over and whispered in Dali's ear, "I think it's really that practice makes perfect. But hey, whatever works."

He kissed her ear, then her cheek. She turned her head, offering him her lips, and he claimed her mouth. Desire caught fire within her, and she caught herself glancing around for a place where they could get some privacy. Merlin, who was clearly thinking along the same lines, peered inside the food stall's window.

Dali followed his gaze, then regretfully shook her head. "We wouldn't be able to move without sacks of potatoes falling on our heads. Tonight, okay?"

"Tonight," Merlin promised her, trailing his fingers along the edge of her collar. Her skin felt like it came alive everywhere he touched, and she trembled.

"On second thought… how about we take a quick trip back to your place instead?"

Merlin grinned. They clasped hands and ran to his car.

The week went by in a whirl of bright colors, alliterative names, and spectacular performances at the circus, and even more spectacular sex at Merlin's place at night. Not to mention kitten cuddling, bugbear antics, cooking together, eating together, cuddling together, talking together, laughing together, even sitting on the sofa and reading together, side by side.

Though they made no more progress in finding out who had dropped the trapeze on them, there were no more 'accidents' either, and Dali began to think that either it really had been an accident, or whoever had done it had given up and wouldn't try again.

Bobby Duffy was as good as his word. He returned her necklace, carefully polished, wrapped in tissue paper, and presented furtively in a box wrapped in brown paper and tied up with string, in time for Sunday dinner with Grandma.

Merlin dressed up for dinner in an actual suit, which made his blue eyes and golden hair stand out like gems on black velvet, and highlighted his muscular shoulders and narrow hips to swoon-worthy effect. Dali had to stop him from going overboard with gifts, but even a restrained Merlin showed up with a bottle of wine, a bouquet of flowers, and a box of homemade marshmallows.

Dali was unsurprised but happy to discover that Merlin and Grandma hit it off. It was one of Dali's favorite things about him: he was genuinely interested in people, and liked to listen as much as he liked to talk. Five minutes after she finished thanking him for the gifts, they were sharing old southern recipes and chatting away about regional differences in barbecue sauce.

When Merlin went out after dinner to bring the car around to the front, Grandma kissed Dali on the cheek. "Didn't I tell you the necklace would bring you luck?"

"So, you like him?" Dali asked, knowing the answer but wanting to hear the words.

"Sweetheart, you walked in here practically glowing! I like any man who makes you happy and treats you well. And he seems very kind, which is the most important thing." She winked. "And right after kindness comes hands that know what they're doing, if you know what I mean."

"Grandma!" Dali whispered frantically, glancing at the door. But when Merlin didn't appear, she relaxed and said, "Well, good. I'm glad you approve."

"I do." But then her face wrinkled a bit more around the eyebrows. "Though... I've known men like him in my time. Kind-hearted, generous, clever, handsome, good with their hands. Men who make women very happy, when they're around."

"What do you mean, 'when they're around?'" Dali asked uneasily.

"Well, they don't always settle down," Grandma replied. "Soldiers, sailors, musicians, traveling salesmen—sometimes there's too much restlessness in their hearts to stay in one place."

Merlin returned, and Grandma smiled and invited him back for next Sunday dinner. But all the drive back, Grandma's words stuck with Dali. Even after they went home and made love, she lay awake in the warm circle of his strong arms, thinking about his restless heart. Now that he was a shifter, there was nothing stopping him from leaving with the circus when they moved on to their next destination.

How could they stay together, if the price was either giving up her life or tearing him away from his?

CHAPTER 16

The wizard-scientist Morgana was pleased with the way her plan was progressing. Despite the concerns of the other wizard-scientists, she had stuck with her plot to build up Merlin's hopes and allow him a stretch of uninterrupted happiness. It would make his despair all the stronger when she destroyed his dreams.

Only one thing hadn't gone exactly as planned: Merlin had not yet stepped forward to claim his position as heir to the circus. Morgana had expected him to do so by now, thus forcing his lover to choose whether to go with him or to break up with him. Morgana could work with either choice, though she'd have preferred (and expected) a break-up. But Merlin hadn't declared himself, and so he and Dalisay were still together.

Now Morgana had to make a choice: should she first destroy the circus and then destroy his relationship, or first destroy his relation-ship and then destroy the circus? Either way, he needed to be left with nothing.

She considered her chosen Dark Knight. Which was he more at-tached to, really? Whichever it was, she should ruin that one first, and then the lesser relationship would be easy to crush in the midst of his despair.

The circus was his family and home. Once he'd lost it, he'd tried to find a replacement, first with the Marines and then with his bodyguard team. But neither had been sufficient. He'd left the Marines and he was unhappy with his team. Moreover, his beloved mother's life was also entwined with the circus. Without it, she too would have nothing. She was elderly, and with luck the shock of losing her life's work might even kill her.

Dalisay Batiste, on the other hand, was merely a girlfriend. Merlin's ability to recognize and bond with his mate had been severed, so even in the unlikely chance that she was his mate, he was incapable of forming a true and lasting relationship with her. Once the circus was destroyed, breaking them up would take no more effort than flicking a finger at a standing domino.

And this was just as well, Morgana thought. She'd put in far more effort in preparations to destroy the circus, carefully laying the groundwork with donations to the proper places, aided with just a little magic.

At last, it was time for the Fabulous Flying Chameleons to meet their doom.

Smiling to herself, she picked up the phone and dialed.

CHAPTER 17

The phone rang while Merlin and Dali were relaxing together on the sofa, drinking afternoon coffee, eating homemade marshmallows, and binge-watching *The Great British Bake-Off*. Cloud lay across their shoulders, with her tail curled around Merlin's throat and her head nestled into Dali's hair. Blue's head and paws were in Merlin's lap, and the rest of him was sliding off the sofa at glacial speed.

The woman he was crazy about, the pets he adored, and marshmallows to satisfy his inner raptor: it was a perfect moment. Which made a tendril of dread curl around his heart at the phone ring. Reluctantly, he picked it up. "Hello?"

Blue fell off the sofa with a thud and a yelp. This startled Cloud, who launched herself into the air, digging in her claws as she went, and knocked the phone out of Merlin's hand. It went skittering across the floor. Cloud, who loved chasing small moving objects, pursued it and batted it under the refrigerator. Blue stuck his nose under the fridge, his tiny wings buzzing madly with his effort to crawl after it.

Dali, wiping tears of laughter from her eyes, used a broomstick to slide it out. She handed the phone to Merlin. "It's for you."

"Hello?" Merlin repeated.

Roland's deep voice had the exasperated tinge it always seemed to have when he was talking to Merlin. "Should I even ask?"

"It all began when my bugbear fell off the sofa," Merlin began.

"I *shouldn't* have asked," said Roland. "Where's your report? And don't tell me your bugbear ate it."

Merlin was relieved that he had a straightforward answer to that. "It's done. I can email it to you right now."

"Our printer's broken," Roland said. "Carter did something to improve it, and now it's printing page after page of a car repair manual in Russian. Can you print it yourself and bring it in?"

"Can't you just read it online?"

"I want to ask questions about it in person. Now, Merlin." He hung up.

Dali winked at him. "Don't worry. I'll be there as backup."

That cheered him up. So did having her by his side when he, she, Cloud (in her purse) and Blue (in the coat) ran into a troupe of cookie-selling Girl Scouts on the way to the car.

"What *is* that?"

"Why's it wearing a coat?"

"Is that blue stuff its fur?!"

The last Girl Scout ignored Blue entirely and directed her sales pitch at Merlin. "We have Thin Mints, Peanut Butter Patties, Samoas..."

His raptor's eager and predictable demand to buy them ALL distracted Merlin enough that he didn't respond to the questions about Blue immediately. To his surprise, Dali answered. "He's a purebred Hairless Saint Bernard, and he's wearing a coat because he doesn't have fur of his own. The blue stuff isn't his fur, of course! It's his little furry sweatshirt."

When they had gotten rid of the Girl Scouts and gotten themselves, Cloud, Blue, Merlin's report, and six boxes of assorted Girl Scout cookies into the car, Merlin said, "You're a natural. You should try running rat roulette some time."

Dali chuckled, but it sounded a little forced. But before he could inquire, she said, "Are the cookies for your teammates?"

"My raptor would love to eat them all himself, but yeah. No way am I eating six boxes of Girl Scout cookies. Take whatever you want, though."

"I'll just nab a few at the office."

But it was not to be. When they parked at Defenders, Merlin discovered that Blue, with incredible stealth for a bugbear so big that he barely fit into the car, had managed to snake every single box into the back seat, slit them neatly open with a claw, scatter the cookies all over the floor, and eat most of the Lemonades, which were apparently his favorites.

Dali stared at the mess. "I can't believe he did all that without either of us seeing or hearing a thing!"

Cloud buzzed down to the floor, sampled a Thin Mint, and spat in disgust.

The Samoa on the seat still looks good, his raptor said hopefully.

"So much for treating my teammates," Merlin said. "At least he didn't eat the report... No!"

As Blue squirmed out of the back seat, printed pages fluttered down. Every one of them was chewed up and wet with bugbear spit.

"Blue!" Merlin yelled.

Blue rushed at Merlin, nearly bowling him over, and began rubbing himself against his legs, stump tail wagging madly in guilty apology.

"How did he *do* that?" Dali said. "It was right there next to us!"

"Same way he gets into locked houses, I guess," Merlin said glumly, gathering up the damp pages. "Magic."

"I'll vouch that none of this was your fault," Dali assured him.

"Don't bother. I'm not a kid being hauled up before the principal. Roland can think whatever he likes."

Merlin knew exactly what Roland would think of his drooled-on pages. And what Pete and Carter and Ransom and even Tirzah would think. Every time he'd tried to do something nice for them that had gone wrong, every annoyed glance in his direction, every yell of "Merlin!" echoed in his mind.

The only reason he could think of *not* to run away with the circus was that Dali might not want to go with him. He tried to think of a tactful way to ask if she could possibly see herself joining the circus, then gave up. He'd figure it out later.

But if it turned out that she wanted to stay in Refuge City, he could always find some other job in the city. He didn't have to stick with a team where he'd never fit in.

At that instant, Merlin made his decision.

"I'm done with Defenders," he said.

Dali stared at him. "Seriously?"

"Seriously." He turned away from her, stabbing moodily at the elevator buttons. "I mean, not this second. I still have to finish my job for you. But after that, I'm giving my notice. I've had a lot of jobs in my life, and I don't have to stick with this one when there's so many other possibilities out there."

The elevator dinged, and they stepped inside. Dali was bent over for some time, making sure Blue was all the way in, so he couldn't see her face. He had the uneasy sense that something was wrong. But when she finally looked up, it was only to squeeze his hand and say, "You need to live the life that's best for you."

The elevator doors opened to show Roland looming in front of them, his arms folded across his chest. He looked down at the tattered report in Merlin's hand with a "Son, I am disappoint" expression. "Seriously, Merlin?"

Carter looked up from the machine he had on the table, then moved to shield it with his body. "Keep that indigo menace away from my stuff!"

Ransom glanced up from a file he was reading. "Put the Girl Scout cookies in a lock box next time."

Tirzah and Pete were there with Caro, his thirteen-year-old daughter. Tirzah and Caro both zeroed in on Merlin at the phrase "Girl Scout cookies."

"You brought Girl Scout cookies?" Tirzah asked.

"Gimme!" demanded Caro, stretching out her hand. Moonbow, her pet miniature pegasus, let out a hopeful whinny.

"Sorry, guys," said Merlin. "Blue ate them while we were driving here."

"Why'd you put them in the back with him?" Pete asked.

"He didn't," Dali began, but it was drowned out in a chorus of complaints from Caro and Tirzah about Merlin's lack of cookies, from Pete about his lack of common sense, from Ransom about his lack of foresight, from Carter about his lack of control over Blue, and from Roland about his lack of an unchewed report.

I am so done with these guys, thought Merlin.

His phone rang. Stepping away from the commotion, he answered it. "Hello?"

It was his mother, but he didn't immediately recognize her voice. She was always so calm, but she sounded frantic. He had to hold the phone away from his ear, her voice was so loud. "We have an emergency! I need you at the circus!"

Alarmed, Merlin said, "I'll be right there. What's going on?"

"We've been set up! Someone's trying to ruin us… and they just might do it."

"Mom, tell me what's happening."

His mother took a deep breath, then another. "We're getting two surprise inspections. From two different agencies."

"What? Which ones?"

"One is from the USDA, on suspicion of violating the Animal Welfare Act. They'll be checking our animals to make sure we're treating them right. The other one is the FBI, on suspicion of not being a real circus, but just a front for criminal activity. And they're coordinating, so one inspector will be backstage to watch the animals, and the other one will be in the audience to see if we're capable of putting on a real show."

"Oh, fuck," Merlin blurted out.

It was a sign of how upset she was that his mother not only didn't reprove him for swearing, but didn't even seem to notice. "And they're doing the joint inspection at our show tonight. In three hours."

Words did not cover the horror of this. He could do nothing but groan.

Kalpana's voice cut in; apparently Mom was on speakerphone. "Actually, it's now two hours and forty-five minutes."

"If we don't pass the inspections, the circus will be shut down," Mom said. "Permanently. And we could go to jail."

The note of suppressed panic in Mom's voice made Merlin realize that he had to step up to the plate. "Mom. Nobody's going to jail. And you're not going to lose the circus. All we need to do is prove that our animals are fine and we're a real circus."

"Yes, exactly," Mom said. "By doing a complete show with only half our regular company because we can't shift with inspectors backstage. And we were already shorthanded with Natalie gone."

Kalpana added, "We're not just proving that we're a real show, we're proving that we can bring in the amount of money we've been claiming on taxes. So it doesn't just have to be a real show, it has to be a *good* show. And we can't do anything drastically different from what our reviews have talked about, or it'll be obvious there's something up."

"So we can't only do the animal acts and cut the human ones," Merlin said with another groan. "Got it. Well—I can be an acrobat and a trapeze artist and a clown and whatever else you need."

"Thank you," said his mother. "I knew you'd come through. The problem is, we don't need one more stand-in. We need ten more. At least. Some of us are going to be stuck pretending to be animal trainers who unlock the cages and lead the animals in and out. Everyone's calling their shifter friends, but most of them don't live in Refuge City and can't get here in time."

Dali's hand came down over Merlin's shoulder and hit the speakerphone button.

"It's Dali," she said. "I'm not a shifter and I can't do acrobatics. But if you could use someone to climb out of a clown car in a red nose, you've got two more stand-ins, not one."

Merlin kissed her, not caring what his teammates—his soon-to-be-former teammates—might think. "You're the best. I'm sure we can find something for you to do."

The familiar sound of wheels over wood came to Merlin's ears as Tirzah came forward. "Hi, this is Tirzah, one of Merlin's teammates. I don't know how useful I'd be since I'm not a shifter either. Also, I use a wheelchair, so I can't do the clown car. But if there's any acts that you can do sitting down, you've got three more helpers."

Merlin was startled and touched. He and Tirzah had always been friends, but he'd never expected anything like this. It could almost make him reconsider…

Pete made a noise like a hibernating bear reluctantly roused from his den, then said, "Four more. I'm Pete, another one of Merlin's teammates. I'm a bear shifter, if that's useful. A cave bear, but I doubt that anyone in the audience would recognize one."

Merlin's jaw dropped. It wasn't only Pete's unexpected offer of help, but that he was willing to transform in public. As far as Merlin knew, Pete had never done that voluntarily.

"Dad!" Caro tugged at Pete's arm. "Please, please, please, can I volunteer? You know Merlin's been teaching me to do acrobatics!"

Pete gave her a quelling look. "You're not getting on a trapeze. I don't care if it has a net."

Mom spoke up. "Pete, is she your daughter? If you're willing, I could show you what the circus children normally do in our acts. I promise you, we never allow them to do anything that could put them in danger."

Pete clearly recognized a genuine Mom voice when he heard one. "Well… Okay. I'll bring her with me, and we'll see."

"Five more!" Caro said jubilantly.

"Six more." Roland gave Merlin a startlingly mischievous smile. "I'm Roland, their boss. I wouldn't be able to show my shift form and I don't think I could fit in a clown car, but if you just need a warm body, you could put me to use."

"Seven," said Ransom. He sounded more resigned than enthusiastic, but he added, "I can juggle."

Carter glared at Merlin. He glared at the phone. He glared at his team. He glared at Blue, who had flopped down and was drooling on his expensive shoes. He muttered "Not my circus, not my monkeys." Merlin was about to tell him he didn't have to do anything he didn't want to do, when he heaved a gigantic, put-upon sigh, and said, "Eight."

Over the speakerphone, his mother's voice rang out clearly. "Thank you all, so much. You're our saviors. It does my heart good to know my son has such loyal friends."

"Come straight over," Kalpana said. "We're holding an emergency planning session. Don't worry about costumes or makeup. We have plenty. And thank you!"

The line went dead. In the silence that fell, Merlin looked around the room. There wasn't a single person in it who hadn't stood up to help him and his family.

"I…" Merlin stammered, at a complete loss for words. "I don't know what to say."

"Save it," Carter advised. "If the future of your crime circus depends on getting people to pay to watch Ransom juggle, you may end up sorry we volunteered."

"No, really," Merlin said, and then ran down again. Finally, he said, "Thank you. Thank you all."

It didn't seem remotely adequate. How could he have ever thought his team didn't like him? They'd instantly stepped up to help him out, and in a way that would genuinely cost them. Tirzah was introverted and disliked interacting with strangers. Ransom went way out of his way to avoid notice. Roland was the least show-offy person Merlin had ever met. Carter was supremely protective of his own dignity. Pete didn't even like *talking* about his cave bear, let alone displaying it to a giant audience. And yet they'd all volunteered to do things that would make them deeply uncomfortable, without him even asking.

And it wasn't just his team. Dali would normally never help criminals foil the FBI. But she hadn't hesitated.

There was one person for whom it wouldn't be a sacrifice. Caro looked positively gleeful.

"Could we disguise the pets and use them in our acts?" she asked hopefully.

"NO!" The reply rang out from everyone's throats, Merlin's included.

"Too much potential for things going wrong," Pete said. "The pets stay here."

"Alone?" Carter exclaimed in horror. "They'll trash the place!"

"We could lock them all in Merlin's office," Roland suggested.

In fact, that was more-or-less what they did. Blue and Cloud were locked in Merlin's office, and Spike, Batcat, and Caro's miniature pegasus Moonbow were locked in Pete's office.

Though they had food, water, toys, and company, Merlin had some distinct misgivings about the whole thing. As he gave Blue a farewell pat, he murmured, "Please don't get bored."

As Merlin ran out with Dali, followed by the rest of the team plus Caro, he reconsidered his earlier resolution to leave Defenders. The last fifteen minutes had completely changed his perception of his team. Sure, they were a bunch of misfits. But so was he. Most importantly, they were a bunch of misfits who liked him and would do *anything* for him—or even for someone they'd never met, but whom he cared about.

Merlin really hoped that would be enough. It would break his mother's heart if the circus was destroyed. And it would break his too.

Could a bunch of totally untrained misfits step into the shoes of highly trained professionals and do their jobs well enough to fool the FBI?

CHAPTER 18

Dali walked into a scene of chaos and panic. The entire company had gathered inside the big top. People were madly rushing around with armloads of costumes and equipment, kittens and baby sea lions were bouncing and flopping underfoot, and a man was struggling into a much-too-small spangled leotard and swearing. The only people who seemed calm were Janet and Kalpana, who were in a huddle over a clipboard.

A little boy gleefully said, "Mom, I'm ready to poop in the tiger cage!" A moment later, a woman strode out with a tiger cub at her heels.

A sense of utter calm come over Dali. This was a situation she felt entirely capable of handling. In the Navy, she'd often had to deal with complex tasks involving many people with different jobs, some of whom were substituting for others, with objectives that had arisen at a moment's notice.

Merlin put his hand between her shoulderblades. "Remind you of anything?"

She nodded, warmed by his understanding.

"You got this," he said.

"Yes, I do," she replied. For the first time since the bombing, she felt completely at home in a job.

Like a fish back in water, she thought. *Or a sailor returning to sea.*

Together they joined Janet and Kalpana. Merlin and his mother hugged, and then he indicated Dali. "This is exactly her kind of problem. She can help."

Dali, Kalpana, Janet, and Merlin sat down together, examining a neatly organized breakdown of the acts, who was in them, and in what form. As Dali helped them sort out substitutions, the rest of the Defenders began to arrive. Merlin waved them over to introduce them and get them assigned to roles.

"Can you ride a unicycle?" Janet asked Pete. "I mean as a bear."

As Caro burst into giggles, Pete looked horrified. "I can't even ride one as a human!"

"Mia!" Kalpana shouted.

A slim woman in a leotard ran over. "Yes?"

"Pete here is going to be the bear tonight, so we can keep you on trapeze with Pia. Can you teach him to ride the unicycle?"

"In two hours?" Mia asked dubiously.

Janet fixed her with what Dali suspected was an alpha stare. "If you want this circus to still exist tomorrow... yes, in two hours."

Mia laid her tiny hand on Pete's muscular forearm and led him away. Over his shoulder, he called, "Tirzah, don't let Caro do anything dangerous!"

"I won't!" Tirzah called back.

Janet smiled at Caro. "You must be Caro. Thank you for volunteering. If Merlin trained you, you must be good."

Caro waved her hand as if to brush off the compliment, but she looked delighted. "Not like you guys. I don't know trapeze. But I can do floor exercises. And I can ride horses."

"Excellent." Janet examined her. "How would you like to ride an elephant? I think you could fit into Shondra's costume, and we need her to be a sea lion."

Caro looked like she would explode with joy. She clutched at Tirzah's arm. "That's not dangerous!"

Tirzah grinned. "Since I assume the elephant is a shifter, I don't see how it could be. Fine by me."

"Renu! Shondra!" shouted Kalpana. Renu and a young woman of about Caro's height and build ran up. "Caro here will be subbing for you as the elephant rider, Shondra." To Tirzah, she said, "Renu's the elephant."

They went off together, Caro saying delightedly, "I'm inviting ALL my friends!"

"I don't know if there's anything I can do," Tirzah said. Indicating her wheelchair, she said in a perfect deadpan, "I can't shift."

Dali snickered, but Janet said, "I have the perfect job for you. I play the talking parrot and Madame Fortuna, the psychic. I have a system for how I 'read the audience's minds,' but I'd need to teach you sleight of hand. There's no time for that. But maybe if you keep your phone in your lap, we could email you information about them in real time…?"

"I can do one better than that," Tirzah said. "I can photograph them from under the table, then do reverse image searches on them to get information. It'll blow their minds."

"Excellent," said Janet. "You have the instincts of a true con artist."

Dali was indignant on Tirzah's behalf, but Tirzah grinned. "Don't tell, but have you ever heard of a hacker called Override? Takes down dirty politicians and evil corporations, exposes corrupt—"

Janet looked blank, but Kalpana exclaimed, "*You're* Override? You're my hero! We have to talk after the show."

Dali cleared her throat, steering everyone back on track. "Moving on. How about the juggling act?"

"That act needs four people," Kalpana said. "My mom absolutely can't do it because she's the only elephant. Ransom… er…"

"How good of a juggler are you, really?" Janet asked bluntly.

Ransom shrugged. "You'd have to judge that, not me."

"Anyone got any balls?" Dali called.

She was answered with a burst of laughter and scattered replies of "Me! I do! Big ones!" Larry Duffy cupped his hands at his crotch, suggesting that he had either a pair of watermelons hidden in his pants or a serious medical condition.

"Thanks a lot, wiseguys," said Dali. "We're auditioning Ransom here as a juggler, and we need some stuff for him to—"

A striped ball, a coffee mug, a donut with sprinkles, and a tennis shoe flew in his direction. Ransom caught them neatly and tossed them in the air, juggling them with impressive deftness. They were followed by a red clown nose, a fake flower that squirted water, and a giant clown shoe. Ransom incorporated them into his juggling routine without missing a beat.

"Very impressive," said Janet. "Let's see how you do with a partner. Hitoshi!"

A flying squirrel, a cat, and a poodle leaped off the back of a sleek black stallion. The horse became a muscular young man. A stark naked muscular young man. Dali averted her gaze for a moment. When she looked up, he'd pulled on a pair of pants and was tossing objects back and forth with Ransom. Donut sprinkles pattered to the floor, but nothing else hit the ground.

"Excellent!" Janet called. "Okay, enough. Ransom, you can stand in for Renu. Hitoshi, Steve, Nora, teach him the routine."

Hitoshi and Ransom caught and put down the juggled objects, one by one. Ransom concluded by stooping down, picking up a discarded paper plate, and catching the last flying object—the donut—on it.

Merlin started the applause. Dali joined in, followed by the rest of his team and the watching circus members. Ransom took a bow. Dali, looking closely, saw something in his eyes that she'd never seen before: happiness, brief but genuine. It transformed him, making him look ten years younger.

He went off with Hitoshi. They both made a wide detour to avoid Pete, who was an immense mass of shaggy brown fur grimly trying to pedal a unicycle and growling to himself.

Janet turned to Roland. "And what do you do?"

There was a mischievous glint in his eyes as he said, "I can lift heavy objects."

Janet gave an admiring glance to his muscles. "I bet you can! Excellent. That'll kill two birds with one stone: you can do the strong man act, which will free up Leopold to stay a lion, and we get to see you take off your shirt."

"Mom!" Merlin said. His ears were turning bright red. Dali couldn't help snickering.

Kalpana's eyes widened with excitement. "Oh! Speaking of his shirt coming off, maybe he can do that twice. We need all our big cats as big cats, so Tawny Lyon has to be a lion. And that means we're missing a target girl. Maybe Roland could do that too."

"What's a target girl?" Roland asked.

Merlin reached out and gave the target wheel a spin. "You get tied to that, and flying squirrels throw knives at you."

Roland shook his head. "Sorry. I feel sick just imagining that."

"Isn't there *anyone* here who doesn't get motion sickness?" Janet said despairingly. "We can't cut it—it's one of the centerpieces of the entire show. Every review raves about it!"

Carter, who had been standing in awkward, appalled silence ever since he'd come in, cleared his throat. Looking like he was volunteering to test a new bulletproof vest, he said, "I'm a pilot. And once I paid for a seat on an aircraft that did parabolas to let the passengers experience weightlessness. They don't call it the Vomit Comet for nothing. I was the only person on the flight who actually had a good time."

"Excellent," said Janet. "Congratulations, you're a target boy. Tawny! Find him a sexy outfit and teach him to smile and wave."

Dali wouldn't have imagined that Carter could look any more pained, but he did. "I know how to smile and wave."

"You don't look it," said Janet, and dismissed him and Tawny with a snap of her fingers. "Now how are we doing?"

"It's looking a lot more do-able, thanks to Merlin's team," said Kalpana. "But if Hitoshi's a juggler, then we're short a horse."

"If we cut him as a horse, then we're also cutting his riders," said Dali, studying their notes. "So that takes one poodle, one cat, and one flying squirrel out of the act, and it leaves Fausto Fratelli, Linda Liu, and Renard Richelieu as humans."

"That works," said Janet. "We need Fausto on trapeze anyway. And I'd hate to lose Linda as a tightrope walker. But Renard doesn't do anything essential as a human."

"You could keep him as a poodle and have him take Claudette's place," Dali suggested. "Then Claudette stays human, and you keep her as an acrobat."

"Yes, good," said Janet. "But we're still short on stagehands. And clowns for the clown car."

"Roland and Ransom could help with the scene changes," said Kalpana. "Roland's too big for the clown car, but Ransom and Carter could double as clowns."

Carter, who was alternating between plastering on a smile when Tawny was watching him and looking like he was being held at gunpoint when she wasn't, let out a yelp of horror.

"If Janet needs you to be a clown, then you're a clown," Roland said firmly.

With a muttered "Fine, fine," Carter spread his arms and allowed Tawny to tie him to the wheel.

Bobby Duffy came pelting up to Janet, followed by four teenagers. "I brought help! They're pigeon shifters, and they're gonna save the circus!"

Then all five of them noticed Dali. The four strangers looked incredibly guilty and nervous, and Bobby shot her a pleading, "don't tell" look.

Dali smiled at the necklace thieves who had started it all. Now that she saw them, it was obvious that they were kids who'd played a prank that had gotten out of hand, not hardened criminals. Besides, if they hadn't stolen her necklace, she'd never have met Cloud. Or Merlin. "Pleased to meet you all. Thank you so much for coming. What can you do?"

In a relieved babble they explained that they had no special skills, but would be happy to be stagehands, clown car clowns, errand runners, and anything else that might be useful. Kalpana and Dali assigned them and sent them on their way.

A disgruntled-looking cave bear rode slowly and wobblingly by on a unicycle. Merlin let out a very sudden, very loud cheer of "YEAH, PETE!" causing Pete to almost fall over. He gave a growl that made Dali's hair stand on end as he recovered his balance and rode on by.

"I can't decide if that's hilarious or strangely disturbing," Merlin mused.

Janet cleared her throat. "Merlin, how do you feel about filling in every role we have left over that won't need you to be in two places at once?"

He leaned over, rapidly scanning the clipboard. "Trapeze artist, clown car clown, acrobat, squirrel ring holder... No problem. In fact, I can't wait!" He patted his mother's shoulder. "Don't worry, mom. The circus is as good as saved."

The stage lights shone on Merlin's hair, turning it to pure gold. He stood lightly on the balls of his feet, poised as if to leap or tumble or grab a trapeze bar and fly through the air. His expression, the light in his sky-blue eyes, every line of his athletic body spoke of hope and joy and freedom. Dali had never seen him happier, or more perfectly *himself.*

It's the circus, she thought. *This is where he belongs.*

Then she thought, *Could it be where I belong, too?*

She'd experienced what the circus life would be like for her, helping Kalpana and Janet run things. And Dali couldn't lie: she enjoyed it. Would it really be so bad to stay on, doing the sort of job she loved, with Merlin by her side?

Sure, it was a crime circus. But their crimes weren't the *bad* sort of crimes. And sure, they never settled down, but they took their home with them. Sure, it was a life devoted to play and fun, but that was good and needed. She'd experienced a life without joy, and it had been no life at all. Sure, some of the members were prejudiced against non-shifters,

203

but the majority of them weren't. And it wasn't like any society was free of bias. Sure, she wouldn't see Grandma much, but that had also been true when she'd been in the Navy. Sure...

There were a lot of *sures.*

Visiting the circus was wonderful, like being at the best party in the world. Joining the circus would be like never being able to leave the party. It was a good life for the people who loved it, but it wasn't a life for her. She'd end up feeling as trapped and frustrated as the circus people would be if they joined the Navy.

But this is Merlin's home, Dali thought. *It's not a trap for him, it's the place where he feels most free.*

I can't be the person who keeps him from the place where he truly belongs. If she really loved him, she'd have to let him go.

CHAPTER 19

Merlin was having the time of his life. As a Marine, as a bodyguard, and flying high on the trapeze, he'd experienced that same pure focus in the face of danger, knowing he was doing something important with his comrades beside him. Only this time he had Dali beside him, and that lifted him higher than he'd ever flown before.

She'd stepped into a scene of total chaos, and turned it into a complex but working machine. She was calm and competent and clever, even when confronted with a totally unfamiliar setting. She was selfless, and she was kind. No one had asked or expected her to volunteer to help out, but she'd done so instantly, without a second thought, because Merlin and his mother and his circus family had needed her.

Dali sent Bobby Duffy to make sure the clown car was running, then sent one of the pigeon teenagers to post a list of jobs backstage. Before she could start another task, he said, "Hey, Dali?"

She turned to him, and the beauty of her dark eyes overwhelmed him.

I love her, Merlin realized. *I'm in love with her. I'd do anything for her. She's the best thing that ever happened to me. She's—*

His raptor interrupted his realization, speaking in a voice that Merlin almost didn't recognize. It was deeper. More mature. It rang out like a church bell, shaking him to the core of his being. *She's our mate.*

Merlin was stunned. And yet somehow, he wasn't surprised. Of course she was his mate. Of course they were meant for each other. Of course they would love each other till the day they died.

My mate, he thought, savoring the words.

The wizard-scientists had managed to delay his recognition of her as his mate, but they hadn't destroyed it. Nor had they severed his ability to bond. And now that he had met Dali, he understood why. They were bound together, soul-deep, heart-deep. No magic or science could ever keep them apart.

"Yes?" Dali said.

Merlin realized that he'd gotten her attention, then stood there silently, lost in his own thoughts. He opened his mouth to say, "I love you."

A little girl rushed by, screaming over her shoulder, "You can't catch me! Nyah-nyah-nyah!" at a pursuing tiger cub and a flying squirrel. Another young flying squirrel dropped down from above and plastered himself across her face like the face-hugger in *Aliens.*

The girl gave a shriek and veered to the side, putting her on a collision course with Pete, who was still grimly practicing his unicycle. He tried to stop, failed, and threw himself to the side, falling with a thud that shook the entire tent. The tightrope walkers fell off and landed in the net, cups of coffee fell off tables, and the little girl pitched face-first into a wall of shaggy brown fur.

"Whee!" she squealed. Then she picked herself up, pried the squirrel off her face and said, "I'm sorry, Mr. Bear. Did I hurt you?"

Pete transformed back into a man to say, "No. Don't worry about it."

Then he gave the unicycle a look of utter loathing before becoming a bear again and climbing back on, grunting and growling in a low mutter.

"You were saying?" Dali asked Merlin, her eyebrows raised in that sardonic arch that he loved. But then, he loved everything about her.

"I—"

"NO I'm not oiling my chest!" Carter said, fending off Pia, who was waving an oil jar at him.

"You have to! All target boys do," she insisted, shoving the jar into his hand. "If you don't, you'll look wrong."

To the universe at large, Carter said, "I don't even work here!"

Merlin tried again. "Dali, I wanted to tell you—"

Kalpana hurried up. "Dali, can you review the clowns for the clown car with me? I'm worried we don't have enough."

Merlin gave up. It was clearly not the time. And now that he thought about it, while "I love you" was at least a universally known concept, "We're true mates" was not, and he needed more time to explain that than he'd have until this show was over.

"Break a leg," said Merlin to them both. To Dali, he said, "It means 'good luck.' In the circus, it's bad luck to wish someone good luck before a performance, so you wish them bad luck instead and that wishes them good luck."

Dali blinked a few times. "Got it. I think."

"And in case no one's said so recently, you're amazing and you're doing an amazing job. It's so great to see you getting to show your stuff. Especially here, my favorite place in the world!"

But she didn't seem happy to hear that. Instead, such a sad expression crossed her face that it worried him. But before he could ask what was wrong, Ransom abruptly dropped the balls he'd been juggling. They went bouncing around the ring as he said, "The inspectors are coming."

For a moment nobody moved. The Duffys had been dispatched to wait outside the fairgrounds to give early warning of the inspectors' approach, but they hadn't showed up yet.

"How do you know?" Hitoshi asked Ransom.

"He knows," said Merlin. Raising his voice, he said, "If Ransom says so, it's true!"

"The inspectors are coming!" Mom called, using her alpha voice. "From now on, obey Kalpana and Merlin as if they were me!"

Her clothes hit the floor as she turned into a parrot.

"Places, everyone!" Kalpana shouted. "Take your places, NOW!"

Clothes fell in piles as the smaller shifters transformed in a hurry. The big ones, who'd destroy their clothing if they did that, had all already shifted. Clowns and acrobats and lions and tigers and squirrels and pigeons rushed backstage, the humans scooping up discarded clothing and stray props on their way out.

Merlin and Dali made a circuit of the ring, picking up any stray items that were left behind while Kalpana paced around in their wake, ticking items off a checklist. They'd nearly finished when a pair of sparrows came flapping in. They landed on the floor and turned into a pair of hairy-backed middle-aged men. Naked. Of course.

"The inspectors are here," said Larry Duffy.

"You've got ten minutes... Wow, you're way ahead of us," said Billy Duffy.

"Thank you so much for your help," said Kalpana to Dali. "I know this isn't your problem."

"Don't worry about it." Dali clapped her on the shoulder. "We can do this."

Kalpana chewed nervously on the end of a long black braid, realized what she was doing and hurled it back over her shoulder, took a deep breath, then glanced at Merlin. "Want to come with me to meet the inspectors? You're much better at charming people than I am."

"Sure," Merlin began, then frowned. His goddamn useless, uncontrollable power might be on, and if it was—

It's not on, said his raptor. *Can't you feel it?*

Merlin realized that in fact, he could. He couldn't have described how he knew, but he did, the same way he knew left from right.

I guess it just took practice, he thought. *Thank God. No more frappuccinos to the face!*

He turned to share his good news with Dali, but she'd vanished backstage. As he followed Kalpana, he decided to tell Dali afterward. She had a lot to do and a lot to remember, and he didn't want to distract her.

Mom flew up and perched on Kalpana's shoulder. In as soft a squawk as she could manage as a parrot, she said, "Break a leg."

"I'll go check on the animal car," Dali said. "If they're not ready, I'll send someone out to stall for time."

Dali headed for the train, and the rest of them went out to meet the inspectors. They consisted of one very intense, no-nonsense white man, who introduced himself as Mr. Varnham of Animal Welfare, and one very intense, no-nonsense black woman, who introduced herself as Ms. Moore of the FBI.

Merlin put on his most charming smile. "Welcome to the Fabulous Flying Chameleons! I'm Merlin Merrick, trapeze artist and jack of all trades, and this is Kalpana Doubek, our stage manager. We'll be the point people to show you around and get you settled in before the show. If you have any questions, just ask us."

"Pieces of eight!" Mom squawked.

Merlin's raptor burst out laughing. Merlin bit his lip.

Kalpana gulped, then said, "This is Goldie. Say hello to the inspectors, Goldie."

"Hello inspectors!" squawked Mom. "I'm Goldie, the amazing talking parrot!"

Mr. Varnham looked very closely at Mom, then grudgingly said, "Seems like a healthy parrot. I notice her wings aren't clipped."

"Oh, no," said Merlin. "That would be cruel. Goldie likes to fly."

"It can be dangerous for a tame bird to be allowed to fly freely, though," said Mr. Varnham. "They don't know to avoid predators."

"She's very well-trained," said Kalpana. "She knows to only fly inside."

"Polly want a circus ticket?" squawked Mom, then imitated a toilet flushing.

Neither of the inspectors looked amused. In fact, neither of them looked *capable* of being amused.

"We'd like to see the animal cages," said Ms. Moore. "Now, please."

They headed for the animal car, with Merlin explaining their train system. The inspectors nodded, unsmiling.

"Surely you're not taking the parrot near the large animal cages!" said Mr. Varnham.

"Er, no," said Kalpana. "Of course not." She handed off Mom to the first person she saw, one of the pigeon shifter teenagers, saying, "Please take Goldie backstage."

Merlin was relieved to see Dali waiting for them outside of the animal car. That meant that all the shifters who'd be animals tonight were in place. She introduced herself as the assistant stage manager and their point person during the show, when Merlin and Kalpana would be busy, and then they all went in to see the animals.

Tawny, Leona, and Leopold lounged in the lion's cage, grooming each other and trying to look as happy as possible. Larry Duffy, playing the big cat trainer, introduced them, discussed their care and feeding, and offered to let the inspectors pet them.

Tawny got up and rubbed her head against the bars, letting Larry scratch behind her ears. Mr. Varnham declined, but Ms. Moore remarked, "Who knows when I'll ever visit a circus again?" and gave her a quick pet. Her expression softened a tiny bit. "Her fur's like velvet!"

"The cages are roomy and clean," Mr. Varnham said, a little grudgingly. "*Very* clean. And the lions seem healthy and relaxed."

Behind the inspectors' backs, Dali squeezed Merlin's hand. He squeezed it back gratefully. Hope was building in his heart. The cages were incredibly clean, far more so than any last-minute cleaning could possibly have managed. The shifters were working overtime to seem as happy and unstressed as possible: the sea lions swam and played in their tank, the flying squirrels glided around and cracked nuts, the tigers lounged and licked their paws, the cats and poodles slept and played, and the horses waited placidly in their stalls.

"We always set up camp by a field where the horses can graze and gallop, of course," Kalpana explained. "They're in their stalls now because they're about to perform."

"The cats and dogs live with their owners," Merlin added. "The cages are just so we don't have to round them up for the show."

"Hmph," said Mr. Varnham, but he could find nothing to criticize. He did, however, fix Merlin and Kalpana with an eagle eye and say,

"Keeping the animals in good conditions is only part of what we're looking for. I can't come to any conclusions until I see how they're treated backstage and onstage."

And then they came to Pete. The cage was big for Mia, but small for Pete, so he was lying down in an attempt to minimize his size. It didn't work. He was enormous, his claws long and sharp as daggers, his black eyes glittering with intelligence and ferocity. Everything about him spoke of the majesty and terror of the prehistoric beasts which had once ruled the earth.

The inspectors stopped still, staring at him.

Pete, who had presumably been instructed to look happy, began nosing at a ball with the same grim determination that he'd had riding the unicycle.

Merlin had to work hard to keep a straight face. Inside his mind, his raptor was rolling around on the ground in hysterics.

"Is that a Kodiak bear?" Mr. Varnham asked. "It's enormous!"

"Yes," said Kalpana. "Yes, he's a Kodiak."

"It's not at the level of a violation of the Animal Welfare Act," Mr. Varnham said. "But all your other animals are in very roomy cages, and comparatively, this one is too small."

"I absolutely agree," said Merlin. "He's grown too big for us, actually. We're in negotiations to donate him to a zoo."

Pete gave a soft growl. Everyone involuntarily stepped back.

"Yes…" said Mr. Varnham, eyeing him and taking a second step back. "Yes, I think that's for the best. He doesn't seem happy here."

Merlin, unable to resist, said, "I think he'll be happier when he's with his own kind."

Pete fixed him with a deadly glare and gave a warning huff.

Hurriedly, Kalpana said, "Mr. Varnham, Ms. Moore, let's get you two set up for the show."

She hustled them out, Merlin and Dali following. They glanced at each other, unable to speak without being overheard. Merlin's amusement faded away when he saw the look on her face. Once again, she seemed so sad. What was wrong?

Cautiously, he said, "How's everything going?"

Dali's dark eyes studied his face. For the first time since they'd met, he thought she was hiding something from him. And he was convinced of it when she put on a fake smile and said, "Fine, Merlin. Everything's fine. Good luck with the show! "A second later, she said, "I mean, break a leg!"

But he had a feeling that the damage had been done.

CHAPTER 20

I'm doing the right thing, Dali thought. *And I have to stop thinking about it, or I'll be so heartbroken that I'll be distracted from my job. The show has to succeed. It'll be my good-bye gift to Merlin.*

She widened her fake smile, then hurried to catch up Kalpana and the inspectors. Once the show started, Dali would be in charge of making Mr. Varnham comfortable and answering any questions he might have, as Kalpana would be in the stage manager's booth above the audience, running the lights and sound. Dali would also be in charge of making sure that Mr. Varnham didn't see anything suspicious.

Kalpana left to escort Ms. Moore to her seat in the audience. Backstage, Dali escorted Mr. Varnham to the chair and tiny desk they'd set up for him. "Here you go. You can see most of backstage from here, and watch how the animals are treated. You'll also be able to see them perform, though it won't be the best view. If you need me, just wave. But please don't move from this spot without some escorting you. We'll have animals taken in and out, and people moving heavy scenery—it could be very dangerous."

"I understand," he said. But Dali caught his wistful glance at the several coffee makers backstage, placed carefully away from the action. Unexpectedly, she found herself sympathizing with him. He was obviously doing his best at a difficult job, and just as obviously liked animals.

"Cream and sugar?" she asked.

For the first time, he cracked a smile. "Yes, please."

She fetched him a cup, then took off. She had to get away from the inspectors and Merlin and… Well, mostly Merlin. It was breaking her heart every time she looked at him.

Focus, Dali told herself. *Pretend you're not planning to break up with him. It's the only way you'll get through this show. And for his sake, you need to get through the show.*

Outside, in the cool night air, she took several breaths to steady herself. A full moon was rising. It was a beautiful night. They'd already passed part of the inspection, with the happy animals in their nice clean cages. They just needed to get through one performance. They could do it.

She could do it.

She owed Merlin that much, at least.

Dali returned backstage and watched with amusement as Merlin and the designated "squirrel trainer" carried a cage full of flying squirrels inside. A light of suppressed laughter danced in his eyes as he opened the cage. One by one, the squirrels were handed tiny knives, which they clutched in their teeth as they scampered up the ladder and into the rigging, where they would wait for their performance.

Mr. Varnham watched this procedure closely, but seemed to find no fault with it. Nor did he frown when the "cat trainer" walked in with a precise line of cats following her, and made clicking sounds to command them to sit down in their designated area, which was a giant cushion.

Max was ready in his ringmaster's outfit, his top hat perched on his head, his giant moustache freshly curled. Roland and Ransom, both dressed in stagehand black, waited on either side of the target.

"Where's the target boy?" Max asked.

"You may have to go fetch him," said Roland.

"No, they're shoving him out of the dressing room now," Ransom said.

Carter emerged from the dressing room where he'd been hiding, looking immensely pained, wearing boots, skin-tight sparkly pants, and nothing else. Eyeliner accentuated his hazel eyes. As he stepped into a well-lit area, his chest glistened. A giggle escaped Dali's lips, and he glared at her. Ominously, he said, "It's not too late to trade places, you know."

Pretending she hadn't heard, Dali picked up one of the headsets, which was how Kalpana communicated from the stage manager's booth. "How are we doing?"

"Fine, fine," said Kalpana. "How are *you* doing?"

"Everything looks good here. I've got Mr. Varnham set up with coffee."

Kalpana gave an unexpected giggle. "I've got Ms. Moore set up with soda and popcorn. She wasn't going to accept it, but I pointed out to her that everyone else had drinks and snacks, and she might stand out if she didn't. She insisted on paying for it, though. I have to respect a woman that dedicated to her job."

"So do I." And Dali could think of another woman who was dedicated to her job. "Hey, Kalpana, can I ask you a personal question?"

"Sure."

"Were you ever in the running to be heir to the circus?"

"Oh, I'm not eligible," Kalpana said. "I can't shift. And you know how much trouble that caused Merlin."

"He wasn't a shifter when Janet chose him, though."

Without bitterness, Kalpana said simply, "Yes, but he's her son. Oh—can you call five minutes, please?"

Dali walked around backstage, outside, and in the dressing rooms, calling, "Five minutes, please! Five minutes till showtime!"

She was answered with a chorus of "Thank you, five minutes!" plus a few groans. Dali also received a remarkably dirty look from Fausto Fratelli, presumably because she was Merlin's girlfriend and thus an enemy by association.

By the time she had finished her rounds, five minutes had passed. The headset light was blinking with Kalpana's call sign. Dali picked it up.

"Call places," said Kalpana. "It's showtime."

Dali ran around calling, "Places, please! Take your places, please, the show is about to begin!"

When she was done, she breathlessly picked up the headset and reported, "Everyone's in place."

As the lights went down in the ring, a familiar presence stepped up beside her, sending a familiar thrill down her spine and warmth to her heart. Merlin whispered in her ear, "It's showtime."

Max strode onstage. From where Dali stood, she could look out from the side and see most of the stage. A spotlight went up on him. He doffed his top hat and made a deep bow, then straightened and said, "Welcome to the Fabulous Flying Chameleons, where humans and animals come together to bring you the most astounding—the most amazing—the most fabulous spectacle you've ever seen!"

Dali had heard his speech before, but it was even more exciting when she heard it from backstage.

"And now for the Wheel! Of! DEATH!!!" Max declared.

Roland and Ransom carried out the target wheel and placed it center stage.

"Looking good, Carter," Merlin whispered. "Very shiny."

"See if I ever fix anything for you again," Carter muttered, giving him a death glare.

With a dramatic gesture, Max announced, "Please give a hand to our handsome and courageous target boy!"

Carter wiped the death glare off his face and replaced it with a surprisingly charming smile. He walked onstage, smiling and waving at the crowd, his oiled chest gleaming. The audience cheered appreciatively, especially the women.

"He forgot to do his shoulders," Dali whispered.

"No, that's correct," Merlin whispered back, vainly turning his coffee mug upside down over his mouth in the hope of coaxing out one more drop. "The squirrels have to land on them, remember?"

Dali swallowed a gulp of laughter at the image of flying squirrels skidding off Carter's shoulders. "Want more coffee?"

"Yeah, but I'll get it. You need to stay here. You want some?"

"Yes, please." She glanced at Mr. Varnham, who seemed mildly bored by the lack of animals except for the cats snoozing on the pillow, and said, "Some for him too. Cream and sugar."

As Merlin took off, Dali watched Ransom and Roland tie Carter to the wheel. Max spun him around, and the flying squirrels swooped down to throw their knives and outline his body. Carter kept determinedly smiling for the whole thing, including when he got untied and the squirrels landed on his outstretched arms and head.

The audience went berserk, clapping and cheering. Carter strode offstage, still covered in squirrels. As he passed Merlin, he muttered, "We will never speak of this again."

Merlin, grinning, said, "Wanna bet?"

The lights dimmed for a scene change. Under the watchful gaze of Mr. Varnham, the "flying squirrel trainer" whistled at them. The squirrels launched off Carter, leaving pink scratches on his arms and shoulders, and scrambled back up into the rigging.

Dali breathed a sigh of relief. "Made it through the first act."

Merlin gave her a quick kiss that sent her nerves tingling deliciously. "Thanks to you."

Don't think of the future, she ordered herself. *This moment is the only moment there is.*

She managed it—mostly—only because she had so much to do, overseeing everything backstage. She breathed a sigh of relief when the cat act went fine, with the Zimmermans marching in formation and pretending to follow the commands of Rosine Richelieu, who played their trainer.

The next act was one of the biggest and most complex ones in the entire show, in which flying squirrels rode cats who rode French poodles who rode horses. Especially since each set of animal required a "trainer" to hang around and pretend to be watching over them and giving them commands from backstage.

But it went off without a hitch. The atmosphere backstage was one of near-manic glee as the act concluded, and the horses (still ridden by poodles, who were still ridden by cats, who were still ridden by squirrels) began to trot offstage.

When the first set arrived backstage, their "trainers" reached in their pockets and gave the horse a carrot, the poodle a doggie treat (Dali didn't miss the poodle glaring, but he gamely crunched it), the cat a cat treat (the cat was either a better actor or actually enjoyed it), and the squirrel a peanut. Mr. Varnham actually cracked a smile when he saw the animals getting their treats—as well he should, given that it had been arranged for his benefit.

Dali could hardly believe it. They were actually pulling it off!

That was when she heard a familiar buzzing noise. Cloud landed on her shoulder.

CHAPTER 21

Merlin nearly had a heart attack when he heard the buzzing of dragon-fly wings. His first, horrified thought was that Blue had followed him. How the hell could he hide a bright blue bugbear the size of a Saint Bernard who knocked over everything in his path?

When he saw that it was Cloud, he felt relieved for a fraction of a second before horror took over again. He lunged to hide the flying kitten, but Dali was quicker. She neatly stepped behind the nearest horse, plucked the kitten from her shoulder, and popped her into her purse.

Merlin shot a quick glance at Mr. Varnham. To his immense relief, the inspector was watching the flying squirrels returning to their carrying case, and had clearly missed the sudden appearance of a kitten with dragonfly wings.

The horses were being led out, depriving Dali of her cover. He darted to her side and beckoned her inside the clown car.

"Good catch," he whispered. "The inspector didn't see a thing."

Dali, her right hand inside the purse, whispered back, "What if she starts meowing?"

"I'll make sure some cats stay backstage to cover it up," Merlin whispered. "Keep her in your purse. She probably just missed you."

Inside the clown car, he and Dali were crouched side by side on the floor. Their body heat warmed the air, fogging the flower-painted windows. It felt like a secret, intimate space for just the two of them.

"Would you think I had a weird kink if I was to say..." he began.

"...that this would be a great place for a quickie? If that's a weird kink, I have it too." But a moment after she said it, she frowned as if she'd said the wrong thing, and the sparkle and heat in her eyes vanished.

She scrambled out, leaving Merlin bewildered. She didn't seriously think it was a weird kink, did she? He climbed out of the clown car, still puzzled, when the lights dimmed for a scene change. Then he had to laugh at his own self-centered-ness; she hadn't been thinking of him at all, she'd just realized that she had work to do. But it was a laugh of relief. Nothing was wrong. It was only that Dali was dedicated to doing her best at everything she did. It was one of the things he loved about her.

The jugglers were the next up. As Ransom started for the ring, he froze so suddenly that the juggler behind him almost collided with him, then whispered urgently to Merlin, "Watch the left-hand tunnel!"

Hitoshi tugged at him, whispering, "Come on, we're up."

Reluctantly, Ransom let himself be pulled onstage. The lights went up on the jugglers, and they began their act.

Dali and Merlin looked at each other, then toward the tunnel. It was one of two dimly lit underground entrances leading into the ring. They could barely see into the opening, but no one seemed to be there. Merlin used that entrance later in the show, to enter as an acrobat, but no one was supposed to be there now. Cloud meowed urgently.

"Shh, shhh," Dali murmured.

Merlin looked from the tunnel to the line of cats marching outside.

Protect Dali, said his raptor.

Obviously, his raptor was right. Merlin rushed after the cats and Rosine, their "trainer," catching them just as they went outside. Speaking softly, he said, "I need some of the cats backstage. Mostly I need the kittens. Tell them to meow every couple minutes. We have a kitten backstage we need to cover up. It's a long story, I'll explain later."

The cats neatly separated. Half of them headed off to wait in their cage with Rosine, while the parents formed another line with their kittens. Merlin took the head of that line and marched them back inside and to their cushion. Mr. Varnham glanced at them, but there were so many animals coming and going that he clearly found nothing odd about it.

Until all the kittens meowed at once, making a piercing wail that seemed to drill into Merlin's brain.

Mr. Varnham whipped around, spilling his coffee, and beckoned urgently to Dali. She handed her purse to Merlin and went to the inspector.

Merlin put the purse over his shoulder and stuck his hand inside it, feeling Cloud's soft, wriggling body. The kitten clearly wanted out. Petting her, he went to the cat cushion and murmured, "Don't all meow at once. One or two at a time. And not all the time. We don't want to hear you onstage, just here."

Mr. Zimmerman nodded, a very un-cat-like gesture that Merlin really hoped was blocked by his own body, then nudged the nearest kitten, who obediently gave a soft meow. Cloud gave a louder one.

Merlin straightened up. This time he avoided the clown car and instead ducked behind a scenery flat, which was also for the clown show and was painted with custard pies flying through the air. Dali joined him behind it.

He whispered, "Sorry. The kittens got a bit over-enthusiastic."

"It's fine," she whispered back. "I told him we'd been training them as a cat chorus and they thought they'd gotten a signal. Thanks for getting them in place."

We make such a good team, Merlin thought.

"I'll go check out the left tun—" he began.

"Merlin! Dali!" Tirzah waved at them frantically. She was waiting in the wings for her entrance in a desk-and-chair set bedecked in artfully draped cloth to ensure that anything in her lap would be hidden. She wore an equally voluminous psychic's robe plus several scarves, one of which was wound around her head in a sort of sorcerous turban.

They hurried over. Tirzah beckoned them in close, indicating her lap. Nestled amongst the cloth were her phone and the furry black shape of her flying kitten. Batcat peered up at them with her enormous yellow eyes and let out a loud meow. It was instantly echoed by a chorus of meows from the kittens backstage.

"How'd she get—" Dali began, then broke off. "The same way Cloud did, I guess."

"One of you has to take her," Tirzah whispered. "I'd hold her in my lap, but she might meow onstage."

A burst of applause signaled the end of the juggling act. Roland and Zane Zimmerman, who had stayed human for the night in case his emergency medical skills were needed, went to carry Tirzah and her desk onstage. They were trailed by a pigeon shifter carefully holding her crystal ball.

The lights dimmed to blue for the scene change. Tirzah whipped off her head covering, wrapped it around Batcat, and thrust the wriggling bundle into Merlin's arms. The stagehands carried her onstage, leaving Merlin clutching a very angry Batcat.

He and Dali once again took refuge behind the custard pie flat.

"I can't put her in my purse with Cloud," Dali whispered. "They'll fight."

Merlin glanced onstage at Tirzah, who was trying to look wise and mysterious as Max introduced her as the world's greatest psychic. "I'll stay here until Tirzah's done. She's only doing Madame Fortuna, so she can take Batcat and go outside after that."

Searing pain lanced into Merlin's thumb. His grip on the bundle loosened involuntarily before he realized that it had only been Batcat biting him. But in that split second, Batcat clawed away the head wrap and zoomed out of it. Merlin made a lunge for her, but wasn't quite fast enough. Batcat triumphantly flew upward and out of their grasp.

"Oh my God!" Dali blurted out.

"It's okay, it's okay," Merlin said, though he didn't feel at all confident that it was. "She's trained to be invisible in public. You can only see her if you already know she exists."

"Oh. Right." Dali let out a huge breath. "I swear, that damn cat took years off my life."

They peered upward. In the shadows overhead, all they could see were a pair of disembodied, demonic yellow eyes.

"Looks like she's perched in the rigging," Merlin said. "I guess she just wanted to watch Tirzah do her thing."

Onstage, Tirzah had one hand raised dramatically and one unobtrusively in her lap. To the audience, it looked like she was gazing down into her crystal ball rather than at the cellphone in her lap.

"I see someone in the audience who just became the aunt of a beautiful baby girl," Tirzah intoned. "Her name is… it starts with an S… it's not Susan… it's not Shelley… it's Sofia! I won't say her last name, for the sake of privacy, but can her lucky aunt Allegra please stand up?"

A woman stood up, calling out, "She's right! Little Sofia was just born—"

"Wait!" Tirzah called. "She was born three days ago, at 6:00 AM. Her older sister Emma was disappointed that she couldn't be there for the birth, but she got over that fast once she saw her baby sister."

The woman in the audience gasped. "How did you know?"

"I am the Marvelous Madame Fortuna," Tirzah said loftily. "I know all!"

Merlin grinned. The advent of credit cards made that kind of scam so much easier. People literally handed over their names when they paid. And then they posted online about their lives.

"Looks like Tirzah and Batcat are doing fine," Dali whispered. "You stay here. I'm going to take a look in the tunnel."

Merlin peered toward it again. It still seemed empty. "No, don't go alone. If there's anything dangerous, I want to be there with you. How about you go ask Ransom if he knows any more details—"

Batcat swooped down from the rigging, making a beeline for Tirzah. Though Merlin knew intellectually that the kitten was invisible to the audience, it was nerve-wracking to see her flying right there in the ring. Tirzah gave a startled yelp, her eyes jerking upward, and flapped her hand in a shooing gesture.

Batcat veered off, and Tirzah recovered herself, saying, "Ah! I had a very sudden, very strong vision. One of you recently became the first person in his family to graduate from college. Congratulations to James, who got his BA with honors in—"

The winged kitten dove down, landed on Tirzah's shoulder, scrabbled in the mass of fabric, and fell off, dragging one of the long scarves with her. Tirzah reached for it, but Batcat ran off. The scarf, tangled in her claws, dragged after her. The audience murmured excitedly.

I wish I was an audience person, said Merlin's raptor. *It must be fun to see a scarf move by itself.*

A flicker of utter horror crossed Tirzah's face, then she nodded wisely, saying, "The spirits are strong tonight."

The audience gasped when Batcat launched herself from the floor, her furry wings beating hard, and flew several circles around the ring with the scarf dangling from her claws. On her third circle, Tirzah reached up and snatched the scarf out of the air.

Merlin, seeing what was coming, gestured at the cats. They began loudly meowing, covering Batcat's yowl as Tirzah unpicked her claws from the scarf. Then she firmly held down Batcat with one hand and rewrapped the scarf around her throat with the other, ad-libbing, "And now you know why psychics always wear so many layers."

The audience burst out laughing, then into delirious applause.

Dali ran for the headset, no doubt to suggest that they end the act on a high note and also get Batcat the hell offstage, but Kalpana was ahead of her. The lights blacked out on Tirzah, then went to the dim blue for the scene change. Roland and Zane hurried out to collect her.

As Tirzah was carried out, she passed close to Mr. Varnham. The inspector held up a hand, stopping the procession, and whispered, "I could see how you did the psychic bit, but how did you make the scarf levitate? I was sitting here watching from backstage, and I couldn't see a thing."

Tirzah winked at him. "Magicians never tell."

Her wheelchair had been parked in a corner backstage, so no one would trip over it. Merlin followed Roland and Zane as they set down her desk-chair beside it.

"That scarf trick was great," Zane said, then took off to change into his clown suit.

Roland said, "Merlin, I'll help Tirzah. You go check out that tunnel. Ransom thinks it's important."

Merlin spotted Ransom changing out of his juggler's costume and into a stagehand's all-black outfit. Someone raised in the circus could do that sort of change in fifteen seconds, but Ransom was doing a reasonable, if slower, job of it.

"Great act," said Merlin. "I especially loved the flaming chainsaws. What's with the tunnel?"

The exhilaration of Ransom's performance faded as he let out a sigh of frustration—more with himself than at the question, Merlin thought. "I don't know. I'd go down with you, but I have to help Roland with the next set change."

"Don't worry about it," Merlin said.

But when he turned to go, he found that his path was blocked. The entrance to the tunnel from backstage was narrow to begin with, and since no one needed to use the tunnel to get onstage for a while, some-one had used it as a convenient location to store some heavy scenery. Renu was waiting there as an elephant, so he couldn't either move the scenery or ask her to move—there was nowhere else she could stand. The only way to get in was through the ring.

Merlin glanced onstage, where his mother was delighting the audi-ence with her talking parrot act.

I can be small, said his raptor. *Tiny. So tiny no one will ever see me!*

Unless his raptor could get down to the size of an ant, Merlin very much doubted that an audience would fail to notice even the smallest velociraptor as it zipped across a brightly lit circus ring.

But that gave him an idea. When Mom's act ended, the lights would dim to blue, and the stagehands would set out the backdrop for the performing sea lions. Merlin knew how that scene shift worked, so if he shrank as small as possible, he could stick behind the scenery as it was moved onstage, and so dart across the ring and into the tunnel, completely unseen.

Well, unseen by the audience. Anyone backstage would be able to see him.

Merlin hurried to Dali, who was getting off the headset with Kalpana. Apologetically, she said, "I had to tell her about the magical pets. She *knew* that wasn't a trick."

"It's fine, it's fine," Merlin said hurriedly. "I was going to show off Blue eventually anyway. Listen, I have to get across the ring as a velociraptor during the next scene shift, can you distract the inspector so he doesn't look onstage?"

And that was one of the many, many things about Dali that made him love her: she blinked a few times, but didn't argue or demand an explanation that he didn't have time to provide. Instead, she simply said, "Of course."

She whispered briefly to the nearest person, who was Bobby Duffy. He grinned and nodded. Bobby picked up a cup of coffee in one hand and scooped up an armful of extra seal balls with his other, and began to hurry on a course that would lead him near the inspector. Just as before he got there, he dropped one of the balls, made a grab for it, and spilled the entire mug of coffee over the inspector's desk. Dali snatched up a handful of napkins and rushed over, mopping and apologizing.

It was beautifully orchestrated, but Merlin had no time to appreciate it. The scene shift lights came on, and he ducked behind the piece of heavy wheeled scenery being shoved along by a cranky-looking, black-clad Carter. Matching his pace with Carter's, he shifted.

As he did so, he realized three things: he was the size of a hamster, which was as small as he could get; he not only hadn't needed to fight with his raptor to get to that size, he hadn't even needed to ask; and he had forgotten to inform Carter of what he was doing.

Carter stared down at him—his head looked as big as a hot air balloon—then shook his head. "I'm not even going to ask."

Merlin kept pace with Carter as he pushed the scenery onstage, waiting for the moment when it would briefly overlap with the flat Roland was moving so he could dart behind that. Merlin saw moving feet, and darted...

...but Roland wasn't carrying a flat. Instead, he had an armful of seal balls.

Horrified, Merlin realized his fatal error. Roland and Carter had been hurriedly trained to take the place of seasoned stagehands who were currently cats or squirrels or sea lions. They knew what needed to go onstage, but not the order in which it normally was placed.

And so Merlin was stranded in the middle of the stage as a tiny velociraptor, with no cover and the lights about to go up.

He started to make a mad dash for the tunnel...

...and the lights came up.

A wall slammed down in front of Merlin, and the light dimmed to a reddish glow. He had no time to stop, but ran into the wall at full tilt. Instead of bouncing off it, the wall moved with him. Bewildered, he kept on running, pushing the wall in front of him. He was vaguely aware of a burst of laughter and applause, and then the light dimmed again and he smacked into another wall. That one didn't move.

Merlin blinked hard, trying to figure out where he was and what had happened. Then the light brightened again as the wall and ceiling fell away. There was a loud buzzing sound, and he looked up at an enormous, furry, bright blue face. An equally enormous tongue came out and licked him from head to toe.

"Yecch!"

Merlin leaped backward. Now everything came into focus. He was in the tunnel. With Blue.

Merlin became a man again. A rather damp man. Resignedly, he petted Blue. "I can't leave you anywhere, can I? At least you stayed here instead of rushing out to find me. Good boy."

Blue's tiny wings buzzed and he wagged his stumpy tail as he licked Merlin's hands.

Merlin glanced around the tunnel. It was equipped with a small table, so performers could drink coffee and water before they went onstage, then collect their cups when they finished their act. It also had a couple chairs so they could sit down while they waited.

And there, under the table, was an overturned red plastic bucket from the sea lion act. Someone must have popped it over him the instant that the lights came up, so all the audience saw was a plastic bucket scurrying across the stage all by itself. No wonder they'd laughed!

He rubbed Blue's ears as he tried to figure out what to do with him. The other end of the tunnel was still blocked by scenery, and Merlin couldn't risk leading Blue backstage unless he arranged for another inspector distraction first.

Still, it wasn't a bad place to be stuck, and not a bad time to be stuck there. He had a great view of the ring, and enjoyed watching Dali in her one and only onstage performance, in which she wore a red spangled dress and threw balls to the sea lions. She'd only agreed to go onstage on the condition that she didn't have to speak, so she just threw the balls while the ringmaster did all the patter.

But despite her stage fright, she looked like she wasn't having a bad time. The tight dress displayed her luscious curves, and her skin seemed to glow under the warm lights. Much as he normally enjoyed the sea lion act, he couldn't look at anything but her.

Which was why he spotted Cloud flying behind a flat, making a beeline for her. With admirable presence of mind, the ringmaster whipped off his top hat and captured the kitten in it before anyone in the audience could see. Max kept the hat pressed to his chest for the rest of the act. Merlin heard faint yowls, echoed by backstage meows, and could tell from a certain tightness around Max's mouth that she must be struggling to escape.

I wonder what's gotten into her, Merlin thought. *She doesn't normally insist on being with Dali every second of the day.*

When the sea lion act ended, the ring went dim and stagehands began clearing out the scenery—all the scenery, since the elephant act was next.

Let's go now, his raptor suggested.

Merlin automatically started to say no, then realized that his raptor was on to something. If he walked out carrying the bucket, he'd appear to be just another stagehand. And since the scene change lights were blue, anyone seeing Blue would assume he was a big dog or small bear who'd be white in ordinary light.

"Keep your wings flat," he said, pressing them down with his hand.

Blue obediently flattened them, panting eagerly. Merlin led him across the stage, his heart thumping. But there was no particular reaction from the audience beyond a few kids murmuring, "Look, a baby bear!" and their parents saying, "No, honey, it's a big dog," and other kids saying, "Look, a big dog!" and their parents saying, "No, honey, it's a baby bear."

Merlin led Blue backstage, edging behind pieces of scenery that blocked them from Mr. Varnham's view, and stepped into the men's dressing room. The looks on everyone's faces when they saw him were priceless.

Everyone began exclaiming things like "What IS that?" and "Is that a bugbear, like in Janet's stories?" and "I always thought they were a myth!"

Merlin couldn't help enjoying the moment. Not only was everyone admiring his marvelous magical pet, but he'd vindicated his mother.

"You should always believe everything my mother says," Merlin said. "She doesn't make things up, and neither do I. Mostly. His name is Blue, and he's my pet. Can you please make sure he stays here? He likes dog treats and getting his belly rubbed."

Blue promptly rolled over with all four legs splayed out in the air like a dead bug. Larry Duffy rubbed his furry belly, and Blue's stubby tail wagged.

"Great, thanks! I'll collect him once the inspectors are gone." Merlin dashed out, then remembered that he needed to change into his acrobat's outfit anyway. He dashed back in, did a quick-change, and dashed out.

He headed straight for Dali. She was standing beside Tirzah, both of them watching Caro ride Renu the elephant, standing on her back in a sparkly leotard and waving at the crowd. She did a flip and landed on her feet. Renu trumpeted, and the crowd applauded.

"Does Pete know she's doing acrobatics on an elephant's back?" Merlin asked.

"No, and neither did I." Tirzah ran the hand not holding Batcat through her curly hair, leaving it a wild mess. "She and Renu must have cooked that up at the last minute. When she said, 'ride an elephant,' I thought she meant like a horse!"

"No, elephant riders always stand. It's more…" He swallowed the word 'dramatic' when Tirzah glared at him, then protested, "I thought you and Pete knew that! But I didn't know she was going to do any flips."

Caro did another one. She was clearly having the time of her life.

Dali turned to Merlin. "What happened? Why did you run across the stage as a velociraptor? Roland had to drop a bucket over you!"

"The other end of the tunnel was blocked," Merlin explained. "Ransom was right. Blue was in there."

"Yes, I saw. But why not just pretend to be a stagehand?"

"It didn't occur to me," he admitted.

Dali looked exasperated, then laughed despite herself. "Well, it's not like you didn't have a lot to distract you. How did he get there, anyway? He can't fly."

Merlin shrugged. "Got me. Magic?"

A loud meow issued from Dali's purse, followed by another from one of the Zimmermans on the cushion. Mr. Varnham, who was intently watching the elephant act, didn't bat an eye.

"Do they follow you all the time?" Dali asked Tirzah. "It must be exhausting!"

"No, they don't," Tirzah said. "This is really unusual. Maybe they somehow sensed the presence of a lot of shifters and wanted to hang out?"

When Renu marched offstage and knelt so Caro could slide off her back, Tirzah wheeled over to her. Merlin couldn't hear what they were saying, but from the gestures and expressions, Caro was getting scolded.

But Merlin had no time to spare for that. The clown car act was next, and he was in it. In more ways than one. He threw on a clown outfit, slapped on white paint and a red nose, and squirmed into a clown car already packed with people. Since he was one of the last in, he got a perfect view of a very unhappy-looking Carter getting literally stuffed inside by Larry and Billy Duffy.

"It's like rush hour at the Tokyo subway," Merlin said. "They have guys with white gloves who help cram people in."

But his mouth was squashed against Carter's red nose, and he wasn't sure anyone could understand what he was saying. He, however, caught Carter's muffled but heartfelt mutter of, "Never volunteer for anything ever again."

The clown car drove around the ring, tooling its horn. When it stopped and the doors opened, Carter leaped out and fled backstage. Merlin rolled out in a somersault and followed him, enjoying the delighted laughter from the audience as clowns continued to exit the car.

The next act was Roland as a strong man. Merlin, who could change and remove makeup very fast indeed, managed to see most of it. He was amused to note that though Roland had escaped the dreaded chest-oiling, the audience members who appreciated men's bare chests were very appreciative indeed.

It fascinated Merlin to watch his teammates performing onstage. Roland, though obviously unused to an audience, was neither nervous nor embarrassed, and was throwing himself into it with good cheer. Tirzah had started out jittery, but had hit her stride when she had to focus on the aspects that were more like hacking than acting. Carter had no stage fright, but clearly found the entire thing deeply embarrassing. Ransom had lit up when he was juggling, as if being forced to stand in the spotlight he was usually so careful to avoid had thrown open some long-closed door in him, letting in a ray of sunlight to the dark room of his soul.

We need to throw things at him randomly in the office to make him juggle them, his raptor suggested.

Excellent idea, replied Merlin silently.

He glanced at the tunnel entrance, and saw the stagehands removing the last of the scenery blocking it, now that they didn't have to shove everything around to make room for an elephant.

"I better go wait for my entrance," he said.

Dali handed him a cup of coffee. "Break a leg."

"You too." He headed back to the tunnel, warmed by her regard, and stood sipping his coffee and watching the act before his, which was Leopold and Leona holding saws in their jaws to saw Mia in half.

The lights went blue, the performers exited, and Merlin set his half-drunk coffee cup on the table. When the lights went up, he sprang onstage, doing a triple flip and landing on his feet center stage, forming a perfect circle with the other acrobats who had done the same from other entrances.

Merlin had always loved performing as an acrobat, and his view of Dali watching from backstage brought him to new heights. He felt like a bird doing a mating dance, displaying his strength and agility solely for her pleasure—and he could see in her expression that it *did* please her. Her lips were parted and her eyes shone, making her more gorgeous and sexy than ever. He wished that after the act ended, he could rush with her straight to bed.

After the show, he promised himself.

Merlin was floating so high on the joy of performing for her that when the lights went to blue, rather than walking out as the other acrobats did, he did another flip and landed on his feet inside the tunnel.

Fausto was there, walking away from Merlin in his trapeze outfit.

Which was a little odd, as he had no reason to be there. But what was *really* odd was the way he started when Merlin came in.

There's something wrong, said his raptor.

"Hi, Fausto," said Merlin.

Fausto turned around. With forced cheer, he said, "Hi, Merlin. Didn't expect you to *jump* back in. Nice act."

That was wrong, too. Fausto had never had a pleasant word to say to Merlin in his life. Merlin stared at him, and caught Fausto's gaze going to the coffee cup Merlin had left on the table, then jerking back to fix on Merlin's face.

"See you," Fausto said, turning to leave.

Merlin picked up the coffee cup and sniffed it. He'd never have noticed it if he wasn't looking for it, but his heightened shifter senses detected a slightly bitter odor.

"What did you put in my coffee?" Merlin demanded, though he had some guesses—salt or Tabasco or something like that. Though the way Fausto was acting, it seemed like it was worse than that. Castor oil, maybe?

He expected Fausto to deny that he'd tampered with the coffee, or to sneer that Merlin had gotten lucky and next time he'd get a good mouthful.

He did not expect what Fausto did, which was to turn around, stare at Merlin in shock and horror, and then run for his life.

Merlin was so surprised that he momentarily froze. Then understanding hit him like a hammer. Fausto hadn't tried to prank him, he'd tried to poison him. Dali had been right all along: Fausto really did want to be heir—enough to kill for it.

CHAPTER 22

As the lights went up on the tiger act, Dali breathed a sigh of relief. They had just a few acts left, Cloud was still in her purse, Batcat was with Tirzah, Blue was in the dressing room, and the show had gone almost without a hitch.

She refused to think about what would happen after that.

Out of the corner of her eye, she saw Fausto bolt out of the left-hand tunnel and rush outside, but she didn't think much of it. People were constantly running around backstage; their whole delicate balancing act of substitutions often required split-second timing.

Nor was she concerned when Merlin came pelting out of the same tunnel a few seconds later, carrying a coffee cup with his hand pressed over the top so it didn't spill. Then she caught the look at his face as he stopped and looked around wildly. Something was wrong.

She hurried over to him. "What's going on?"

"It's Fausto!" Merlin said. The inspector glanced up, and Merlin lowered his voice. "You were right all along. He tried to kill me—he poisoned my coffee—he dropped the trapeze on us!"

Dali felt an odd shock of alarm and relief combined. An attempted murderer was on the loose, but at last, they knew who it was. There was no more need to jump at shadows. "I just saw him run outside."

Merlin started toward the door, but Dali grabbed his hand. "Don't go after him alone! He might have a weapon."

"Right." Merlin nodded decisively. "I'll get a group together. You warn everyone else. And find someone who can do trapeze to take his part. The show must go on!"

"Okay," Dali said, feeling a little dazed.

"And if anyone doesn't believe you, send them to the men's dressing room. I'm going to leave the coffee there. They can smell it themselves." Merlin strode to the birdcage where Janet was watching everything as a parrot, opened the door and held up his arm for her to hop on, then went with her into the dressing room.

His confidence and quick planning made Dali feel better. She immediately got on headset with Kalpana.

"Fausto?" Kalpana said incredulously. "Seriously?"

"Yes, seriously." Out of the corner of her eye, she saw Merlin emerge from the men's dressing room with three strong men, then knock on the door of the women's dressing room. "Who else can do trapeze?"

"With Fausto out? Nobody. They're all stuck in their shifted forms. We could cut the act to two, but they've trained with four. I'm not sure they could go to a two-person act on the fly."

"You keep thinking about it," Dali said. "I have to warn everyone."

As she hung up, Merlin and his group, which now included three strong women, headed outside. Janet flew from his arm and perched atop her birdcage, her feathers fluffed up and her beak clacking.

Mr. Varnham waved at Dali. Reluctantly, she went to his desk.

"Er, can someone escort me to the bathroom?" he asked.

"Yes, of course," Dali said, uncertain whether this was the greatest stroke of luck ever or the worst. "Hang on, let me get someone."

She found Bobby Duffy, who was scowling at not having been included in Merlin's team, and whispered, "Can you please take Mr. Varnham to the bathroom and back? And make sure he doesn't see… anything."

"Sure," said Bobby, perking up a bit at having *something* to do. He collected Mr. Varnham and went out a side door.

Dali went around warning everyone who hadn't already been warned by Merlin. She felt slightly silly crouching down and explaining a murder plot to a bunch of cats, but it was nice to not have to worry about Mr. Varnham watching.

"Hey!" whispered a girl's voice. It was Caro, still in her spangled elephant rider outfit. "I heard you telling Kalpana you need another trapeze artist."

Tirzah chimed in before Dali could. "You are absolutely not doing trapeze. For one thing, Pete already said no. For another thing, you don't know how."

"Oh, I didn't mean *real* trapeze," Caro assured them. "I mean I could pretend to be on a trapeze."

"How do you pretend to be on a trapeze?" Dali asked, baffled.

At that moment, one of the doors that led outside opened, and Fausto came in. Before anyone else could react, Janet let out a screech of rage and flew at his face. Fausto went over backward with the parrot clinging to him, clawing and pecking. Dali lunged forward, sat on his chest, and pinned his arms, one with her right hand and one with her left forearm.

Then the solid man's body she sat on was gone. Dali hit the floor with a painful thud. A flying squirrel wriggled out from under the heap of clothes and leaped upward, flaps of skin spread to glide away.

Tirzah snatched him out of the air and popped him into Janet's birdcage. The squirrel that was Fausto chittered angrily, flinging himself against the bars.

"Can he shift and break it?" Dali asked.

"It's wrought iron," Janet squawked. "He'd squash himself. Stick him in the dressing room closet. I'll go tell Merlin's team we caught him."

A clown took away Fausto's cage. Dali held the door open for Janet, and she soared out into the moonlit night.

Pete came in a moment after Janet left. The massive cave bear was being led in on a leash by his "trainer," growling softly to himself. Dali was somehow unsurprised to see Spike, his prickly green flying kitten,

236

fly in after him through the open door.

With the same practiced ease that had allowed Tirzah to grab Fausto and get him in a birdcage before he could shift, Caro captured the cactus kitten and passed him to Tirzah, who resignedly held him with one hand and Batcat with the other.

Caro ran to her father. "Dad, I don't know if you heard but Fausto tried to kill Merlin, so we locked him in a birdcage. That leaves us one trapeze artist short, so I was thinking—"

Pete growled loudly and shook his shaggy head.

"Not of *actually* doing trapeze," Caro said hastily. "Of course not! I don't know how. Um, and also you said no. But Moonbow showed up a little while ago, no idea why. Moonbow!"

Her miniature pegasus fluttered out from a shadowy corner, his opalescent wings seeming to glow in the dim backstage lights.

Only on a night like this would I not notice a miniature pegasus flapping around, Dali thought.

"So if we open a panel in the tent to let in some moonlight, he can go full-size and I can ride him, but the audience won't see him because he'll be invisible to them, so I'll look like I'm floating in mid-air. And I'll pretend I'm on a trapeze," Caro concluded. "It'll be completely safe. I ride him all the time! Please, Dad?"

Pete made a low rumbling sound that meant either *Oh I guess so but be careful* or *Absolutely not.*

"Dad?" said Mr. Varnham, stepping back in. "The bear is named Dad?"

Caro gulped, then said, "Yep. The bear's name is Dad. It's 'cause he has a dad bod."

Pete growled again.

"Is it safe for you to be so close to him?" asked Mr. Varnham. "He sounds angry."

"No, Dad loves me." Caro petted him. "Right, Dad?"

Pete nuzzled her with a tenderness that convinced even Mr. Varnham.

Merlin returned with the group he'd left with, with Janet on his shoulder, just as the tigers exited (Mr. Varnham shrank back into his chair as they passed him) and Pete grumpily climbed on to his unicycle and rode it into the spotlight.

Much as Dali would have enjoyed watching Pete's act, she was distracted by Caro tugging at her sleeve. "Ask Kalpana if we can get moonlight inside the tent!"

"I'm not sure your father said yes," Dali whispered.

"Well, I can't ask him to be more clear," Caro pointed out. Rounding on Tirzah, she said, "He really does let me ride Moonbow."

"That's true," Tirzah admitted. "But…"

"Merlin, I can take Fausto's place in the trapeze act by riding Moonbow while I hold on to the bars and—"

"—and he'll be invisible, right," Merlin said. To Dali, he said, "The big top panels do open."

Dali got on headset with Kalpana and began hurriedly updating her on Caro's idea.

Music began to play, and there was a burst of laughter. Dali glanced onstage. A very annoyed-looking Pete was now dancing on his hind legs.

"Oh, I wish I had my phone to video this," Merlin said. Since few of their costumes had pockets, phones were stashed in the dressing rooms.

"I'm sure Pete will be extremely glad you don't," said Tirzah, then snickered. "Though I do have mine."

"I have to get up in the rigging before Dad finishes dancing if I'm going to do this," Caro said to Tirzah, her voice rising as she got increasingly frantic. "Please, please, please!"

Moonbow hovered in mid-air, madly flapping his wings. He gave a hopeful whinny, making Mr. Varnham glance around curiously; there were no horses backstage.

Tirzah gave a huge sigh. "Merlin, you'll take care of her, right?"

"Of course," he promised her.

"Go," said Tirzah. "If it turns out Pete didn't give you permission, it's on me."

"Thank you, thank you, thank you!" Caro flung her arms around Tirzah, then practically flew up the ladder.

Merlin kissed Dali, then ran for the ladder at the opposite end of the stage. The music stopped, and Pete ambled offstage in the scene shift lights. He glanced at Tirzah, who tilted her cell phone to display the message:

CARO RIDING MOONBOW. I SAID OK. HOPE YOU DID TOO.

Pete heaved a huge sigh that blew sawdust around on the floor and made Mr. Varnham give a nervous twitch, then sat down with a good view of the stage. His "trainer," who had already taken out some kind of bear treat to feed to him, thought better of it and stuffed it back in her pocket.

"Opening panels," said Kalpana over the headset. Moonlight flooded the stage, and Dali heard the audience go, "Ahhh."

What followed was pure magic.

Kalpana brightened the stage lights only slightly, to enhance rather than distract from the silvery moonlight. Merlin soared through the air, his hair bleached to silver-gold, the light seeming to shimmer on his skin. He seemed to use the trapeze more for balance than for necessity, as if he could fly unassisted. Every movement was grace and strength and beauty combined. Dali could have watched him forever.

Caro rode her pegasus, now full-size in the moonlight, holding the trapeze bar or releasing it to catch another artist's hands. She and Moonbow flew like a single being, her long black hair flying out behind her in an echo of Moonbow's opalescent tail.

The three trapeze artists had to shape their act around Caro and Moonbow, and that meant slowing it down, focusing more on grace and precision, less on speed. The result was that they seemed to be doing a ballet in mid-air. It was the most beautiful thing Dali had ever seen.

When it finally ended to rapturous applause, the trapeze artists climbed down the ladders. Moonbow, again the size of a kitten now that the moonlight had vanished, flew down.

Caro was radiant. She hugged Tirzah, then Pete. Her father nuzzled her and made a sound that could only be interpreted as pride.

Merlin swept Dali up in his arms and spun her around. She felt as weightless and joyous and free as if she was on a trapeze.

Almost the entire company joined in the final act, in which the animals taught the humans to play tricks and tossed them treats. The mood of giddy joy continued as Dali and Merlin crouched onstage, letting a sea lion teach them how to ring a bell.

And with that, the show was over. Dali took her bows with the rest of them, and looked out across the ring to see a standing ovation.

Afterward, Ms. Moore came backstage to join her colleague. She looked completely different, practically glowing with delight. Spotting Merlin, she said, "I absolutely adored the show. I can't speak for Mr. Varnham's report, of course, but it's obvious to me that this is a real circus, not some kind of front. You had a packed house that would easily account for all your income if that's the number of tickets you normally sell—and I assume you do, because the show is brilliant! I'm bringing my wife and our daughter next week!"

Mr. Varnham also seemed much happier than he'd been when he'd come in. "I enjoyed it too. Your animals are well-cared-for, well-trained, and happy. My report will have all the details, but just keep up the good work and you have nothing to worry about. In fact, I'll come back too. I'd like to see the show from the audience."

"We change our acts a fair amount, so people can see it again and again and never get bored," Merlin said. "So next week's show won't be exactly the same as this one. Just so you know."

"But you're keeping the flying scarf, right?" asked Mr. Varnham.

Tirzah, overhearing, said, "That's up to the spirits."

Once the inspectors and audience had left, the circus company and Merlin's team gathered in the ring for a meeting. Janet, back in human form, carried in the birdcage containing a furiously chittering Fausto.

An uproar immediately began at her entrance, but was quelled when she raised her hand, looking around the circle with what Dali now recognized as her alpha stare.

"News travels quickly," she said. "I know you're aware of two pieces of news, one very good and one very serious. First of all, you were all amazing. We pulled together, we put on the show of a lifetime, and we saved the circus!"

A cheer went up, from which the Fratellis notably abstained, glaring at Janet and Merlin.

"Secondly, Fausto put *something* in Merlin's coffee," she went on. "Normally, I'd assume this was a prank. But he fled the scene instead of laughing it off, and no one who's smelled the coffee can recognize what's in it. There was also a previous attempt on Merlin's life."

The Fratellis began shouting angrily, but were again silenced by her stare.

"I'm sending the coffee to a lab for chemical analysis," Janet said. "We need to find out what's in it before we make any decisions. They should have the results by the end of the day tomorrow. In the meantime, I'm keeping Fausto under house arrest, since he's already tried to flee."

She opened the cage. The squirrel scrambled out, and immediately became a very angry, very naked man.

"I didn't do anything!" Fausto yelled. Pointing at Merlin, he said, "I never touched his coffee! I never even saw his coffee! And I never ran away! He made it all up just to screw with me!"

"You were right there," Merlin protested. "In the stage left tunnel. I caught you when I exited after my acrobat performance."

"I was never in the stage left tunnel in this entire show!" Fausto shouted.

Dali, Caro, Zane Zimmerman, Larry Duffy, a pigeon teenager, and Janet all spoke simultaneously. "I saw you."

Fausto stared at them, his mouth open. He looked utterly shocked. "But…"

"That's enough," said Janet. "Fausto, put on some clothes. You're under house arrest in your room. Once we find out what was in the coffee, you'll get a chance to give your side of the story."

Fausto angrily pulled on a pair of jeans, then was escorted out. The rest of the company broke off into groups and began to wander out or clean up, talking excitedly.

Soon the only people still in the ring were Merlin and his team, Dali, Caro, Janet, Kalpana, and the magical pets.

Merlin hugged his mother. "We did it! We saved the circus!"

"Son, you did good." Her bright, bird-like glance took in the rest of them. "So did you all. Thank you for helping out. We couldn't have done it without you."

"It was our pleasure," said Roland.

"Speak for yourself," muttered Carter. Then, catching Janet's eye, he said, "That is, of course I'm always..." he seemed to choke on the next word, then finally managed to get out, "...happy to help a teammate."

Janet chuckled. "Not everyone's cut out for the circus. It means even more that you stepped up when it wasn't something you're comfortable with."

"I'm glad I could help," said Pete. "And I'm also glad that Dad and his dad bod are retiring to the zoo."

Caro burst out giggling. "You don't want to ride a unicycle again? Or waltz on your hind legs?"

"Never again," said Pete with feeling. "And next time you need to ask permission for something, try to do it when I'm not a bear." Then he patted her shoulder and said, "I watched your trapeze act from the wings. You were fantastic."

She beamed. "Thanks, Dad."

"We'd love to have you and your pegasus step in, any time," Janet said. "But do ask your father first. And, Ransom, if you ever want to try a new career, we'd love to have you as a juggler. I'm serious."

He looked at her, his dark eyes wide and startled, seeming to seriously consider it.

"Where'd you learn to do that?" she asked.

A shadow came over his face, and he retreated back into himself.

"Nowhere as nice as here."

"And Dali," said Janet. "You were marvelous."

"You really were," Kalpana said. "Normally Janet runs things backstage, but you stepped into her shoes like you'd been wearing them forever. And they're very big shoes. Metaphorically, I mean," she added quickly, casting a glance at Janet's average-sized feet.

"I do mean to retire, eventually," Janet said. "Not from the circus, of course! Just from everything but Madam Fortuna and the talking parrot act. So Kalpana's been looking for someone she can train to run backstage. If you'd like to join us, you'd be very welcome."

Dali fought down a wave of emotion that threatened to overwhelm her, and managed to get out, "Thank you."

Merlin, giving her a worried glance, said, "Mom, we're all tired. Let me take Dali home. We can come back tomorrow."

They walked to the car in silence, with Cloud in her purse and Blue ambling at Merlin's heels. Or maybe Merlin said some things, but Dali couldn't hear them. Her mind and soul and heart felt like they were tearing themselves apart.

Say yes, urged one part of her. *Join the circus and stay with Merlin. Maybe you'll like the life more than you think. You know you loved tonight!*

Say yes, said another, darker part. *Make him happy. It's not the life you want, but his happiness is more important than yours.*

Yet another dark part said, *Say no. Tell him you'll only stay with him if he stays here in Refuge City. He always puts other people ahead of himself. All you have to do is ask, and he'll sacrifice his happiness for yours.*

"No!" Dali spoke aloud without meaning to.

They were standing in the dark and empty parking lot in front of his car. Merlin already had his keys in his hand.

"Dali, please just tell me what's going on," he said.

She wanted to delay, to beat around the bush. At the very least, she wanted to wait until after the car ride. But she'd have to tell Merlin to drive her to her own home, not his, and then he'd know anyway.

"I want to break up," she said.

CHAPTER 23

Merlin had been riding high on saving the circus, finding out who'd tried to kill him, and having a wonderful night with Dali by his side. Her words brought him down to earth like he'd fallen off the tightrope without a net to catch him.

"What?" he said, though he'd heard her perfectly.

"I want to break up," she said. "I'm so sorry, Merlin. You're a great guy. But this isn't working out for me."

No no no! His raptor sounded frantic. *She's our mate! She'll always love us! This can't be happening!*

His raptor was right: this *couldn't* be happening. Merlin's mind raced, seeking a problem he could solve. Was she worried he'd run away with the circus, leaving her behind?

"If it's because of the circus…" he began.

"It's not because of the circus," she said.

Her voice was tight, her lovely dark eyes brimming with tears. But she had to be telling the truth. Dali was honest down to her bones; hiding the existence of shifters and magical animals was as far as she'd go with deceit. Merlin couldn't believe she'd lie about something as important as their relationship. If she said it wasn't about the circus, then it wasn't about the circus.

"Then why?"

She dashed the tears from her eyes with an impatient gesture. "We're too different. You're funny, and I'm serious. You love excitement, and I love pushing papers."

"What you do involves way more than pushing papers," Merlin said. "And it *is* exciting—weren't you excited tonight?"

He'd meant to go on that they were different in a good way. That they balanced each other like a pair of trapeze artists. But before he could say anything more, she looked as stricken as if he'd stabbed her in the back, then burst out, "Stop arguing! You're only making this harder—" She gulped down tears, but he knew what she'd meant to say: *harder on me.*

Merlin felt like someone had taken a sledgehammer to his heart, smashing it into a million pieces of broken glass. The fragments cut him inside. But he *couldn't* make it harder on her. This obviously hurt her too.

He swallowed. "All right. Should I drive you to your apartment?"

"Yes, please."

"Pete can take over protecting you. He and Tirzah will already be there. Just call him, all right?"

"I don't want Pete," she began, then gave a sigh that sounded halfway to a sob. "I mean, I don't need protection. We know who dropped the trapeze on us, and he's locked up. And whoever was after Cloud must've given up by now."

"We don't know that," Merlin said. "Maybe they just haven't made their move because I was guarding you. Call Pete, okay?"

"All right." She wrapped her arms around herself and shivered. They were still standing beside the car, and her breath made clouds in the air.

Merlin took off his jacket and handed it to her, then opened her door for her while she put it on.

The drive to her apartment felt longer than any drive he'd ever taken in his life. The whole way there, neither of them said a word.

CHAPTER 24

She'd done the right thing. So why did it feel so wrong?

Dali locked her apartment door and released Cloud from her purse. The kitten flew out, yowled, and swatted Dali across the cheek before landing on the floor, folding her translucent wings, and skittering under the bed.

"What's with you?" Dali asked.

All she could see of Cloud were a pair of gleaming sapphire eyes. The kitten hissed, then retreated farther under the bed.

Her apartment had never felt so lonely. She and Merlin had never gotten around to painting her dishes, and they hadn't spent much time there so he hadn't left anything at her place. The only trace of him in her cold white room was the jacket she'd forgotten to return when he'd dropped her off. She'd have to give it to Pete or Tirzah to pass on to him.

That reminded her that she ought to call Pete. But between his presence and Tirzah's electronic monitoring, she was perfectly safe in the apartment building. And she couldn't bring herself to explain why she was calling.

If she'd done the right thing, then why did she feel like she'd just stabbed herself in the heart?

Dali wasn't sure how long she sat in her chair, staring at the wall, alternating between an icy numbness and utter misery. And guilt. The look in Merlin's eyes when she'd told him she was breaking up with him would haunt her for the rest of her life.

It'll haunt me, *but* he'll *get over it,* she told herself.

If she'd set them both free, why did she feel so trapped?

The knock at the door nearly made her jump out of her skin. Instantly, she regretted not calling Pete as soon as she'd gotten in. Cautiously, she went to the door and peered through the peephole.

It was Merlin.

A rush of love and regret and uncertainty nearly swept Dali off her feet. She opened the door and let him in.

"Merlin…" she began, then stopped, not knowing what to say. *I'm sorry? I take it back? I need more time to think?*

"Come with me," he said. "We need to talk."

It sounded more like an order than a request. That wasn't like him. She must have really knocked him for a loop. He even moved differently, his usual light-footed grace changed to the slightly awkward body language of your average civilian with a desk job.

She'd done that to him. Guilt overwhelmed her.

"Of course," she said.

Cloud hissed and spat from under the bed, then scrambled out and flew at them, wings buzzing like a chain-saw. Merlin ducked, and Dali snatched the kitten out of the air and stuffed her into her purse.

"I don't know what's gotten into her. She swatted me across the face earlier." Dali touched her cheek, and withdrew blood-stained fingers. "Look at that. She actually drew blood!"

Merlin glanced at her cheek. "Those magical animals can be temperamental. Bring her along. Maybe a ride will calm her down."

Dali left with him, keeping the struggling Cloud inside her purse. They walked down the hallway and took the elevator in silence. With every instant, Dali's misery grew. They moved out of sync, not touching, their usual camaraderie and sexual awareness of each other gone. Merlin could have been any man. He could have been a stranger.

Dali wished she hadn't agreed to come. But why wouldn't she? Even apart from the romance they'd shared, Merlin was a friend. And she was the one who'd ended their relationship. She at least owed him an explanation.

He took her to a rental car, as ordinary and anonymous as the ones Ransom used, and clicked to unlock it.

"Where's your car?" Dali asked.

"I totaled it. I was upset over our breakup, and thinking about it distracted me. I went off the road and into a tree."

Dali stared at him, horrified. She'd not only broken his heart, but she was responsible for the destruction of his beloved car! "Oh, Merlin, I'm so sorry. I shouldn't have let you drive."

"Yeah," he said. "I guess you shouldn't have."

He got into the driver's seat and started up the engine, then gestured to her to get in. She scrambled inside, Cloud hissing like a teakettle from within her purse, feeling like a fool for having expected him to open the door for her. She wasn't his girlfriend anymore, so why should he?

"You're not hurt, are you?" she said uncertainly. There wasn't a scratch on him, but not all injuries were visible.

"No."

"And Blue—is Blue okay?" As soon as she asked, Dali once again felt like a fool. Of course Blue was fine. If he wasn't, Merlin would never have left his side.

"The bugbear's fine," Merlin said indifferently. "I left it at the house."

Dali should have felt relieved, but the sense of surreal wrongness only grew. Why was he calling Blue "it" instead of "he?"

Just moments after she'd broken up with Merlin, he'd opened the car door for her and offered her his jacket.

She glanced in the rear-view mirror. Cloud's scratch was shallow, but it had left a line of blood across her cheek. Why hadn't Merlin remarked on that the instant he'd seen her?

He'd been so insistent that she call Pete for protection, so why hadn't he checked on that? If he'd called Pete himself, Pete would have told him he hadn't heard from her. If he'd assumed she'd made the call, shouldn't he have expected *her* to call Pete to inform him that she was leaving with Merlin?

At the moment she'd hurt Merlin most, the moment when he'd have been most justified in blaming her, his first instinct had instead been to protect her. He'd spoken up when he'd thought she was putting herself down, and he'd stopped arguing when she'd said that was making it harder on her. Could a few hours to stew over their breakup have changed him enough to make him blame her for him crashing his own car?

Cloud squirmed under her hand and nipped her fingers with needle-sharp teeth.

"Ow!" Dali exclaimed, then said, "Sorry. Cloud bit me."

Merlin glanced at her. "Doesn't that purse zip up? If you leave a little opening, it won't suffocate."

At that, Dali's doubts coalesced into horrified certainty.

"I don't know who you are," she said. "But you're not Merlin."

CHAPTER 25

Merlin's raptor hadn't stopped yelling at him since he'd dropped off Dali, shouting stuff like *Go back and bang on her door* and *Buy her a sofa and deliver it yourself,* and *Call her call her call her call her* and *Make her homemade marshmallows and present her with a box of five hundred* and *Make her homemade truffles and present her with one box and a certificate for a lifetime supply.* Merlin was getting a splitting headache to go with his crushing heartache.

More to make his raptor shut up for thirty seconds that because he thought it would help, he said, "Fine. I'll make her truffles."

But Blue was underfoot the entire time he was getting the ingredients out, whining and making barking grunts and grunting barks, banging into Merlin and even nipping him a few times. He probably missed Cloud and Dali. No amount of petting calmed him down. Merlin finally had to shut him in the bedroom for fear that he'd knock down a pot of molten chocolate over himself.

The truffles demanded enough focus that they worked as a distraction. But not enough to shut out all other thoughts. The house felt so empty and silent without Dali.

How can your mate break up with you? Being mates was supposed to mean you'd love each other forever.

That was when Merlin remembered that he'd never had a chance to tell Dali that they were mates. He'd never even told her he loved her!

Was *that* why she'd broken up? Had he somehow failed to convey the depth of his feelings? Did she think he saw their relationship as a passing fling, not something true and deep and forever?

Seized with new hope, he ran to the phone. He picked it up, then remembered the truffles and ran back to the kitchen. He'd roll them in their appropriate toppings, box them up, and drive to her apartment with them.

Merlin had almost finished rolling the truffles when there was a knock at the door. His heart leaped at the knowledge that there was only one person for whom it would make sense to come over rather than calling at this hour. He dashed to the door, then remembered that there were in fact a couple of other people who might knock on his door for much less friendly reasons. Merlin checked the feed on the camera Carter had installed outside his window.

Dali stood outside his door.

Merlin flung open the door, only barely stopping himself from flinging his arms around her too. She stood a little awkwardly, her body language closed off, without her usual confidence and sensual ease.

She hasn't come to tell me she's changed her mind, he thought. *She's just come to talk.*

But that realization didn't dampen his hope. Once they talked, maybe she *would* change her mind.

"Dali, come in. I made truffles. I was going to bring them over to your apartment, but you beat me to it." He spun around, rushed to the kitchen, quickly laid them on a plate, and presented them to her. "The one covered in light cocoa powder are milk chocolate, dark cocoa powder are dark chocolate, the ones with a bit of candied Buddha's palm are lemon, the crushed peppermint candy are peppermint—of course—and the ones with the green square on top are pandan."

Dali stared at them like they were alien artifacts. "Panda?"

"Pandan," Merlin said, making himself slow down. He must've been talking way too fast for her to mishear that word.

She gave him another blank look, then said, "I don't want candy."

They're not "candy," they're homemade truffles, his raptor said, sounding aggrieved. *How can she not want homemade truffles?*

Shush. She's probably too upset to eat.

"Sorry," Merlin said. "Bad timing. Would you like something else? Hot chocolate? Hot tea? A glass of water?"

He could hear that he was babbling, but there was something so strange about her, it was throwing him off. The way she stood… her expression, something about her expression…

"I want to talk." She was still standing at the door. She hadn't even closed it behind her. It was a cold night, too.

"Sure. Want to sit down?"

"No, I don't want to sit down!" She sounded so angry that Merlin felt the force of it like a slap.

She'd spoken loudly enough to alarm Blue. He started growling and yelping from the bedroom. There was a thud as he banged into the door, then a bunch of nails-on-chalkboard sounds as he scrabbled against it with his blunt claws.

"Sorry," Merlin said again. "I had to lock him out because I was cooking with lot of hot ingredients, and he was all over the place. I was afraid he'd get hurt. Shall I let him out?"

"No." Dali was as beautiful as ever, but her eyes were cold, not warm. So cold that he couldn't feel the sexual heat that had always crackled between them, from the first moment they'd met. "I came here to tell you not to contact me. Ever. When I say it's over, I mean *over.*"

This isn't right, his raptor broke in.

I know, Merlin said silently. It was the least right moment of his entire life.

"I don't want you in my life," she went on, each word as precise as a dagger of ice to the heart. "I want a man, not a boy who'll never grow up. There's no room in my life for you and your lies and your ridiculous stories."

There was a moment of dead silence. Absurdly, Merlin found himself fixated on her eyebrows. Those marvelous, expressive eyebrows of hers that had never moved once since he'd spotted her on the closed circuit camera.

She turned to go.

Merlin grabbed her arm and yanked her back inside, kicking the door shut behind her.

She stared at him, eyes wide and eyebrows unmoving, then let out a distinctly fake-sounding scream.

"Don't bother," Merlin said. "Who are you, and what have you done with Dali?"

The person wearing the shape of the woman he loved glared at him. But it wasn't Dali's glare.

Once the penny had dropped, it was obvious. Merlin couldn't believe she'd fooled him for even a few minutes. Her body language was all wrong. She'd looked puzzled when he'd mentioned Buddha's Hand and pandan. She'd refused his truffles and hadn't even looked tempted by them. He'd seen her beauty, but he hadn't wanted to kiss her or touch her; the spark between them was gone.

Most of all, she'd been cruel to him. Dali would never be cruel. Even when she was breaking up with him, she'd done her best to be gentle and not blame him. Her tears had been as much for his pain as for her own.

And she loved his stories.

What had this person done with her?

Make her talk, urged his raptor. *Let me take over. I'll bite her till she gives in!*

Merlin was seriously tempted. But it wasn't necessary. The air shimmered and the arm he held seemed to squirm unpleasantly within his hand. Then he stood facing a middle-aged woman with white hair and cold blue eyes. She wore something halfway between a doctor's white coat and a psychic's flowing robe, embroidered in black with magical and scientific symbols.

"You're a wizard-scientist," Merlin said. "Why am I not surprised?"

"I am Morgana," she said. "And I have come to make you an offer."

Tell her to fuck her offer, said his raptor. *Tell her if she doesn't tell you where Dali is, this second, you'll bite her head off. Literally.*

Merlin wanted to do that so much, he actually had to bite his tongue to stop himself. But he'd had a lot of practice reading people's faces, and what he read in Morgana's, in addition to arrogance and cruelty, was intelligence. This woman was a planner, and she was a good one. She hadn't charged in with all guns blazing, she'd walked in wearing his true love's face.

He had absolutely no doubt that Morgana had already set up some kind of fail-safe in case he did the obvious thing and threatened her. She had to have a gun to Dali's head. And much as that image put him into a near-blinding rage, it also made him hold his tongue.

If he wanted to save his mate, he couldn't just be aggressive. He had to be smart, too. Her life might depend on it.

"What's the offer?" Merlin asked.

Morgana looked down at his hand like it was covered with watermelon frappuccino. "First, release my arm."

Merlin was glad to do that. He wanted to touch her about as much as he wanted to pet a slug. "Well?"

She smiled. It wasn't a nice smile. "How are you feeling tonight?"

Furious, said his raptor. *Protective. Scared for Dali. Is she locked up? Is she tied up? Is she hurt? Is she afraid? Stop talking and bite Morgana's head off, now now now now now!*

Merlin bit his tongue again. This time he actually tasted blood.

Stop it, he told his raptor. *Do you want to save Dali? Then stop yelling and help me think!*

To his surprise, his raptor promptly said, *She didn't expect you to recognize her. She must've been planning to twist the knife and go. And maybe come back again as herself, with her offer? She wanted to make you miserable, and she wanted to make sure you wouldn't call Dali and find out she never said those things.*

"Lousy," he said. "My girlfriend dumped me. Kind of takes the shine off saving the circus."

As he spoke, his mind was racing. Who'd sicced those inspectors on them, anyway? He suspected that the culprit was standing right there in front of him.

"Yes, you did save the circus." A sour expression crossed Morgana's face, then melted into pleasure. "It will go on. But you will never be able to go back to it again."

That genuinely startled Merlin. What had she done? But he pushed that curiosity aside. He didn't want her monologing for ages about whatever clever plan she'd concocted to ruin his life; he wanted to get to Dali as quickly as possible.

But Morgana was already talking. "Remember how friendly Rosine Richelieu was, and how she promised to speak to her friends on your behalf? That was me, raising your hopes and making sure you'd assume you had help instead of campaigning on your own behalf."

"Shit!" Merlin blurted out. He hadn't realized she'd infiltrated the circus. Had she harmed anyone there?

Morgana smiled, no doubt assuming he was upset about her under-mining him as heir. "The trapeze? That was me. And Fausto, poisoning your coffee?"

Merlin winced. He didn't like Fausto, but nobody deserved being falsely accused.

"Me." The wizard-scientist's smile widened. "And when you went to Fausto's room to tell him you'd made up the whole story and poisoned your own coffee, and gloated over his downfall? That was me, too. And guess who overheard?"

Merlin, horrified, didn't have to guess. Morgana clearly went for whatever would cause the maximum pain.

"Mom." His voice came out choked. "Oh, my God."

"Yes. Well, your mother plus a few witnesses. I had to be sure she wouldn't cover up her beloved son's crimes."

"She wouldn't," Merlin whispered. "Not if it meant convicting an innocent man."

"Yes, you're quite correct," said Morgana. "It turns out that all it takes to destroy a mother's love is to discover that her son committed an unforgivable crime out of greed. The entire circus hates you now."

Merlin felt like the floor had crumbled under his feet. But he forced that feeling aside. No matter what happened to him, he had to save his mate.

His frustrated anger escaped in the sound of a low hiss as his raptor very nearly took control of his body. Merlin only barely managed to wrest back control and stay human.

Morgana flinched slightly, but stood her ground. "Keep in mind that if I don't report back to my minions within a certain timeframe, they'll kill your mother and your ex-girlfriend."

The entire world seemed to white out in a blinding flash of incandescent fury. When he came back to himself, Morgana was holding up her hand in a mystic gesture, and the air sparkled around her in what he assumed was a magical shield. His knuckles were bruised and bleeding where he'd apparently slammed them into the shield. When he forced his fists to unclench, he saw that his fingernails had bitten into his palms.

I knew it, he thought. *It's useless being stronger than her. I have to be* smarter *than her. I have to trick her, somehow. But how?*

Nothing came to him.

"Dali," he said. "I'll listen to your offer. But I want to see Dali first."

Morgana gave him a sharp look. "She doesn't love you, so what do you care?"

Merlin gritted his teeth. Why couldn't he have been targeted by a different type of wizard-scientist? The one who'd gone after Pete had turned into a pteranodon and attacked him. Merlin would have much rather dealt with that than with this manipulative woman who knew all his weak points. It was almost as if she'd been designed to frustrate him—even her power was similar to his.

His power.

The power he'd recently gained some control over, at least enough

256

to tell if it was off or on. It was off now. But what if he could get it to turn on?

Morgana already knew him. His power should be completely useless against her.

But he had a feeling that maybe it wasn't. Maybe, just maybe, he'd never been able to make it work the way it was designed to.

Help me, Merlin thought. *For Dali.*

For our mate, his raptor agreed. Unexpectedly, he added, *You needed the mate bond to make your power work right. I know that now. When they tried to sever the bond, it fractured your power. But now the bond is strong. And so are we.*

Of course, Merlin thought. No wonder he hadn't had any trouble recently getting his raptor to agree on what size to become. He was in tune with his truest self now: the self who could love and be loved. And, he hoped, that would enable him to unlock the limits of his other power too.

Together, they reached deep into themselves. Merlin could feel how to turn his power on now. But he needed to make it work just a little bit differently, give it that little twist that would enable it to get past the difficulty of a person already knowing him. And then one more twist, to make it not about perceiving him as the *person* she expected, but as the *Merlin* she expected...

He looked into Morgana's cold blue eyes, willing her to see the same chill in his own. Willing her to believe that he was the man she wanted him to be—the one who would betray everything and join with her.

"I know she doesn't love me," Merlin said. "But if I've lost every-thing—if I'm maybe going to leave everything—then I want to know for sure where I stand. Take me to her, and then we'll talk."

She examined him carefully, then gave a brisk nod. "Fine. Just keep in mind what happens to her if you try any tricks."

"I'm not trying anything," Merlin said, holding up his bloody knuck-les. "Once was enough."

He followed her out the door, his mind whirling. Had she forgotten about poor Blue, still locked in his bedroom? Blue, whose barking must have been trying to warn him?

In a flash of realization, he understood why Blue had appeared in the tunnel where Morgana-as-Fausto had poisoned his coffee. His smart, loyal, magical pet must have been trying to warn him about her.

Probably all the magical pets had showed up at the performance to try to warn their owners about Morgana. They'd been captured and imprisoned by the wizard-scientists, so they probably knew their scent or auras or something like that. If only he'd had the sense to try to figure out why Blue was there, instead of dismissing his presence as simple loneliness!

"I'll send a minion to collect your beast," Morgana said casually as she unlocked her car. "I don't want him shedding all over the back seat."

Merlin had to think fast. His power was making him more believable, but he still had to say things she'd find it *possible* to believe. Would the wavering-on-the-brink-of-the-Dark-Side Merlin be willing to sacrifice his pet, or was that a bridge too far?

"What are you going to do with him?" Merlin asked.

"Nothing harmful," she said. "You saw yourself that the magical creatures in our lab were well-fed and in good health."

Well-fed, healthy experimental subjects, he thought with an inward shudder.

"How about this, then," Merlin suggested. "*If* I decide to take your offer, Blue is part of the deal. I keep him, but if you need any blood samples or fur snippets or anything like that, you're welcome to them."

He caught the flash of greed in her eyes at that. Once your mark started saying stuff like "*If,*" they were already in your pocket. They just didn't know it yet.

"Agreed," she said.

He didn't know if she was lying or not, and didn't care. Whatever got him to his mate.

Morgana drove on, taking him deeper into the dark night and whatever dangers lay ahead.

CHAPTER 26

Dali sat alone in an empty warehouse, alternating between worry for Merlin and fury at Morgana.

As soon as Dali had realized that the person she was with wasn't Merlin, Morgana had revealed her true form and paralyzed Dali with a weird magical gesture. She'd been forced to sit in the car, silently seething, until Morgana parked and a couple of big men unloaded her and carried her into a warehouse, where they handcuffed her to a chair; apparently the paralysis went away as soon as Morgana stopped actively maintaining it.

Dali had entertained a brief fantasy of being able to escape by removing her prosthetic hand, but unfortunately neither Morgana nor her minions had failed to notice that she had one. She was handcuffed by her right wrist, and the chair was bolted to the floor. Which was alarming all by itself.

Even worse, the warehouse contained several empty cages, one large enough for a big dog and several sized for kittens, all secured with locks made of an odd silvery metal. That must be the shift-silver Merlin had mentioned, which prevented mythical shifters from shifting and stopped magical creatures from escaping. Cloud was imprisoned in one of them, sticking her paws through the bars and alternating between pitiful meows and ominous howls.

Cloud let out a particularly nerve-shredding yowl, making both the guards wince.

Much as Dali didn't want to attract the guards' attention, she had to comfort her kitten. "It's okay, baby. I'm here with you. Just sit tight."

Sure enough, the guards sneered at this. One repeated her words in high-pitched mockery, and the other said, also imitating her voice, "Don't worry, baby, the crippled woman handcuffed to the chair is going to save you!"

Dali took some satisfaction in looking at the bloody bites and scratches on the guards, which they'd gotten while transferring Cloud from her purse to the cage.

But it didn't last long, lost in a tide of worry about herself, about Cloud, and about Merlin. Sure, Morgana wanted Cloud. But Dali was convinced that the wizard-scientist wanted Merlin, too. For all his strength and skills and cleverness, could he evade a woman who could look like anyone in the world and paralyze you with a snap of her fingers?

The door opened, and Morgana walked in with Merlin at her side. The sight of him gave Dali a rush of totally irrational relief, followed by fear for him.

But most of all, what she felt was love. Every moment they'd ever had together came back to her with a piercing clarity, along with the desire for more moments. She wanted so much to jump up, throw her arms around him, and never let him go that she almost believed that the force of her desire would allow her to rip the chair up from its bolts.

Dali realized then that she'd left him not out of love, but out of fear. She'd known they were both far too willing to make sacrifices of their own lives for the sake of others, and she'd been so afraid that they'd do it again that she'd walked away from the greatest love she'd ever known.

She couldn't let herself be ruled by fear. If she had to be ruled by something, she wanted to be ruled by love.

Dali was about to call out to him that she loved him and she was sorry when their eyes met. She didn't know how she knew what he wanted, but without a single movement, without even a flicker of his eyes, he was telling her to keep quiet and follow his lead. Dali knew it with as much certainty as she knew that she loved him, though his actual expression showed a weariness and despair and bitter determination that made her heart hurt.

But Merlin had been raised by con artists. He'd run rat roulette when he wasn't old enough to drink.

Morgana's the mark, Dali thought. *And I think I'm the plant.*

She hoped she'd be able to figure out what con Merlin was playing, and be word-perfect with her lines without any rehearsal. A single slip was likely to be deadly for both of them.

"See?" said Morgana. "Your ex-girlfriend is unharmed."

"She's bleeding," Merlin pointed out.

"A minor scratch," said Morgana. "One that I had nothing to do with. She told me herself that her own magical beast attacked her."

"Well, I want to check her myself." Merlin strode to her side and took her chin in one hand and the back of her head in the other, tilting her head around as he peered at her blood-smeared cheek. Though his touch was impersonal and his expression revealed nothing, the crackle of sexual energy that went through her nearly made her jump.

How could I have believed in Morgana for a second? This *is Merlin*, Dali thought.

"Satisfied?" asked Morgana.

"Not yet." He lifted her left arm and checked it, running his hand over the join between the prosthetic and her wrist, then knelt and began patting her down.

Dali fixed her gaze on Morgana, not Merlin. The wizard-scientist was visibly bored and irritated.

Finally, Merlin straightened up. "You're right, she's not hurt. Are you going to release her once I've heard your offer?"

"Yes," Morgana said smoothly. "My interest is in you and her magical beast, not the woman herself. I merely wanted to keep her from interfering while I presented my offer."

Sure you're going to release me, Dali thought, but held her tongue. Her attention was on Merlin, the wizard-scientist, and her two guards. Even if they weren't shifters, they were big strong men, and they both had guns. Not even Merlin's biggest velociraptor could take out one wizard and two armed men before one of them got off a spell or a shot.

"Fine," Merlin said. "Let's hear your offer."

Morgana smiled. "First, let's review your situation. You're alone in the world. Your ability to form a mate-bond has been severed."

What the hell is a mate-bond? Dali thought.

"Your latest lover wants nothing more to do with you," Morgana went on.

"No, wait," Merlin protested. "Here she is—maybe she's changed her mind."

Dali *thought* she knew what Merlin wanted her to say, but she hoped he'd give her some kind of clue.

Without pause, he addressed her earnestly. "I came here to rescue you! At serious risk to myself! I'm not saying you owe me, of course, but, well…"

"You're not saying it, but you sure implied it," Dali snapped. "It's because of you that I got kidnapped! I never should have gotten in that car with you. I mean her."

"Doesn't sound like she's changed her mind to me," Morgana remarked. "And she's not the only one who doesn't want you. Your team would be glad if you quit. The circus has declared you outcast. Your own mother has disowned you. "

What? Dali thought. But Merlin just nodded, looking even more depressed, so she kept up her stone face. Given how much she wanted to punch Morgana in the face, that took some doing.

"You've never belonged anywhere, in your entire life," said Morgana. "Not on your bodyguard team, not in the Marines, not in any of the jobs you did before the Marines, not in the circus, not even in your own blood family."

Low blow, thought Dali. She was more certain than ever that Merlin wanted her to play along, but she had to clench her jaw tight to avoid shouting out in his defense.

"So, to sum up, you have nothing and no one." Morgana paused for effect before saying, "Am I wrong?"

The sheer misery on Merlin's face struck Dali to the heart. Sure, he had a plan. But what Morgana was saying had to hurt anyway. Dali *had* broken up with him. He *had* been unwanted by his horrible bio-parents. And what was that thing about the circus and his mother?

"No," Merlin said in a voice of numb despair. "You're not wrong."

"But it doesn't have to be that way," said Morgana. "Not if you join us. We'll give you a place, and we'll never abandon you. You're important to us. We want you to be one of our Dark Knights, who will help us build a world in which we will rule. You will be powerful, and you will have a home."

Merlin hesitated, then took a slow step toward her. Then he stopped, wavering.

"And you will have freedom. You can do anything. Say anything. Whatever you say, people will believe it—or face the consequences. If you tell them they're a dog, they'll bark."

He took another step closer to her, then bowed his head in surrender.

Morgana extended her hand as if she expected him to kiss it. "Kneel before me, Merlin, and I will make you the first and most powerful of our Dark Knights. Kneel, and I will name you Deceit."

Merlin sank down to his knees.

Then he sank further down. Much further. In the blink of an eye, he was a velociraptor the size of a kitten. Before Morgana could react, he sank his fangs into her ankle.

Morgana let out a piercing shriek of shock and pain. Her men tried to aim their guns at Merlin, but he shrank further, to the size of a hamster. As she flailed around, screaming, he used his talons to rapidly clamber up her robe.

But Dali only saw this out of the corner of her eye. She'd made her move the instant she saw Merlin shrink.

When he'd touched her hair, he'd pulled out one of her hairpins, and when he'd patted her down, blocking everyone's view of her body with his own, he'd picked the handcuff lock with one hand. So she was free to leap out of the chair, rush the nearest guard, and disarm him while he was distracted by Morgana's screaming.

Dali had learned that move in boot camp and faithfully practiced it. She'd always trusted that it would work in an actual combat situation, and was pleased to find that it did. She slammed the butt of his own gun down on his head—another move she'd learned in boot camp—and that worked too. He crumpled to the ground.

But one guard remained. He couldn't shoot at Merlin without hitting Morgana, so he swung his gun toward Dali.

Instantly, Merlin was a velociraptor the size of a man. His long tail cracked like a whip, knocking the gun from the guard's hand.

Morgana, no longer distracted by a tiny velociraptor climbing her robe, made a quick gesture. Merlin froze in place.

"Dammit!" Dali yelled.

As she backed up so she could cover both Morgana and the guard, something grabbed her ankle. She kicked out, dislodging the clutching hand; it belonged to the guard she'd hit with the gun, who had failed to stay unconscious.

In that instant of distraction, the other guard rushed her. He had the element of surprise and was much stronger than her. Despite her struggles, he managed to pin her hands at her side. Dali gave a hard, painful twist and upward yank of her left arm. Her prosthetic hand popped off, leaving her arm free.

The guard, who had obviously forgotten that she had a prosthetic, let out a yell of horror. Dali almost laughed; he must've thought her actual hand had come off! Before he could recover from the shock, she struck him across the neck with her left elbow (boot camp again), then body-slammed him into the row of cages.

With a vengeful howl and a buzz of wings, Cloud pounced. She stuck out her paws, yanked his fingers through the bars, and sank her teeth in the nearest one while clawing the hell out of the others. The guard let out a shrill scream.

Dali spun around, bringing her gun to bear on Morgana.

And froze in place.

If she could have moved her lips, she'd have sworn a blue streak. As it was, all she could do was watch while Morgana, her brow furrowed in concentration, said, "Guards! Restrain them!"

The guard Dali had hit over the head got up, glaring at her. He was joined by the guard whose hand Cloud had scratched and bitten.

"How do we restrain a dinosaur?" the bitten guard asked sulkily.

Morgana looked at them like they were idiots. "Hold a gun to the woman's head. Then I'll release Merlin. If he doesn't turn into a human and cooperate, shoot her."

"Oh." The bitten guard pried the gun from Dali's hand, then pressed the barrel to her head. The touch of cold steel made her shiver involuntarily.

Morgana gestured. Merlin unfroze, then became a man. Without pause, he said, "I'll cooperate! I'm going to go sit in that chair there, and you can cuff me, okay?"

"Do it," she ordered.

Merlin sat down in the chair, and the other guard handcuffed him by both wrists with his hands behind his back.

"And keep the gun on him, too," warned Morgana. Then she gestured, and Dali unfroze.

It's hard for her to keep people frozen, Dali thought. *Especially more than one person at once.*

But she couldn't figure out how to make use of that knowledge when she had a gun to her head. And their enemies were taking no chances: Morgana indicated another chair, and cuffed Dali herself when she sat in it, so the guard could still keep a gun to her head. He didn't lower it once she was cuffed, either.

The guard who'd thought he'd pulled off her hand picked up her prosthetic gingerly, by one finger. "I oughta stomp this to bits."

"Have fun trying," Dali said, though she really hoped he wouldn't. It had been very expensive. "You'll bruise the hell out of your foot. Might even break it."

With a disgusted look, he instead dropped her hand in her lap like it was a dead rat.

Merlin's golden hair was disheveled and he was cuffed to a chair, but he gave her a reassuring smile. "You were fantastic. I had no idea you could fight like that. How have we never sparred together?"

Dali didn't see how they were going to get out of this, but Merlin's impossible yet genuine cheer gave her hope. "Guess we were too busy with other stuff. Too bad."

"It's not too late. We still can."

"What are you talking about?" Morgana said angrily, stepping back to face Dali and Merlin. "You're not going anywhere. And even if by some miracle you did escape, you're not going to do anything together, ever again. She doesn't love you, remember?"

"Boy, are you wrong about that." Dali turned her head so she could look Merlin in the eyes as she spoke. "I love you, Merlin. I'm sorry I broke up with you. I was scared that our lives were incompatible, and… I was scared. But I'm not scared anymore. I love you, and I want to be with you. We can work it out."

His eyes shone like a cloudless sky on a sunny summer day. "I love you too. And we *will* work it out."

"You're not working anything out," snapped Morgana. Her cold eyes fixed on Merlin. "So you found one person to lean on. Good for you. But you have nothing else. You're swimming alone in a stormy sea, and she's your life preserver. And when I kill her before your eyes, you'll have to take my hand or drown."

Dali saw the flash of fury and terror in Merlin's eyes. But when he spoke, his voice was calm and steady. "I'm not alone. It doesn't matter what kind of tricks you played at the circus—once I explain what you did, my mother and my friends will believe me, not you. My team does respect me and care about me. I teach Caro gymnastics. I have friends all over the world. Killing Dali won't get you anything from me."

"Then maybe I'll kill her just because I feel like it," snapped Morgana.

"I don't think so," said Merlin.

"Oh?" Morgana said. "And who's going to stop me?"

Merlin just smiled. And then Blue, who had come padding up behind her, unnoticed by the guards who were intent on Dali and Merlin, bent down and bit Morgana's ankle. Her other ankle, the one that the velociraptor hadn't bitten before. She went down with a scream.

"Blue is," replied Dali. Now that she could stop trying not to look at him or give anything away, she didn't need to let Merlin hog *all* the comebacks.

Morgana rose from the floor with an ear-piercing screech, taking to the air on flapping leathery wings. She had become a gray-green flying reptile with a long, sharp beak: a pterodactyl. Blood dripped down her scaly ankles and off her sharp claws.

Merlin's cuffs fell to the floor as he became a hamster-sized velociraptor. Before either his guard or Dali's could react, Merlin became the twelve-foot raptor again, knocking the guns from their hands with simultaneous blows from his head and tail. He was so fast that Dali had no time to be afraid, but only to marvel at his agility and precision. Even his maximum-size raptor moved with the grace of the acrobat that he was.

But as he lunged for the guards, they both shifted. The one Cloud had bitten became a dinosaur bigger than Merlin with spines down its back and a vicious spiked tail, and the one Dali had hit over the head became a shaggy black dog the size of a horse, wreathed in gray smoke and with eyes of flame.

What is *that thing?* Dali was more unnerved by the black dog than by the dinosaur, even though the dog was smaller. *That's not any kind of animal that ever lived. It looks like some kind of dog-demon!*

Then she had no room in her mind for curiosity, but only fear for Merlin. He stood in front of her, shielding her from the three creatures as they all attacked at once.

The pterodactyl who was Morgana flew at him from above, darting in to stab at him with her sword-like beak, then veering upward before he could retaliate; the warehouse had a very high ceiling, with more than enough room for her to evade him. Dali wondered if Morgana, who liked to plan ahead, had brought them to it in case she had to fight in her flighted form.

Meanwhile, the spike-tailed dinosaur attacked with vicious swipes of its tail. The black dog was hard to see clearly, with its cloud of smoke, and it seemed to materialize wherever Merlin wasn't looking, biting at him.

Merlin was more agile than any of them, and fought with a protective fury. But he was stuck in one place, as he wouldn't leave Dali, and soon his sleek black hide was streaked with blood.

Dali struggled furiously, but to no avail. Cloud was throwing herself against the bars of her cage and yowling, but she couldn't get free either. And Blue seemed to have vanished as mysteriously as he'd appeared. Dali hoped he was sneaking up on their enemies, but she couldn't imagine that one bugbear could do much good against three monsters. On the other hand, they needed all the help they could get.

And then she spotted him on the other side of the warehouse, moseying across the floor in what did indeed look like an attempt to sneak up on the fight. Dali wanted to scream at him to hurry up, but she held her tongue. The element of surprise was their only hope.

Morgana the pterodactyl was starting to swoop upward again. To make sure she didn't spot Blue, who was extremely easily visible given that he was bright blue and the rest of the warehouse was gray, Dali let out a piercing shriek.

Morgana's gray-green head whipped toward her.

"Hey!" Dali yelled. "What ever happened to your sneaky, clever plans? Now you're just trying to beat us up like some kind of common thug! You're not as smart as you think if the best you can do is turn into a pterodactyl!"

As Dali kept on yelling, behind Morgana and the other attackers the big double doors of the warehouse slowly and soundlessly swung open.

The hot red-gold glow of firelight flooded the warehouse. For the first time since she'd entered it, Dali felt warm. A great bird who seemed entirely made of flame arrowed through the doors, leaving behind a trail of fire, and went straight for the pterodactyl.

Not it, Dali thought as her face cracked in an incredulous smile. *Him. That must be Roland, the phoenix.*

A ferocious roar shook the building as the cave bear that was Pete charged in. The shaggy brown beast slammed into the spike-tailed dinosaur, biting and clawing.

Then a huge black dog stalked inside. Wisps of gray smoke rose from its body, and its eyes were like windows into the flames of Hell.

"Behind you!" Dali yelled. "Merlin, Pete, enemy behind you!"

The black dog swung its head toward her. Dali shrank back from the pits of flame that were its eyes. It shook its head in a surprisingly human gesture, then leaped to attack the other black dog.

Dali's bewilderment gave way to realization. So *that* was what a hellhound was. She hoped her warning hadn't distracted the others too much.

Finally, Carter strode in. He wore a long black coat over a suit and carried a gun in one hand and a briefcase in the other. He cast a quick glance over the fight, saw that he couldn't fire without risking hitting one of his friends, and made a wide circuit of the fight to get to Dali. Despite the battle going on all around him, he calmly reached into his coat, pulled out a tool Dali didn't recognize, and lowered it to her handcuffs. They fell to the floor with a clang.

She grabbed her prosthetic and jumped up, gasping, "Thank you!"

"No problem."

"What can I do to help?" Dali asked, then trailed off.

Pete the cave bear was crouched atop the fallen spike-tailed dinosaur, growling. Merlin and Ransom, both still in their shift forms, had the other hellhound cornered.

The only people still fighting were Roland and Morgana. Morgana dodged a swipe of Roland's fiery claws and dove toward Merlin, her vicious beak aimed straight down. Roland flew to intercept her, flame streaming out behind him. They met in a fireball so big and bright that Dali had to cover her eyes. When she opened them, nothing remained in the air but the phoenix, and a little ash sifting down.

"I think we're good," said Carter.

He used his gadget to unlock Cloud's cage. The dragonfly kitten flew out and into Dali's arms, nuzzling her and rubbing her face into Dali's chest. Dali held her close with her left arm while she put her left hand back on.

The phoenix landed on the floor. For an instant that was seared forever into Dali's mind, he became a man still wreathed in flame. Then the fire vanished, and he was Roland, looking a little tired but unhurt.

"Pete, get off him," Roland ordered. "Hellhound, dinosaur, shift back now, kneel down, and put your hands behind your heads."

Pete clambered off the dinosaur, growling. Once he was off, both the guards shifted back to battered, bleeding men who sullenly obeyed Roland's orders. Roland cuffed them with handcuffs that had a line of shiftsilver running through their steel. Pete stayed a bear and Ransom stayed a hellhound to keep watch over the prisoners.

Roland continued, "Carter, call the shifter police and tell them to come for a hellhound and... some kind of big dinosaur."

Shifter police? Dali thought. But she didn't waste time wondering about that, but ran to Merlin.

He shifted back to a man before she reached him, then staggered. She caught and steadied him. His clothes were covered in blood, making her heart miss a beat.

"Merlin's hurt—he needs help!" Dali shouted.

"I'm fine," Merlin said. "Don't worry about me."

Roland hurried to his side. "Merlin, sit down."

Merlin didn't try to go to a chair, but sat down on the floor. Dali kept her arms around him. "Lean on me."

Blue padded up and nuzzled him. Carter knelt down, produced a pair of scissors from his coat, and cut off Merlin's shirt. His chest and shoulders were gashed and bleeding, but to Dali's immense relief, none of the wounds looked life-threatening. Carter opened his briefcase, which turned out to be a first-aid kit in the world's most inappropriately expensive case, and he and Roland began bandaging Merlin's wounds.

Merlin leaned his head against Dali's shoulder, and she stroked his hair and held his hand.

"You saved me," she said. Then, no longer caring about who heard her or what they might think, she said, "I love you."

"I love you too," said Merlin. "And I'm pretty sure you saved me a couple times too."

They caught each other up on how Morgana had tricked them. Dali saw red when Merlin told her Morgana's plot to destroy the circus and set him up. She burst out, "That woman was the worst!"

"I know. I have to talk to my mom. And everyone. Undo the damage she did." Merlin glanced up at Roland. "How about you wait for the shifter cops, and Dali and I go back to the circus?"

Roland frowned, his hands still full of rolls of gauze. "You should go back to the office, actually. There's a puncture wound that an actual medical professional should take a look at. I can call the paramedics on the west coast team…"

"We have a paramedic at the circus," Merlin pointed out. "I'm sure he can handle a pterodactyl beak stab wound as well as Shane or Catalina or Ellie."

"In that case, let's go now. I have the biggest car—you can lie down in the back seat." Roland straightened up. "Carter, can you stay and talk to the police?"

Carter shook his head. Dali expected him to say he wasn't on the team and it wasn't his job, but he looked agitated rather than put-upon. A small muscle twitched at his temple as he said, "Roland, I have to go before they get here. I told them I was you over the phone. Shifters are a small community—someone might recognize me—"

"Go, go," said Roland. Carter practically ran out. A moment later, Dali heard the motor revving as he sped away.

Before Dali could ask what that was about, Roland glanced at Pete and Ransom. "Can you both shift for a moment? They're cuffed with shiftsilver, they're not going anywhere."

Pete shifted back to a man. Ransom didn't.

Roland looked closely at the huge black dog. "Are you all right?"

The hellhound made a sound that made the hairs on the back of Dali's neck stand up before she recognized it as the world's scariest version of a dog's whimper of pain.

Merlin struggled in Dali's arms, trying to stand up. "Roland, he's hurt—we have to get him help."

"I can handle the prisoners," Pete said. "And I'll explain everything to the cops. I can't believe I'm saying this, but Merlin's right. The rest of you should go to the circus."

Roland crouched down and lifted Merlin from Dali's arms.

"I can walk," Merlin protested.

"This is faster," Roland said as he strode out with Blue following him, whining anxiously. Dali walked beside him, with Cloud perched on her shoulder. The hellhound that was Ransom padded silently at their heels.

Dali opened the back door of Roland's car and got in, and he helped Merlin lie down with his head in her lap. Cloud jumped down and nestled into Merlin's shoulder. Blue scrambled in and sat on the floor, resting his head on Merlin's chest.

Roland said, "Ransom, you have to shift back. If you can't—"

The hellhound became a man, pale and swaying.

"Sorry," whispered Ransom, and fainted.

Roland caught him before he hit the ground, then lowered him down and checked him for injuries.

Merlin rolled over and propped himself up on one hand. "Where's he hurt? I don't see any bleeding. Maybe a head injury?"

Roland gently felt around Ransom's head. "No, doesn't look like it.

There's no blood or swelling." He stood up, tilted the passenger seat as far back as it would go, and buckled Ransom into it. As he got in the driver's seat and began heading away from the warehouse, he said, "I think he overused his powers. He's the one who found you."

"How'd you know we were even missing?" Dali asked.

"I set off Carter's house alarm on my way out," Merlin said.

Roland nodded. "We all came running, and we found your house empty, your car still there, and Blue gone."

"Huh." Merlin scratched behind Blue's ears. "I left him inside. I wonder how he got there?"

"Same way he got to the circus, I expect," Dali said. "However that was. It's not like he can fly."

Roland shrugged. "Well, I wish he'd waited till we got there. Maybe we could've followed him. As it was, we had nothing to go on. So Ransom found the address. By the time he got it for us, he was in so much pain, he couldn't drive. But he insisted on coming anyway. 'Just in case,' he said. So I drove him. I told him to stay in the car. When he came in anyway, I figured he was feeling better."

A police car drove past them in the opposite direction, sirens blaring.

"There they are," said Roland.

"The shifter police?" said Dali. "I thought shifters were secret."

"They are," said Merlin. "But there's a few high up in law enforcement, and they pull strings to create small units where every officer in them is a shifter, then assign them shifter-related crimes. Something like this is probably going to be completely off the record, and the prisoners will stand trial in a shifter court. A normal jail couldn't hold a hellhound or a kentrosaurus."

Dali patted his shoulder. "I love that you know what kind of dinosaur that was."

"Of course I started *really* studying them once I could turn into one," Merlin said. "But even when I was a kid, I was interested in prehistory. Did I ever tell you how Natalie and me helped return a stolen trilobite to a museum? It all began when Leona Pride, the lioness, got the bright

273

idea of using the French poodles to scam a dogfighting ring…"

As Merlin went on, Dali felt herself slowly begin to relax. There was no way he was seriously injured when he could talk like that. Morgana had fled, and her minions were under arrest. The circus had been saved.

Most of all, Merlin loved her. They'd figure out their future, and she'd listen to his stories for the rest of her life. She knew she'd never tire of them, with the bone-deep certainty with which she knew that they'd never tire of each other.

CHAPTER 27

Getting pecked by a pterodactyl was no picnic. And though Merlin knew that Ransom's powers took a toll on him, he'd never seen his teammate actually pass out before. Not to mention that he had a difficult conversation coming up with his mother—and he wasn't even thinking about the one where he explained to her that he was not in fact a heartless, conniving sociopath who'd frame an innocent man out of greed and petty dislike.

But despite all that, Merlin was happy. His enemies were defeated. Dali was safe. His teammates cared about him. He had a flying kitten curled up on his shoulder and licking his face with her little sandpaper tongue, a bugbear resting his furry head on Merlin's chest, and his head in Dali's lap. She had her prosthetic hand wrapped protectively around his, and her other hand was stroking his hair.

How could he be anything but happy, when Dali loved him?

"What's a true mate?" she asked. "Morgana mentioned it, and you seemed to know what it was."

"Oh, sorry," Merlin said. "I was going to tell you about that earlier, after the performance, but... er..."

"I broke up with you," she said, wincing. "Merlin, I am so sorry—"

"Don't worry about it. Anyway, your true mate is your true love. It's the person you're totally compatible with, who you'll always love and never fall out of love with."

"Till death do you part," she said, nodding. "That's us."

That's us.

All the weight of ancient shifter lore, all his angst over mates, and the wizard-scientists' greatest science and magic brought to bear to try to prevent him from ever having a mate, and Dali had recognized and accepted that they were true mates so simply and easily, before he'd even gotten the chance to explain any of the context.

But that was Dali. She was like a knife that cut through impossible knots, all the way through to the heart of things.

That's us, echoed his raptor.

"There's a *little* more to it," Merlin said. Seeing the stiffness of Roland's neck as he drove, Merlin decided not to get into it in his earshot. He still remembered Roland saying, "If I ever had a mate, she's dead." He went on, "But yeah. That's us."

Ransom stirred, his hand dangling by the side of his seat clenching into a fist. Merlin could see him in the rear view mirror, his face white and tense with pain. He struggled to sit up, mumbling, "I can't shift— he'll know me—"

"Easy." Roland put his hand on Ransom's chest. "It's me, Roland. You're safe."

Ransom's dark eyes opened wide, glassy and unseeing. He sat bolt upright, pushing Roland's hand aside, and said urgently, "She's dying! I can—I have to—turn around, turn around, you're going in the wrong direction—"

He slumped back down in the seat, his eyes falling shut again. When he opened them, he looked infinitely weary, but present. "I lost it. I had it for a moment, and then I lost it."

"Lost what?" Merlin asked.

"A woman… I could see her so clearly, but now I can't even remember what she looked like."

"It sounded like you were having a nightmare," said Dali.

"No. It was real." He leaned forward, resting his head in his hands.

"I can't *remember.*"

"Maybe it'll come back to you," said Roland. "Don't push it."

"Hey, Ransom?" said Merlin. "Thanks for finding us. I know it wasn't any fun."

"Yes, thank you," Dali said. "I really appreciate it."

Ransom mumbled something into his hands that might have been "you're welcome" or "don't mention it" or possibly "never again."

"We're taking you and Merlin to a paramedic at the circus," Roland said.

Ransom lifted his head slightly. In the rear-view mirror, Merlin caught a faint glimmer of humor as he said, "I know."

They pulled up to the circus gates. Merlin had lost all track of time, beyond that it was very late at night or else very early in the morning; either way, he'd expected that given the situation with Fausto and him, at least some people would still be up.

He hadn't expected everyone to be up and at the gates, waiting for him. A very angry-looking Fausto included.

"Maybe Roland had better explain," Dali suggested. "He has a natural air of authority, and he's less emotionally involved than me."

Roland got out and stood in front of Merlin's door, unobtrusively blocking it with his body.

Just in case he needs to defend me from an angry mob, Merlin thought. It touched him, though he knew the worst that would happen was getting placed on house arrest.

But when the crowd parted to let someone through, he realized that explanations might not be necessary: the people who came forward were Zane Zimmerman with four stretcher-bearers, followed by his mother. She waved Roland aside, saying, "We already know what happed. Pete called us from the warehouse. Not that it was necessary. Everyone knew that *person* couldn't have been my son!"

"You sure didn't know I couldn't have poisoned his coffee," muttered Fausto.

Over her shoulder, Mom said, "On the contrary. The fact that you

277

had previously been seen doing something very out of character helped us realize that there was an imposter on the loose." Then she squeezed partly into the car and touched Merlin's cheek. "I can't wait till you quit this dangerous job of yours!"

"About that," Merlin said. "I want to talk you. Can you wait till Zane gets through with me?"

"Of course." Mom extracted herself from the car and snapped her fingers at the stretcher-bearers. "Step quickly! There's two men to be taken to the infirmary."

"I can walk," said Merlin.

Dali's eyebrows conveyed her steely determination to not let him, as did his mother's frown and Roland's head-shake. Outnumbered, Merlin let them lift him on to the stretcher. To his irritation, he saw that Ransom had quietly gotten out of the car on his own two feet, forestalling any attempt to make *him* get carried away. It was especially frustrating because he was certain that Ransom felt worse than he did.

In the infirmary, Zane did a quick check of them both, then said to Ransom, "Your vital signs are stable. I can't find anything obviously wrong. Has this happened before?"

Avoiding Roland's gaze, Ransom admitted, "Yes."

"What did you do then?" Zane asked.

"I lay down for a while."

Roland looked like that answer gave *him* a headache. "Of course you did, you were already on the floor!"

Ransom didn't reply to that, but cast a pleading glance at Zane, who said, "Then do that again," and gave him the bed beside Merlin.

After that, Zane removed Merlin's bandages, thoroughly cleaned his wounds, and re-bandaged them. It hurt more than getting the injuries had, and it took a while. Dali held his hand, Cloud licked his face, Blue lay across his feet, and his mother distracted him by making him, Dali, and Roland recount to her exactly what had happened.

When Zane finished, Merlin said, "Mom, I have something I need to talk to you about."

"I'll just check my inventory," Zane said. Merlin knew perfectly well that he meant "I'll pretend to count pills while I nearly break my ears eavesdropping." But he didn't mind. This was something the whole circus would find out about anyway.

"Shall I..." Roland began.

"No," said Merlin. "You and Dali may as well sit in. It involves you both. That is, it definitely involves Dali. And it involves you too, Roland, you just don't know why yet."

His mother snapped her fingers. "Enough stalling, son."

Merlin plunged in. "I realized some things during the performance earlier. One is that there's exactly one person at this circus who could step into your shoes, and it's not me. It's Kalpana."

His mother looked stubborn. "Of course Kalpana's wonderful. But..."

"Who's been helping you with literally everything? Who runs the show every night from the booth? I've been gone for years—have things fallen apart, even a tiny bit? No, because Kalpana's been here, actually doing the job that's supposedly mine."

"That's all very well and good, but she's not a shifter. If, hypothetically, I named her heir, she'd have the exact same problem you did."

"I don't think so," Merlin said. "I think me not being a shifter was an excuse. I didn't realize it till I came back here as a shifter, and nothing changed. Fausto's jealous and some people just don't like me, but I think most of the opposition honestly doesn't think I'm right for the job. The reason they're so set against me as heir is because they love the circus and they want it to succeed."

"That's their problem, not yours," his mother replied with a sniff.

"Mom, they're right," Merlin said. "Your heir needs to be detail-oriented, with excellent organizational skills, who can manage a large group of people and keep them all working together smoothly. Be honest: does that sound like me?"

Fiercely, she said, "You can be anything you want to be!"

"I know." Merlin squeezed her hand. "And I know you love me. I know you're my mother in every way that matters. You don't need to give me a job I don't want to prove it. And I *don't* want it. I love the circus, and I love performing in it, but I've *done* that. I want to do something else now. I want to stay here in Refuge City and be a bodyguard."

Then, for the first time uncertain, he looked up at Dali. "That is— unless *you'd* rather join the circus? If you do, I'd be happy with that too. But if it's all the same to you, I choose the Defenders."

Dali's eyebrows rose in an arch that suggested equal parts delighted surprise and exasperation. "Merlin, why on earth didn't you tell me any of this earlier? I broke up with you because I *didn't* want to join the circus, and I thought it was the only place where you'd be happy!"

"Not at all," Merlin said. "I can be happy in lots of places."

His mother took a deep breath, then slowly let it out. She leaned over and kissed his forehead. "Then be happy in the job you choose. And next time, dodge better!"

"I promise," said Merlin. If Dali ever needed him to place his body between her and danger, he'd never hesitate. But sometimes you had to tell parents what they wanted to hear.

Dali jumped in before Mom could start scolding him over his care- lessness. "Janet, Merlin told me that you know a lot about the history of shifters. The wizard-scientists claim to be descended from ancient enemies of King Arthur. Do you know anything about them?"

Roland leaned forward, interested. "Or any shifter-related Arthur lore that might possibly be helpful to us."

Mom looked pleased; she enjoyed being consulted for her knowledge of legend and myth. "This is the first I've heard of your wizard-scien- tists, I'm afraid. The legend of Merlin is that he was the first shifter, and all shifters descend from him. He was a friend to animals, both ordinary and mythic. He had a pet owl who spoke prophecy, and he gave King Arthur his beloved dog Cavall. But on the eve of the battle of Camlann, the sorceress Morgana cast an enchantment over the owl and the dog, so the owl couldn't warn Merlin and the dog couldn't protect

Arthur. Arthur was killed and Merlin vanished forever."

Blue let out a mournful whine. Merlin petted him. "Not me, Blue. Just my namesake."

"It's interesting that magical animals have sought you out," said Mom. "It's almost unheard-of for them to adopt humans. Given what happened when the original Morgana took the pets out of the picture, I suggest that you be careful with yours."

"I would anyway," Merlin said, putting his arms around Blue and Cloud.

"So you think the pets may have some protective abilities?" Roland asked.

"They definitely do," Dali told him. "Blue and Cloud both attacked our enemies. And I think all the pets came to the performance to try to warn us about Morgana."

"It's more than that," said Ransom unexpectedly; Merlin had thought he was asleep. "They're important in ways that we haven't discovered yet. That's all I know, though."

"Changed your mind about wanting one?" Merlin teased.

"No," Ransom said, and rolled over and put a pillow over his head.

"What were those qualities you said were needed to run a circus?" Roland asked Merlin. "Detail-oriented, excellent organizational skills, able to manage a group of people and get them working together smoothly? There's another person here who has them."

Everyone looked at Dali, who said, "I don't want to run a circus, though."

"How would you feel about running the Defenders office?" Roland asked.

Yes yes yes, said Merlin's raptor. *She can fix everything and not chase off the clients and we can be together even more!*

Roland went on, "It's very similar to your old job."

Ransom removed the pillow to say, "And we *really* need you."

"If you can run a circus, you can run an office," Mom said.

"Our office *is* a circus," Merlin said, grinning. "Complete with a fake psychic, a juggler, an acrobat, a strong man, a target boy, and a dancing bear."

Dali looked like the sun had risen in her eyes. She nudged Merlin. "If I take the job, will you bring hot chocolate to my desk on cold days?"

Heartfelt, he said, "I'll bring you anything, anywhere, any time. And I'd love to have you on the team. We all would. It might even make Carter happy."

"Then I accept." She smiled at him, then at the rest of them. Roland gravely shook her hand.

"Good," said Ransom, and put the pillow back over his head.

Roland's phone rang. He stepped away to take the call, then returned and said, "Well, I have good news and bad news. The bad news is that Morgana's shifters were just criminals she hired. They're going to a special jail with shiftsilver locks, but they don't know anything about the wizard-scientists or their plans."

"And the good news?" Merlin asked hopefully.

Roland smiled at Dali. "Pete and Tirzah say welcome to the team, and Carter says me hiring you is the only reason he'll even consider setting foot in the office again."

"Woo-hoo!" Merlin exclaimed.

Without removing his head from under the pillow, Ransom yanked Merlin's pillow out from under his head, and laid it atop his own.

"Keep it down in here," Zane said, walking over. "The patients need their rest."

Mom and Roland left, but Dali stayed, lying down next to Merlin and snuggling in. She retrieved a pillow from another bed first.

"Go to sleep," she whispered. "Zane was right. You need it."

Merlin *was* tired, but he hated to waste this time in sleep. He whispered, "I want to enjoy every second I have with you."

Dali kissed him. "I'm not going anywhere. True mates, remember? You'll have all the seconds in the world."

For the first time, his future felt less like a wild rollercoaster, fun but totally unpredictable, and more like a ride that was just as fun, but was headed toward a destination where he wanted to go.

All the seconds in the world, his raptor said dreamily. *One... two... three...*

Warmed by Dali's body and the love that surrounded him, Merlin fell asleep.

CHAPTER 28

Ever since she'd lost her hand, Dali had known that your life could change in an instant. But she'd only thought about it in the sense of the changes being terrible. But the moment those pigeons had stolen her necklace had set off a chain of events that had changed everything for the better.

Sitting in the audience of the Fabulous Flying Chameleons' final Refuge City performance, Dali mentally ticked off the ways that everything had changed.

She'd gotten back in touch with her Navy buddies. As Merlin had predicted, none of them thought less of her—in fact, it turned out that some of them had worried that *she* thought less of *them!* They now checked in with each other almost every day over email or text or phone. She might be retired, but the Navy would still be a part of her life.

She and Merlin had moved into a larger apartment that had opened up in Tirzah and Pete's building, and managed to compromise on decoration by dividing it up room by room. When they proudly showed off the final result, Tirzah suggested that they photograph it for a magazine article called "Opposites Attract."

Managing the Defenders office, not to mention the Defenders themselves, was definitely a challenge. But then, she'd always loved a challenge.

She'd cracked down on food-stashing and coffee-mug-abandoning with an iron fist, posted clear rules about what was and wasn't allowed in each room of the office, and turned a certain horrifying disaster area into an actual working kitchen/break room where people could cook, eat, and relax.

Dali had also hired the two most responsible of the pigeon teenagers as cleaners, since they already knew about shifters and clearly needed good honest work. It had been a definite win-win. Ara and Mason got money to save for college, and the office actually looked professional. Mostly. Not even Dali could bring herself to ban the pets, so clients were occasionally puzzled by the discovery of blue hairs on the sofa.

She'd even had a chance to plan and coordinate a team mission. Merlin's raptor had never let up about the barista's sofa, so Dali had presented Roland with a plan for retrieving it.

As the least intimidating member of the team, Tirzah had approached the barista after work and said that she worked at a security agency, she'd been in the Starbucks when the barista's evil sofa-stealing ex had showed up and gotten his just deserts in the form of a frappuccino to the face, and she'd like to help out, woman to woman. With the barista's enthusiastic permission, Roland and Pete had knocked on the evil ex's door, loomed over him, and repossessed the sofa. And then the whole team had ceremonially moved it back into the barista's apartment.

The barista had been delighted and posted an enthusiastic review for Defenders on Yelp, the evil ex had left an angry comment to her review that attracted hundreds of jeering rejoinders, Merlin and his raptor had been thrilled, and Dali had enjoyed the deep satisfaction of a difficult job well-done.

A month ago, Dali and Merlin had driven her grandmother to their own apartment to tell her about shifters in a more private space than the retirement home. Merlin had proved it by turning into a hamster-sized velociraptor. Grandma had taken the news with surprising equanimity; Dali suspected that was mostly due to Merlin's charm and Dali's clear

285

happiness at being with him, though the presence of Blue hadn't hurt.

"I had a hound dog named Blue when I was a little girl," Grandma said, patting the bugbear. "He had big sad eyes like this creature, too."

"How'd you get him?" Merlin asked. And then they were off, trading stories about dogs they had known.

After the visit, Merlin stayed in the car while Dali walked Grandma inside.

"I was wrong about what kind of man he is," Grandma said thoughtfully. "He's got other things to do with his restless heart than run around the country."

"You mean, he runs around as a raptor instead?" Dali asked.

"Yes. Much more practical. This one's a keeper." Once again, she said triumphantly, "I told you my necklace would bring you luck!"

Dali kissed her wrinkled cheek. "You were so right."

And now Dali was back at the circus, in the audience for a change. Cloud perched on her shoulder, intently watching the show. Blue sat in the aisle beside Merlin, his stubby tail thumping the floor.

Merlin sat beside her, his arm flung over her shoulder, suffusing her with his body heat, their ever-sizzling chemistry, his protective strength, and his love. Even though she could touch him and be with him all she pleased, his presence was still a marvel to her. Especially when she thought back to how discouraged and lonely she'd been only a few months ago.

"How did I ever get this lucky?" she whispered in his ear.

He knew immediately what she meant, and whispered back, "*I'm* the lucky one."

The lights went down, and the small but enthusiastic audience applauded, then applauded again for the curtain call. And then the house lights went up, and Janet came forward to invite everyone to join the closing night party in the ring.

The Fabulous Flying Chameleons liked to conclude their engagements by doing a final show for a private audience composed of local shifters and non-shifter friends and family who knew about shifters.

The audience for tonight's performance was a bunch of Refuge City shifters and their friends, the Defenders, Pete's mother and daughter, three of Caro's friends from the apartment building, and Dali's grandmother. It also included some non-locals: the west coast branch of Protection, Inc. and their mates and children, who'd flown out for the occasion.

By the time Dali and Merlin and Grandma got down to the ring, it had already been set up for a shifter party, with tables of circus-themed food and drink, plus plenty of toys and climbing equipment for kids (and adults) who wanted to play.

Birds and flying squirrels zoomed and fluttered and glided overhead, and raccoons and opossums and humans and other beasts with grasping hands tried out the trapezes, which had been lowered for the sake of nervous parents, though the net remained underneath.

Dali settled her grandmother down in a comfortable chair with a table for her food. Grandma wore her lucky necklace, and the pigeon teenagers kept shooting her guilty looks while staying as far away as possible. Janet came over and introduced herself, Pete introduced his mother to them both, and soon the three old women were chatting away.

Merlin and Dali set out the goodies they'd brought for the party, which they'd transported in a lockbox to protect it from roving bugbears. They'd spent a happy weekend cooking, and had produced everything from Filipino nata de coco pastries to peach cobbler from Grandma's recipe to truffles in twenty different flavors. No sooner had they arranged everything on platters than the entire Defenders team, plus Caro, descended to fall upon their homemade treats like a bunch of starving wolves.

Carter bit into a Buddha's Hand truffle. "Put some of these in my next box, Merlin."

"That was an apology box," Merlin said. "You're not getting one every week!"

"I'm sure you'll have something else to apologize for," said Carter. "I want some of the raspberry ones too."

Kalpana gave a sigh of happiness as she ate a truffle. "Merlin, you outdid yourself. This tastes just like Dad's hot chocolate."

Kalpana, who normally dressed plainly, practically glowed in a striking green pants and tunic with a flowing pink scarf. Going against all tradition, she'd convinced Janet to hold a company vote on the heirship with Kalpana and Fausto as the contenders. Kalpana had won, and Fausto had accepted it with a mutter of, "At least it's not Merlin."

Fausto was currently a flying squirrel, and Dali suspected he was enjoying himself more that way. No velociraptor, regardless of size, could annoy him while he was in the air.

"Come on, Dali," Merlin said. "I want to introduce you to the west coast team."

He escorted her to a group of men and women, plus three babies and a whole bunch of magical pets. Blue wagged his tail and panted happily. Cloud took one look at the other pets, arched her back, buzzed her wings, and hissed. Merlin quickly plucked her from Dali's shoulder and kept a firm grip on her.

"This is Dali Batiste, my mate," Merlin said. "She was a yeoman in the Navy and now she's our office manager. She ran the entire show backstage when we had the inspectors, and she saved my life, and..."

A handsome man with shoulder-length black hair said, "I remember what it was like to meet Grace."

He squeezed the arm of the woman beside him. In contrast to his black silk shirt and dress pants, she had pink-and-purple hair and wore Army boots and a 1950s dancing dress with a cherry print. She held a baby in one arm. A pink-and-purple flying kitten perched on her shoulder.

He went on, "I couldn't stop talking about how wonderful she was to anyone who'd listen, and some who didn't. But let us introduce ourselves, and then you can go back to telling us how fantastic your mate is."

Merlin grinned. "Okay, Rafa. It's a date."

"I'm Grace Chang," said Rafa's mate. When Dali shook Grace's hand, she noticed calluses, little scars, and very short nails painted with black glitter. This was a woman who worked with her hands. "You ran this show? I'm so impressed! I'm a stage manager, and I kept thinking what a fun challenge it would be."

"Kalpana's the stage manager," Dali said, indicating her. "You should talk to her. She could show you the booth."

"Oh, thanks, Dali. Join us when you get the chance if you want to talk shop. Rafa, mind taking Gabriel?" Grace passed the baby to Rafa, who cuddled him against his broad chest. Her pink-and-purple kitten spread his wings and flew to Rafa's shoulder as Grace headed off in Kalpana's direction. To Dali's delighted astonishment, the kitten's bright coloring got darker and darker until he was almost invisible against Rafa's black hair and shirt.

"I'm Rafa Flores, a lion shifter," he said, and gave Dali a firm hand-shake. "Navy, huh? Represent! Me and Hal were SEALs."

Hal, a big man carrying a baby clutching a teddy bear, said in a rumbling voice, "Pleased to meet you. I'm Hal Brennan, the west coast boss and grizzly bear shifter. This is my mate, Ellie. She's a paramedic."

Ellie, a plump woman with curling hair who was also carrying a baby, said, "And this is Haley, and that's Elliot, and that's Bob."

"Sorry, which one is Bob?" Dali asked. The babies were clearly twins and crawling age, with their mother's sandy-blonde hair and their father's hazel eyes.

Ellie laughed. "I've got Haley, and Hal's got Elliot, and Elliot's got Bob. Bob is the owbesloque."

Merlin reached over and scratched the teddy bear behind the ears. It opened round owl's eyes and blinked at them.

"It's alive!" Dali exclaimed, then took a closer look. Its paws had blunt hooked claws like a sloth, which it was using to hang on to Hal's arm, and a squirrel's tail that she had initially mistaken for a fur wrap around the baby. Then she remembered what Ellie had called the creature, and laughed. "Oh, it's an owl-bear-sloth-squirrel. How cute. Your kids must love him."

Elliot squirmed, making an unhappy noise. Haley promptly echoed it. Both babies were wriggling and staring downward. Following their gaze, Dali saw that a nearby area had been set up where kittens and poodle puppies and baby sea lions and tiger cubs and flying squirrel kits were playing together, pouncing on each other, nosing around balls, and dozing in furry piles.

"Nick?" said Hal, glancing at the man near him.

Nick, a young man with tattoos and intense green eyes, detached Bob, allowing Hal to set his son down with the baby animals. Ellie did the same with Haley. A moment later, a pair of bear cubs crawled out of their onesies and joined the group. Nick considered Bob, then set him down beside a tiny jungle gym. Bob reached up with his sloth claws and dangled from it, watching the twins closely with his golden owl eyes.

"Best babysitter ever," said Ellie.

"Bob saved our lives," said Hal. "Every parent of twins needs an owbesloque."

"Hey," said a man. "Who gives your twins panther rides whenever they want?"

Dali nearly jumped out of her skin. She could have sworn the tall man with ice-blue eyes had materialized from thin air.

"Shane..." Hal said with a sigh. "Will you ever stop doing that?"

"Probably not," said Shane. He looked Dali over, his cool gaze approving, and offered his hand. "Shane Garrity. Your kitten and mine look related."

Dali was about to ask where his kitten was when a soft gray head peered out from behind his neck. Shane held out his hand, and his little kitten spread gray moth wings and landed on it, soundless and light as a feather.

"This is Shadow," said Shane.

Cloud stretched out her neck, curious but not aggressive. Merlin opened his hands and let the two kittens sniff each other. Though their wings were different, their fur was very much alike. They flew off together, up toward the rigging. Halfway up, they were joined by a fluffy black kitten with wings like a Monarch butterfly. As the three kittens began to circle and playfully chase each other in the air, they were joined by Batcat and Spike.

"Is the butterfly kitten yours too?" Dali asked Shane.

"Nope," said a woman cheerfully, walking up to them. She was short and curvy, with brown skin and black hair. "She's mine. Well, more mine. Shane's my mate, so we kind of share all the cats."

"You have more?" Dali asked, craning her neck to spot them.

"Rogue, Natasha, and Jessica Jones. But they're back at home. They're not magical, and they don't like to travel." The curvy woman stuck out her hand. "Hi! I'm Catalina Mendez. I'm a bodyguard and a leopard shifter."

Shane smiled at her fondly. "And a superhero."

"I was experimented on by Apex, the black ops agency that the wizard-scientists took over," Catalina explained. Gleefully, she said, "So I have powers!"

Dali was interested to see that Catalina, like Merlin, talked about being experimented on with a total lack of angst, unlike everyone else in that situation. But before Dali could ask about it, Catalina threw her arms around Merlin.

"Merlin, I'm so happy for you," Catalina said. "You finally got a flying kitten of your very own! Isn't it great having a furry little darling to perch on your shoulder and chew on your hair?"

Merlin chuckled. "It is, but she's not exactly mine. At least, she's only mine the way Shadow is yours. She's really Dali's pet, though she does perch on my shoulder sometimes."

"Oh no." Catalina's face fell. "But I'm sure some day…"

Merlin whistled. Blue, who had been napping on a pile of sawdust, woke up with a startled grunt, then galloped to Merlin's side, his wings buzzing madly as if they'd give him extra momentum. Proudly, Merlin said, "*This* is my magical pet. His name's Blue."

Dali had already taken a liking to Catalina, but it only increased when Catalina said with utter sincerity, "Oh, what a good dragonfly doggo!"

"He's a bugbear," said Merlin. He dropped to his knees, and Blue made a sincere effort to climb on to his shoulder and perch.

"I love him!" said Catalina, petting him. "Oh, good for you, Merlin. You got the best of both worlds."

"Both worlds?" said Shane. "Perching on shoulders *and* getting drooled on?"

"Cat world and dog world. And bonus bear world." Catalina grabbed Shane's arm. "Come on, let's have some fun!"

The two of them ran to the ladder, which they climbed with feline grace, then joined the group that was taking turns swinging on the trapezes.

Merlin caught her hand and introduced her to Ethan, a Protection, Inc. bodyguard with sandy hair and blue-green eyes like Hal's mate Ellie; in fact, he explained, they were twins. His own mate was the beautiful and very pregnant Destiny, also a bodyguard.

"Though not right now," Destiny said cheerfully. "I'll be back soon-ish, though. All us parents and parents-to-be made the rest of the gang promise to pitch in with the babysitting."

A tiny snow-white kitten with robin's egg blue wings swooped down briefly to bat at her earrings, then returned to the kitten games above.

Grace came back then, with Kalpana in tow.

"Come on, Dali," Grace urged. "Kalpana's going to show me her stage manager's booth. Managerial geek girls unite!"

Dali couldn't resist. Waving good-bye to Merlin, Destiny, and Ethan, she headed for the booth with the two women, where they had a very satisfying time examining the equipment and telling stories about disasters onstage and onboard caused by people failing to do as they were told. They exchanged emails and phone numbers, and promised to stay in touch.

Things change in an instant, Dali thought again. She'd not only gotten her old friends back, but made new ones.

When she returned to the party, she found that she wasn't the only one who'd made new friends. Tirzah was in a huddle over a laptop with an elegant blonde woman who introduced herself as Fiona, one of the Protection, Inc. bodyguards. Dali said hello, then left them to their way-over-her-head tech talk.

Merlin caught up with her as she passed by Hal and Roland, deep in conversation over the rewards and difficulties of being the boss of a bunch of rowdy shifters. She told him her thoughts on new friends, and he grinned and replied, "I was just thinking the same thing. Come look at this set of new pals."

He indicated a gawky young man who couldn't be more than twenty-one, and had pulled up a chair to join Grandma, Janet, and Pete's mother Lola.

"Who's he?" whispered Dali. "Some local shifter?"

"His name's Manuel, and he's semi-local," Merlin replied. "He's a protégé of Nick's, going to college in New York."

The three white-haired women seemed utterly charmed by Manuel's earnest manner as he asked Janet's advice on putting on a production of a musical he'd written. It was, he explained, called *Howl* and was an exploration of the real lives of werewolves, written by a werewolf.

"It's got serious themes, but I want it to be fun, too," said Manuel.

"Like *Hamilton*," said Lola. "My Caro just loves that musical. Can't stop playing it."

"Isn't that the rap musical?" Janet asked doubtfully.

"Oh, it's not all rap," said Lola. "Lots of it is very hummable. I could play you some on my cell phone."

"Manuel, do you have any songs on your phone we could listen to?" Grandma asked. "I mean from *Howl*."

"No, I haven't recorded any of it yet." Hesitantly, he said, "I could sing you something, though…"

"Yes, please," said Grandma.

"We won't be critical," Janet assured him. "We know it's a work in

293

progress."

"Come on," Lola said. "I want to be able to say I heard it before it was even recorded!"

Manuel cleared his throat a few times, then began to sing in a pleasant tenor. The song was a heartfelt tribute to the joys and responsibilities of being in a pack, with clever rhymes and wordplay.

Nick, the young man with green eyes and tattoos, came up beside Dali and Merlin to listen, along with a woman with flowing silver hair. She too had tattoos that wound up one arm in an abstract pattern, but hers glittered silver. Dali had never seen anything like them before, and had to stop herself from staring.

When Manuel finished, everyone broke into applause. He ducked his head, embarrassed, then caught sight of Nick and said, "Applaud Nick. If it wasn't for him, I'd still be stealing cars in a werewolf gang."

"No fucking—" Nick began. Three pairs of disapproving eyes turned on him, and he gulped and said, "No way. He was always meant for better things."

The silver-haired woman offered Dali a hand. "Hello. I'm Raluca, Nick's mate."

As they shook, Nick said, "And the best fu—best fashion designer on the west coast. You want a special outfit? Call Raluca, she'll fix you up."

Raluca was indeed dressed very beautifully, but Dali's attention wasn't on her clothes. It was on the miniature blue dragon that fluttered down from the rigging to land on Nick's shoulder. It gave an inquiring chirp, then a trill as it stretched out its long neck to nuzzle Raluca's cheek.

"Wow," Dali breathed out. "A *dragon!*"

"A dragonette," said Merlin. "Rescued from guess where."

Raluca said, "Her name is Doina."

"*She's* the dragon," Nick said, indicating Raluca.

Dali remembered Merlin's first aid kit, with its little vial of the antidote for a poison that only affected dragons. Raluca was one of the people Merlin was looking out for, along with his team and the circus and anyone else who he encountered. Dali was his one-and-only, but he had more than enough kindness and protective instincts to go around.

An elegantly dressed man with golden hair strolled up, arm in arm with a redheaded woman bedecked in jewelry, with a diamond dragonette perched on her arm. They introduced themselves as Lucas and his mate Journey. Their dragonette, Treasure, flew off with Doina.

Dali gazed up at the dragonettes and kittens swooping and diving in mid-air. She murmured, "It's so magical. It's hard to believe that it's real."

"I know what you mean," said Journey warmly. "Lucas and I have been together for years now, and sometimes I'm still just struck by amazement at how my life turned out."

Merlin put his arm around Dali's waist, strong and secure and warm. "Me too."

As the party went on, the two teams drifted together again. The west coast team started teasing the east coast over their impromptu performances.

"I can't believe I missed it," Rafa said. "Pete as a dancing bear! Now that's once-in-a-lifetime spectacle."

"Yes was," said Pete. "And now it's over. Thank God."

"Not e," sang out Caro. She waved a phone at the group. "Guess who en a buddy to come to the show and secretly tape all the best bits?"

Pete m ab for his daughter's phone, but she ducked under his arm, laug

"Get it, Pete called.

"Get it y Tirzah said, snickering. "I for one am delighted that my brilliant nce was immortalized on tape."

"And Batc magical pets said Dali. "Well—maybe. I don't know if the

"They do it video."

Batcat. And D know they exist," Caro assured her. "I got

"That video nicycle. And Carter covered in oil."

"I totally agreed," said Carter.

They looked at their other team members. Carter demanded, "Aren't you going to help?"

"I'd love to see it," said Merlin. "I missed a lot of it, since I was busy wrongly accusing Fausto—" Cupping his hands around his mouth, he called up to the air, "Sorry, Fausto!" In a normal speaking voice, he went on. "And other stuff."

"I don't mind if anyone sees me being a strong man," said Roland. "It's not as if I was oiled."

"I wouldn't mind seeing myself juggling," said Ransom, rather wistfully.

Pete and Carter glanced at each other, then spontaneously worked together, creating a pincer formation to go for the phone.

"Help!" yelled Caro between bursts of giggles. "Help, I'm under attack!"

Shane seemed to materialize out of nowhere, neatly confiscating the phone out from under Carter's nose. "Got it. Hmm. Too bad we don't have a projector, so we can all see…"

"Give me that," said Dali.

Shane passed her the phone, evading Pete's grab for it. Dali fed it over Carter's head to Grace, who caught it and yelled, "Kalpa Help me in the booth with the projector! Rafa! I need a blockade!"

Grace and Kalpana ran for the ladder to the stage mana ooth, Grace stuffing the phone into her Hello Zombie Kitty p safe-keeping as she went. Rafa body-blocked Pete's rush after Carter tried to dart around him, and Rafa shouted, "Guys! I n e help here!"

Merlin and everyone on the west coast team w either pregnant or holding a baby fell into place, forming all and blocking Carter and Pete's access to the ladder.

Grace and Kalpana reached the booth, where a m ad been left on; a chorus of amplified triumphant giggles . A mo-ment later, a video clip began to play on the rin showing the world's most disgruntled dancing cave bear.

Pete sat down on the floor and groaned. Carter joined him when the clip of his oiled chest outlined by flying squirrel throwing knives appeared. Caro's friend hadn't recorded the entire performance, but they'd gotten all the most embarrassing parts.

When Caro herself appeared, gracefully flying through the air on the full-size Moonbow, her Grandma Lola called out, "Just beautiful, princesa."

Pete got up and put his arm around Caro's shoulders. "We'll keep a copy of that one. But the ones of me must be deleted."

"No way," said Tirzah. "I'm saving copies deep on the dark web, where you'll never, ever find them."

"Email them to me," said Grandma Lola.

Pete sighed.

When the clips ended, the groups again drifted apart. Blue wandered off to play with Fiona and Justin's three-headed Cerberus pup, Trio, and Ethan's frost-puppy Snowy. Catalina and Shane went to try out the flying trapeze.

Dali looked up wistfully.

"Want to try?" Merlin asked.

Dali held up her left hand. "Not unless you want a repeat of how I scared the living daylights out of Morgana's minion."

He laughed, then said seriously, "I could hold your wrists instead of your hands. Like this." He demonstrated, gripping her wrists. "Now you grab mine. See? Like that."

His grip was strong, and she'd seen him fly through the air with ease. But more than that, she trusted him. He'd never suggest that she do anything unsafe, and if he thought she could do it with his help, she could.

She took his hand. "Let's go flying."

A few minutes later, Dali was soaring through the air, delighting in the sense of speed and freedom, while Merlin held her wrists and softly sang a snatch of "The Daring Young Man on the Flying Trapeze." His golden hair floated around his face, his sky-blue eyes sparkled, and his ease and grace and strength were on full display.

High above the crowd, it was as if they existed in their own perfect little world. It wasn't frightening—she could never be afraid while Merlin held her—but it was thrilling, exhilarating, and altogether wonderful.

"You're especially sexy in mid-air," Merlin said softly.

"You too," said Dali. "Let's find a closet or something when we get down."

"Good idea."

They didn't find a closet, so they snuck out of the big top and went hunting around the empty fairgrounds, clutching hands and giggling like a pair of teenagers. Merlin turned a corner around a food stall and burst out laughing.

Dali, following, also began to laugh when she spotted what he was looking at.

It was a clown car.

The wheels were off, and it seemed to be in the process of being broken down for parts. But it was unmistakably a clown car.

"Well," she said. "The windows are painted over, so it's definitely private."

"Come on," Merlin said. "Just to say we did it in a clown car."

"I can't resist such a romantic invitation," Dali said, and climbed inside.

It was small enough inside that they couldn't move without touching one another. Getting fully undressed would have been difficult, and she doubted they'd have had the patience to do so even if they'd had all the space in the world. The hunger in Merlin's eyes was a blue blaze, and Dali felt hot enough to set the air on fire. They pushed aside the clothes that were in the way, their fingers clumsy with need, and he slid into her like a key into a lock.

They moved together, rocking rather than thrusting, overcome with passion. Two bodies and hearts and souls united in love and ecstasy. A spark built within her, setting her every nerve alight, until it roared into a wildfire and they both went up in flames.

Dali had completely forgotten where they were until she emerged from the lazy haze of satisfaction and tried to stretch out, and accidentally elbowed Merlin in the neck.

"Ow!"

He tried to move aside, and that was how she discovered that his hand was pinning her hair.

"Ow!"

They managed to emerge without too much more damage, and fled to the train to clean up in a bathroom.

"Well," Merlin said, "We can now say that we've had sex in a clown car."

"It was pretty great while we were doing it," Dali said, brushing out her hair. "But now I know why most people prefer beds."

When they returned to the party, they passed by a man with copper-colored hair and startling black eyes, who had earlier introduced himself to Dali as Justin, Fiona's mate. He was speaking quietly to Ransom in a corner. Both men looked so serious that Merlin and Dali glanced at each other, then walked close enough to overhear.

"If you ever want to talk to anyone," Justin was saying. "I was experimented on by Apex. It leaves a mark." He indicated his eyes. "Literally, in my case."

Ransom made a sound halfway between a laugh and a sob. "You think me talking to you will make me *feel better?*"

Patiently, Justin said, "It doesn't have to be to me. But yeah, I think you should talk to someone who can understand."

Ransom closed his eyes briefly, seeming to struggle with himself. When he opened them, they were unfocused, gazing into some far-off distance. "I—I'm sorry. I have to go."

He turned and hurried away, stumbling and bumping into things as if he was half-blind. Dali and Merlin went after him. Before they could catch up with him, he'd gone backstage. They saw nothing but the door to a storage room closing.

Merlin knocked. "Ransom? Are you okay?"

There was no reply.

CHAPTER 29

Ransom stumbled away, barely registering where he was going. His mind's eye was focused on a vision of the woman he'd seen after he'd passed out at the warehouse, the woman whose face and story had slipped away with waking like he'd tried to grab a handful of smoke.

He wasn't going to lose her again.

A door was in front of him. He opened it, went in, and fumbled to lock it behind him, still holding on to the vision with all his strength. Any interruption, and it would be gone.

He barely spared a glance for where he was—some kind of storage space—other than to assure himself that it was empty. Only then did he throw wide the doors of his mind.

Ransom saw her as vividly as if he was in the room with her. She was short and slim, with a lithe strength to her small frame. An acrobat's build. Her face was elfin, her tousled hair dyed in a streaky rainbow.

She didn't look anything like the women who got on the covers of magazines, with her boyish body and sharply angled face. But she had something those women lacked: she was *alive*. A feeling of intensity, of vivacity, of *presence* radiated from her.

As Ransom drank her in, he knew things about her.

Her name was Natalie.

She was Merlin's friend who'd left the circus.

And she was dying.

He pushed his vision to widen, and then he saw that she was in a doctor's office.

"So," Natalie said. Her voice was high and clear, and surprisingly calm. "I have a year to live."

"I know this is a lot to take in," said the doctor. "But you need to focus on what you can do for yourself, to make sure you get that year. The electrical shock that damaged your heart left it too weak to cope with any kind of excitement or surprise. So no playing sports, no scary movies, no wild parties, and absolutely no stress. Try not to get excited or angry or frightened—those kinds of strong emotions could be very dangerous for you."

"Are you saying I could literally drop dead if I do anything fun?" Natalie asked.

"I wouldn't put it that way," said the doctor. "There's plenty of fun things that wouldn't strain your heart. Think of it as bringing peace and quiet and serenity into your life. I recommend that you take up some kind of gentle exercise, like tai chi."

"That's really not my style." Natalie stood up. "Thank you for your honesty."

"Wait, wait," said the doctor. "We're not done yet. I need to set you up with more specialists, and more testing, and lifestyle counseling, and a support group, and—"

"Thanks, but I'll pass," Natalie said. "I have to get going. I've got a lot that I want to do, and I don't have much time."

She headed for the door.

"Are you—wait, you can't just walk out!" The doctor jumped up. "Where are you going?"

Natalie tossed back her rainbow hair and grinned at him. "To ride a rollercoaster!"

The door banged shut behind her. It sounded like a gunshot going off next to Ransom's head. The impact flung him out of the vision and back into his body.

He slowly became aware that he was kneeling on the floor of the storage room, his mouth dry, his hands shaking, drenched in cold sweat. The pain behind his eyes felt like a hammer trying to break his skull from the inside.

But he could take it. If he'd been at the office, he'd have waited for his hands to stop shaking and changed his sweat-soaked shirt, then walked out like nothing had happened. He didn't have a change of clothes here, but he could go out the back and be gone before anyone noticed he'd left the party.

One of these days, they're going to notice, growled his inner hellhound. *Then they'll know how broken you really are.*

Ransom might have argued with his hellhound, but he had something much more important to think about.

Natalie.

The vision of her haunted him. She was like a splash of color in an ash-gray world. The lock of blue hair hanging into her eyes. The arch of her feet in their bright red ballet slippers. The stubborn thrust of her chin. The frustrating way that shadows had played over her face, making it impossible to discern the color of her eyes.

I have to find her.

The thought startled him. But it wouldn't let him go.

I have to meet her.

It wasn't that he was attracted to her. Or, well, it wasn't *just* that. Sure, she was beautiful. But with her rainbow hair and "seize the day" attitude, not to mention that she was a target girl in a crime circus, she was the opposite of a match for him. If he even had a match, which he didn't.

But beyond the mere biological fact of sexual desire, he was fascinated by her personality, her dire situation, and the way she'd reacted to it. When faced with death, the ultimate terror, she'd spit in its face and laughed at it.

She was so *alive.*

He'd never met her, and yet it broke his heart that she was dying. It

302

was so unfair. And it made him feel helpless. He wanted to save her, but what could he possibly do to heal a damaged heart?

Nothing, growled his hellhound. *For all you know, she's dead already. You'll never even get to meet her. It's hopeless.*

Usually his hellhound's words just ground him down. But this time they kindled a spark of defiance in his heart.

Oh? Ransom returned. *Let's see about that.*

It was sheer contrariness that gave him the strength to try. His power, never easy or enjoyable, got harder and more painful and more debilitating if he used it too many times too close together. Normally after a vision like this, he'd try not to use it at all for a few days, and certainly not for anything even remotely as difficult as what he planned to attempt.

You can't do it, growled his hellhound. *It'll be excruciatingly painful, and you'll fail anyway.*

Ransom tuned him out. His focus narrowed as he bent his concentration to a single question:

How can Natalie can be saved?

He threw open the doors of his mind.

Information battered him like an avalanche, tossed him about like a flood. It felt like his head—his entire *self*—was being torn apart, his mind scattered like confetti. The pain was beyond bearing, and the sense of being a tiny speck in a vast and uncaring universe was worse.

But he held on until he had all the answers he needed. Only then did he try to get out.

He couldn't find the way out.

The doors wouldn't close.

He was lost inside his mind.

An eternity passed, or maybe just a second.

Then Pete was there, calling his name. Pete held out his hand, and Ransom grabbed it like a lifeline.

And then he was back in reality. In the store room. With his entire team standing over him or crouched around him. He and Pete were sitting on the floor, and Pete gripped his hand.

Ransom yanked his hand back, horrified at the thought of what Pete might have seen.

With a gentleness that belied his words, Pete said, "I didn't look at anything inside that mess of a head of yours. I just found you and pulled you out."

Looking into his teammate's straightforward gaze, Ransom knew it was true. If Pete had learned his secret, he sure as hell wouldn't have touched him.

"What the hell, Ransom?" Carter demanded. "We had to break down the door! What were you doing in here?"

Ransom couldn't answer. He felt exactly as bad as he'd expected, and from the way his vision was going black around the edges, he was probably going to pass out at any second.

But it had been worth it. He had his answers.

Natalie *could* be saved... and only he could save her.

He didn't know how he could do it, nor was it at all certain that it would happen. It was only a possibility, and a small one at that.

And along with that possibility came a certainty: if he and Natalie met, his team would learn his secret.

Would he give up everything he had and make everyone he cared about hate him, just for a tiny chance at saving the life of a woman he didn't even know?

He tried to speak, but saw by the puzzlement on their faces that even with their sharp shifter hearing, his voice had been too weak for them to understand.

Forcing himself to speak more loudly, he said, "A *pen*. I need a pen."

Roland produced a pen from his pocket, then uncapped it for him. Ransom's hands were shaking badly, but he managed to scrawl down the thing he most needed to remember across his forearm: Natalie's current address.

And then, at last, he let everything go black.

A NOTE FROM ZOE CHANT

Thank you for reading *Defender Raptor!* I hope you enjoyed it. It's the second book of the *Protection, Inc: Defenders* series. The first book is *Defender Cave Bear.* The next book, *Defender Hellhound,* is coming soon.

Protection, Inc: Defenders is a spinoff from the seven-book series *Protection, Inc.* The entire series is available now on Amazon. It begins with *Bodyguard Bear.* If you read the whole series, you'll catch the first appearances of the Defenders characters.

If you enjoy *Protection, Inc.* and *Defenders,* I also write the *Werewolf Marines* series under the pen name of Lia Silver. Both series have hot romances, exciting action, emotional healing, brave heroines who stand up for their men, and strong heroes who protect their mates with their lives.

Please review this book on Amazon, even if you only write a line or two. Hearing from readers like you is what keeps me writing!

Printed in Great Britain
by Amazon

81276616R00181